THE
DEAD
GIRLS
CLUB

THE
DEAD
GIRLS
CLUB

A Novel

DAMIEN ANGELICA
WALTERS

CROOKED
LANE

NEW YORK

Copyright © 2019 by Damien Angelica Walters

Published in the United States by Crooked Lane Books, an imprint of The Quick Brown Fox & Company LLC.

Crooked Lane Books and its logo are trademarks of The Quick Brown Fox & Company LLC.

Library of Congress Catalog-in-Publication data available upon request.

ISBN (hardcover): 978-1-64385-163-1
ISBN (ebook): 978-1-64385-164-8

Cover design by Melanie Sun
Book design by Jennifer Canzone

Printed in the United States.

www.crookedlanebooks.com

Crooked Lane Books
34 West 27th St., 10th Floor
New York, NY 10001

First Edition: December 2019

10 9 8 7 6 5 4 3 2 1

For all the girls whose names we know,
and those whose names we don't.

Little girls are cute and small only
to adults. To one another they are not cute.
They are life-sized.

—Margaret Atwood, *Cat's Eye*

CHAPTER ONE

NOW

There's nothing special about the envelope. Standard #10 size, 24-pound white paper stock, available in any office supply store. My name and address written in capital letters with black ink. Deliberately generic, so neat it appears typed, but the giveaway is a tiny smudge on the *d* in *Maryland*. No return address.

Early-September sun peeks through the window blinds behind me, cutting bars of light and dark across my desk, and a plane rumbles overhead on its way to or from nearby BWI Airport. I have a letter opener in one hand and a small pile of unopened mail before me. To my right, a messy pyramid of opened envelopes and their contents; on my left, a laptop with an unfinished game of solitaire on the screen. I was decompressing when Ellie, the receptionist, brought in the mail after my last appointment, a fifteen-year-old with complex PTSD as a result of years of abuse. Doesn't matter how thick your skin or how well your patient is doing, you never grow accustomed to hearing certain things.

The envelope is unbalanced, and as soon as I slice open the top, it's clear there's no letter within. Curious, but not overly so, I fish out something small wedged in the corner.

A thin silver chain unspools with a quiet hiss. A small half-heart pendant, its clasp broken, tarnished by nearly thirty years' worth of time, the edge in the shape of a lightning bolt so as to fit its opposite. With a trembling finger, I turn it over, knowing what I'll see—an *ST* with half an *E* and *NDS* below, and another bisected *E* and *VER* beneath that. *Best friends forever.*

"Please," I say, my voice too loud, too ragged.

My free hand flutters to my bare neck; my gaze darts around the room.

On the corner of my desk sits a framed photograph. Me in heels, a black dress, and red lipstick, my shoulder-length hair pulled into a sleek chignon, the hundred bobby pins taming it in place invisible against the dark strands; Ryan in a charcoal suit, one arm snaking my waist, his hair secured at the nape of his neck, one stray pale curl hanging at his temple. All evening fancy and champagne flutes. A gala six months ago for the opening of Silverstone Center, a substance abuse treatment center for girls. The picture ended up in the newspaper, and objectively I can see why. We look good together. His light to my darkness. We're shining with happiness. Security. Honesty. That woman looks like a stranger right now. I nudge the frame so only Ryan's visible. Nudge it again so he's staring at the wall. A coward's tactic? Call me Baum's lion.

I flip the envelope, revealing a smeared, illegible postmark. An accident or done on purpose?

I've done everything possible to keep that summer, to keep what transpired, tucked away in a tiny, impenetrable box, but the necklace, this necklace, is the key. The lock shatters. I'm no Pandora, unleashing evil into the world. This is a private apocalypse. *Devastation for one, ma'am?* A potent vintage.

The heart, the other half of which once hung around my neck, even after, is a cheap thing of nickel, stainless steel, or some other inexpensive alloy. Originally affixed to a cardboard square and purchased by two girls who saved their allowance. *Best friends forever.* We meant it, she and I. We meant it with every bone in our bodies and every true and good thing in our souls. We didn't know forever didn't always last that long. We had no way of knowing that day was the beginning of the end.

The necklace is an impossibility, yet here it is on my palm, the weight an anvil. I can still smell the basement of the empty house: the new paint, the old moisture trapped within its walls. Can feel the carpet rough against my skin and Becca's hand in mine. Hear her saying my name. *Heather.*

I scrape a nail across the front of the charm, dislodging several gritty flecks. They crumble between my fingers and leave reddish-brown streaks behind. Another plane passes, and I let go. The chain hisses again; the heart clinks. It lands faceup on the desk, the letters an accusation.

Nothing good will come of this. I feel it in my bones. Know it in my gut. I grab the hands of the clock to stop them from spinning, but it's too late. You can't unopen an envelope. Can't undo the damage you've done. The box is open, no way to hide what's inside. Not anymore. The tangle of truth and lies and imagination makes no sense, but we make up stories when it hurts too much to tell the real ones. The ones with teeth; the ones that keep us awake at night. They're the ones that leave scars.

Not trusting my legs to carry me to the bathroom, I reach for a tissue, ball it up, and scrub the red marks from my skin. I keep scrubbing, even when they're gone.

The last time I saw the pendant, it was on Becca's neck. Her eyes were closed, her arms at her sides. I sat beside her for what felt like hours, my fervent apologies filling the air, my tears turning the changed world to a blur.

Long before the Dead Girls Club, long before the stories of the Red Lady, Becca was the one person I could tell everything to, no matter how hurtful or ridiculous, the one I knew would always be by my side, the one I promised to help, no matter what. She was my best friend.

And I killed her.

Sorrow thickens my throat and I rock back and forth, the tissue crumpled in my fist. It wasn't my fault. I didn't mean it. Didn't mean to hurt her.

I didn't.

I inhale. Exhale. Nudge the necklace into one of the pockets in my bag and toss the tissue. I want to shout, to rage and tear my hair. Instead, I growl, long and low. It's not loud enough to seep through the walls, so I don't have to worry about Ellie or the other psychologist with whom I share the space hearing.

Doesn't take a genius to figure out why I chose this career, why I don't see anyone over eighteen. I don't have any photographs of Becca, but I remember her pale eyes and her even paler hair. I remember the two of us talking about Ted Bundy, our heads tucked close together, the sleepovers, the giggling until late in the night. I remember—

I make twin fists. Pinch the tip of my tongue between my front teeth. I can't afford to do this right now. There isn't much time before my next patient arrives. After that, back-to-back appointments until the end of the day. I need to do what I'm good at. I need to listen. I need to observe. Memory lane can wait.

Here's the thing: I refuse to believe the dead can buy postage stamps.

But someone obviously did.

The only two possibilities are so remote, so absurd, I can't even take them seriously. If Rachel or Gia, the two other members of the Dead Girls Club, knew, why would they wait so long? Why didn't they tell the police? Then or now?

All four of us—me, Becca, Rachel, and Gia—were thick as thieves at the end of the school year. Before summer's end, we were no longer friends and Becca was dead. I don't think I ever spoke to Rachel or Gia again.

I scratch my temple. *I can't call the police, but . . .*

My fingers hover over the keyboard. The clock isn't just ticking, but ticking down. Once I start this, there's no going back.

"I didn't start it," I say aloud.

I wonder if things would've been different if they'd found her body. That's when a *missing girl* becomes a *dead girl*. That's when she gets interesting.

Focus, Heather. Focus.

The necklace was on Becca and she wasn't moving. She was dead. And now—

My desk phone rings. I jump and answer it.

"Elijah's here, Dr. Cole," Ellie says.

"Thank you. I'll be up in a minute," I say, arranging my voice into a professional cadence. I've worked hard for that voice. I've worked hard, period. No way in hell am I going to let anyone take that or anything else away from me.

Necklace or no necklace, they don't know what happened.

*   *   *

By the end of the day I feel like the Hulk, every nerve exposed, waiting for the explosion. On the inside, anyway. On the outside, I'm Dr. Cole of the tailored slacks, the crisp button-down shirt, the trim waist, the tasteful silver watch and wedding band, the polite *good-night* to Ellie, the shiny black Jeep Cherokee waiting in the parking lot. A typical Wednesday.

Bag over my shoulder, steps wide and confident, I scan the lot. No one's skulking about or sitting in their car, staring at me. And most of the cars are already gone. Route 100 is quiet. Frequent glances in my rearview mirror assure me that no one follows me onto Interstate 97.

Our house in Edgewater, thirty minutes from my Linthicum office, overlooks the South River, a tributary of the Chesapeake Bay. Fifteen minutes from downtown Annapolis and all the restaurants and local seafood you could ever want, but our neighborhood's quiet. Only one road leads in or out, and after I make the turn, the sound of traffic vanishes, like a blanket's been settled over it all.

I pull into the driveway, not bothering with the garage, even though there's plenty of room with Ryan's side still empty. When his truck is parked there, it feels too small for both our vehicles, even though I know it's not. I step out of the car, a small dog lets loose with a series of high-pitched barks, and an engine revs. The rich smell of grilling meat hangs heavy in the air. It feels even warmer now than it did this morning.

September's always a funny month. One foot still in summer, the other in autumn.

Nothing waits in the mailbox other than a sale flyer and a gas-and-electric bill. A little bit of tension eases from my shoulders as I walk the stone path to the front door. The house, a Craftsman with cream-colored siding, black shutters, and a wide covered porch, has four bedrooms, two and a half baths, a two-car garage, and a secluded backyard ending at the river. It's bigger than two people need, but ten years ago it was in sorry shape, so we got it for a steal.

The interior of the house, filled with a mix of furniture inherited from his grandparents and pieces found in consignment shops or on Craigslist, is even quieter than the neighborhood. Normally it's welcoming; today it's suffocating.

I refuse to look in the mirror above the small table in the foyer, can't bear to see the liar reflected there. Balancing from one foot to the other, I pull off my heels, then take the stairs two at a time up to my bedroom, my bag bouncing against my shoulder blade.

Small velvet squares in the bottom drawer of my jewelry box cup my earrings, and in the back row in the corner, beneath a plastic bag holding spare buttons to a jacket I no longer own, is my half of the heart. Did part of me know this day would come? Is that why I've kept it all these years?

As I search the outside pocket of my bag, I think I've lost Becca's half and my shoulders get tight, then my fingertip hooks the chain. Maybe they won't match. Maybe this is a coincidence of monstrous proportions. Maybe I mentioned it sometime, somewhere, and someone picked up on it. Fixated on it. One of my former patients occasionally sends cheap medallions, all of them pseudo-religious in nature, though the religions are usually headed by online gurus who push detox cleanses and herbal supplements.

I could say such things a dozen times, a thousand, and still wouldn't believe them. Besides, the proof is here in front of me. Time and tarnish notwithstanding, the halves fit together. There's power here. It bound us then, it binds us now. Inescapable. Irrevocable.

We crooked our fingers together when we put them on for the first time, Becca and I. A pinkie swear. *Best friends forever.*

I said it that last night. She did, too. And we weren't lying. My chest tightens. I yank the heart apart, dropping mine back into the jewelry box and holding Becca's by the chain. The heart spins a slow circle like a hypnotist's pocket watch.

Tell me your story. Where have you been? What have you seen? Why are you here? Who sent you?

There were only two people in the basement that night, but did we examine the rest of the house first? Could someone have been hiding; could they have seen the whole thing? What we—what I—did, what the Red Lady made me do? I shake my head. Not possible. We would've known. We would've heard.

And they would've stopped us.

I gather the necklace in my palm and finger the broken clasp. The two ends are still hooked together but hanging from one side of the chain. It wasn't broken that night. It was on her neck when I . . .

If someone else was there, did they yank it off?

The garage door purrs, and I return the necklace to my bag. Meet Ryan downstairs and fold into his arms, ignoring his protestations that he's sweaty and grimy.

"Rough day?" he says into my hair, and I answer with a nod. In his arms everything feels right and normal and true. When I let go, he cups my face and kisses me on the forehead, the tip of my nose, my lips.

"If I don't shower, my clothes are going to stage a rebellion," he says. "You know things are bad when you can smell yourself."

"Swamp ass," I say. "So very sexy."

I start dinner, focusing my attention on seasoning chicken breasts and fetching a bag of frozen broccoli. Gourmet cook, I am not. Hanging out in the kitchen has never been anything I enjoy, much to my mother's chagrin when she tried to teach me.

After dinner, after our teeth are brushed and we've turned in for the night, I roll onto my side, rearranging the pillow until it's comfortable.

Ryan does the same and we link fingers, the rasp of his rough carpenter's skin, calluses and scars aplenty, a comfort. In the light from the bedside lamp, his green eyes appear gray, his blond hair brown. I twine a finger through one of his curls, pull it between thumb and index finger until it's straight, let it go. A simple act, yet it's the tether I need.

His face and physique, all long hair, cleft chin, and lean muscles, say California surfer as much now as they did when we met at an acquaintance's party, the ink fresh on my bachelor's degree. I took him for a pot-smoking perpetual student. How wrong I was. Only two years older than me, he already had his own home improvement business. "I was the kid out mowing lawns every summer and shoveling sidewalks every winter, saving every dollar," he said on our first date. A coffee shop, him with an espresso, me with a latte. Almond biscotti and blueberry scones. Knuckles brushing together. Knees nudging under the table. Ten minutes in, wanting a second date. Hoping he did, too.

Here and now, he takes a strand of my hair, mimicking my actions, although I've no curls to subdue and he rubs my scalp in small circles. I listen to the soft whisper of skin against skin and the branches of the oak tree outside tapping against the roof.

"Do you want—"

"I was thinking—"

"You first," he says.

"No, go ahead."

"Want to talk about it?" he says.

"Talk about what?"

"Your rough day?"

"No," I say, the word too blunt. "Just one of those days."

"No more weird phone calls?"

A few weeks back, while working late, I received a call with shallow breathing on the other end of the line. I hung up, and thirty seconds later the phone rang again. More breathing.

"No, no calls. Just things that were hard to hear." He shows no indication of detecting the lie within my words, and I'm grateful I've used the excuse before.

"Anything you can talk about?"

"Did you ever hurt any of your friends when you were a kid?" I say.

"All the time," he says. "Football in the street, acting like assholes on the docks."

"No, I mean . . ." I rub the tip of my nose. "Intentionally."

"Indian burns, snowball fights, dunking in the river," he says, ticking each item off on a finger. He traces a line from his philtrum to the center of his chin with a thumb and index finger. "One time . . ." He shifts a little. Frowns. "My buddy Christian and I beat the shit out of each other. Bloody noses, black eyes, the works. Don't remember what prompted the fight, but I meant every punch. It felt good to hit him, to hurt him." His fingers make a slow circuit around his mouth again. "I haven't thought about that in years. What a little asshole I was. Does that make me Hannibal Lecter?"

"Depends," I say with a grin, despite the cold waltzing the length of my spine. "Did you eat him afterward?"

"With or without fava beans? 'Cause that's important, right?"

"Could be."

I debate whether to ask him if he talked to Gerald Kane yet about the outstanding check for their basement renovation but don't want him to think I'm prying. Bringing it up today would be a crappy thing to do, too. Can't guarantee I wouldn't be trying to pick a fight, release some aggression. Why bring that home to him? Into our bed?

I don't want to talk anymore, don't want to think either, so I peer through my lashes. "Come here, Mr. Morrison."

"On my way, Dr. Cole."

He scoots closer, traces my lower lip with his thumb. I pull it into my mouth, and for a time we let everything go in favor of the crash and pull of our bodies. Afterward, he curls in a comma behind me, hand resting on my hip.

"In a scorched landscape," he says, "she plunges into danger to save the lives of two children. Panic and faulty wires abound. Will she succeed? Will she fail?"

"Mmmm," I say, nudging him gently with an elbow. "Not fair, taking advantage of me when I'm falling asleep. Can I have a hint?"

"Already?"

I growl but play his words over in my head, trying to match them to a scene in a movie. The first time we played our game, we'd been dating for about six months. No lead-in, nothing. Walking out of the restaurant, he leaned close, dropped his voice, and said, "Two faces, a blind attorney, and his ex-lover get tangled up in what could be a real estate investment deal gone wrong."

I was equal parts confused and amused, and even after a dozen hints, although he said I would only get three—"What's the point if it isn't hard?"—I gave in. It was *Primal Fear.* I argued his initial clue wasn't fair. He cited Agatha Christie, said I had to read between the words.

He usually wins. He has an uncanny ability to remember nearly everything from a movie the first time he sees it: side characters, subplots, lines of dialogue. Even if we've watched the flick more than once, I can barely recall a main character's full name.

The rules are easy: three hints (one of which, if I'm lucky, will be a quote I recognize); no searching online or the movie collection in the family room; no asking anyone else for help. The only rule I've ever set: no horror movies. A boyfriend once tried to trick me into watching one, even after I told him I hated them. He thought it would be funny. Five minutes in, a killer was chasing a woman through the woods and I was breaking up with the boyfriend.

Now, I tick movies off in my head, knowing there's a better-than-average chance I'm searching in the wrong direction. *Aliens*? Only one child. Same with *The Terminator.* The volcano movie with Pierce Brosnan, the title of which I can't remember, is a potential choice because it has two kids, but I don't remember any faulty wires. *Jurassic Park*? Two kids, yes, but Sam Neill's Dr. Grant saved the kids, and does technical sabotage count as faulty wiring?

"Yes, I already need a hint." I say. But he's asleep. I wiggle free from his grasp, turn off the bedside light, and stare at the ceiling. My guess is it's an old movie. He stumps me with those, having watched legions of them with his paternal grandmother. Such a silly thing, the game. Silly, yet monumental. Part of the scaffolding of a marriage, along with the knowledge you collect over the years: the way your partner takes their coffee, their shirt size, whether they prefer onions in their salad or not. But no matter how well you know a person, there's always something they hold back, something they never tell anyone. I try not to wonder what secret he keeps, but I know it's nothing like mine.

He doesn't know a thing about Becca, not even her existence in my life, and he never will. "Honey, when I was twelve, I killed my best friend" isn't scaffolding. It's a sledgehammer.

I hold up my hands, turning them from palms to backs. Short, neatly trimmed and unpainted nails. Long, slim fingers. Piano fingers, Nana called them. No marks or scars. Not that a murderer's extremities should look a particular way.

In stories, blood smells of old coins. An apt description. What those stories fail to mention is that the smell lingers, not on your skin, but in your memory. You can't ever wash it away.

The shadows in our room are too big and I'm drowning. Drowning in the darkness, in the quiet, in the after-love haze, in the fear that the necklace's appearance signals the beginning of the end of everything.

I skim the hollow between my collarbones, remembering how the heart nestled there once upon a time. I bite the side of my thumb to keep from laughing or crying or both and slip from the bed. In the hall bathroom, I squirt soap into my palm and work up a thick layer of lather. Rinse, then soap again.

"Out, damned spot," I say, the water masking my voice.

I don't view my reflection in my mirror. And I don't cry.

*   *   *

While I'm in the bathroom putting on the day's makeup, Ryan gives me a quick kiss. "Love you. I'm getting ready to head out."

"Can I get a movie hint?" I say.

"Going up?" he says, and mimes pushing a button.

"That's not much. That's not even a real hint."

"Oh, it definitely is, and it's all you're getting," he tosses back.

I rub my lower lip while he walks away. Scorch. Plunge. Panic. Faulty wires. And an elevator? "*Die Hard*?" I call out.

His feet pause on the stairs. "Guess again," he says. "And choose wisely. You only have two left."

When the door to the garage closes, I rest my hands on the counter beside the sink and stare at the drain, a knot behind my rib cage.

I will not lose my husband over this. I will not lose anything at all.

* * *

"But Cinderella's stepfather locked her in her room because he said she was bad and she couldn't come out until she was a good girl," Cassidy, my first patient of the day, says. "And Cinderella really wanted her mommy, but he said no."

My office is the size of a spacious living room, its one window facing the parking lot, four stories below. In addition to the typical office furniture, I have beanbag chairs and a small armchair covered in cartoon cats and dogs. Framed posters for *Finding Nemo*, *WALL-E*, and *Star Wars* line the walls.

Cassidy's a bright eight-year-old who's been coming to see me for three months. She's perched on the cartoon chair, and I'm at my desk. I typically don't sit here, preferring to be next to or across from my patients, but at our first session, Cassidy refused to speak. When I moved to the desk, she began responding, always with fairy tales. Her grandmother, currently waiting in the reception area, told me Cassidy watched the animated Disney movies with her mother.

Stories are powerful, and Cassidy's contain a wealth of information, of truth. While she continues, I fetch the half heart from my bag and turn it over and over, as if I were a magician and it a coin, as if truth could be guided from finger to thumb and hidden up a sleeve.

Becca told stories, too, full of whimsy and imagination. Harmless. At least until the Red Lady. From the very beginning, *her* stories were different. I bite the side of my thumb hard enough to leave an imprint of my teeth.

"Dr. Cole?" Cassidy asks, staring down at her lap. "I don't want to talk anymore today. Can I color instead?"

"Of course."

She scampers over to a small table in the corner and its collection of coloring books, blank paper, crayons, and colored pencils. I should sit next to her, talk to her about what she's drawing, but I can't bring myself to do it. Not today.

I drop the half-heart into my desk drawer, flipping it over so the letters aren't visible, and swirl the chain into a loose spiral. No golden ratio here. The metal, cool and slippery, reminds me of blood on my hands, of Becca's cold skin. I shut the drawer hard enough to make Cassidy jump. One apology later, she's back to her drawing.

On the drive to work, I was thinking back to the house, wondering again if someone else was there that night, someone who saw but didn't intervene. An adult would've stepped in as soon as it became clear where things were headed. The knife would've made it obvious it was no longer a game. But another child? Maybe not.

No one else knew about the empty house and how we sneaked inside. Not our parents. Not a neighbor. Only the members of the Dead Girls Club—me, Becca, Rachel, and Gia. And no one else knew about the Red Lady. I know Rachel and Gia weren't talking to us at that point. Hell, I wasn't talking to any of them, not even Becca. Not until she asked me to go. Asked me to help her. And of course I went. She was my best friend. Even then.

But what if they went back later? After? What if they saw her body? I press my lips together, shake my head slowly. Impossible. There was nothing to see. Her body was gone. Wasn't it?

I cross and uncross my legs. Thump my foot on the floor.

Sometimes you cope with trauma by opening yourself up and pulling it out—my recommendation to every child passing through my office door. But sometimes you bury everything so deep you forget it's there because it's the only way you can make it through the day. *Physician, heal thyself?* Bullshit.

I remember many things in vivid detail, but there's also a lot I don't remember at all. What if someone else was there and I didn't see them? Or don't remember seeing them? Time has taken some of the memories, but others . . . Dissociative amnesia can occur from severe stress or trauma, and killing your best friend definitely qualifies.

I pinch the bridge of my nose. I can't allow myself to fall apart. I have to view this as I would a case. Concerned, but not overly involved. Not emotionally involved. This is what I'm trained to do. Put the puzzle together and see the picture as a whole.

Cassidy's focused on her crayon and paper, so I open a browser. Type in REBECCA LILLIAN THOMAS. It's been a long time since I've read the official story, but I know it by heart: Lauren Thomas, Becca's mother, killed her in a drunken rage. They didn't find her body, but it didn't matter. There were signs of a struggle in the house. There should've been a countrywide media circus—the case was ripe for tabloid frenzy—but three days after her arrest, a fourteen-year old was found murdered in the woods behind her home in northern Baltimore County. She came from a good two-parent family. Sunday dinners and after-school clubs. Her school picture revealed shiny hair, big eyes, perfect teeth. The right kind of dead girl. And you can bet her death—at the hands of a neighbor with a history of sketchy behavior—made the national news.

Instead of the expected *Baltimore Sun* archives, there's a new link, a new story. Five months old—new enough, anyway. I skim it, landing on the important phrases: *Pleaded guilty to killing her daughter in 1991. Paroled after serving—*

My vision narrows to the letters on the screen, and I clench my jaw so hard my molars grind. Lauren Thomas is out of prison. Becca's mother is free.

CHAPTER TWO

THEN

The ride to the mall took forever. Maybe because it was Friday, June seventh, the last day of seventh grade. Maybe because there was traffic. Or maybe because me and Becca were so excited we could hardly sit still; we finally had enough money saved for the necklaces.

My mom listened to the same radio station we did, so when "Baby, Baby" came on, she turned it up loud and the three of us sang along. Lots of people said it was the best song of 1991. At that minute, it was for me, too.

At the mall entrance, I had the door open before the car stopped all the way. When I got out, my hair caught on the seat belt and I had to yank out a bunch of strands, squinting at Becca the whole time. She'd made me take out my braid this morning because she said it looked better down. If hers had been down to her waist instead of her shoulders, she'd have understood what a pain it was.

We were practically opposites. Becca was smallest-kid-in-the-class short and had almost white hair and eyes like the sky mixed with clouds. Last year, Jeremy Dixon hadn't stopped calling her "ghost girl." She said it didn't bother her, but names always hurt. Plus, she hated that she looked like her mom. She had an aunt—her mom's sister—who'd died when Becca was a baby, and she looked like her, too. I'd seen a picture once. But Becca was the prettiest.

Mom called me lanky, which meant tall with long, skinny arms and legs. I'd gotten my height from my dad. Everything else—my thick hair, mud-colored eyes, and caterpillar eyebrows—came from her and Nana, who was mostly Italian.

"Thank you for giving us a ride, Mrs. Cole," Becca said.

"You're welcome. And girls? Seven o'clock on the dot."

"Yes, Mom," I said, adding syllables where there weren't any extras.

"Mrs. Cole?" Becca said.

"Yes, dear?"

"Please be kind," she sang, extending the last word.

"And rewind." Mom sang, too. "Have fun, be careful, love you both!"

Normally we'd make a beeline to the food court, but normally Rachel and Gia were with us. We hadn't invited them today because we wanted the necklaces to be ours first. They knew we were best friends and we knew they were best friends, but we didn't want them to copy.

Soon as we got to Claire's, we went to a spinning jewelry display case in the back.

Becca spun it once. "Oh, no, they're gone."

"What do you mean, gone? There were a bunch."

"I know. They were hanging right here. I remember." She pointed to a metal peg holding an enameled butterfly pendant.

"Maybe they moved them. We could ask."

But the woman behind the counter was all scrunched forehead and squished-together eyebrows, like we were planning to steal.

"Never mind," I said. "Let's not."

Becca scanned the lower section of the case. I took the top. We went peg by peg, and when we were down to the last few, she said, "Found it! The last one, too."

Becca worked the cardboard square free from the peg and inspected the hearts, chains, and clasps, her lower lip caught between her teeth. I checked, too, but if anything had been broken she would've spotted it.

The clerk sighed when I pulled out my wadded-up dollar bills. But I ignored her. After Becca had the bag, she said, "Have a nice day," all syrup-sweet.

Outside the store, Becca unwound the necklaces and hooked the right heart around her neck while I tried to do the same with the left. My hair kept getting in the way, and Becca ended up helping me.

"Forever," she said, crooking her pinkie.

I fitted mine into hers. "Forever."

My eyes got hot and watery for a second, which was silly, so I bit the inside of my cheek until it stopped, and said, "Bookstore?"

"Definitely."

We took the steps to the second floor two at a time and split up in the bookstore. Horror was my favorite, but I read science fiction and fantasy sometimes, too. Becca read anything about mythology, true crime, and anatomy. At home, she had one book with photographs, and all the shiny wet purple-pink-red organs and yellow globs of fat made me gag.

The new Stephen King book wasn't coming out until August, so I flipped through a bunch of others. Nothing seemed very interesting, but I didn't have enough money left anyway. My mom hated most of what I read but said she'd rather have me read morbid books than not read at all. My dad, on the other hand, swiped them when I was done or read them first and passed them to me.

When I found her, Becca was sitting cross-legged in an aisle, back to the shelves, a book open on her lap.

"Whatcha reading?"

"Look," she said, holding up a page showing a big pair of metal pincers that reminded me of tongs my dad used on the grill. "They used these to rip boobs off women they thought were witches. They did it super slow, so it would really hurt."

"That's gross," I said, hunching forward.

"Right? And . . ." She turned to another page, holding up a picture of a spike with a big metal pyramid on top. "They made people sit on this."

"La-la-la, I can't hear you," I said, but I sat down next to her anyway.

She read to me about people strapped to wheels, how their arms and legs were hit until they broke, about people boiled alive, about people with sticks shoved under their nails. I kept making little yip sounds, trying to keep them muffled so no one would come and kick us out for making noise.

When she closed the book, she said, "Why are you so grossed out? Ted Bundy and John Wayne Gacy were way worse."

"Yeah, but . . ."

"We talk about stuff like this all the time," she said.

She was right. We'd been talking about serial killers for years. Then she'd come up with the idea for the Dead Girls Club last summer, after she saw one of my books about a bunch of kids with a club in a secret hideaway. We didn't have a treehouse or anything. Nowhere special—yet.

The name came from all the true crime books Becca read. Her basement was full of them, and they were always about dead girls. This year, a woman named Aileen Wuornos had been arrested for killing six men, but most of the time, it was men who killed and girls who got killed.

Some of the books had pictures, too. Sheet-covered bodies and blood-stained floors. Knives, baseball bats, and handcuffs. Big metal barrels and crawl spaces underneath houses. Photos of killers before and after they were caught. The worst one was Ted Bundy because he looked normal, but he did gross things to the women's bodies after he killed them.

There were so many killers, I didn't think we'd ever learn about them all. Sometimes Becca read us their stories; sometimes she told us about stuff from the news. Sometimes she told scary stories. I never liked them as much, though, because real people were always scarier.

"They're different," I said.

"They still killed people. Remember about Ted Bundy and the bottle and the other stuff? What he did? And the two guys with the van and the tools?"

"Yeah, but they did stuff like that because they were messed up in the head. The people doing the torture thought they were right."

"Maybe they were. We weren't there, so how do we know? Maybe they were saving everyone by doing what they did."

"Doesn't make it right."

She got to her feet and slid the book back on the shelf. "Doesn't make it wrong, either."

I pulled a face. "Come on, my mom'll be here soon and we still have to get your stuff. Maybe we can get her to order pizza."

*   *   *

My mom waited outside while Becca packed up for spending the night. Her mom wasn't home, so her house was super quiet. She lived in the same kind of row house I did, only on a different street. We had the same middle bedroom, too, but Becca had a twin bed, not a double.

While she got her underwear and pajamas, I plopped on her bed, knocking off one of her sketchbooks. A waterfall of loose pages dislodged, all pen-and-ink drawings: people in old-fashioned clothes, a little girl with ribbons in her hair, an older girl with her hands on her cheeks like the kid in *Home Alone*, a woman on her side, hair covering her face.

I bent to pick them up, but Becca said, "No, I got it," as she rushed over to sweep everything up into her arms.

One slipped free from the others, and I caught a glimpse of someone with long hair like mine, but Becca snatched it away, turning it over.

"Just wanted to help," I said.

"I know, but I want to keep them in order."

She patted the edges until they were in a neat pile and put the stack on her desk underneath a Lisa Frank notebook, one with a rainbow kitten cover.

"How come I can't see them? You always show me."

"They aren't ready yet."

"I bet they're still good."

She swiped her hair back. "You can see them when they're finished."

"Promise?"

"Yes."

Becca could draw as good as a real artist. When we were little, we'd made construction paper books—I wrote the stories and she drew the pictures—and tried to sell them to some of the neighbors. They were monster and ghost stories and were supposed to be creepy, but we were too little to know how to make things scary.

I had one of her drawings hanging over my bed, a picture of my dog, Roxie. My mom said when I was a baby, Roxie slept on the floor next to my crib. I cried for practically a month straight when she died. Becca's drawing was perfect, down to the spots on Roxie's nose and her goofy bat ears. She made it for me right after Roxie died and didn't even have to use a photograph.

While she was in the bathroom getting her toothbrush, I tiptoed to her desk. The picture wasn't of me, but a woman with hair so long it curled on the ground. Her eyes were colored in black, her arms wide open. I knew the drawing was finished because it had Becca's signature in the bottom right corner, a big *B* and then a curlicue. It didn't look like it, but it was supposed to be her name.

"Every artist has a signature. This is mine," she'd said when I asked about it.

Why had she told me it wasn't finished? Her footsteps clomped in the hallway. I put the drawing back fast and sat back on her bed. She gave me a funny look, lips all pushed out, when she came in but didn't say a word.

My mom didn't order pizza, but she made stuffed shells and garlic bread, which was almost as good. Dad and I play-fought over the last piece of bread, earning a "Please, Joe" from my mom. He won but tore it in two pieces for me and Becca.

"Thank you, Mr. Cole," she said.

"Thank you, Dad," I said, but I'd taken a bite of the bread, so I had to talk around it. My mom shot me a look, and I tried to look sorry, because I wasn't showing my chewed-up food on purpose. When she wasn't paying attention, my dad winked.

He started telling Mom about work, which was always boring, until he told her about an accident at a job site with a crane, not one he was driving. The guy busted his head open falling in a hole or something, so they had to pour new concrete, and now Dad was going to start working on that job, for a fancy new building near the old cemetery. Then Mom told him about her day at the dentist's office where she worked part-time. Even more boring.

After, with a bag of salt-and-vinegar potato chips, we went to my room to listen to music. But I voted for Whitney Houston and Becca wanted Mariah Carey, so we ended up playing the radio, on our backs on the floor, feet resting against my mattress.

Becca rabbited her feet, then pointed her toes. "I wish I was allowed to hang posters. *She* says it would ruin the walls."

"My mom gave me stuff that doesn't mess them up. If you want, I can give you some, too. It doesn't tear the paper either."

"She'd still get mad."

I didn't say anything. It wasn't the first time we'd talked about it, but I felt guilty. In addition to the picture Becca had drawn of Roxie, I had posters of Whitney and Madonna and Paula Abdul. But it wasn't just the posters. My room was painted bright blue and I had polka-dot sheets. Becca's was pale yellow, which she hated, and her comforter and sheets had ugly flowers. The only picture on her wall was a framed print of fruit in a basket. Once we stayed in a hotel in Ocean City with almost the exact picture. It was pretty awful. I didn't understand why her mom was so weird about it all.

"Do you have a mirror?" she asked.

"Duh, right there." I pointed to the wall over my dresser.

"No, a small one."

It didn't take me long to find one in the bathroom.

"You have to hold it like this"—she held the mirror at boob level and bent her head over, her hair spilling down in pale, shiny curtains—"and look down."

"Why?"

"Just do it."

I did, but my hair spilled forward, covering the mirror. She gathered it into a ponytail at the base of my neck and said, "Try it again."

I was Silly Putty stretched the wrong way.

"That's what you'll look like when you get older," Becca said.

"Gross, I'm all squishy. Here, you do it and pull your hair back so *I* can see."

"I look even more like my mom," Becca said, her words deflated balloons.

"I bet you don't. Show me."

"Fine," she said, holding her hair back and tilting the mirror.

Her mom's twin was staring up from the glass, but I said, "Your face is way better than hers."

"Right. I wish I looked like my dad."

I rubbed my palms on my thighs, not sure what to say. Becca's mom said he'd left before Becca was born because he didn't want to be a father. A pretty crappy thing to do. He never even called or anything.

She stuffed a chip in her mouth and spoke around the crunches. "Even though I hate him. I hate them both," she said.

I didn't think I could ever hate my parents, but I might be mad enough to if my dad had left and never knew me. If my mom didn't even try to make him.

She turned and peered through her hair. "Hey, have you heard of . . ."

"What?"

"Never mind, I'll wait until tomorrow when we're all together. At the house."

"Oh, come on. You can give me a hint."

"Hmmm," she said, tapping her chin. "One hint. She's called the Red Lady."

I hoped it wasn't just a made-up story, or if it was, I hoped it was good, with a name like that. "What did she do? Kill her whole family? Her parents?"

"Nope, that's all you get."

"Not fair. I won't tell them you told me."

No matter how much I asked, she refused to say another word.

I crossed my arms and said, "It's probably just something like the angel."

"It's not like the angel at all."

A couple months ago she'd told me a story about how an angel tried to kidnap her when she was really little. Her mom had to fight the angel to save her, a real fight ending with the angel's hair and wings torn off. It was made-up, like all of Becca's stories, even though she said it really happened and she'd just remembered it.

"Hey, Becca? What if we can't break in the house?"

"We're not breaking in. Jeez. We're just walking in like normal."

"But what if you can't get the key?"

"I'll get it."

"But what if you can't?"

She sighed, dropping her head. "Let me braid your hair."

"It was in a braid this morning. You took it out, remember?"

"That was earlier. Please?" She touched the half-heart. "Best friends forever?"

I groaned but gave her the brush from my dresser. Sitting in front of her with my legs crossed, I said, fingertips to my half of the whole, "Best friends forever."

Humming "Vision of Love," she started working out the tangles at the ends.

"I want hair like yours."

"No you don't. I want to cut it all off, but my mom says it's too thick and I'll end up with a giant mushroom on my head. *Ouch.*"

"Sorry." She yanked a tangle of hair free from the brush and waved it in my direction. "*Hello, I'm Mr. Octopus. Nice to meet you, yes indeed.*"

"What are you doing?" I said.

"Nothing," she said with a giggle as she separated my hair into several sections, more than she'd need for a braid.

I reached for the mirror; she nudged it away with her knee. I tried to feel my hair, but she smacked my hand. "Nope, stop. I'll let you see it when I'm done."

"Don't make me a porcupine," I said.

She giggled again. "You're not going to chicken out tomorrow night, are you?"

"No, but I still think it's a bad idea."

"It'll be fun," she said.

"Unless we get caught." A super-skinny braid fell forward, and she snatched it back. "Bec-ca," I said.

"Hea-ther," she mocked, tugging a bunch of my hair. "Stop moving."

As soon as she finished, I grabbed the mirror. My head was nothing but braids in all different sizes, some flat against my scalp, others sticking up.

Becca's shoulders hitched. "You're a wildebeest!"

"Am not," I said. I wasn't even sure what a wildebeest looked like, but it had to be awful. Tears pricked my eyes. I shouldn't get upset over hair, but I couldn't help it. I worked my fingers through the bottom of a braid, untwisting the strands as fast as I could; Becca rolled on her back, holding her belly, laughing so hard she wasn't making a sound.

* * *

"I love them!" Rachel lifted the heart off my neck to turn it over and back again. I waved her strawberry-blonde hair away; as always, it needed brushing. "They're so pretty. Gia, we should get some, too."

"We got the last ones," Becca said.

"Oh," Rachel said, the excitement vanishing from her blue eyes.

"We can find them somewhere else," Gia said, and Rachel brightened again.

We were outside Gia's house. It wasn't dark yet, but the edge of the sky was starting to change. Since we were all together, our parents didn't care if we stayed out late. We were old enough to know not to talk to strangers or get in anyone's car or help find a lost pet. And it was Saturday night. We were allowed to stay up later.

The four of us set off, me and Becca in the lead, our sneakers tapping along the sidewalk. It was warm out; not too hot, but still sticky.

My dad said our neighborhood was shaped like a tic-tac-toe, only with four lines each way, not two, inside a rectangle. Me, Rachel, and Gia lived on left-to-right streets and Becca on an up-and-down. Our row houses were all the same, with three bedrooms, bay windows, and

24

fenced-in backyards. A road with the elementary school made up the bottom piece of the rectangle; a bigger road, the top; and a shopping center, the right. On the left was a field with little hills on each side.

We got near the end of the street, and Mrs. Keene, who had watched me and Gia when we were babies, was on her front porch and waved as we walked past.

"She looked prettier before she cut off all her hair," Rachel said.

Becca poked my arm. "See?"

"What?" Gia said.

"Heather wants to cut off her hair," Becca said.

"But you can't," Rachel said. "It's pretty."

I shrugged. Everyone said the same thing, but they didn't have to brush it or wait a gazillion hours for it to dry.

When we went down the hill to the field, Rachel said, "What if someone sees us?"

"Sees us what," Becca said. "Walk across the field? People do it all the time."

"But what if someone's there now?"

"Hel-lo," Becca said, sweeping out one arm. "See anyone except us?"

"No," Rachel said. "But I don't think we should do this."

Becca came to a stop. The rest of us did, too.

"Then go home," Becca said, and started walking again without looking back.

We all followed.

The long grass swished across my ankles, making them itch. They used to play little league baseball and soccer games here, but the county had built a bigger field a couple miles away.

Instead of climbing the hill on the other side, Becca walked alongside it. Near the end, close to a big fence separating the field from a sidewalk running along the road, the hill curved down. Becca led us single-file down a narrow path until we were past the field, behind a bunch of single-family houses. They all had tall wooden fences, not the chain-link kind we had, so no one could see us. Most of them had big trees, too.

"It's this one," Becca said, pointing to the house at the end.

No fence, but it was surrounded by thick hedges taller than my dad. Becca pushed through a small gap halfway down. I went second, the branches scraping my bare arms and legs. Gia came out next, then Rachel, brushing her face and shoulders.

The house was gray stone with tall windows. More hedges surrounded the porch. There were so many trees in the yard, it made it darker than it really was. A FOR SALE sign, with Becca's mom's name and phone number printed in big blue letters, was stuck in the ground right next to the driveway.

"What if somebody sees us?" Rachel said, kitten-soft.

"They won't," Becca said, fishing the key from the pocket of her shorts. "Look at all the trees and bushes."

I'd have bet we could dance in the middle of the lawn without being noticed. It wasn't just private. It was hidden, like we were in the middle of nowhere. I'd lived here all my life and I'd never even known this house was here.

"I can't believe your mom didn't catch you taking the keys," Gia said.

"I was careful. It's not like she checks all the keys every night. Besides, Heather and I already checked it out."

I scratched my side. Such a lie. My heart was a moth near a porch light, even when we got inside and locked the door. The daylight disappeared, leaving us in shadow. Since nobody lived here now and we didn't break a window or kick in the door, we weren't technically breaking in, but we knew we weren't supposed to be here.

It was warmer than outside, the air all stuffy. It smelled of paint, and the quiet was bigger than the house itself. We stood in the foyer, still as cats in a sunbeam.

"I can't believe we did it," Gia said, her eyes wide. The gloom made them darker than usual, black instead of brown.

Rachel was blinking too fast, but Becca didn't look scared or worried at all. It *was* pretty neat, like being in school when almost everyone was gone, but better.

"Let's check out the upstairs," Becca said.

The steps went straight up to a wide hallway with six doors, all open but one. We went room by room, our footsteps whisking on the dingy carpet. The four bedrooms, all with window blinds firmly shut, were huge.

"My mom said the people who lived here were old," Becca said.

"Where are they now?" Rachel asked. "Are they . . ."

"Nah, they're still alive."

Back downstairs, the foyer opened into another hallway, archways on either side leading to empty rooms with heavy curtains. The kitchen cabinets were the color of mud, the tile floor patterned in bright-yellow-and-green flowers. Big-time ugly. No wonder it was still for sale. I'd thought it would be creepy, and it was, but it felt sad, too, like it knew its owners weren't coming back.

Becca opened a door beside an empty refrigerator-sized space and said, "Come on. We can turn the light on down here and no one will see."

Even with the fluorescent tubes buzzing overhead, the basement was dreary. The carpet was the same shade of brown as the kitchen cabinets and wood paneling covered the walls, like my Nana's basement. Dark curtains covered the tiny, high windows, and there was a small half bath back by an old dryer. It smelled like a bunch of wet towels left overnight in a washing machine. Rachel and Gia wrinkled their noses, too, but Becca didn't seem to notice. She sat cross-legged in the middle of the room, and after a second, the rest of us did, too. It was a lot cooler down here, and even with the carpet, the floor chilled my legs.

"We would get arrested if anyone found us here," Rachel said.

Becca huffed out a breath. "No we wouldn't. We're not damaging anything. They'd just make us leave."

"And call our parents," Gia said.

"Maybe," Becca said. "Don't be such a chicken. It's cool."

Gia pursed her lips. "You'd never be able to get the keys again."

"I doubt that, *Georgina*," Becca said.

"Don't call me that. You know I hate it."

"But it *is* your name."

"Fine, *Rebecca*," Gia said.

"Hey, did you see Mrs. Talbot on the last day of school?" Rachel said.

"No, why?" I said, glad we wouldn't have to listen to the same argument Becca and Gia'd had a thousand times.

"She had on this sweater so tight you could see her bra through it. I want those kind of boobs," Rachel said.

Becca got up, palmed her flat chest, and arched her back. Swinging her hips, she paraded the room. Rachel cracked up, rolling on her back and kicking her heels.

"Becca, you're obsessed," I said.

"So what? I want big boobs, too. Don't you? Big, massive boobs."

"But everyone would stare at them all the time," I said.

Gia crossed her arms over her chest super slow, and I wanted to take back what I'd said. She had real boobs, not just bumps, and the boys were always looking. She said she stayed in her room when her older brother Matt had friends over because they stared, too. She was also the only one who'd already turned thirteen. Rachel, Becca, and me all had late birthdays. Gia was the only one who was biracial, too. Her dad was white, her mom Chinese, and sometimes people asked what she was, but they were jerks.

I mouthed *I'm sorry*. "Are we going to start sometime tonight, or are you going to keep doing that?"

"I'm going to keep doing this." She whirled around. "Or, I could go like this." She dropped her shoulders to where they should be, lifted her chin, and took small steps. "*Children, get in line. Come, come, come. Quiet little mice.*" Becca might not have looked like our kindergarten teacher, but she sounded identical.

I giggled. Raised my arm. "Miss Langan, I have to go potty."

"Me too," Gia said, waving for attention.

We all loved Miss Langan, Becca most of all, because she'd never teased her about her invisible friend Sarah the way some of the kids had.

Once Becca and I started to play together, she didn't need to pretend to have a friend anymore. I didn't think anyone else remembered Sarah, maybe not even Becca.

"Bec?" I said. "It's going to get too late if we don't start soon."

"Fine," she said, plopping down. The rest of us scooted in, making a small circle. With a clap, she said, "This meeting of the Dead Girls Club is now in order. So, have any of you heard of the Red Lady?"

I did a little up-and-down shoulder dance. The last story she'd told was about a guy who'd had a bad day at work. After his family went to bed, he stabbed them all—his wife, two sons, and baby daughter. She wasn't even walking yet. For about a week, I kept watching my dad, wondering if he ever had a day bad enough to make him want to stab me and Mom. I decided not, but you never knew, Becca said. You never knew who was secretly a monster.

Gia and Rachel shook their heads, and Becca said, "I didn't think so. Not many people have, and most who have are gone."

"Gone?" Rachel said.

Becca slipped her finger slowly across her neck. "Gone."

"Why's she called the Red Lady?" Rachel said.

"Are you going to let me tell her story or not?"

"Okay," Rachel said, pulling her legs to her chest.

"She lived a long time ago when women wore long dresses and had to cover their hair. When men made all the rules and women had to do whatever they said."

I guess I made a face, because she fixed me with a glare. I didn't mind when she told us about things from long ago. It had been cool when she'd told us about Jack the Ripper, but with the name Red Lady, I'd expected something else. Not boring history.

"Did she have a real name?" Rachel asked.

"Yeah, but nobody remembers it."

"So how—"

"Rach! Let her tell the story," I said.

"Just asking," Rachel mumbled.

"The Red Lady lived in the woods near a village, and if you needed help, you could go to her. She could make someone fall in love with you or make your enemy have an accident or make your plants grow taller. She could do almost anything you wanted if you were willing to pay her price. And the more important or dangerous the spell, the more she asked for. Like she'd do a small spell for a chicken or some eggs, but for bigger things you had to give up something important.

"Even though she did spells, she wasn't a riding-a-broom and warts-on-her-nose witch. She was more powerful than that. And smart, too. Women sometimes went to see her not for spells, but about regular problems. She would give ways to fix them, ways without using magic. But when the women talked to their husbands, the men would say the ideas were theirs. The men didn't know they were really the Red Lady's because the women were careful, so it was okay for a while. See, the men were afraid of the Red Lady, afraid of her power, but they left her alone because they were afraid of what she might do if they didn't.

"Some of the women decided they didn't want only the men to be in charge because that wasn't fair or right, so they asked the Red Lady to help. At first she didn't want to, because if the men found out they'd blame her, but the women wouldn't stop asking. So she agreed. But since the spell she had to do was complicated, her price was that they had to send their oldest daughters to her to learn magic."

"Cool," Gia said.

"Right?" Becca said. "Except the parents had to give them up completely. The girls would live with her and be her daughters. The women said okay, but one of the women was only pretending."

"Like a spy?" Rachel said.

"Exactly," Becca said. "She told the mayor's wife about the deal, and the wife told the mayor, and he hated the Red Lady more than anyone."

"Why?" I asked.

"Because when he was younger, he liked her but she didn't like him back. Ever since then, he'd been trying to figure out how to get rid of her but was too afraid to do it by himself."

"Jerk," I said.

Gia looked over at me and said, "Big time."

"So the mayor got all the men together but twisted the story around, saying the Red Lady wanted to kill, not teach, the girls, and that she wanted to be the one in charge. And they believed him," Becca said. "So they arrested her and they held a trial. She reminded everybody about the spells she'd made for them, even the ones they didn't want anyone to know about, and all the other ways she'd helped, but they didn't care. They found her guilty."

"Why didn't the other women help her?" I said.

"They couldn't. The men wouldn't even let them go to the trial. If they stood up for her, they'd be put on trial, too."

"But weren't they her friends?" I said.

"Maybe, but they were scared," Becca said. "And it was way different back then. Or maybe they weren't her friends enough. Maybe they didn't care what was going to happen because it wasn't going to happen to them." Becca leaned back, palms flat on the floor, arms straight. "Anyway, they found her guilty and sentenced her to die." She glanced at us one by one. "By being buried alive."

Rachel shuddered, Gia bit her lower lip, and I curled my toes tight and gnawed at a cuticle.

"That's not even the worst part. First, they dug a deep hole right in the middle of the village. Then they stripped off all her clothes, tied her ankles together, and cut off her hands with an ax."

We squealed.

"Because a witch needs her hands to make potions, right? And to dig herself out of a hole. Then they cut out her tongue."

Rachel moaned. "Why would they do that?"

"They were afraid she'd say the spells and use her magic."

"And everyone went along with it?" Rachel asked.

"They did," Becca said. "The Red Lady was quiet the whole time, even when they cut off her hands. She couldn't say anything after they cut out her tongue, but she didn't even moan or cry."

I ran my tongue around the inside of my teeth, wondering how it would feel to have a stump there instead. Would you be able to eat? Make any noise at all? Would it slip down and make you choke? I rocked my hips and slid my hands under my thighs, pressing them hard into the carpet.

"They put her in the hole, threw her hands and tongue in, too, and took turns filling it in. They made the women and even the little kids drop some dirt in so everyone would be part of it. And the Red Lady watched them the whole time. She didn't move, not even when the dirt started covering her mouth and nose, and that was worse than the watching. There was no way she could breathe and she should've been flopping around trying to get air, but she was perfectly still.

"Finally, when they had the hole filled in, they went back to their houses, pretending everything was okay. They told themselves she was a witch, not a woman, and things would be better with her gone.

"But then everyone who helped fill the hole had bad dreams, even the kids. They dreamed they were in the hole with her, and even though the dirt was going in their mouths and noses and choking them, her mouth and nose were dirt free and she was smiling. Everyone woke up choking, their mouths full of dirt for real. But they were so scared, they didn't tell each other. And the hole was exactly the way they left it, all filled up. The next night, they all had the same dream again and woke up with even more dirt in their mouths. They told each other then and went to the mayor, since he was the one who decided she should be buried alive. They said he had to do something, but he said they were lying, it was because they felt guilty, but she was evil and they'd done the right thing.

"That night the dreams and the dirt came back. They went to the mayor again, but he was dead, his mouth full of dirt. So they decided to dig out the hole and let the Red Lady out. They were scared, but they were too scared not to. They all took turns digging, but when they got to the bottom"—she spoke so low we had to lean close—"there was nothing, only an outline of her shape in the dirt, stained dark from her blood."

"That's it?" Gia said. "But did they keep having the dreams? And what about the dirt?"

"I didn't say it was the end, but it's all I'm going to tell you right now."

Rachel said, "That was awful."

"Come on," I said. "I want to know more."

"Me too," Gia said.

"Nope," Becca said, stretching her arms overhead. "It's getting late and I have to get home."

I groaned. "Not fair, Becca. Not fair."

"It's a reeeeally long story. I don't think I'll finish it next time, either."

I groaned again. Gia, too.

"You probably won't even like the rest."

"Ugh," I said. "Don't say that."

"Does it get worse?" Rachel said.

Becca quirked the corner of her mouth, and like that, we were hooked.

CHAPTER THREE

NOW

"Yes, Lauren was released five months ago," the husky voice on the other end of the phone says. I can tell she's smiling, too. A firm believer in rehabilitation, Alexa Martin.

"Where is she now? Did she move back to Towson?"

"You know I can't tell you."

"No, I know. I was . . . What's her mental state like?"

"Given the parole board's decision, it's good. She's happy to be out. I know you have a personal interest in her, but she's served her time." Alexa's tone is gentle, patient. I recognize it all too well, although she's had a dozen more years than I to perfect it. "She's not the woman you knew. I've told you before, but it's the truth."

I curl my fingers around the half-heart until the edges dig into my skin. "You should've told me she was out. You promised you would."

"To what end? Truly? And it was years ago when you asked. I thought it better to keep it all quiet."

I squeeze tighter. *Oh, really? Better?* What if I'd run into her while running errands? Or what if I'd stumbled upon an article detailing her release? Or what if she decided to send me a necklace in the mail?

Keeping tabs on Becca's mother had never been my intention, but ten years ago I met Alexa, one of the staff psychiatrists at the prison where

Lauren was serving her time, at a professional development seminar. I'd known who she was beforehand, and while I had no intention of seeking her out, when I came back from a break, the seat next to her was empty, and I mentioned how much she resembled the actress Charlotte Rampling. It's a good story, anyway.

Over drinks a month later, Lauren's name spilled from my lips. I kept to the official story, admitting I was a childhood friend of her daughter's, and it's been easy enough to bring her into the conversation now and again. Alexa's far too professional to divulge in-depth details, but reading between her words has given me enough over the years. At least until now.

"Is she still your patient?"

"Heather."

"I know, I'm just shocked, that's all."

"You knew it was a possibility."

"A remote one, yes, but . . ."

"She's paid her price, that's all I'm going to say."

We hang up with a promise to get together soon. My fingers grip the half-heart even harder. Just because Lauren's out doesn't mean she sent this to me. For one thing, how would she have gotten it? If she had it all along, why wait until now? It doesn't make any sense. I want to understand, but I can't. Why spend years in prison if you know—

I rub the confusion from my forehead, put the necklace in my desk drawer, and pull up a browser. I find the same article about her release and archived articles about the crime. She probably won't be on social media, but I check anyway. Thirty minutes later, with no luck whatsoever, I shell out sixty bucks to a pay site claiming they can provide information on anyone. Unfortunately, the results can take up to twenty-four hours.

Okay, then.

Before knowing Lauren was released, I'd thought Gia and Rachel were the only ones who could be involved. Again, it makes no sense for them to wait until now, but I can't completely ignore the possibility. So while still logged in to my oft-neglected Facebook page, I search for Gia Williams. A few profiles have no pictures; others obviously aren't her. Maybe she got married and changed her name. I try Georgina Williams. The second profile listed has GIA in parentheses, the picture unmistakable. Small and curvy; straight, dark hair pulled back in a messy bun; wide, full-lipped smile.

Most of the pictures show her and a man with a dark, close-cropped beard. Climbing Arizona-hued rocks; in diving gear beside a cerulean sea; roasting marshmallows over an open flame, a tent in the background. I stop at a photo of them standing beside a FOR SALE sign. He's holding a bucket with gardening tools; she has a tape measure and paintbrush. The house, a pale-blue Cape Cod. Two-car garage. Nice front yard.

The first comment says, CONGRATS! NOW YOU'RE OFFICIALLY AN ANNAPOLITAN!

You've got to be kidding me. Annapolis? We're next-door neighbors. Of all the places in Maryland she could've moved to. And we're not exactly sitting next door to the old neighborhood. Annapolis is about forty-five miles away from Towson.

The picture is dated July of this year. Two months ago. Curious timing. Maybe a little too curious? More pictures show outings with other women, dinners with other couples. They all show a woman content and happy with her life, not a woman who'd poke old secrets like a bad tooth. But what the world sees—what you present to the world—doesn't mean a damn thing.

I could send her a friend request. Play catch-up. But I need to be smart about this.

It takes a little longer to find Rachel McAffrey, now Anderson—she isn't friends with Gia, and her page is as frequently updated as mine. But I learn she's married with a son and she's an attorney, which seems out of character for the Rachel in my memory. A little more digging reveals she practices family law. The house in her profile picture's background catches my eye and, if I'm not mistaken, isn't far from where we grew up.

A few minutes later, I have their addresses. Rachel's is exactly where I thought, and Gia's is so close we must've run into each other at some point. Annapolis is a small place. Starting points. For what exactly, I don't know yet. I may not have made the first move, but I'm not going to sit idly by while waiting for the second.

I tick names off my fingers. Lauren. Gia. Rachel. There's no one else I can think of.

Except the Red Lady.

Leaning back in my chair, I cross my ankles. The Red Lady. What a wretched story; what a wretched beginning to the end. Before her, my friendship with Becca, Gia, and Rachel was the stuff of every healthy childhood. All that laughter, all that sugar and spice. Look closer, though, and you'll see the sharp teeth and smell the cruelty lurking beneath the surface.

I type THE RED LADY into the search bar but don't press enter. I know what I'll find: nothing. She was only ever a story. Becca's story. And yet.

And yet.

Red Lady, Red Lady.

I rub the side of my abdomen, frowning at the memory of chanting. The four of us were still talking then. Still friends. The Dead Girls Club. Four girls with a penchant for the macabre. Reading from true crime books about serial killers and imagining what it felt like to be killed in such horrific ways. The bloodier, the better. Gruesome, certainly. Our parents would've been as horrified by the eager tone of our conversations as our subjects: Ted Bundy, John Wayne Gacy, Ed Kemper. The names of their victims never summoned as easily. They made good press only when their pictures were lined up, a grim tableau of numbers. The more the merrier, so to speak. A bigger headline.

They came first: the killers, the Dead Girls Club. The Red Lady came after. She was Becca's boogeywoman, her avenging angel, her desperate wish for another, better life. The product of fraught emotions, her stories and overarching theme didn't always follow the expected logic. What began as a story became something more, and what started as a chain around my ankle turned into a noose around my neck. Maybe Becca and I were damned from the first mention of her name.

How exciting, how grim, that first story. Even now, the thought of choking on all that dirt sends a chill through me. At least I think that's how the story went: a deep hole, a dying woman. But when you recall an event, you aren't remembering the event itself, only the last recollection. A memory of a memory. And if the mind wants something to be real, it can rearrange facts and occurrences to suit. Sometimes we make up stories to explain things to ourselves; sometimes we do it to hide the truth.

Index finger held rigid, I jab the enter key.

My search results: an Alabama ghost; an Upper Paleolithic–era human skeleton; Sekhmet, an Egyptian deity. I've seen the links before. Never the correct red lady, because she never existed, neither as ghost nor historical figure. And yet.

Tell a story enough, it becomes something else. To the mind at least. It felt true. It all felt horribly true. And deep inside, in a tiny part of me that's still twelve years old, she feels as real now as she did then. If I take her away, what's left? Cold-blooded murder.

She made me do it. I didn't want to. I would never have hurt Becca like that.

My eyes burn, and there's a dry click when I try to swallow. I scrape the edge of my thumbnail along the skin around my index finger until I peel away a pale comma. The small wound stings but doesn't bleed. I scrape until it does, then blot it with a tissue.

There wasn't as much blood that night as I thought there'd be. That's a truth I remember. Another truth: I have no memory of burying her body. But I know I did it. I must have; I've a strong memory of digging, of washing dirt from my hands.

I open my drawer, swirl the necklace's chain. Feel a tightness in my belly at the liquid sound it makes. I close the drawer, catching the tip of my pinkie finger. I shake it off with a hiss.

This is not my fault. And I can't change what happened then. If I could, I would've already. All I can do is move forward. One way or another, I'll find out who sent the heart to me. Then I'll figure out what to do.

* * *

Ryan's singing Linkin Park, which usually means good news. I shrug off my shoes and force myself to relax as I walk into the kitchen. He has a pot on the stove, a bowl in one hand, mixing spoon in the other.

He turns with a smile. "Hey."

"Hey yourself," I say. "Something good happen?"

"Indeed. I got a call today from Eloise Harding."

"Should I recognize the name?" I say, pulling a glass from the cabinet and peering over his shoulder into the bowl. Olive oil, red wine vinegar, a scatter of spices. "Looks good."

"Remember the four-million-dollar house with the cupula on Sharps Point Road?"

"I think so. That big gray one with the wraparound porch?"

"That's the one. Eloise Harding lives there, wants her guest bathroom renovated, and as she put it, I came highly recommended."

"That is good. I'm happy for you."

He scans my face. "What?"

"What do you mean?"

"I thought you'd be happy. It could be a big deal."

"I said I was, and it sounds like it could," I say. Could, but isn't yet. And I know the Kane check didn't come today because I checked the mail. He forgot. Again. I fetch plates, carry them into the breakfast nook, and return for silverware.

"This isn't just for an estimate," he says. "She hired me over the phone. I'm going tomorrow morning to start measuring."

"I thought you were helping Mike this week with their kitchen rehab?"

"I still am, afterward. Mike's fine with it."

I'd hope so, since Ryan isn't charging his brother a dime. A knife turns in my hand, catching the light and my reflection, and I shiver.

"Look," he says. "I know it isn't a paycheck now, and I called Gerald again today. He's sending the check tomorrow."

The oldest excuse in the book, but I say, "It's fine."

"I can tell it isn't."

"Please," I say. "I don't want to fight. I am happy for you. It was a long day, I'm tired, and I want to change out of these clothes."

"Right," he says, turning away.

I pinch my lower lip between my teeth. "I'm sorry," I say, pushing softness into my words. "Today was a rough one."

He turns back, his head cocked. "Another one? You okay?"

"Mm-hmm." The lie is battery acid and sandpaper, and I'd like nothing more than to drop to my knees and spill the whole story. But at this point, where would I start? The necklace? Or the murder? "I'm . . . edgy and out of sorts. I'll finish setting the table when I come down."

"The chicken should be ready by then. Do you give up yet?" he says, stiff but not exactly angry, and it takes me a second to understand. Our game.

"Can I get another hint?"

He grins, and I pretend there's no strain behind it. "Going up, or going all the way down with a little help?" he says, spinning one finger in a circle.

"That's helpful," I say.

Turning back to the counter, he starts humming, but I can't hear him once I'm out of the room and upstairs. It would be different if we had kids; the house would never be quiet. Luckily Ryan and I were on the same page. It's for the best, really. I don't think I'd be a very good mother.

I mull Ryan's hint while I change into a T-shirt and leggings. The spinning finger. A helicopter? Tied somehow with an elevator and faulty wiring? I leave my earrings on my dresser, not wanting to open my jewelry box.

Children in an elevator. Children in an elevator hanging below a helicopter. Fire. The pieces come together, revealing a small but significant section of the whole, and I walk back downstairs with confidence. "*The Towering Inferno?*"

He makes a small bow. "The lady wins this round. Ball is now in your court."

To be fair, if it hadn't been one of his favorites—he has a quirky predilection for disaster movies, especially the old ones—I wouldn't have had a clue.

My phone vibrates with a new email, and I do a double take at the subject line: INFORMATION YOU REQUESTED. I open the file attachment with a mix of dread and anticipation. Let's see what sixty dollars buys.

Apparently, a list. Phone numbers and addresses for over a dozen Lauren Thomases. And I don't even know if the right Lauren is here. I should've known better. Nothing's ever that easy.

"Everything okay?"

Ryan's a foot away, holding a plate of chicken, and I turn my phone so the screen isn't visible. "What?"

"You were frowning."

"No, everything's fine," I say, taking the plate from his hands.

Everything's perfectly fine.

*　*　*

Viewed at a quick glance, the four-story Silverstone Center with its old brick, dormer windows, and room-sized porch could be a bed-and-breakfast, like many others in Annapolis, and to be fair, it was before the owners sold it, after it proved too out of the way. Tourists wanted West and Main Streets, restaurants and crab cakes, the shops and harbor, all within easy walking distance.

But the reason for the failure made it perfect for its new purpose: a private substance abuse facility funded primarily by a family whose teenage daughter had overdosed several years prior. Look past the well-manicured hedges and see wire mesh in the windows, an intercom next to the front door, a keypad beside the back. Wrought-iron fencing with spiked posts enclosing the front lawn. Since its opening, I've worked a half day here every Friday.

Although it's not yet nine AM and the sky is clouded with gray, there's a girl sitting on the lawn beneath a tree, a book in her lap. She glances up as my car creeps down the driveway—not for her benefit, but because the path is narrow. She's not in any of my group sessions and I don't know her name, but she reminds me, painfully so, of Kerry Wallace, a patient I couldn't save. A patient targeted by bullies. A patient who ultimately took her own life.

The car lurches forward and my teeth snap on my tongue, just short of drawing blood. I ease my foot off the gas pedal. Seems all my skeletons are coming out to play.

The staff entrance in back is a reinforced steel door. A tiled, oatmeal-colored hallway leads to another locked door. Once inside, tile changes to charcoal carpet, dove walls, and pleasant lighting. This section of the first floor is all administrative; even I have a small office. As I pass the office of the facility's head of psychology, I peek inside, offering up a Venti caramel macchiato.

Nicole Matheson's face lights up, her green eyes catching the overhead. "And this is why you're my best friend," she says, one blush-pink silk-clad arm reaching over the cherrywood desk for the cup. I sit in one of the leather chairs across from her desk while she takes a sip, making a small noise of pleasure. Though we didn't become close friends until a few years later, I've known Nicole since college.

After a few minutes of non-work-related chitchat, Nicole tucks an auburn strand behind her ear and slides a file across the desk. "Samantha, the new girl."

I thumb the cover open, scan the first page. Fifteen years old, opiate abuse, stealing from parents, skipping school. Nothing unexpected.

"Keep an eye on her," Nicole says. "She's smart. Manipulative. A bit aggressive verbally with the other girls. Could be something more going on."

Not unexpected. Drug abuse in kids is often a blind for something else.

Nicole and I part ways and I prepare for my sessions, steeling myself for potential trouble. But the new girl, all dirty-blonde hair, narrow hips, and American Eagle jeans, doesn't say anything more than *hey* when she enters the room. She takes a chair and flips it around, sitting wide-legged. Other than a brief wave to decline talking, she doesn't shift position.

Nicole's not in her office when I leave, but her car is still in the lot. As I reach mine, the skin on the back of my neck prickles. There's no one around in any direction, but there are plenty of trees with trunks large enough and bushes dense enough for a person to hide behind. A light breeze stirs the air, and I swear I hear my name whispered underneath. A husky, otherworldly voice. Skin crawling, I get in the car, locking the doors.

There's no one hiding or lurking. Or whispering. It's only my imagination. Still, I pull out of the parking lot too fast, and I don't look back.

* * *

My parents still live in the same house in Towson where I grew up. The Saturday traffic's light, so I make it there in under an hour. Turning onto their street puts a stone in the pit of my stomach, and I wish Mom and I had decided to get together elsewhere. Even shopping, which I hate, would be preferable to the onslaught of images rushing in: four young girls traipsing up and down the streets, walking to each other's houses under a bright summer sky, glee trailing behind us. Giggles, whispers, gruesome stories rolling off our tongues. I should've canceled today altogether.

But I parallel-park in front of the house, shove the unease—and the memories—down deep, and don an untroubled mask. My mom hugs me and doesn't hold on too long, something she does when she knows there's a problem, so my subterfuge works. I kick off my shoes, having nearly six inches on her in my bare feet as it is.

She's in palazzo pants and a flowy shirt, accentuating her body's slight roundness, a softness she didn't have when I was a child, but her arms and her heart are as strong as ever. The overhead light gives her skin a warm glow, and while she's over sixty, her hair threaded with gray, only a few wrinkles kiss the corners of her eyes and faintly bracket her mouth. Genetic luck, she says of her unlined forehead. I'm not quite as lucky, but I'm doing okay.

In the dining room she has pasta salad, bread drizzled with olive oil and herbs, and a tray of melon and prosciutto set out on the table along with a bottle of sparkling water. As I'm sitting, she's already dishing out food.

"The dressing's a new recipe. Your dad loves it, so hopefully you will too, and if not, pretend for my sake."

I wait for her to finish filling her plate before I take a bite, tasting garlic, rosemary, and pepper. Of course it's delicious.

"Long week?" she asks. "Good one, I hope?"

I nod and spear pasta with my fork. She doesn't request anything more. Patient confidentiality notwithstanding, we drew that line in the sand a long time ago. "But I'm proud of you, of what you do," she told me then. "Don't forget that."

"So where's Dad today?"

"He's playing golf."

I almost drop my fork. "Golf?" When I was a kid, he called it the most boring invention ever.

"Oh believe me, I teased him about it."

We're clearing the table when I say, "Do you remember Becca? Becca Thomas, who lived on Barron Drive with her mom?" As soon as the words are out, I want to pluck them from the air. It makes perfect sense to ask, but still. I'm a glutton for punishment.

She pauses, holding a plate and blinking, then gives a little shake of her head as she turns to the dishwasher. "Yes, I remember her. Why?"

"I have a patient with a similar history and thought, I don't know, maybe there's something I can refer to for help. Or something." I'm talking too fast and know it. "My memories are a little vague. There's a lot I can't remember at all."

"Good," she says, and her vehemence surprises me. She rinses another plate, then fixes me with a frown. "You were young, and her . . . it was hard on you."

"What do *you* remember?"

She shuts the dishwasher with a thud, and I follow her into the living room. The furniture has changed since I was kid—gone are the floral prints, swag curtains, and overstuffed sofa—but the layout is exactly the same.

"Do we really need to talk about this?" she asks.

I want to say no and change the subject, but I say, "Please."

"I was—*we* were—shocked," she says, sitting on one end of the sofa. I take the other, nudging a striped throw pillow out of the way.

"And?"

Her lips pinch tight. "We didn't know about her mother. Becca seemed like a normal happy kid, like you and the rest of your friends. If we'd known how bad things were, we never would've let you spend the night there. Never." She practically spits the word. "Nothing ever happened when you were there, did it?"

I blink, and in the brief darkness see Becca spitting into an open bottle of wine.

"No," I say. "Her mom stayed out of our way." I tuck the pillow in my lap and wrap my arms around it.

"We did everything we could for you. You know that, right? Do you remember Dr. Sakalauskas?"

"Yes," I say, remembering a kind, calm woman with a slight Eastern European accent. I remember knowing I couldn't tell her what happened, so I pretended to know nothing. I also remember months with a tutor instead of school, my parents trying extra hard to act normal and me doing the same until eventually things . . . settled. I learned how to hide the guilt, shame, and distress. By the time I went back to school, I appeared to be myself again. At least on the outside.

None of which matters now.

Mom shifts on the sofa. "Did I tell you I bought a new—"

"Her mom's out of prison," I say, my arms tightening around the pillow.

She stares down at her hands, gives a small shake of her shoulders. "Okay," she says, rising to her feet, cheeks flushed. Upset, yes, but not surprised. "I don't want to talk about this anymore. It isn't healthy."

"You already knew, didn't you? Mom, I—"

"No. Find some other way to help your patient. I'm sure you can. What happened was a long time ago. Best to leave it in the past."

I wish I could.

"Okay," I say, raising both hands. "But before I forget, can I look though the old photo albums?"

Her eyes pinch at the inside corners, her lips thin, and I swear she's going to say no, but she waves toward the stairs. "They're up in the middle bedroom."

She doesn't come with me.

My old bedroom is now a craft space slash reading nook slash home office. Inside the closet, the albums are side by side on the top shelf. All are labeled on their spines, so 1990/1991 is easy to find—Mom is nothing if not organized.

The photographs are tucked into plastic sleeves, three to a page with a paper margin filled with notes in my mom's delicate handwriting. So MUCH SUN! Me in a tank top, my shoulders vivid red. SOMEONE IS ANGRY! Me again, sulking in a chair, not looking at the camera. HAPPY BIRTH-DAY! Dad and I at the dinner table, a huge cake in the center.

One picture shows Becca from the back, her hair unmistakable, and another's too filmy to see her face. My heart sinks as I turn the pages. I'm more than halfway through when I find what I'm looking for.

We're on my front lawn. Shorts and T-shirts. Arms linked. Chins up. Wide, happy smiles. My hair in a braid looped over my shoulder, the tail resting near my waist; hers is hanging free. This is the Becca I remember the fiercest. From the lighting, it must have been early evening. I slip the photo from its protective sleeve. More of my mom's writing on the back: JUNE 1991. This picture was taken not long before our big fight.

Footsteps approach. From the doorway, Mom says, "I forgot how long your hair was."

"Too long. She loved to braid it. And unbraid it, too." Savagely, I blink away tears. "You never have friends like you do when you're a kid," I say, once I'm sure my voice won't quaver. "I think I read something like that in a Stephen King book."

"I've never understood why you read those."

"Kids like scary things. I wouldn't read one now if you paid me, but anyway," I say, drawing out the word as much as I can, "it was your fault for letting me."

Her brows arch. "Let you? The first time I caught you with one, you'd snuck it out of our bedroom."

"What? No, Dad lent it to me."

"No, he did not. He left it on our nightstand and you took it without asking. When he realized it was gone and you had it, he and I had a very tense discussion because I thought you were too young. You were only about ten, I think, maybe even nine. By then you'd read more than half of it, so he thought we should let you finish and if you got scared, so be it."

I rub my forehead. I clearly remember my dad giving me *Carrie* and telling me I might like it. It was the first adult horror novel I'd ever read. I wouldn't even have considered it if not for my dad. "Are you sure?"

"Absolutely."

My fingers curl the photo, but I catch myself before it creases. "Can I keep this?"

She blinks twice. "Take whatever you want."

"This is enough." I flick the picture against my thumb. "We were so silly, weren't we?"

The front door opens, and my dad calls out, "Barbara, I'm home!"

"We're up here," Mom says.

Dad thumps up the stairs. "Hey, bug."

I wrinkle my nose at the nickname and hug him in return. He smells faintly of cigarettes, a habit he's been trying to break for years.

"Did you have fun?" Mom says.

"Yeah, Dad, how was golf?"

"You two. It wasn't that bad. I may have even had fun," he says. "But the storm's finally rolling in. They're calling for thunder and lightning, maybe even some flash flooding in your area."

"I should head out then," I say, sliding the photo into my pocket. "Ninety-Seven is a bitch when it rains."

"I'll fix up a container of pasta salad for you to take home to Ryan," Mom says. "I promise I'll be quick."

When I leave, with repeated admonitions from both of them to drive safely, the sky is gunmetal, air thick with the scent of the impending squall.

Becca always loved the rain.

I push the thought away and get in my car. Turn at the end of my parents' street and pass the field, but instead of continuing straight, I make another turn. At the end of the street, I pull to the side with the engine running.

The house looks completely different. For one thing, it's visible from the street now; the hedges are gone. In their place is a low border of hostas. No room for kids to hide. Without the heavy greenery, the stone appears lighter. Then, the porch was fairly small; now it spans the length of the facade, with a white railing and squared columns supporting the roof. Wicker lawn furniture with flowered cushions sit on either side of the front door. That's been changed, too. Once solid wood, now it has an oval of etched glass in the center.

I close my eyes. Hear the susurration of our voices and footsteps breaking the silence. How many times did we sneak in it that summer? It's a wonder we never got caught.

There might've been signs of a struggle at her house, but that last night we weren't there. We were here. The fine hairs on my nape rise. You don't need flickering lights or doors slamming shut, the parlor tricks of a poltergeist, to be haunted. The true ghosts are made of deed and word and live deep inside the marrow and bone.

She begged me to help her. And then her eyes closed.

My own snap open. "Stop it," I hiss, my voice loud and ragged. The photo is a weight in my pocket. I slip it out, shove it under my purse on the passenger seat.

She begged me.

I shake away the thoughts, jam the car in drive, and pull away as the first drops of rain strike my windshield.

* * *

With Ryan still out like a light, I slide out of bed, throw on leggings and a long-sleeved T-shirt, and grab my keys and purse, bagels and cream cheese on my mind. No rain today, but no sun either. A drowsy sort of day. I'm near Panera Bread when I turn toward Gia's instead. It's not the best idea, I know, but I'm so close and it'll only take a few minutes. What's the harm in driving by? If Ryan wakes and sees I'm not there, he'll text me. I can tell him Panera was crowded. Won't even be a lie. Not on a Sunday.

The neighborhoods in West Annapolis are nice, most of the houses old but heavily renovated. Modest yards. SUVs with roof racks for kay-aks and paddleboards. Cedar swing sets peeking over wood fences. An A-frame at the end of Gia's street has a shiny blue-and-white FOR SALE sign in the yard. I drive slow, gaze panning left and right.

I recognize Gia's house from her Facebook photos. They've placed two Adirondack chairs, stained deep blue, on the front porch, a small table between. A hanging basket of flowers. Garage doors closed tight. No cars in the driveway. Front porch light still on. I drive to the bottom of the street, turn, and make another pass, driving even slower. Even though I'm not doing anything wrong, I feel conspicuous. Guilty.

I park by the house for sale. Great idea number two. Why not make it three? Mouth dry, I act casual as I get out of the car and walk up to the front door. Peek in the window. The furniture inside is staged, so the owner's already moved. To anyone who might be watching—and this neighborhood seems even quieter than mine—I'm interested in the property. After making a show of looking over the fence into the back-yard, I take to the sidewalk.

My heart beats double-time. I feel like a stalker, but I'm not. I'm investigating. I slow my steps, eye the neighborhood. I should go back. Get in my car. But no one's around.

Fingers taut, I approach Gia's house. Two steps lead to the porch. Four to the front door. While it's solid wood, there are narrow glass pan-els on each side. No curtains. Inside, a long hallway leads to a kitchen. To the left, a living room. To the right—

Behind me, a door shuts with a heavy thud and I jump. I don't see anyone, but it's warning enough. Tonguing sweat from my upper lip, I make myself walk a normal pace down her steps, away from her house. Once I shut my car door, I giggle. *Good one, Heather. Very clever.* Maybe I should've knocked on her door, said I was in the neighborhood. Checking out old friends. Accidentally, of course.

I rub the end of my nose with the side of my index finger. This peeking around does me no good. What can I hope to learn? Her taste in furniture? An accidental meeting, though . . . that could work. A way to get in front of her. To actually talk. To feel her out, so to speak. And no, she might not want to talk to me, but it's at least worth a shot. Since we live so close, I should be able to manage something. Just not here. This was a fool's game.

My phone chimes with a message from Ryan: MORNING. I text him back with a quick AT PANERA, WANT ANYTHING SPECIFIC? I'm waiting for his response when a shadow falls across my lap and three raps sound on my window. I drop my phone, biting back a yelp.

The man beside my car is in his midfifties. Short gray hair, slim build, navy-blue polo shirt. Narrow chin, deep brackets around his mouth, dark eyes. My instinct is to gun it, peel away from the curb fast, but I lower my window.

"You lost?" he says, without a trace of kindness. A smell of aftershave lotion, the kind with a ship on the bottle. My dad used it when I was little.

"No, but thank you for asking."

"I saw you looking at the house." He nods toward the FOR SALE sign. "And walking."

Neither are questions. Did he see me on Gia's porch?

"I'm in the market for a new house, closer to work," I say. "This neighborhood is one I've been thinking of. I have friends who live here."

He clears his throat, or maybe it's a scoff of disbelief. "The realtor's number is on the sign. If you want to see it, all you have to do is call."

Whatever would I do without you, Captain Obvious?

My phone chimes again. "It was nice to meet you, but I need to take care of this."

He taps the side of his fist on the car window's ledge and steps away, leaving me barely enough room. My stomach is fluttery, my fingers trembling.

Fuck you.

Fuck.

CHAPTER FOUR

THEN

"What if you had to eat a bug? What would you eat?" Gia said.

We were in the house, sprawled on the basement floor, and it was almost as dark as the first time we'd sneaked in, on account of the rain. We'd been lucky and made it inside right before it got bad and had been smart enough to take off our shoes so we wouldn't track in mud.

"That's disgusting," Rachel said.

"A ladybug," Becca said. "They'd be crunchy."

Gia and I cracked up, while Rachel made puking sounds.

I said, "An ant. A teeny, tiny, baby ant."

"But if it's so small, you might not be able to chew it," Becca said. "It might crawl back up. Or come out of your nose!"

Rachel shook her head. "I'd never ever eat a bug, no matter what."

"You have to pick," Gia said.

"Fine," Rachel said. "I'd pick a cricket."

"They're huge," Gia said.

"Yeah, but some people eat them," Rachel said.

Gia rubbed her chin as if she had a beard, and said, "I pick Heather to go next."

I already knew what I was going to ask. "What if you had to move someplace else? Where would you go?"

"Alaska," Rachel said. "To see penguins."

"Penguins aren't in Alaska, dummy," Becca said. "They're in Antarctica and you can't live there. It's all ice."

"Oh," Rachel said, and her face got all sad-hurt.

"I'd live someplace warm," Becca said. "Like Florida."

"But they have flying cockroaches," I said.

"So?"

"What if they flew in your hair and got stuck?" I said.

"I don't want to *what if* anymore," Rachel said. "Becca, can you tell the rest of the story now?"

"Yes, tell the rest," I said. I'd tried to get Becca to tell us—or at least me—more, but she wouldn't.

"Please," Gia said, her hands clasped together under her chin.

Becca leaned back on stick-straight arms.

"Come on, Bec," I said.

"Yeah, come on," Rachel said.

Becca grinned slow and wide, like a Cheshire cat. "O-kay. I can't tell you the rest—I told you it was long—but I can tell you some more."

She stared at the ceiling, her mouth working for what felt like forever before she said, "The people decided to dig the Red Lady out, but when they dug the hole, it was empty, remember?" She waited for us to say yes. "They left it like that and no one talked about her. Like nothing had happened. But they all had dreams, remember that, too?"

Again, she waited for us to respond.

"Good. So the dreams stopped, but everyone felt like they were being watched all the time, no matter where they went. Then they started hearing their name whispered. At first they thought it was a neighbor or something, but no one else was ever there. One night a woman woke up and thought it was her son, but he was asleep. The voice kept saying her name, so she followed it outside, thinking maybe someone was hurt. The next morning a neighbor found her in the hole, dead, mouth full of dirt."

"Gah," Rachel said, covering her mouth.

I tugged on my lower lip and ran my tongue across the back of my teeth. I wondered if the woman was dead first or if the dirt killed her.

"But the worst part?" Becca said.

"What?" Gia said.

"They found a long, smeary trail of blood on the ground leading to the hole. They buried the woman and filled the hole back in, but that night, the man who found the woman heard the voice, too. He went to look and *bam*, gone. They found the hole open and him in it the next day. No matter how many times they filled the hole, it kept happening. And even though people knew they shouldn't follow the voice, knew it was a trick, they couldn't help it. It was like they had to go, and when they did they ended up dead. They tried tying each other up at night, but it didn't help. They'd find piles of rope where people should be. They tried putting cotton in their ears, but it didn't work either because they were hearing the voice only with their minds.

"One man packed up his family and left. For two days, nobody heard the voice, but the morning after that, they found the man's wife in the hole, cold and dead. The next night, his son, and the night after, the man."

"She wouldn't let them leave," I said.

"Right. Every morning someone else turned up dead until everyone was gone."

I clapped. I shouldn't have been happy, but they shouldn't have buried her alive. And Becca was right about the women who were supposed to be the Red Lady's friends. It didn't matter if they were scared; you always helped your friends.

"So that's it? Everyone died?" Gia said. "Then what? Did the witch go away?"

"I didn't say it was the end of the story," Becca said. "It's the end of this part."

"Wait," Rachel said. "If the witch didn't have hands, how could she have put the dirt in their mouths? She wasn't even alive anymore, was she?"

Gia grunted and clutched her belly. At my frown, she said, "I have cramps."

"Ugh, I have my period, too," I said.

"Me three," Becca said.

We all looked at Rachel.

"I don't have mine," she said. "But I can tell it'll be any day."

"That's so weird, right?" Gia said. "That we all get it the same time?"

"Nah, my mom and I get it close, too," I said. "She said it happens when girls are around each other a lot."

"I hate it," Gia said.

She'd had it the longest, since she was eleven. I'd had it for six months, Becca a little longer, and Rachel only two months ago. Afterward, her mom wanted to have *the talk* with her. Talk about embarrassing. We already knew about sex. My parents had told me when I was nine because I'd heard a kid at school talking about a vagina kiss, so I'd asked what it was. All our parents would've had heart attacks if they'd known we'd found a magazine in the field last year and knew a lot more than anyone had told us.

"I want to use tampons," Gia said. "But my mom said no."

"My mom said the same thing," I said. "She said I was too small inside."

"I used one of my mom's once," Becca said. "And you can't be too small, because babies come out and—"

"You did?" I said. "You never told me."

"I didn't have any pads left. What was I supposed to use?"

"What did it feel like?" Gia asked.

"Kinda weird at first, but it was gross when I took it out. It smelled like raw hamburger."

"That's what pads smell like anyway," I said.

"Yeah, but it was different," Becca said.

"Hey, I think it stopped raining," Rachel said. "Want to walk around?"

"Not if it's muddy out, no," I said.

"Want to watch a movie?" Gia said. "We rented *Dick Tracy* from Blockbuster."

"Please be kind," I said.

"And rewind!" Becca finished.

"I'm serious," Gia said. "And maybe you can tell more of the story after?"

"Maybe," Becca said.

But when the movie credits rolled, she said she had to go home, so I went with her because it was close to dinnertime. Halfway to my house, it started showering again and she grabbed my wrist.

"It's only rain," she said as I tried to pull away.

"I don't want to get wet."

"We're already wet!" She jumped in a puddle on the sidewalk, the way we did when we were little, splashing water everywhere.

"I'm getting soaked," I said, peeling my shirt away from my body. As soon as I let go, it stuck to my skin again, a soggy lasagna noodle at the bottom of a pot.

"So go home then," she said.

"You won't be mad?"

"Uh-uh." I couldn't tell if she was serious or not, but my hair was plastered to my back and my socks were a sopping mess. When I got to the end of the street, she was still outside, face turned up to the sky, all of her blurry, but not so I couldn't tell she was happy.

*   *   *

It rained the rest of the week. Becca ate dinner with us Friday night and ran home after to change her shirt because she spilled spaghetti sauce on it. While I was waiting for her to get back, a neighbor brought over my mom's Avon order. Mom asked if I'd borrowed any money from her wallet, which I hadn't, and then she sent me out to ask my dad for some. He was taking pictures of a crunched bumper on his car where some-ass-hole-hit-it-in-the-parking-lot-and-didn't-even-leave-a-note. Becca came running up the sidewalk at the same time.

"Hey, girls," my dad said, lifting his camera. "Say cheese!"

We linked arms, and right before Dad snapped the picture, Becca grabbed my braid and pulled it forward. My mom was tapping her foot when I brought her the money, and she shooed us upstairs so I could pack for spending the night with Becca.

When we got to Becca's, her mom was upstairs and didn't even come down to say hello. I'd never tell my mom, though. She'd get upset.

We went down to the TV room in the basement; the living room was all fancy furniture and a big glass case of creepy antique dolls. If you looked at them the wrong way, their eyes followed you. Becca said they'd been in her family for a long time, but she couldn't wait to smash them to pieces. I'd help her, too.

After we watched *Full House*, we put on MTV and danced around until her mom yelled to turn it down because she had a headache. Becca turned it super low and said, "She can't even hear it up in her room, no matter how loud it is."

Her mom had never been the chaperoning-on-field-trips kind of mom. But if she gave us a ride somewhere, she'd never minded if we told ridiculous knock-knock jokes like *knock-knock, who's there, Europe, Europe who, no, you're a poo* or sang along to the radio. I wasn't sure when she'd stopped letting us, but the last time I'd ridden in their car there was all this silence, so big it hurt my ears.

Becca rubbed her side and her shirt lifted, revealing three scabbed lines like healing cat scratches, but she didn't have a cat.

"What are those?" I said, my voice low.

"Nothing," she said, pushing her top back down fast.

I tried to grab for her shirt, but she shoved me away, hard enough I had to pinwheel my arms to keep from falling.

"Stop!" she said.

"Sorry, sorry."

She tugged her ear. "It's nothing. I scratched myself the other day. It's not a big deal."

"Then why are you acting like it is?"

"I'm not," she said, turning so I couldn't see her. "You are."

"Do they hurt?"

She blinked at me a few times, then went upstairs, walking the way my mom did when she was late for work. She was getting out mint chocolate chip ice cream when I went up.

"I'm sorry," I said.

"Okay," she said, but she didn't sound okay at all. I wasn't sure if she was mad about the scratches, but I didn't want to ask and make her even more mad at me.

We were only there for a couple minutes when Becca's mom thudded down the steps. We hurried but weren't finished scooping the ice cream, then Becca dropped the scoop in the sink and had to rinse it off.

"What are you girls doing?" Mrs. Thomas said, leaning against the doorway, holding an empty glass.

"What's it look like?" Becca said. "We're getting ice cream."

"Don't eat all of it. I might want shome, *some*, too." When she spoke, her mouth was trying too hard to make the right shapes.

I moved as close to the counter, as far away from her, as possible. I wanted to run back down to the basement, but Becca was between me and the door. And anyway, I'd never leave my best friend like that.

Becca and I kept hurrying as her mom pulled a bottle of wine from the refrigerator. After she filled her glass, the wine sloshing near the top, she petted my hair. I hated when people did that without asking, but I held still, even though my hands were shaking.

"You're a good kid, Heather," she said.

"Thank you, Mrs. Thomas," I said, the words barely above a whisper.

"And sho polite."

When she let go of my hair, I exhaled long and slow. Becca shoved the ice cream container, lid only half closed, toward me, and I put it in the freezer.

"Are you girls watching television?"

"Come on," Becca said, nudging my foot.

"I'm not finished talking to you."

"Our ice cream's going to melt," Becca said.

Mrs. Thomas laughed, the sound like a glass dropped on pavement. "Go then," she said. She took a couple steps forward, moving in a zigzag rather than a straight line. Wine crested the edge of the glass and ran down her hand.

"Let's go," Becca hissed, and slammed the basement door shut behind us.

I tensed, waiting for her mom to yell, but she didn't. We sat between the coffee table and sofa, ate our ice cream, and didn't say anything. Her mom banged around in the kitchen, opening and closing cabinets, before thumping up the main staircase.

Becca dropped her spoon in her bowl. "I wish she'd stop. I hate her this way."

I hated her that way, too.

Becca stalked over to the shelves and came back with a book I recognized from the picture on the front. Rachel said Ted Bundy was cute, which was gross because he was a killer and old enough to be our dad, but his eyes freaked me out.

When Becca finished reading aloud the part about the bloodstained sheets on Lynda Ann Healy's bed, she said, "You can't ever tell anyone about her. Promise?"

I knew she wasn't talking about Lynda Ann Healy. "I told you a gazillion times, I won't."

"Promise again," she said. "Cross your heart and hope to die."

I made an X over my chest. "I promise. Cross my heart and hope to die."

She grabbed her bowl and told me to bring mine. We could faintly hear her mom's television playing and didn't speak while we rinsed our dishes. After, she grabbed the wine bottle from the fridge.

"What are you doing?" I said.

"Shhh." She unscrewed the cap, spit in the bottle, and pushed it toward me.

I stepped back. "I can't do that."

"If you're my friend, you will," she said.

"I am your friend."

She shoved the bottle in my direction again.

"Fine." I had to try three times, but I spit a little. My mom would kill me if she knew. It didn't matter that Mrs. Thomas was the way she was.

"Ugh." She took the bottle back and spit in it twice more. "Want to go to the house?"

"What about your mom?"

"She's probably asleep and won't wake up, or if she does, it'll only be to get more spit-wine."

"I don't know," I said. I half wanted to go and half didn't. Her mom was acting really strange tonight—I'd never been scared of her before—so maybe going wouldn't be such a bad thing. But it was late and the house seemed safer when it was all four of us, not just two.

"Oh, come on. I've done it by myself."

"You have?" I said.

"Yes."

But she'd be too scared to go in the house by herself, wouldn't she? Except sometimes when she was lying, her face said she was, no matter what her mouth said. This time, I couldn't tell.

"What if I promise to tell you more of the story?" she said.

"Gia and Rachel will be mad."

"Not if you don't tell them."

Five minutes later, shoes on, we were outside. The neighborhood was all shadows and cricket chirps and we walked fast. By the time we got to the house, we were panting. When Becca locked the door behind us, my arms went all-over goose bumps. The house was pitch-black. I waved in front of me and felt air on my nose but couldn't see at all. There was nothing in the dark that wasn't there in the light, but it felt different. It felt alive. It felt hungry.

"Scared?" Becca said.

"No," I said, but my mouth was dry and papery.

"Liar."

We fumbled through the darkness, Becca in front, groping the walls. I grabbed her hand and squeezed. "Let's go back," I said.

"What are you talking about?"

"It's creepy," I said.

"It's not that scary."

"Yes it is. I can't see anything."

"We're near the kitchen," she said. "Once I turn the light on, it'll be fine, and we're together, so . . ."

I squeezed again, trying to make her stop, but she kept moving. "Don't you remember the house in Florida where Ted bashed all those girls in the head? They were together, too."

"They were sleeping, and there's no Ted Bundy in Towson."

"How would we know?" I said.

"Because there'd be bodies and missing girls."

"There was one last year."

"She ran away and they found her and brought her back," Becca said. "Hold on, here's the basement door. Don't push so close; I'll fall down the steps."

The dark turned the sound of her fingers moving along the wall into skittering mouse feet. I pressed my knuckles to my mouth, pushing my lips into my teeth. With a tiny click, a pool of yellow light appeared at the bottom of the stairs.

"See? We're fine," she said.

Even with the light, the basement was shadowy and gray, especially in the corners. It smelled even worse than it had the other day. I tried breathing through my mouth, but it tasted like wet, smelly socks.

"Becca, it smells really bad."

"You'll get used to it in a few minutes. It's like when you poop. At first it stinks, and then you can't even smell it." She sat down, curling her fingers around my wrist so I had to, too. The floor was even colder now.

"We didn't check the rest of the house," I said. "What if someone's hiding upstairs?"

"There's nobody here except us."

"If there's a killer hiding here and he gets us," I said, pulling up my knees and resting my chin between, "it's your fault."

"Have you ever thought about it?"

"About what? Killers hiding in this house? I just did."

"No, I mean killing someone," she said.

"You're joking, right?"

She touched the tip of her tongue to the bow of her lip and scratched the house key back and forth across the carpet.

"Right?" I said, trying to ignore the key. All I could think of was being buried alive, scratching at the coffin to get out and no one would ever hear.

"No," she said, setting the key aside. "I'm serious. Have you?"

"No. That's awful. I thought we came here so you could tell me—"

"I have."

"No you haven't," I said.

"Yes I have," she said. "And I bet I could get away with it, too."

I snorted. "Ted Bundy couldn't."

"I'm smarter than he was."

"But you're not crazy. You have to be crazy to do that to people." I swirled my finger near my temple.

"Maybe, maybe not." Her face went blank, like someone took a squeegee and wiped it away.

"Becca, that's not funny."

Her eyes were empty and reminded me of a house with no one home. She was only goofing off, but it gave me the heebie-jeebies. I pinched her arm. "Becca, stop, that's freaky."

Her face rearranged itself the right way. "Pretty good, right? I practiced in front of the mirror."

"Why would you even want to do that?"

"Why not? It's fun." Becca moved her jaw from side to side, looking at the ceiling. "Anyway, what Red Lady story should I tell you?"

"It better be good, after all that."

"Okay," she said, scooting closer. "So you already know when the people in the village buried the Red Lady, they didn't kill her. That's why the hole was empty. If she was dead, they would've found her body."

"Uh-huh," I say.

"Everything they did to her made her stronger. She was kind of a ghost, but not, and could go wherever and do whatever she wanted. After everybody in the village was dead, she disappeared."

"Where did she go?" I said.

"No one knows. No one saw her for a long time. I think she was hiding so everyone would forget about her."

"Did they?"

"Yeah, but she was there, watching and waiting, getting stronger than she'd ever been."

I darted a glance into the dim corners. Gnawed the edge of a fingernail. "But she couldn't cast spells anymore, could she? She still didn't have hands, right?"

"Right, or a tongue, but she didn't need spells anymore. She could do things just by wanting to, and if she talked to you, she talked to you in your mind." She tapped her head. "Maybe I'll just tell you this story and not Gia and Rachel. I have plenty of others I can tell them."

I rubbed the heart between my fingers. She lifted hers and kissed it. "Best friends," she said.

"Forever," I said.

"So years later, there was this girl about our age, and she lived with her dad, her little sister, and their old dog. Even though her dad worked a lot, they were pretty poor, so she got picked on. Not calling her names, but throwing rocks at her and pushing her down so she got all bruised up. The leader was a boy who hated her."

I scrunched my face. "Why?"

"Don't know. He just did. The girl didn't tell her dad and made her sister promise not to tell either. She didn't want to be a crybaby. She didn't even cry when the kids knocked her down, which made them even madder. That's what they wanted most of all, to know they hurt her."

Becca tucked her hair behind her ears. "Then they got the idea to feed her dog poisoned meat."

I growled and brought a finger to my lips, teeth pinching the skin. She knew I hated when animals got hurt. Even Cujo, a rabid dog that killed people. "Did the dog . . ."

"Yes, and the girls' hearts were broken. The dog was pretty much their best friend. The kids laughed about it, said it was just a stupid old dog. For the first time, the girl cried in front of them. All they did was laugh even more and said they were going to kill her little sister next and then her dad.

"So she asked the Red Lady to help her."

"How? And how did she know about her?" I said, my finger mushing the words.

Instead of answering, she said, "The girl asked every night for two weeks. She promised she'd do anything, give her anything, to protect her sister and her dad. One night, when her dad worked late and her sister was asleep, she went in the backyard, and the Red Lady stepped out of the shadows."

I felt a sting and tasted blood. When I pulled my finger free, a tiny drop of blood welled to the surface of the ragged cuticle.

"She had long, thick hair like yours, except hers went all the way to the ground. Her skin was bone white. Her lips were cherry red and her eyes were all black, like they were colored in with a marker. Like shark eyes. And you can't look at them. If you do . . ."

"What?" I said. "What happens?"

"They'll find you in the morning with a mouth full of dirt."

"Dead?"

"Dead."

I hunched my shoulders all the way to my ears.

"Instead of hands," Becca said, "she had bloody stumps, and when she opened her mouth, more blood dripped out. Worst of all, when she walked she left a trail of blood, and since her hair was so long, it dragged through it."

"Ugh," I said, but my voice barely made any noise at all.

"It's not her fault. The blood is the one thing she can't fix. She's always bleeding because of what the people did to her. And sometimes you won't see her, but you'll see the blood and know she was there. But then it goes away, disappears, so no one else will know she was there.

"Anyway, the Red Lady waited to see if the girl would run away, but she didn't. Even though she was scared, she was more scared of the kids. The girl told her what they did to her dog and asked if she could bring the dog back and keep her sister and dad safe. The Red Lady said, in the girl's mind, she couldn't bring the dog back—once an animal is dead, it's dead forever—but she could keep them all safe if the girl was willing to pay her price."

I exhaled, long and low. "What was her price?"

Becca leaned close and said, "Her eyes."

I swallowed. Hard.

"That's what the Red Lady does," Becca said. "If you ask for help, you have to really mean it. She'll know if you don't. And she won't help everyone. She decides who sees her, who she helps or not."

"What did the girl say?"

"She agreed, and the Red Lady vanished." Becca clapped once, and I jumped. "The next day they found the bullies buried in a hole, all the way to their necks, their mouths full of dirt. The leader was the only one alive. When they pulled him out, his tongue was cut out so all he could do was make weird noises. Then he died. When they did the autopsy, guess what they found in his stomach?"

"What?"

"His tongue."

"She made him eat it?"

"Uh-huh. A couple nights later, the Red Lady came to see the girl. She was ready to give up her eyes, even if the Red Lady had to scoop them out, but all she did was say a few words, and the girl couldn't see anymore. Just like that."

"Then what?"

"Her sister and her dad were safe. The girl had to learn how to do things without being able to see, but she wasn't dead. And sometimes she felt the Red Lady watching over her."

I shivered, and Becca giggled.

"Would you," I said. "If she was real, would you ask her for help?"

Becca went still. "She is real."

CHAPTER FIVE

NOW

I hang up the phone, cross off another wrong Lauren Thomas, and drum my fingers on my desk. I've winnowed it down to three possibilities: one never answers her phone, one has a disconnected number, and the number for the last belongs to someone else. I have their addresses, but I'm not going to play drive-by. It was a juvenile idea to begin with. A gut I-don't-know-what-else-to-do reaction. So, what do I do? Not sure knocking on a door is any better—to be honest, they're both less-than-brilliant ideas—but I can't think of anything else. And something is better than nothing.

I'm pulling up directions for the next address when Ellie tells me my next patient is here. I close Google Maps and check the filing cabinet, but the slot where Trevor's file should be is empty. I flip through the files on either side and nope, not there either.

Ellie answers after one ring.

"Do you have Trevor's file with you?"

"I don't think so," she says, and I can hear her frown. "Why?"

"It's not in the cabinet. I'm sure I gave it to you last week so you could update his insurance information." I try to keep the irritation from my voice, but I suspect I fail.

"No, I remember, but I put it back," she says, her words in a rush.

"Could you please double-check?"

"Absolutely."

I flip through the files again. I swear I remember giving her Trevor's. But I also remember her returning it while I walked another patient up front. There's a slight knock at my half-open door, and I look up to see Ellie there with worry heavy on her face.

"I don't have it up front," she says, clutching her hands. "I'm so sorry. Can I help you look?"

I wave her in, and she stands so close I can almost taste her perfume, floral and sweet. In her early twenties, she's petite and usually wears her fair hair in a ponytail. A spring temp while our previous receptionist was on maternity leave, she became permanent once Trisha decided to stay home with her baby.

Luckily, it takes only a few minutes for her to locate the file. Although Trevor's last name is Andrews, she'd misfiled him in the Ws.

"I'm so sorry. I must've been rushing and put it back in the wrong spot."

"No worries," I say.

As she leaves, she glances at my desk. I curse myself for not turning over my list of Laurens, but Ellie's gaze doesn't linger long.

* * *

My eleven o'clock patient cancels, leaving several hours free on Tuesday. Outside, it's nothing but blue skies and crisp air, the kind of day that makes you want to play hooky. I nod as I pass Christina Bennett, the other psychologist here, in the hall and tell Ellie I'm off to the gym. Instead, I plug the first Lauren's address into my GPS and turn as directed, ending at an apartment complex in Parkville, not far from Towson. According to my list, the Lauren whose number doesn't belong to her anymore lives on the top floor. The label on her mailbox shows her name, so it seems she still lives here.

Five minutes later I'm back in my car, scratching off another name. This Lauren was most definitely not the right one, nor was she happy to have anyone knock on her door, even someone supposedly visiting a neighbor for the first time who got the building number wrong. I'm equal parts frustrated and relieved. Two names left. Two possibilities. What if neither is the right Lauren? Then what?

Lauren's the obvious choice. But is she too obvious?

And *obviously* whoever it is wants something from me. Money? We've got a little in savings, but we're not rich. Instead of giving me the necklace, wouldn't they have sent a picture along with a list of demands? Because if I throw the necklace away, it's over and done with. Never mind that I haven't. They don't know that.

I should return to the office, but my thoughts are Lovecraftian nightmares flailing for purchase, and I can't focus. Ten minutes later, I'm in the old neighborhood. I park at the bottom of the street closest to the field, grateful my Jeep Cherokee is one of those SUVs you see everywhere and never notice. No identifying bumper stickers or window decals; I doubt my parents would even know it was mine.

The field appears as it did last month, last year, last decade: a wide-open, neglected space depressed into the earth as though created by a giant's foot. Big fence at the far end, closest to the road. The fenced-in backyards of single-family houses along one side. Lots of trees there, too. Too-tall grass slaps against my jeans. The whole thing seems smaller than I remember, the rises on either side shorter. But that's always the way.

The pathway near the end isn't as well trod anymore, but the grass conceded defeat a long time ago. Beneath my feet, brittle weeds crunch and pebbles scatter. A small animal scurries away on my left. The field smells caustic and biting with cat spray, and I weave around several piles of dog feces hardened into brown-black fossils. I keep my shoulders squared, steps purposeful, but as I get close to the base of the hill I slow, searching the ground until I find a hefty stick.

I think I'm in the right spot. Or close enough. I kneel, stab the ground with the end of the stick, cutting free a tiny, hard clump. I try again. Another clump. A third time, but it's not the hoped-for charm. The stick is useless, the ground rock-hard. Ankle creaking, I rise and survey the field with fresh eyes. The earth is undisturbed, so the secret it holds is still safe. Somewhere beneath me is a knife.

Becca, are you here, too?

I fingertip a temple, but there's nothing. She has to be, though. I couldn't have carried her much farther. Not without being spotted.

Back in my car, on the road, radio turned up. Generic pop. Four-beat rhythm. Female voice, midrange. My thoughts tentacling in all directions, but not flailing. Searching for my next move. Rachel's house isn't far from here, and the likelihood of running into two nosy neighbors has to be slim to none. And I'm here. One quick drive, one quick look.

Except Rachel's there, getting into a silver Audi SUV, cell phone to her ear. Hair pulled back into a French twist, not a strand out of place. Black slacks, ivory cardigan. Purposeful steps. Chin raised.

Could the timing be any more perfect? A U-turn would be conspicuous, so I keep going, music off, counting on her distraction. She drives in the opposite direction; I do a messy three-point turn, finishing in time to see her making a right.

The movies make following someone look easy. It's not if you don't want to get caught. I let cars in between us, happy I'm not in something small and low. Rachel nears a shopping center. My guess, the grocery store, Target, or maybe Bed Bath & Beyond. But she passes all three. I hang back too far and move my head like a dodging boxer. For a few panicky seconds, I'm sure I've lost her, but a flash of silver as another car turns right proves me wrong. But I'm too far back and the road curves in fifty yards. She'll be out of sight. Plenty of places to turn off.

I blow through two lights I pretend hadn't switched from yellow to red, slowing so I don't get left behind at the next, which is very definitely red. Rachel scoots to the right lane and takes the on-ramp to 695, one car between us, and I cut off a Honda to make it in time. The driver taps the horn. I wave.

Now I'm thinking White Marsh. The Avenue is a popular spot. Open-air shopping. But she zooms by the exit and merges onto 95 South. Stays right to merge onto 895. The same route I take home. Maybe she'll take an exit off 895.

She doesn't.

When we hit the Baltimore Harbor Tunnel, I'm three cars behind. Once I read an interview with Stephen King, who passed through the tunnel while here on a bookstore visit, and he commented how creepy it was. The tunnel, not the visit. I've driven through it so many times I don't think much about it, but he's right. The ceiling is low, the lanes narrow, and the roar of moving engines fills every square inch. Even with the windows shut and vents closed, the thick stink of all the trapped exhaust is impossible to block.

After the toll plaza, Rachel keeps going straight, toward Annapolis. The speed limit's sixty-five, which means most folks go eighty-plus in the left lane. She drives in the middle, keeping with the flow of traffic. I'm four cars back. I keep waiting for her to switch to the right lane and take an exit, but it doesn't happen. I clench the steering wheel so tight my knuckle bones are mountains about to split the skin.

Maybe she knows I'm following her. Maybe she's trying to mess with my head. If so, she's succeeding. For the life of me, I can't come up with a reason why Rachel would want to punish me for Becca all these years later. The Rachel I remember was timid, a follower. She was best friends with Gia, so any sort of jealousy of my friendship with Becca seems absurd. And if she saw something, there's no way she could've kept quiet. She would've shouted or shrieked or something. Unless she was too shocked. Maybe she didn't even realize what she saw?

I shake my head. That's even more absurd.

We're close to the exit for Benfield Boulevard when brake lights flash. I crane my neck and see police cars and an ambulance. Traffic merges to the leftmost lane and it's a disaster, everyone trying at once. Horns beeping, then blaring. Inching forward, I keep one eye on Rachel's vehicle, the other on the road and the cars. Four cars between us becomes five, then eight, then a dozen, then so many it's ludicrous. A sea of red, all surging closer to the accident, a tractor trailer and a sedan, all mashed to hell.

My skin feels two sizes too small and I stink of adrenaline. Sour and ripe. I can't see Rachel's Audi anymore. She's too far ahead. The accident's fresh enough that the cop's still putting out cones to separate us from the road debris. If I'd been a half mile behind where I was, I'd be stuck for hours. As it stands, it's awful enough, but we're still moving. No way to get ahead, though, to close the distance between me and Rachel.

When it's my turn around the cones, I hit the gas hard, but it's no use at all. I've lost her.

"Fuck, fuck, fuck!"

My phone chimes and I grab it, never mind the state's no-handheld law. A message from Ellie.

"Fuck," I say again, but this time it's barely a whisper. I'm going to be late.

* * *

Two psychologists, a teacher, and an accountant walk into a bar: the opening to a bad joke. Yet here we are, walking into Davis' Pub for dinner. An Annapolis institution, it was originally a general store in the twenties. In the forties it became a lounge; in the late eighties, a pub. The food is good and cheap, but an appearance on Guy Fieri's *Diners, Drive-ins and Dives* in 2012 opened the door to tourists, so to speak, and helped its popularity.

The four of us, all friends from college, sit at a table in the back. Nicole and I, the psychologists, take the booth side, while Kelly and Jenn, high school teacher and accountant, respectively, take the chairs. A routine we have down to a science. Nicole's traded her usual tailored silks for jeans. Jenn and I are wearing jeans, too, but Kelly's in Lululemons and sneakers.

I came close to bowing out tonight, but Ryan was catching the latest World War II movie with Sean, his youngest brother. And tonight's a good thing, seeing friends who've only ever known me as an adult. But I feel off-kilter, waiting for them to see there's something wrong with me. That *I'm* wrong. I know I'm no different today than I was before the necklace arrived. Same guilty hands. Same guilty heart. Hiding in plain sight. Yet before, the truth belonged to me and me alone.

We order drinks and two crab pretzels to share, another routine. None of us need to scan the menu, but we do anyway. Nicole scratches above her right ear, fingertip disappearing into her hair, while she reads. Jenn twists the end of her French braid, and Kelly scowls, no doubt stressing over her diet, not that she needs to worry, not with her meticulous habit of counting calories and six days a week of power yoga.

Jenn starts a story about her son's school science project. I catch Nicole's distant expression, and we share a secret smirk. She often quips that we spend so much time seeing messed-up kids that we're too terrified we'll screw up our own to have them. We both pretend she's wrong.

The pretzels arrive, and when we're down to the last few bites, Nicole says, "Did you hear about the girl's body they found in Towson?"

I drop my fork. Luckily, Kelly's loud "Yeah" offers aural camouflage, but my blood rushes in my ears. I haven't watched the news, haven't heard anything, and my tongue sticks to my soft palate. *Not like this. Please.*

"It's the one who's been missing. Has to be," Jenn says.

"Yeah, that's what they're saying," Kelly says. "But they won't say, not till the autopsy." She glowers. "The kids in my classes have been talking about it nonstop."

I unstick my tongue. "Missing girl?"

"The eighteen-year-old?" Jenn says. "The one who's picture's been everywhere?"

"Oh," I say, sinking back against the booth. "Her." I did read about her online, but my mind is a blank when it comes to the details.

"Yes, her," Jenn says. "Some kids playing in the woods found her body. Can you imagine? That would mess you up a little. Out playing one minute, face full of decomp the next."

"Jenn, you're awful!" Kelly says. "And they didn't fall on her. They found her. Huge difference."

Nicole palms the table edge. "Lucky for them. Falling on a body would require at least another year of therapy."

Laughter all around, the kind that's too loud and too high. Four of us, talking about one of our own, dead—most likely murdered by a man. The Dead Girls Club, Redux: The Second Chapter. I can't help the smile.

"Cough it up, Heather; what's funny?" Kelly says.

"Oh," I say, blushing. "I was thinking about when I was a kid, how my friends and I would talk about serial killers and dead girls and . . ." I wave a hand. "Does it ever change? How much of a woman's world is shaped by violence?" That which we suffer, that which we suffer unto others.

"Way too much," Nicole says.

"The boyfriend definitely did it," Jenn says, after the waitress delivers our entrées. "If he didn't, why'd he split a week after she vanished?"

I think of a body, of someone running away. I'll have to go back to the field. And I'll have to take a shovel. I can't risk anything being found.

"It's always the boyfriend," Kelly says, leaning forward, the ends of her hair dangerously close to the ketchup squirt on her plate.

"Or the husband," Jenn says. "One a day, right? Isn't that the statistic?"

Nicole says, "It's three, here in the U.S., anyway. When they catch him, I hope they throw away the key, but I know that's too much to hope for."

"Right. He'll get a few years, if that. Then they'll let him out," Jenn says.

Nicole fans her fingers near her head. "Unless he gets off on a technicality. Some pretty little horseshit we're all supposed to swallow as plausible."

"Ha! The girls in my homeroom think he's too cute to be guilty. And we all know that if he comes from money, there's always a magic technicality," Kelly says, a French fry pointing skyward for emphasis. "The kids I know with money act like entitled little assholes."

"His parents have money," Nicole says. "They were raving about what a good kid he is, how this is all a misunderstanding. Pleading for him to come home so they can straighten it out, like he's the victim. God forbid his life gets ruined."

"Is he an athlete? A swimmer?" Kelly says. "Being groomed for the Olympics? 'Cause if so, he'll never be convicted. I'd stake money on it. Juries love the nice boys."

"Boys' lives are always more important than girls'," Jenn says. "No matter what happens. It makes me sick."

"Amen," Nicole says. "In the immortal, and terrifyingly true, words of Margaret Atwood, 'Men are afraid that women will laugh at them. Women are afraid . . .'"

"'That men will kill them,'" we say in unison.

After we've finished and said our goodbyes to Kelly and Jenn, Nicole and I stand outside chatting and enjoying the mild temperature until she stifles a yawn. "Okay, lady. Time to call it a night. Where are you parked? I'm there." She points up and across the street.

"I'm up there," I say, indicating a spot farther down.

There's a figure near my car on the sidewalk side, standing in an arc of shadow the light from the streetlamp can't pierce. I can't tell if the person is short or hunching down. They move toward the back of my car and disappear from sight. My fingers crook into painful claws.

"Earth to Heather?"

"Sorry, I thought I saw somebody standing by my car."

With a flash of concern, she turns to look.

"It's nothing," I say. "It was just the shadow from the light."

"Want me to walk with you?"

"No need," I say, but she's already moving.

The shadows are darkest at the rear of my car; easy to hide in the space between my bumper and the car parked behind. When we get there, Nicole wastes no time but stomps to the back. I'm only a few seconds behind. There's no one there. No one walking up the street, not this side or the opposite. The back seat's empty. Trunk, too. The locks on the doors are still engaged.

"I told you," I say. "Just a shadow."

"Better safe than sorry." She hugs me, turns to go, and half-turns back. "You know you can talk to me, right? No matter what it's about?"

"Of course," I say. "See you on Friday. Drive safe," I add as she runs across the street to her car.

Funny. *You know you can talk to me.* My mom said the exact same thing once, and I kept quiet then, too. Guess I've always been better at keeping secrets.

Even from myself.

I'm in my car, ready to put it in drive, when a bit of red beneath my wiper blade catches my eye. Thinking it's a leaf, I reach for the knob to turn on the wiper, but halt halfway there. It's not a leaf. It's a piece of ribbon, four or five inches long, once red, now faded to a watery pink, edges frayed. And it wasn't there when I arrived.

Becca had one like it in her hair that night, holding it back. It doesn't mean this one is hers, but ribbons don't fall from the sky, and the way it's positioned—tucked under the blade, not stuck to the windshield—says it isn't detritus. It's deliberate. My palms go slick, and I alternate wiping them on my pants. It can't be hers. It can't. A sound comes from my throat more akin to a dying animal than a human.

Is this from the person standing by my car? I wipe my skin dry again. Fight a lump in my throat. This is worse than the necklace. This feels confrontational, not passive. The car isn't cold, but I'm shivering and can't stop.

My hand twitches toward the knob, returns. I can't pull my gaze away from the ribbon. It was in her hair. And it was the same color as the—

I can't sit here. I have to get home. I open my door, not wanting to touch the ribbon, but I can't swipe it away. Tugging the sleeve of my shirt down, I use it as a barrier between fabric and fingertips. Not perfect—I can still feel the ribbon's rolled edges—but better. I go even colder, all over, and feel a presence behind me. Mouth dry, spine locked, I pivot slowly, so slowly.

No one's there.

I practically jump into my seat, locking the door as I shake the ribbon free. It moth-flits in the air and settles onto the passenger seat. I cover it with my purse, trembling as realization threads through my veins. They knew exactly where to find me.

* * *

There's no nightmare, only a sudden jolt from sleep to wide eyes. A split second later, I realize my hands are wet and sticky and the air is laced with the iron-rich smell of blood. Am I hurt? But there's no pain anywhere. With arms extended and a knot in my chest, I scoot off the bed. Ryan doesn't even stir. Is *he* hurt?

I try to say his name but can't make a sound. I turn, a puppet on a marionette's tangled strings. I listen. Hear nothing. Listen harder. A soft snore. And another. My shoulders sag.

I nudge the door to the hallway bathroom with my foot and flip the switch with several clumsy swipes of my elbow. Blinking in the sudden bright, I hip the door closed.

My skin is spotless, but I feel the blood, wet and sticky, between my fingers, under my nails. I inhale the sharp tang of copper, but no red streaks my inner thighs. I wipe myself with a tissue; no blood. Yet the sensation and the smell linger.

I turn on the tap and grab the soap. One, two, three washings. Rinsing my skin under water so hot it leaves my skin bright red.

I tap my fingers over my lips, cheekbones, the hollows of my lids. My face, yet a stranger's, too. I envision an orange, the outside perfect and unblemished. Begin to peel it away and what lies beneath? Perfect fruit or rot and ruin?

I squeeze the edge of the sink. I didn't mean to hurt her. I didn't. It's not what we thought would happen. I swear it with every bone in my body. But I could apologize ten thousand times and it wouldn't be enough.

I bestow a practiced grin to the mirror. It's garish, something from a Gothic film, me in the role of the woman locked away in a tower. But I've kept my wits for almost thirty years. Over ten thousand days. I can keep it together for one more. For as many *one mores* as it takes. I can do this.

There's no going back to sleep—my alarm's set to go off in less than two hours—so I grab my robe and pad into my home office. I do some more poking around Rachel and Gia's Facebook pages, looking for anything to help engineer an accidental meeting. Rachel posts the occasional meme, articles about scientific breakthroughs, heartwarming stories about people beating the odds. Gia's posts are far more interesting. Lots of intelligent political thoughts and strong opinions. From a recent picture of the Annapolis harbor, I springboard to her Instagram. Snapshots of places from her travels. No selfies. Food porn. Fresh fruits and veggies, all bright and tantalizing.

Then I spot it amid recent pictures of the kiwi, the carambola, the jackfruit: the background, the lettering on a sign above a pineapple display. I recognize it from a smaller, upscale grocery chain with only one location in the area.

The most recent picture was posted last Saturday. The previous, also on a Saturday. I tap my toes on the mat beneath my chair and return to Facebook. Both pictures were posted in the late afternoon. Back on her Instagram, I check the older pictures. Different store, but still taken on Saturdays. I sit back with a sigh. This I can work with.

*　*　*

At two thirty, the parking lot at the grocery store is packed. It's another gorgeous day to be outside; warm, but not hot, with a sky so blue it seems like it was painted. The kind of weather September does best. I circle a few times until a spot fairly close becomes available and sit with the engine off, idly picking at a cuticle and fighting a yawn. Wednesday night wasn't a one-off; I haven't slept well all week.

I know the likelihood of Gia shopping at the exact same time I'm here is slim, no matter the timing of her photos. But if I see her, I need to hang back. Keep track without following. Then at some point, maybe while in the corner near the frozen food, bump into her. Literally or figuratively, it doesn't matter. Act surprised. She's an old friend. Catching up is a great thing. Invite her for coffee right away. No, exchange numbers and email and then text or write in a few days. If she sent the necklace, she won't expect that. It might shake her up.

When a white-haired woman, a grocery bag looping her wrist, gives me a look, I realize I've been sitting here long enough for her to go into the store, buy what she needs, and return. As she gets in her car, I get out of mine.

I push a cart through the aisles, gaze skimming from shoppers to shelves. The music seeping from hidden speakers seems too loud, the people's voices shrill and demanding. The air smells of rotting vegetation, of turned milk, of fish. I grab a few things—bananas, pasta sauce, green olives—so my cart won't be empty. No Gia in any of the aisles, not even after I make a second circuit of the store. And is it my imagination, or is that woman standing at the cheese display looking at me? Is the man by the eggs staring? And what about the woman behind the deli counter?

This is preposterous, seeing specters in everyone. None of these people know me, know what I did. I leave the cart at the end of an aisle and, in the Barnes & Noble café three doors down, order a large latte in a to-go cup, but I sit at a table in the back. All I smell is coffee; all I hear are soft murmurs.

Maybe whoever is doing this left the ribbon to make sure I knew. Maybe they feared I didn't get the necklace. Maybe—maybe they can go fuck themselves. If they know what I did, aren't they being foolish by provoking me? I got away with it once, yes? I'm a hell of a lot smarter now. My bravery feels ready to shatter into a thousand pieces, but it's all I have right now. I sip my latte. Swallow. Repeat. When the cup's half empty, I'm feeling good. Strong and confident. *I will not let them win. I will not—*

"Heather? Heather Cole, is that you?"

The speaker moves into my line of sight. Are you kidding me? It's Gia.

I don't have to fake the shock. I feel it in my jaw and my shoulders. On shaky legs, I rise, hoping what feels like a pleasant expression is indeed one. In black leggings and a scarlet sweater, she looks even younger than she does online. Her hair is loose, hanging to her shoulder blades in a glossy curtain. And she's still got me beat in the curves department.

"I can't believe it," she says. "I haven't seen you in forever, but I knew it was you. You look exactly the same. Only taller."

"You do, too."

"Only not much taller."

We hug and I smell lavender. Not perfume, maybe conditioner or lotion. She keeps hold of my arms, just below the elbows, a moment longer.

"What are you doing here?" she says. "Do you live close?"

Her voice sounds genuine and there's no artifice in her smile, but it's way too soon to tell anything.

"I live in Edgewater, over the bridge on Route Two." I tip my head in the correct direction.

"I think I know where that is. We moved here a few months ago; I'm still trying to figure out my way around. We, meaning me and my husband, Spencer. Wild, right? Both of us ending up here? Of all the places in Maryland we could've moved to. Have you lived here long?"

"About ten years. Do you have a few minutes? Want to sit down?" I say, indicating the empty chair.

The corners of her eyes crinkle slightly. "I do and I'd love to. Let me grab a drink first. Do you want something else?"

"No, I'm good, thanks."

There's no line and she orders her drink from the barista, makes a quick sidestep to the bakery display and points, glances over at me, and points again. When she returns to the table, she has a steaming mug and two cinnamon coffee cakes.

"If you don't like them, I'll eat both," she says. "Spencer teases me because I have a huge appetite and eat more than he does."

"I love them," I say, which isn't a lie.

"So—"

"So—"

We grin, and for a moment we're nothing more than two old friends.

"So, where to start? How are your parents?" I say, picking off a piece of streusel crumb that melts on my tongue.

"My dad passed away three years ago—cancer—but Mom is fine. Healthy and happy. Matt—you remember my brother, right?—he still lives in Maryland, too, in Bel Air, with his wife and their four kids."

"Four?"

"Right? I never thought he'd ever have one, let alone more, but he's like father of the year now. Kind of funny. Makes me feel old, though."

"And you?" I say, even though I already know.

"No, Spencer and I decided early on before we got married. What about you?" She glances down at my hand, my ring.

"No kids. Yes husband."

"So what do you do now that you're a grown-up?"

I watch her closely when I say, "I'm a child psychologist." There's no sign of anything amiss, though. Her expression remains naturally curious. "And you?"

"Physical therapist."

So we both work with broken people, helping patch them back together. Curious, that. The conversation spirals into all the minutiae you cover when you haven't spoken in years. We eat our cake and drink our coffee in between. She sits forward, forearms resting on the table. No disinterest, no drumming fingers, no obvious signs she wants to be anywhere else. And no animosity.

"Are you and Rachel still friends?" I say, when there's a lull.

"No, we fell out of touch after high school. You know how it goes," she says with a small shrug. "You start to go in different directions, make new friends."

Not sure if it's my imagination or if there's a sudden change in the air. A heaviness of time and memories.

To hell with it. "Should we talk about serial killers or tell ghost stories, like old times?"

She's taking a sip when I say it, and after she chokes it down, she says, "I completely forgot about all that."

"Light as a feather," I say.

"Stiff as a board."

Her eyes are wistful. Becca's name lingers on my tongue, but I don't want to let it out yet.

"Cell Block Tango" starts playing from her purse, and she pulls out her phone with an apologetic grimace.

"This has been great," she says, silencing the music. "But I've got to get going. We're going to dinner tonight with one of Spencer's coworkers, so I need to shower and stuff. But I'm serious about getting together. What's your number?" Her fingers hover over the screen.

I hesitate again. It makes perfect sense for old friends to exchange contact info, but is she too eager for it? I clear my throat and give her my number; she texts so I have hers. We hug again and she squeezes my hand.

"I'm so glad I ran into you. I'll check my schedule and send you some dates for dinner. Deal?"

"Deal."

We're still smiling when she walks away. I let mine fall once she's out of sight and sit with my empty cup, tracing a fingertip around the lid. What are the odds? I came here to find her and she finds me instead? It doesn't feel right. But I sensed no dishonesty whatsoever. She's either an incredibly good actress or she's genuine. And I'd bet money she'll send me dates for dinner. Her voice was too earnest for lip service. Besides, what better way to keep an eye on me than to keep me close?

I pick at the skin of my thumb until a small piece rises, a skin periscope, and scrape it with the edge of a nail, enjoying the blood and the sting. Anger floods my veins, not a wall-punching surge but a steady wave, filling every cell. No matter how this ends, it wasn't my doing. Whoever it is, they didn't have to send the necklace, didn't have to turn back the clock. It's been almost thirty goddamn years. I crush my cup, leaving bloody smears on its waxed surface.

I hope like hell Gia isn't the one doing this. Because I like her.

I fucking like her.

* * *

I turn up the radio while I drive home so I don't have to hear my thoughts. The mail is still in the mailbox—no check for Ryan. No Ryan in the kitchen or the family room either. Halfway upstairs, I hear his voice in his office, so I keep quiet. The last thing I need to do is screw up one of his job prospects. In our bedroom, I exchange my jeans and V-neck for a slouchy sweater and leggings but leave my makeup on in case we decide to go out for dinner. Ryan's voice draws near then away again. He's pacing, which means I was right, a business call. The bane of being self-employed. Your job never stops, not even on a weekend. I stand just inside our bedroom door, not listening to him, but not *not* listening either. His voice moves farther away. The hallway's empty. His office, too. Craning my neck over the railing at the top of the stairs, I see a shadow moving across the wall, hear the soft tap of sock-clad feet.

His voice rises and falls, pauses, then sounds again. The shadow approaches and retreats as he moves the length of the front hallway. He's taking care to speak softly. A little too much care. The word *furtive* pops into my head, and although I feel like a sneak, I take two steps down, slow and quiet.

"Okay," he says. "No, it's fine." Silence as he listens, then, "I completely understand. Thank you for getting back to me, I appreciate it."

He draws closer to the staircase, and I make a beeline for the bedroom. By the time he comes upstairs, I'm flipping through the stack of paperbacks on my nightstand. From behind he gives me a hug, pressing a kiss to my neck.

"Hey, babe," he says.

"Hey yourself."

"What do you want to do for dinner tonight? I was thinking maybe the Boatyard."

"Not sure. Who was on the phone?" I say.

"Huh?"

"The phone? You were talking to . . . ?"

"Oh yeah, Mike, talking about his kitchen. Didn't want to bother you, so I went downstairs," he says.

"Gotcha. How's Karen?"

"She's good," he says, letting go. "Let me get a couple emails sent before I forget, and then we can figure out dinner."

I stand there, tapping the spine of a book against my palm. He lied. Why, I don't know, but that wasn't Mike on the phone. Ryan was too professional. I know that's not the way he talks to any of his brothers. I know him. I want to follow him into his office and ask again, but maybe I'm wrong. Maybe I'm so on edge I'm hearing things. This is Ryan, after all, and he has no reason to lie to me. No reason at all.

CHAPTER SIX

THEN

"Can you please get the jelly?" my mom said.

Becca jumped up from the kitchen table, where we were putting goldfish crackers in sandwich bags. Mom had eight pieces of bread spread out on the counter, four with peanut butter already smeared on.

"Thank you," Mom said, bumping Becca's hip with hers.

"Do you need bags?" I asked Mom.

"Sure."

I pulled four out of the box. I didn't get a hip bump, and it felt like a tiny punch in the stomach. Right that second I wanted Becca to leave. I was sorry about her crappy mom, but she couldn't have mine. But that made me the worst best friend in the world, so I threw a goldfish on her side of the table and stuck out my tongue. She did, too, almost her normal self again.

Once Mom finished, we loaded the sandwiches in our picnic basket, along with a bunch of Hi-C Ecto Coolers, which she called the most disgusting drink ever. Me and Becca took turns carrying the basket and a blanket. It was bright and sunny today and not too hot.

We got to the field before Rachel and Gia and already had the food on the blanket when they got there. When we were mostly finished eating, Becca slurped the last bit of her drink. "Who wants to hear another story?"

"Can we talk about something else? You've been telling stories about her all week. And they're all kind of the same. Somebody asks her for help and she does. Then they have to give something up like their eyes or a leg or something. They're getting boring," I said. It was partly true and partly not. I didn't mind the stories that much, but I hated that she was all Becca cared about. Hated that Becca acted like she was real.

Rachel and Gia wide-eyed each other.

"This story isn't the same at all, but you can leave if you want." Becca's voice was quiet, her words piercing.

She was my best friend in the world, but right now she looked like she hated me.

"I-I don't want to leave," I said.

Becca's face was unreadable, Rachel blinked fast, and Gia frowned. All three kept staring at me, and my stomach tightened.

"Okay," Becca said finally. "There was this town in the middle of nowhere, and there were three girls, older than us, who heard about the Red Lady. And they hated their history teacher. He was tough, and most of the time they failed the tests he gave them. Sometimes he'd give them a test on things he didn't even teach. All the kids hated him, but the girls hated him the most because he accused them of passing a note in class and said they were cheating. They got Fs on the test and suspended for three days.

"They all got punished, too, so they couldn't watch TV or talk on the phone for a month. But one girl got punished for two months, and every night she sat in her room, getting angrier and angrier. See, they hadn't been cheating. She was giving her friend a tissue for her runny nose. The teacher even saw what it was when he took it, but he didn't care. Since he thought they were passing a note, he pretended it really was one."

"Jerk," Gia said.

Who cared about a teacher and cheating? I played with my shoe-string, flicking the plastic end against my shoe until Gia elbowed me.

"Right? So they wanted to get back at him, but they knew the Red Lady didn't care about cheating or suspensions. She cared about important stuff. So the girls decided to make themselves believe the teacher had done awful things, sex things, to them. They wrote it down and read it aloud. They told stories over and over until it was like he really did it all. They pretended they were too afraid to tell their parents or anyone. And when they asked the Red Lady for help and she came, they wanted her to kill the teacher.

"But she knew the girls were lying. It made her remember how the villagers came to her for spells and then turned against her like *that*"—Becca snapped her fingers—"so instead of killing the teacher, she followed the girls. She wanted them to admit they lied, but they wouldn't. So she'd hide underneath their beds and thump her stumps against their mattresses, press her bloody mouth against their favorite shirts, whisper their names.

"And they still refused to say they were lying. They told their parents what the teacher supposedly did and *they* called the police. The teacher was arrested, and it made the Red Lady angrier, because even though the girls were lying, everyone believed them." She tossed a couple goldfish crackers in her mouth and brushed crumbs from her hands.

"All the kids were questioned," she said, talking around the crackers. "And more girls said the teacher did things to them, too. The sheriff knew they were lying because their stories were either too messed up or too perfect, but he didn't say anything."

"Why not?" I said, tugging my shoelace again. Okay, maybe the story was a little interesting, but I still wished we were talking about something else.

"Because he didn't like the teacher either, and no, I don't know why. The Red Lady started showing up in his mirrors, too, and in the back seat of his car, and in the middle of the road. So he told everyone the girls were lying, but it was too late.

"He told the girls to tell the truth, but they said they were, and there was nothing else he could do. So the Red Lady left him alone, since he tried to do the right thing.

"She didn't leave the girls alone, though. She followed one everywhere, breathing on the back of her neck, saying in her mind she was a liar and until she told the truth, the Red Lady was going to stay with her every minute of every day for the rest of her life. And if she wanted her to go away, all she had to do was look in her eyes. She was there when the girl took a shower, when she ate dinner, everywhere. And every morning the girl found streaks of blood in her room next to her bed, so she knew the Red Lady was watching her while she slept, but then it would just disappear.

"She couldn't take it anymore. She begged the Red Lady to stop, but all she did was laugh. So the girl jumped off a bridge and broke her neck."

Gia gave a high-pitched squeak, Rachel a little hiss. Becca ate another goldfish. Chewed and swallowed slow.

"Then she did the same thing to the next girl, and *she* slashed her wrists in the bathtub. The third girl, the one whose idea it was in the first place, ignored the Red Lady for as long as she could. She thought she was stronger and smarter than the other girls. But one night she was driving, and the Red Lady showed up in the passenger seat, showing her bloody smile. The girl lost control and drove into a tree.

"She didn't die, but she broke every bone in her body. In the hospital she kept screaming the Red Lady was going to get her, and she only stopped when they drugged her. She spent the rest of her life in a nuthouse, screaming anytime she was awake. By then, the Red Lady wasn't even doing anything to her anymore.

"But when she was an old lady, the nurses found her dead in her bed, mouth full of dirt. See, the Red Lady never ever forgets. Ever. If she wants you to look in her eyes, if she wants you to see her, eventually you will. Even if you're old and think you're finally brave enough or safe enough to look."

Rachel said, "Why didn't they just tell the truth?"

"Because they told the lie so much they believed it," Becca said.

Clouds moved over the sun, turning the day dark. I knew Becca's story was fake, but I went all shivery.

"Can we go hang out inside instead?" Rachel said.

"We should sneak back in the house," Gia said. "See if we hear anyone else like we did on Sat—"

Becca sat straight up. Gia turned bright red.

"You went there without me?" I said.

"Yeah," Becca said. "On Saturday, when you went to your grandparents' house."

"Why didn't you wait?" I said. This was different than when she and I had gone alone Friday night. We were best friends. We did stuff together without Rachel and Gia all the time. And they did stuff without me and Becca. But the three of *them* going without me? That felt wrong, really wrong. They'd never done anything without me before.

"We didn't plan it, we just went," Becca said. "We weren't even there long; Rachel thought she heard someone in the house."

"I did."

"Did not," Gia said.

"Were you even going to tell me?" I said.

"We were only there for a couple minutes. It's not a big deal," Becca said, turning away from me, toward Gia. "You know, there is something else we could do, something more than the stories."

"What?" Rachel said, and at the same time Gia said, "What do you mean?"

"There's a ritual we could do," Becca said.

"Like looking in a mirror and saying Bloody Mary three times?" I said. Everyone knew that didn't work. Nothing like that did.

Becca's nostrils flared. "Sort of. But you don't need a mirror."

"A séance?" Gia said. "Or light as a feather, stiff as a board?"

"Nope, it's way better," Becca said.

I wanted to remind them that when we'd done the séance last summer, Becca had blown out the candles and pretended it was the spirits, even though we all saw her do it. And when we tried light as a feather, stiff as a board, we dropped Gia and she hit her head.

"What do we have to do?" Rachel said.

"A bunch of stuff. And if it works, the Red Lady will step out of the shadows and show you her face."

"Then what?" Gia said.

"That's it. She isn't going to do anything, not if you're not doing anything wrong. You get to see her and then she goes away."

"Are you sure?" Rachel said.

"Positive."

"So when can we try it?" Gia said.

"How about Saturday?" Becca said. "We'll do it at the house."

"But I won't be here, remember?" Gia said. "We're leaving for Ocean City on Friday and won't be back until *next* Friday. You know that. I told you."

Rachel groaned. "Gi-a."

"It's not my fault you forgot."

"We'll wait for you," Becca said. "The Red Lady isn't going anywhere."

* * *

My mom was out running errands when we got back to my house. I put on MTV, but I was the only one watching. Everyone else started talking about what body part they'd give up if they needed to ask the Red Lady for help. I said I wouldn't give up anything.

Then Becca said, "What if your parents were killed and the person got away with it?"

"I don't even want to think about that," I said, glaring at her. But even then I wouldn't ask the Red Lady for help. Not that she was real, anyway, because she wasn't.

"I would give up my boobs," Gia said. "Nobody would have to die either."

"You can give them to me," Becca said, making grabby hands.

Gia squealed, and the two of them ran around like we did when we were little. We'd pretend our hands were poison, and if you got touched you had to act like you were dying: grabbing your throat, flopping down, gasping for air.

"Yeah, but what if?" Gia said.

"La-la-la, I can't hear you," I said, covering my ears.

Becca yanked one wrist and Gia the other. I squirmed away.

"You have to tell," Becca said. "What would you give up?"

Rachel stood in front of me and pointed one finger. "Eyes, fingers, or toes? Or boobs," she said with a giggle.

90

"Toes," I said.

"What about your hair?" Becca said. She was smiling, but it was funny. Not happy; kind of mean.

"Sure," I said. "My hair, then."

"I mean all of it," Becca said. "And it would never ever grow back again."

"Like bald?"

"Yes," Becca said.

"No way," I said.

"I thought you wanted to cut it off," Rachel said. "Becca said you did."

"I want to cut it short, not all off."

"Nope," Becca said. "You said cut it all off."

"I meant cut it shorter, to my shoulders, not all off," I said.

"That isn't short," Rachel said.

"It is for me."

"We could do it," Becca said, her voice quiet.

"What?" I said.

"Cut it. It would be fun."

I grabbed my braid. "Uh-uh. My mom would kill me."

"It's your hair," Rachel said.

"I know, but it's too thick. It won't look right."

"We could cut it so short it wouldn't matter," Becca said. Her mouth was too open, her teeth too big, like she was ready to bite.

My stomach clenched. I knew they really wouldn't do it, but their faces said they would if I let them. Maybe even if I didn't.

Ignoring them, I plopped on my back on the floor between the coffee table and television, my head propped up with a throw pillow. I craned my neck and saw a faded yellow butterfly on the underside of the table. A crayon ghost, drawn by a smaller girl. I always forgot it was there. It made me kind of sad, made me think one day it would fade away to nothing, and by then I wouldn't remember it had ever been there at all.

Becca flopped down beside me but didn't say anything. Gia and Rachel did the same on her other side. When my mom got home, we were still not really talking, just watching MTV. Then Gia and Rachel left, so it was just me and Becca.

Mom came out of the kitchen, wiping her hands on a dishrag, and said, "Girls, I'm making chicken and macaroni and cheese for dinner. Becca, would you like to stay and eat with us?"

"I can't tonight, but thank you."

"Of course," Mom said. "And I hope you know you're welcome to have dinner here anytime."

Becca smiled, but when my mom turned away, it fell off. She got up, put the pillow back on the sofa, and headed to the front door.

"You don't have to go yet," I said.

"No, I do."

"Come on, stay. You said your mom was probably working late tonight, and you love my mom's mac and cheese."

"Uh-uh."

"Why not?"

She met my gaze. "Because I don't want to."

I stepped back. Crossed my arms. "Okay. Please be kind?"

She made a strange face, like the way an old person looked at you if you made too much noise.

"What's wrong with you?" I said.

"Maybe I don't feel like being funny," she said, and pulled the door shut.

After dinner, I went up to my room and practically tripped over Becca's backpack in the middle of the floor. I tossed it over one shoulder and thumped downstairs.

"Becca left this, so I'm going to take it over to her house."

"Come right home after," Mom said. "Or call if you're going to stay there."

"Okay," I said.

When I got close to Becca's and saw her mom's car, I slowed my steps. I was getting ready to knock when her mom yelled. I couldn't tell what she was saying, but she sounded angry, and not you-forgot-to-unload-the-dishwasher angry. Becca shouted back, then things got quiet. I knocked, but not too loud.

Her mom opened the door a crack. She didn't tell me to come in, just called Becca and pushed the door shut again. I scuffed the toe of my sneaker on the welcome mat. Maybe they should've had one saying Go Away.

Becca opened the door the way her mom had. "What?" she said, her voice flat.

"You left this"—I lifted her backpack—"at my house."

She grabbed the backpack with her left hand, which was weird. She was right-handed, same as me. But her right arm was bent and held against her chest.

"Thanks," she said.

"You're wel—"

She closed the door. I stood there for a minute, waiting to see if she'd reopen it, but she didn't.

CHAPTER SEVEN

NOW

I pad into the kitchen and stop in the middle of the room. The counter is crowded with more food than Ryan and I could eat in a day, let alone one meal. Bacon, waffles, toast, French toast, sausage. Jam, maple syrup, butter, Tabasco sauce.

From his place at the stove, where he's scrambling eggs, Ryan says. "I made Sunday breakfast. And I might have overdone it. A little."

"I see that." I shamble to the coffeemaker and fill my largest mug. Wait for him to finish the eggs, load a plate, and carry it into the breakfast nook. For a time, we eat in companionable silence, and I feel safe in a way I haven't for days.

"Don't forget, you still owe me a movie trailer," he says, getting up to top off our mugs.

"I know," I say, but I did forget.

When he returns, he says, "I know you can't talk details, but is work okay?"

"Uh-huh. Why wouldn't it be?" I say, taking a too-big sip of coffee and scorching the roof of my mouth in the process.

"No reason, just wondered."

He takes a bite of French toast, but I sense he's waiting for something and steel myself for a conversation about money or the missing check. I hope not, because I don't want to have that discussion this early on a Sunday.

"Babe?" he finally says. "Who's the red lady?"

The world tilts on its axis. My vision turns hazy, and I think I'm going to faint—how Victorian—before everything sharpens into focus. Wood cabinets, steam from my mug, the sweet smell of syrup. The here and now. I try to keep from choking on a mouthful of eggs that now taste of sawdust. *Please, let me have misheard. Please, please, please.* I swallow and arrange my voice into an even cadence. "What?"

"The red lady. You were talking about her last night in your sleep."

"I was talking in my sleep?" I spear a triangular piece of waffle, sure Ryan can hear the pounding of my fear, see the panic.

"Yeah, you do it every once in a while. It's kinda cute."

"What did I say?"

"Something about a red lady and her face. I didn't catch the rest 'cause you were mumbling."

He waits, open and curious. My thoughts tumble over each other. I was talking about the Red Lady? What did I say? What did I reveal? A sudden compulsion to tell him everything surges inside me, but I push it down. It's too late for the truth. I've been lying for too many years.

"She's . . . she was a story my friends and I told when we were kids. Not a big deal." I take a sip of coffee.

"I almost woke you up because you seemed scared."

"Scared?" My voice is nonchalant with only a glimmer of interest. It sounds convincing as hell.

"Yeah, you were saying 'no' and twitching around. You don't remember it at all?"

"No. Honestly, she was just a ghost story, an urban legend sort of thing." I can't prevent the defensive tone. "I was talking to my mom last weekend about some of my old friends. Guess it stirred up memories."

He cocks his head. "No other reason?"

"For the dream? No, not that I can think of."

"Okay," he says. "Just asking. Anyway, can't remember if I told you already or not, but I'm going back to Mike's today." He pinches his fingers together. "We're this close to finishing his kitchen, and I just want to get it done."

While he showers, I put away the extra food. He kisses me on his way out, and I say, "Did I say anything else last night?"

"No. Nothing I could make out, anyway."

I search for duplicity and see none. Guilt curdles on my tongue. This is my husband, for god's sake. Yet I can't help the suspicion. What else have I said? What else has he heard? As I watch him drive away from the kitchen window, I catch a glimpse of myself in the glass.

Red Lady, Red Lady, show us your face.

My arms landscape with goose bumps. I don't remember dreaming about the Red Lady, don't remember dreaming about anything at all. It makes me feel weak. I should be made of stronger stuff. I've been through worse. God, have I been through worse.

I finish cleaning the kitchen and take a quick shower. Grab my keys and GPS the address for the Lauren who doesn't answer her phone. I cleared a couple hours from my calendar tomorrow afternoon, but Ryan will be at Mike's for a while. My laundry can wait.

*   *   *

The neighborhood was probably nice once, but those days are long past. Even after my key fob chirps, I tug the handle of my car door, just in case. The apartment building smells strongly of soiled diapers and stale beer, and on the wall leading to the bottom-floor units, there's a brown streak I hope isn't what I suspect. The fluorescent lighting in here doesn't do much to improve the gloom from the overcast day.

I knock on the door quickly, and from inside a woman says, "Just a minute!" I step back, arms stiff.

Her voice comes closer, the words low, but heavy with irritation. The woman who opens the door, holding a cell phone at shoulder level, is a gray-streaked blonde, about the right age. But the slight resemblance to

Becca holds more to the coloring and build rather than her actual features. Pale skin, slim in a wiry way. Eyes pinched and sharp. Alert. No recognition. I'm about ninety-nine percent sure it isn't her. But it's been a long time. Who's to say this isn't how Becca would've aged if she'd had the chance?

"Yeah?"

"Hi, I'm looking for Lauren Thomas," I say.

"You got her."

"Originally from Towson?" I restrain the urge to wipe slick palms on my thighs.

Her eyes narrow. "What's this about? You from CPS? If so, I already told the lady on the phone what I saw. Them kids are home alone all the time."

"Oh, no," I say. "I knew Ms. Thomas when I was a kid," I say. "It's been a long time, but I was friends with her daughter."

"You got the wrong person."

"I'm sorry to take up your time," I say. But I don't move away. "I'm Heather, by the way." Nothing on her face save annoyance.

"Whatever." Her cell phone is on its way back to her ear when she holds it out again. "If you find her, tell her to stop listing my address as hers, all right?"

"I'm sorry?"

"You ain't the first person to come here looking for her."

I jolt back a half step. "I'm not?"

She sneers and says, "That's what I said, didn't I?"

"When? Who was it?"

"A couple months ago, and my boyfriend answered the door, not me. It was some lady, that's all he said."

She's already closing the door when I stick out my foot. It works, and the door bounces back.

"What the fuck, lady?" she says.

"Please. Do you know what she looked like? The woman who came here?"

"I don't know a goddamn thing, and even if I did, I ain't telling you shit. You don't move your foot, I'm calling the cops."

I yank my foot clear, and she slams the door as I'm about to apologize. I hightail it outside in case she decides to make good on her threat anyway, and there's a man standing next to my car, back to me as he peers in the driver side's window.

"Hey," I say, when I'm only a few feet away. "That's my car."

He turns like a plastic skeleton, all jerk and jiggle. Tall, painfully thin. Dirty-blond hair. Scabbed skin. He reeks of body odor and rotting teeth. My guess: meth.

"Can I borrow a couple bucks?" he says.

"No," I say. "Please move. I need to leave."

He leans against my car instead. "Why you gotta leave? Can't you stay and talk?"

"No, I can't. Move."

"Sure you ain't got money?" he says, taking in the purse hanging over my shoulder. "All I'm asking for is a dollar or two."

"Get the fuck out of my way."

He steps a little to the side, but close enough that my shoulder brushes his when I reach for the door. His hand lands on my bicep, squeezes. "Why you gotta be that way?"

This close, his breath is noxious, full of nicotine and decay. I wrench my arm free, unlock the door, and fling it open, practically throwing myself inside and locking it behind me. I start the car and race out of the parking spot, sending him staggering to the side. His mirth follows. I'm hot and blotchy with fear and anger. My shirt's sticking to my back. My armpits are damp. But I'm fine. He was just a pain in the ass. He didn't hurt me. Nothing I haven't encountered before.

As the apartment complex disappears in my rearview mirror and my physical reaction fades, the import of what this Lauren Thomas said hits me again. There's someone else, another woman, looking for Lauren. Not just me.

* * *

Monday afternoon, I'm getting ready to leave the office with directions to the last Lauren Thomas on my list when a text arrives from Gia with a bunch of dates. SEE, I'M SERIOUS! reads the accompanying message.

My thumb hovers over the delete button. This is what I wanted, but I wanted it on my terms. I pick at a finger, stopping short of drawing blood this time; there's already a healing scab. Although most of the dates are further out, she has this Sunday listed and Ryan and I have nothing planned.

BRUNCH THIS SUNDAY? I message back, adding a smiley face.

It's too soon, but what the hell. Cat and mouse. While waiting for her response, I open my desk drawer, peek down at the half-heart necklace. If Gia's doing this . . . she'll pay.

I'm closing the drawer when she texts ABSOLUTELY! After we set a time and location, I head out, asking Ellie to tell callers I'll answer them tomorrow, barring an emergency.

This Lauren lives in a run-down rowhouse in Dundalk. Postage-stamp front yards. Street parking. The instant she answers the door, it's clear she isn't the right one. This woman is tall and broad hipped. Dark haired. Swallowing my disappointment, I use the same query I used yesterday, but she crosses her arms and cocks a hip.

"I'm sorry to bother you," I say. "One last question, please. Has anyone else come looking for her?"

"So what'd she do?"

"Excuse me?"

"The other Lauren? If people are looking for her, what did she do?"

"Oh, nothing."

"Right," she says, stretching out the word.

I don't bother to wait for her to close the door. When I'm halfway down the sidewalk, an engine revs. An old grayish-blue Chevy that's seen better days pulls away from the curb across the street with a belch of smoke. I step back instinctively, although my Jeep is a barrier between me and the street.

Inside, doors locked, I crumple the list of Laurens and throw it on the floor of the passenger seat. I canceled patients for this? What do I do now? Is it worth trying another pay site? What if I get another list with the same names I already have?

No, somehow I have to convince Alexa Martin to give me the information. If I want to find Lauren, I don't have a choice. I rub my chin. Maybe I'm running in circles for no reason. Maybe I should step back, do nothing. Let Lauren or whoever it is come to me. Oh yes, that's brilliant. Just brilliant. Reactive instead of proactive.

A curtain twitches in the front window of this Lauren's house, and I start my car. Since Alexa no longer works at the prison full-time, she should be in her office. I could stop by, say I was in the area. Maybe if I catch her unaware, she'll be more willing to divulge details. At this point I'll take anything.

* * *

"I'm sorry, Dr. Cole, Dr. Martin is with a patient," Corinne, Alexa's receptionist, says, her lips set in a way that maintains I should already know. She's the sort who'd be at home as the headmistress in an English boarding school. Nothing gets past her.

Nonetheless, I keep my easy smile. "Does she have any free time afterward?"

"Unfortunately not. She's leaving soon for Florida and has back-to-back appointments until then."

"Oh, yes, of course."

This I do know. Alexa goes south to visit her sister every September for a few weeks. Maybe I can use her prevacation chaos to my advantage, get her to drop her guard long enough to give me what I need.

"Will you let her know I stopped by?" I say. "And have her call me when she has a chance?"

Corinne says she will, but her gaze is already turning away, and once the phone begins to ring, I've lost her.

Today has been an utter waste of time, and I'm no better off than when I got out of bed. Frustration is a stone in my gut.

Traffic's a bitch, but even though I get home late, the lights downstairs are out and the house is silent. I'm not overly quiet closing the door or slipping off my shoes, but I don't call out in case Ryan's napping. I called when I was halfway home, and he said he had a long day, his first full day of what I can't help but think of as *The Great Eloise Harding Bathroom Renovation*. Awful of me, I know.

Keeping my steps soft, I pause at the top of the stairs. Our bedroom light is off, but the overhead in Ryan's office is on, his door half open. I hear the tapping of keys, a pause. The creak of his desk chair. A long series of keystrokes, a longer pause. A sigh. More typing.

"I'm home," I say.

"In here," he says.

I nudge his door open all the way. His laptop is now closed, his chair pushed back from the desk. He smiles, but it looks forced.

"Good day?" I ask.

"Not bad, just long. You?"

"Same. Anything in today's mail?"

I specifically don't mention the check for the Kane job, but his eyes pinch at the outer corners.

"No," he says.

"I didn't mean anything. I was just asking."

"Uh-huh."

Irritation bubbles behind the cauldron of my ribs. "Seriously, Ryan. If I wanted to ask something specific, I would've. All I wanted to know is if there was anything in the mail, you know, maybe for me?"

He blinks. "Okay. No, there was nothing for you today."

I respond with a curt nod and head into our room to change. I asked a simple question and he acted like I was the goddamn Spanish Inquisition. I pause with a hand on the corner of my dresser, the other against my forehead.

Maybe I'm making mountains from molehills.

Maybe I just wanted to pick a fight.

* * *

"I'm sorry I couldn't see you," Alexa says. "But I wasn't expecting you to drop by," she says. "Things are a little busy at the moment." I hear her riffling through paper, opening a file cabinet, closing a desk drawer.

"I should've called, but thought I'd take a chance. I had a doctor's appointment that didn't take as much time as I expected." The lie rolls off with ease.

"When I get back, let's get together for lunch or dinner. Unfortunately, I can't fit it in between now and when I leave."

I wheel my chair so I'm facing the window. Cross my legs. Here goes nothing. "So, something interesting or maybe just odd happened the other day."

"Oh?"

Her interest is merely polite, I can tell, accompanied by the shuffling of more paper.

"I saw Lauren."

Silence on the other end. A drawn-out silence with a long exhale after.

"You saw Lauren?" Each word is pregnant with disbelief.

"Yes, on Saturday. Here in Annapolis."

I can even picture the meeting. Me coming round the corner in a store. Target, maybe, or Kohl's. Her standing in the center of the aisle, eyes widening when she sees me, when she realizes I see her and know who she is . . . I uncross my legs. Plant both feet on the floor. Enough of that mental fuckery.

"At least I think it was her," I say.

"Did you talk to her?" Her words are tight.

I regret my subterfuge—I do—but I say, "Is she close to me? I guess that would solve it, wouldn't it? Or at least help?"

"Heather."

"I'm not asking for anything other than that."

I hear a series of faint clicks that might be the tap of her fingernails. "I think you must've been mistaken. That's as much as I'm willing to say. This preoccupation you have with her isn't healthy."

"I know, I'm sorry. I'll let it go."

After we say our goodbyes, I spin toward my desk. I may not know exactly where Lauren is yet, but now I can guess she isn't living nearby.

That's something. I exhale through my nose. Bullshit. It's still nothing. Alexa isn't going to give me anything else, no matter how hard I try. There has to be another way. There has to. But I can't think of a damn thing.

I stare out at the parking lot, find my car. No one's nearby. A woman gets out of her vehicle on the other side of the lot. Her wavy, flyaway hair reminds me of Rachel's when we were girls. I close the blinds. Peek through the slats.

What do I do next? I have to do something. But what? What?

I pinch the bridge of my nose. Maybe stop thinking about Lauren for a minute. Sometimes the best solutions come when you're not actively thinking. What about Rachel, then? I scoff. As if that's any better. Blank walls every way I turn, with someone lurking just out of sight.

I scan Rachel's social media again, but there's not a damn thing there to work with. I'm definitely not going to skulk around her house. I can't exactly sit in the parking lot of the law firm where she works either. I can't take a holiday from my own life to shadow hers. I got lucky with Gia, but I can't count on that sort of thing happening twice.

I pick at a cuticle. Drum my fingers on my chair's arms. Rachel practices family law. What if . . .

My fingers still. What if I make an appointment with her, pretend to be contemplating divorce? If nothing else, it would put me in front of her. Ryan would never know. It's not a good idea—it's a terrible one, as a matter of fact—but it's the only one I've got.

Before I can second-guess myself, I pick up my phone. Ten minutes later, I have a consultation set for next Thursday. I quell the unease in my gut, reminding myself it's a fake appointment, merely an excuse to get in front of Rachel, to look her in the eye. I'd never leave Ryan.

So. Back to Lauren. I find another website advertising INFORMATION ON ANYONE! This one's a hundred dollars, but I plunk in my credit card information. I can't think of any other way—short of hiring a private detective—to find Lauren. There has to be something I'm missing. In this day and age, no one can hide completely.

After, I make a pit stop in the bathroom, and Ellie's in my office at the filing cabinet when I get back. She turns fast, face pink.

"I was putting this back," she says, holding a file. "Trying, anyway."

I fish out the keys. I won't ever tell Ellie, but if she were to yank the top two drawers at the same time, there's a good chance the whole thing would unlock. A quirk I discovered via accident.

"Dr. Cole? Your finger's bleeding."

"A terrible old habit," I say as I fetch a tissue and blot the torn skin. I squirt a bit of hand sanitizer into my palm. It burns when it hits the wound, but I soldier on. Apply more sanitizer. Rub until the wound bleeds anew.

"What file is it?" I say.

Ellie closes the drawer hard enough to rattle the files inside. "Sorry?"

I tip my head toward the cabinet. "The file?"

"Oh, it was Jacob's. I forgot to bring it back in this morning, and then it got tucked under some other papers, I'm sorry—"

"No harm done," I say.

I'm about to ask her to add today's notes to another patient's file, but my notebook is blank. Nothing from the session? That's not like me at all.

Ellie leaves without another word, her steps small and quick. Never mind the lack of notes. Something doesn't seem right. Ellie returned Jacob's file this morning. I swear she did. But nothing's out of place in the cabinet. And Jacob's file is in order. There are notes dated today, a few anyway. Nothing's missing from my desk. The necklace is still in the drawer.

But the color in Ellie's cheeks, the way she spoke. Am I being paranoid? Or do I need to keep an eye on her, too?

I sit. Steeple my fingers. An email arrives from the information website, and my stomach lurches with anticipation. I scan the attached list, comparing it to the old. Not even one new addition. The same Laurens. The same information.

I groan behind clenched teeth. I feel as though I'm a puppet dangling from someone else's strings. And I don't like it at all.

End of day, I shove my laptop in my bag. Check my pockets for keys. My office phone rings and I think about not answering, but I put on my professional voice and say, "Dr. Cole speaking."

Silence on the other end.

"This is Dr. Cole. May I help you?"

The silence grows even larger.

"Is someone there?"

There's a hint of movement. An exhale.

"Who is this?" I say, trying for forceful. In control. I can hang up anytime. But I clutch the phone even tighter, ignoring the tension in my fingers, my other hand splayed like a starfish on my desk.

An inhale. A syllable, unintelligible. The voice feels wrong. My spine turns arctic, my mouth Saharan.

Who are you?

What are you?

Then they're gone. Hissing through my teeth, I drop the phone as though it's poison. Bite the side of my fingernail, loosening a bit of cuticle. Bite it again, pulling until it hurts. Until there's blood.

We had to bleed.

My arms are awash in goose bumps.

When we did the ritual, she said we had to bleed.

CHAPTER EIGHT

THEN

"Take off your shoes and sit inside the circle," Becca said.

One by one, we stepped over the thirteen candles Becca had arranged and sat cross-legged. I sat facing the staircase, Rachel to my right, and Gia across from me. In the middle was a plate with another candle, unlit, matches, a needle, and a bunch of Becca's mom's scarves. The room smelled of fruit, baby powder, and vanilla. The corners were all shadowy.

A couple months ago, I'd read a book where people were trying to summon the devil and they did a ritual inside a circle of candles. *Thirteen* candles. I'd told Becca about it, too, so I knew that's where she'd gotten the idea. In the book, the main guy used a knife to cut their palms and they all drank the blood. When the devil came, he ripped off all their heads, but I didn't think the Red Lady would do anything to us. I didn't think she'd show up at all, even if she was real. Which she wasn't, no matter what Becca said.

Becca took the open spot in the circle, her back facing the shadowed end of the basement, and said, "If you want to see the Red Lady, you have to make yourself bleed, and then you have to be blindfolded and say the right words. You have to prove you can do it, prove you want to see her."

Rachel was breathing fast, her lips parted. Really scared, not fake scared. I glanced at the needle and stifled a grin. When we were ten, Becca and I had pricked our fingers to be blood sisters.

"If we wear blindfolds, how will we see her?" I said.

"Do you want to accidentally look in her eyes?" Becca said. "And wake up with dirt in your mouth? Or not wake up at all?"

"I don't," Rachel said.

"But how will we know she's here if we can't see?" Gia said.

"We'll know. We'll see her here," Becca said, tapping the side of her head.

Yeah, in our imaginations. But I said, "How do you know?"

Her gaze locked onto mine, and we stared without speaking, like in a don't-blink contest. I didn't know why I was trying to make her mad. Rachel and Gia were watching us, but they kept quiet. In the past week and a half, I'd seen Becca once and not even for that long. Every other time I'd called, she'd said she was too busy to hang out. But she wasn't now that Gia was back from her vacation and it was time for the ritual. She'd even had Rachel call me this morning to tell me to come to the house after dinner; she hadn't called me herself.

Becca looked away first and picked up the matches. "I just do. If we're lucky, she might talk to us, too." She lit the candle on the plate and turned the needle in the flame. "So we don't get lockjaw," she said. "Hold out your hands."

Rachel held hers against her chest. "But it will hurt. You never said we had to do this."

Becca tilted her head, the way my dog Roxie used to. "Are you scared?"

"No. I mean, a little, but . . ." Rachel said.

A muscle in Becca's jaw twitched. "If you don't want to—"

Gia put out hers. "I'll do it."

"I will, too," I said. Not that I wanted to, but I wanted it all over with.

"Fine," Rachel said.

I hissed when Becca jabbed my finger, surprised she'd picked me first. Gia made a little squeak, and Rachel yelped.

"Now squeeze some blood on your palm."

"What about you?" Rachel said.

"I will, but I need to do your blindfolds first. Now rub together, like this." She mashed her palms together.

"Gross," Rachel said.

"It's just blood," Becca said.

I was the last person Becca blindfolded. After, if I angled my head back, I could see a sliver of candlelight beneath the edge of the scarf. Becca pricked her own finger, blew out the candle stub, and scooted in between me and Gia.

"Everybody move in so we're close," she said. "We have to hold hands tight so our blood touches." Hers slipped into mine, the blood wet and sticky. "Don't let go, no matter what. Not until I say so. Don't take off your blindfolds either. Say exactly what I say and how I say it." She sat up a little straighter. "Red Lady, Red Lady, show us your face."

Rachel laughed.

"Do you want to do this or not?" Becca's said, her voice a rubber band snapping on skin.

"Sorry. I'm sorry."

"Okay," Becca said. "Red Lady, Red Lady, show us your face."

She shook my hand, so I said it, too, even though it didn't make any sense. With our blindfolds on, how could the Red Lady show us anything? And since we weren't supposed to look in her eyes, it made it even more ridiculous. How could you look at a face without seeing their eyes?

We said the words once, twice, five times, ten. Each time, Becca squeezed tighter and her voice grew louder. The carpet scratched my legs, but I kept still. After the twelfth *show us your face*, Rachel fidgeted, and I nudged her knee with mine.

My nose tickled. I squished it into my shoulder, but the tickle didn't go away. I sneezed, my hands jerking free. Silence hung in the air. Then Rachel giggled, and Gia joined her. Becca exhaled, more like a snort, and got to her feet.

"Sorry," I said as she stomped up the stairs and turned the light on. She stomped back and blew out the candles.

"I didn't do it on purpose," I said.

"Don't be mad at her," Gia said. "It wasn't even working."

Becca grabbed the scarves in a fist.

I went into the half bathroom to wash off the blood. Gia and Rachel went after me. By the time we were done, Becca had everything picked up.

"It's okay," Rachel said.

Becca kicked the wall. "No, it isn't. She was supposed to be here. She should've been here. We didn't do it right."

"But we did what you told us to," Gia said.

"It was supposed to work," Becca said, hefting the backpack over her shoulder. The rest of us followed her upstairs.

Once outside, I tried to walk next to her, but she kept going faster, so I gave up. She didn't even say goodbye when she split off down her street.

*   *   *

I called Becca after I ate a bowl of cereal but hung up before I pushed the last number. I wasn't mad at her anymore. Not exactly. I was upset because she was mad, but I was also happy. Maybe now she'd stop being so obsessed. Maybe everything would go back to the way it was.

When I called again a couple hours later, she said the word *hello* like *homework* or *I hate you*, but I pretended things were fine.

"Want to come over?" I said. "My mom bought more Ecto Coolers."

"I have stuff to do."

"I don't know why you're mad at me. I told you, I didn't sneeze on—"

"I'm not mad, but we have to do it again, the ritual. I think I know what we did wrong."

"O-kay," I said slowly. "What if Rachel and Gia don't want to?"

"I already told them."

I traced circles on the wall. She'd called them first? In the background, there was a yell and a thump, then the sound muffled as Becca covered the phone. Even so, I heard another yell, definitely her mom.

"I have to go," Becca said, the words all running together.

"Maybe—"

The phone disconnected with a click.

"Becca?"

My mom came around the corner, saw me frowning, and said, "Everything okay?"

"Yeah, it's fine," I said, running the pendant back and forth along its chain, the metal *whisk*ing with each pass.

* * *

Becca opened her front door, and the skin on her cheek was all purple and red. Not just a little mark, either.

"Holy crap," I said. "What happened?"

"I banged into the doorway," she said. "It's not a big deal. There wasn't even any blood. Come on up, I want to show you something."

I followed her upstairs, but it almost felt like she didn't care that I was there, even though she had called me and said I could come over.

Two steps into her room, I stopped. A bunch of drawings of the Red Lady hung on the wall above her bed. One showed the four of us blindfolded, sitting in a circle, hands clasped together, the Red Lady in the center. Another was of her in a hole, blood dripping from her mouth, dirt covering the lower half of her body. In another, she stood beside the hole, her mouth open in a scream, blood leaking from her wrists. One from the back showed her hair trailing in a long streak of blood.

The last one, hanging in the middle, was Becca with the Red Lady behind her, arms spread wide, blood puddling their feet. I stepped closer. The Red Lady was smiling, but it wasn't nice at all. Her shark's eyes bored into mine. From the stories I knew, she was scary, but in this picture she seemed worse. She seemed evil and wrong. Her hair hung in dark vines over her shoulders, and several tendrils were wrapped around Becca's shoulders, too.

Real Becca had a *Mona Lisa* face, like she knew a secret. "That's my favorite," she said, pointing.

I wanted to rip the picture to pieces, and I backed away until I bumped into her dresser. "Is your mom mad at you for hanging them up?"

She blinked like something hurt. "I don't let her come in here any-more," she said.

I knuckled the end of my nose. "What are they?"

"Hel-lo, what do they look like?"

"I know, but when did you draw them?" I said.

"I've been working on them for a while," she said, scratching an ear-lobe. "Do you like them or not?"

"They're . . . I don't know, scary."

"Yeah, but I thought you'd like them. You always like my drawings." Her mouth went *Mona Lisa* again.

"No, I do like them, but she doesn't look like I thought."

"What did you think she looked like?"

"Not so bloody, maybe?" I said, cocking my head.

"They chopped off her hands and cut out her tongue. Of course she's bloody."

"I don't think we should do the ritual again," I said.

"Why, are you scared?"

I stared at the Red Lady's face. Her open mouth said she wanted to bite, and it didn't matter that she was a story. I *was* scared. "Maybe."

"She isn't going to hurt us. And she doesn't always look so scary. Most of the time she looks sad." Becca rummaged through a stack of paper on her desk. "See?"

She gave me an unfinished pictured of the Red Lady inside a window. Her lips were closed, her head bowed.

"You should hang this one up instead."

"But it isn't done yet."

"So? It's better than that one." I nodded toward the wall.

"What do you think it was like, being buried alive?"

"Awful," I said. "Ugh. Can we talk about something else, please?"

"Like what?"

"I don't know. Anything. When was the last time we talked about something else? I want to talk about music or the movies or a book."

"You said you liked the stories. And remember what it was like after you saw *Edward Scissorhands*? That's all you talked about forever. I didn't say anything because we're friends, and that's what friends do, right? They don't tell each other to shut up."

"That's not fair," I said. "I never told you to shut up."

"Same difference."

It wasn't at all, but I didn't know how to make her understand. The eyes of the Red Lady on the wall followed me the way the ones in the dolls did.

"Maybe she's the only thing I want to talk about," Becca said. "If you were really my friend, you wouldn't be mad."

"I am your friend."

The corner of a box stuck out from beneath her bed, and I said, "What's that?"

"Go look."

Inside were a bunch of the construction-paper books we'd made when we were little. I snickered at the titles: *The Ghost. The Witch's House. The Ice Dog. The Fire Cat.*

"We were such dorks." I pushed the box back and sat on the edge of her bed with my back to the Red Lady. "So where did you get all her stories?"

"Oh," she said. "That book at the mall."

I chewed my bottom lip. "I don't remember seeing her in it."

"You didn't read it all, but I did."

But she said it without looking at me, and I knew she was lying. She was making it all up herself. For one thing, there was no way she'd had time to read all those stories and remember them while we were at the bookstore. For another, it was all too weird to be anything but made-up.

"I won't tell Rachel and Gia," I said.

"Won't tell them what?"

"That you're making it up."

"I'm not. I don't understand why you don't believe me."

I didn't want to call her a liar, so I said, "Want to watch a movie or something?"

"Yeah, sure."

We went in her basement and watched MTV for a while, but every time I talked to her, even to say something silly, she only sort of dipped her head. She kept rubbing the bruise, her face turning angry and then kind of sad. When I lied and said I had to go home and check the dryer for my mom, she just said, "Don't forget to lock the door on your way out," and didn't even walk with me upstairs.

* * *

"I know what we did wrong," Becca said.

The candles were in a circle in the basement again, and she was in the middle holding the matches. The mark on her cheek was still dark. She caught me looking and flipped some of her hair forward, not that it hid much, but I got the point. "We weren't sitting the right way," she said, lighting the candles.

I thought she was joking, because how could that make any difference, but her face was serious. Once again, Rachel was scared, twisting her fingers and biting her lip. Gia was all wide-eyed and excited.

We sat the same way we did before, Rachel next to me with Gia on her other side. But after Becca pricked our fingers again and put on our blindfolds, she said, "Turn so you're facing out, with your legs crossed, and leave room for me."

Once Becca sat down, I had to scoot again. Our folded legs were squished, Rachel's knee practically on top of mine. Everyone, even Becca, moved a little bit, trying to get comfortable as we linked hands. Because of the way we were sitting, our arms from shoulder to elbow were pressed tight to our bodies, and from elbow to fingers rested on our thighs, like dolls stuck in wrong poses. I wrinkled my nose. If they wanted to do this a third time, I was going to say no, no matter how angry they got. They could do it without me.

"Red Lady, Red Lady, show us your face," Becca said.

We joined in, my voice not nearly as loud. I waited for Becca to knock my leg or something, but she didn't. After a while, her voice got faster and so did Rachel's and Gia's. Mine, too, until the words were oatmeal in my mouth. It sounded like there were more than four of us here, like we weren't even speaking English anymore, and goose bumps pebbled my arms.

The room grew warmer. The candles smelled even worse this time, all flowery and fruity and Christmas trees. It made me feel queasy, but if I threw up Becca would never forgive me. Rachel started shaking. I tipped my head back, peeking under the blindfold's bottom edge. The light flickered and a shadow moved past. I jerked my hands, but Becca held tighter. Rachel's slipped a little, but she held on too. I turned my head from right to left but saw only the candles. Past them, the candles made dark shapes flit on the walls.

The air grew thick, and I smelled something other than the candles, something meaty and rich. Something moved on the carpet with a soft rasp. I knew it was only my imagination; there was no such thing as the Red Lady. But I saw her in my mind. Fierce and terrifying with her black, black eyes; her mouth, open and bloody; her arms and the empty places below her wrists. Her rage burned me with its heat.

"Red Lady, Red Lady, show us your face."

Rachel moaned softly around her words. Sweat stuck my hair to my scalp. Gia's voice was husky, Becca's excited and higher-pitched than normal. I wanted to stop, to run away, but I couldn't pull free. It was as if our skin was glued together.

This wasn't real. She was a story, nothing more. But I couldn't move anything except my mouth, my voice a thousand miles away. Like the rest of me, I had no control. My ears went stuffy and my tongue stilled, clogged by something felt and not felt at the same time. Behind the blindfold, the world grew darker. A weight pushed against my chest, my belly ached, and my mouth, wrists, and side hurt. Someone laughed, sharp and cruel. The carpet beneath me felt wrong. It was cold and damp and rough, and from far away, there was a soft thumping sound. Something moved in front of me again, rustling slow and soft, and I heard my name whispered—not with my ears, but in my head.

Then, in the space of a heartbeat, the sound was gone and the carpet was carpet again. I yanked off my blindfold. The others were doing the same. I blinked, confused by the darkness.

"Why are the candles out?" Rachel said, her voice quivering. "Who blew them out?"

"Hold on, I have a flashlight," Becca said.

There was a click and a beam of light appeared. Rachel had her knees tucked up to her chin, Gia was crouched in front of her.

"Can we put the light on?" Rachel said. "Please?"

The darkness returned as Becca crept up the stairs, flashlight sweeping from side to side. When the overhead light came on, I shielded my eyes. Rachel burst into weird hiccup-like tears. Gia gig-gled. Something, maybe a sob, built in my throat, but I gulped it down. Becca wasn't angry, which surprised me. As she gathered the candles and blindfolds, she said, "It worked this time. The Red Lady was here. I felt her."

Rachel said, "I felt her, too."

"Me too," Gia said.

"What about you?" Becca said to me.

The weight of their gazes was crushing. All I had to do was say yes, but I couldn't. No matter what I'd thought I heard or felt, it wasn't real. It couldn't be. The Red Lady wasn't real. It was Becca, tricking me some-how. Tricking us all. "I didn't feel anything."

Gia frowned. "You didn't?"

I shook my head. Inside, I was numb.

"How do you explain the candles all going out, then?" Gia said.

"I don't know. A breeze?" I said.

"Inside the house?" Gia said.

"But the rest of us felt her," Rachel said. "And you were the first one to let go."

"I was afraid I was going to puke from the candle smell. That's all," I said.

Becca narrowed her eyes. "It doesn't matter. Maybe the Red Lady didn't want Heather to know she was here for some reason, but the rest of us felt her. Help me clean up, okay?"

While we put the rest of the stuff in the backpack, they didn't talk to me, only to each other.

"I felt her right in front of me," Gia said. "She touched my arm."

"She touched *my* face. What about you, Becca?" Rachel asked.

Becca said, "I smelled her, too. She smelled like blood."

"Me too," Gia said.

"Me three," Rachel said. "It was gross. But sad, too."

They had to be lying. There was no way anything had happened for real. It was only our imaginations. And the pain I'd felt in my belly was probably just a cramp.

They were still talking after we crossed the field. We passed Gia's house first, then Rachel's. On the way to mine, Becca stayed quiet. I did, too. I had one foot on the sidewalk leading to my front porch when she said, "Tell me the truth. What did you see?"

"Nothing. We had blindfolds on, remember?"

She blew hair out of her face. "You know what I mean."

"I told you," I said, crossing my arms. "I didn't feel anything, and all I heard was the chant."

"I don't believe you. You let go first."

"Because I thought I was going to get sick." I scraped the heel of my shoe on the pavement. "Anyway, nothing happened. There was no one else in the basement. Don't know why you're making it such a big deal."

She stepped close enough for me to feel her breath. "Because it's important. I wanted you to feel her, too."

"Gia and Rachel did. Isn't that good enough?"

She got even closer; this time I pulled back a little so our noses wouldn't bump. "But they're not my best friend. You are."

"Just because nothing happened to me doesn't mean I'm not your friend. Best friends are more important than stories," I said.

She had a funny expression, not angry or upset, but a little sad. "She's not just a story. And you know it. She talks to me sometimes."

"Who?"

"The Red Lady."

"You're so lying."

"You don't have to believe me if you don't want, but she *is* real."

"Believe whatever you want," I said, turning on my heel and going inside. When I peeked out the peephole, she was gone.

* * *

I didn't talk to her again for three days, then she called and told me to come to the elementary school playground. I almost said no but didn't want to be left out.

Rachel and Gia were sitting on the wood chips beneath the monkey bars; Becca showed up a couple minutes later, blinking a few times when she saw me. I dragged my fingers through the wood chips to the dirt below. If she didn't want me here, she shouldn't have told me to come. But she slipped through the metal bars and sat down next to me, so maybe she'd just had the sun in her eyes.

"Did anyone else have a weird dream last night?" Becca asked, pulling strands of her hair over to help cover the bruise, now the color of a plum.

Rachel and Gia both nodded.

I chewed my fingernail. "I don't know. If I did, I don't remember."

Becca's mouth made a funny shape. She could not believe me all she wanted, but I was telling the truth. I'd woken in the middle of the night, dizzy and with a gross taste in my mouth, but I didn't remember any dreams.

"If you had one like mine, you'd remember it," she said. "I was being buried alive."

Rachel said, "That's what I dreamed, too."

Gia nodded a bunch of times. "And there were people laughing."

"Like it was the best thing they ever did," Becca said. "I could taste the dirt and I tried to scream—"

"But you couldn't because . . ." Rachel twisted the bottom of her T-shirt. "You couldn't talk."

"Because your tongue was gone?" Becca asked.

"Yeah," Rachel and Gia said at the same time, their voices too loud.

Rachel scrunched her nose and said, "But how could we have had the same dream?"

Becca traced her teeth over her lower lip. "Because the Red Lady wants us to. She wants us to know how scared she was and how awful it felt. So we don't forget it, so we don't forget her."

"I won't ever forget," Gia said.

"I don't want to dream about it ever again," Rachel said.

They sounded like soap opera actors and I wanted to laugh, but their faces were serious. Maybe they weren't lying, but if they had dreamed about her, it was on account of the ritual and what they imagined happened. Nothing magic or mysterious. I remembered the phantom pain in my side and the way the carpet had turned bumpy, but I bit the inside of my cheek until I tasted blood. Then that reminded me of the smell, and I grimaced.

"What?" Becca said.

"I bit my cheek," I said. "See?" I stuck out my tongue.

"Gross," Rachel said.

I hooked my knees over the monkey bars and swung upside down, reaching out and making monster groans with my bloody tongue sticking out. Rachel shrieked and pulled away. Becca hung beside me, fingers bent into pincers, snagging Gia's shoulders every time she got close. And for a little while, everything seemed normal again.

CHAPTER NINE

NOW

I drive to Silverstone through a mist of rain, the day as gray as my mood. Nicole's door is open, and when she glances at my empty hands, I say, "I'm sorry. I stayed up too late last night, it was raining when I left, and I wasn't even thinking."

All three are truths, two in a manner of speaking. I couldn't fall asleep, and although I left in time to stop at Starbucks, I was thinking of other things: of strange phone calls, of brunch this Sunday with Gia, of a half-heart necklace that once belonged to my best friend.

She waves me off. "Not a big deal. How has Samantha been for you?"

Samantha? Then it clicks. The girl with the chair. "She's been fine. A little rough around the edges, but you know how that show is sometimes."

"Okay, but please watch her with Abby. I've heard a few rumors she's been antagonizing her. No one will confirm it, of course, and Abby says she hasn't, but she never likes to rock the boat."

"Will do," I say.

My cell phone rings and I jump, but let the call go to voice mail since I don't recognize the number. They don't leave a message. I can tell Nicole wants to keep chatting, but I say I need to prepare for my sessions.

"Call me later if you want?" she says, and I toss an "Okay" over my shoulder.

The girls are already in the meeting room when I get there. Samantha's sitting next to Abby, leaning close, the two speaking in fervent whispers. According to Samantha's file, her background is similar to Abby's—financial stability, private schools—but they couldn't be more dissimilar. Abby's the only girl in the room who resembles a child more than a young woman: cheeks rounded, body more straight than curved. It makes her appear younger than she is. Her eyes, though, belong to someone decades older.

A few months ago, her parents discovered she was trading oral sex for pills. They were, of course, shocked. Abby went to private school and wanted for nothing. She did her homework, called if she was running late. You'd never have guessed she'd been abused by a close family friend when she was young. She never said a word until she was caught with drugs. Never said a word because her abuser had said he'd kill her family if she did and she believed him. Why wouldn't she? We teach kids to listen to grown-ups.

I get closer and hear Samantha say, "My cousin knows somebody who saw him, the real Slenderman."

"There isn't a real one," Abby says. "He's just some Internet thing, and those girls killed their friend because of him."

"I'm telling you, he's real," Samantha says. "And that girl didn't die. They'll just have to try again when they get out of jail. Sometimes there has to be a sacrifice."

"Samantha!" I say, harsh enough to make the others fall silent and stare at me. "That's enough. We have more important things to talk about here."

"Sorry," she says, but she's smirking.

After I leave, I realize I forgot to tell Nicole what happened. But I doubt urban-legend nonsense counts as antagonizing. I doubt Samantha believes Slenderman is real. She's a little too old. When you're twelve, it's different. You can believe in something so strongly you make it real, and then you can't tell any difference between the truth and the story.

*   *   *

120

My drive to Evelyn's, a neighborhood restaurant close to Gia's house, doesn't take long. I'm early, but its's okay. I'm comfortable. This place is a known entity for Sunday brunch. The restaurant serves only breakfast and lunch and the food is good, the portions hearty. It's sunny and warm enough to sit outside, so I ask for a table out front. Every time the door opens, out waft the aromas of bacon, syrup, and coffee, and I order a cup of the last.

I sip my drink, one hand traveling to my waist. I woke with marks, four of them, along my side. Not deep enough to draw blood, but close; the red is pebbled with darker spots about to break the surface. Even now, as I touch gently through my clothes, the marks sting, and I've been unable to escape the flow of memories. Becca tried to hide scratches on her body from me, but I saw them. Bruises, too. Were there other wounds, other signs I missed or can't remember? Probably. Kids are very good at hiding the marks of dysfunction. And they usually only get better as time goes on.

I know things were worse for Becca that summer, for whatever reason. Maybe puberty, maybe her mom falling deeper and deeper into her glass. Maybe both or neither. Whatever the underlying issues, they both paid the price. And then some. I should've told someone, never mind what I promised Becca. I promised I'd help her, too, and I didn't do that either. I'm drenched in guilt, no matter who took the official blame.

Please be kind and rewind.

We never said goodbye, not once, not even at the end. But it wasn't supposed to end that way. It wasn't supposed to end. Tears thicken my throat, and I wash them away with a big, too-hot swallow.

Gia rounds the corner, beaming when she sees me. I rub my palms under the table and gird my mental loins. She's in a striped top and slim-fitting navy-blue pants. Hair in a loose bun. After we order breakfast—French toast and bacon for me, the same for her plus a yogurt parfait—she says, "It's so good to see you again."

My eyes prickle again. This shouldn't be easy. This shouldn't feel good. I bite the inside of my cheek until my teeth leave impressions.

We end up chatting about husbands and work and parents and life and nothing and everything. More than half my food cools on the plate, but I don't mind. I'm down to the last three bites when a family approaches and with them a girl about thirteen, give or take a year in either direction. She has pale hair, pale eyes, and delicate features, and the resemblance to Becca is slight but enough. A second too late, I realize I'm staring. Gia smiles, but there's neither good humor nor cruelty there.

"She reminds me of . . ." I say.

She nods. "It's strange. Until I saw you in the bookstore, I hadn't thought about her in years. Now I can't get her or that summer out of my head."

She reaches over the table, and her hand on the back of mine is warm.

"I understand," I say. "I've been the same. That summer shaped us in many ways. It was the last time we were all friends." In for a penny, in for a pound. I drop my voice. "Do you remember the Red Lady?"

She scrunches her face. "She was the witch story, wasn't she?"

"She was."

"I don't really remember details, but I remember the gist." She, too, lowers her voice. "And sneaking in that empty house? What were we thinking?"

"Oh, come on," I say. "It was fun."

"Our merry little band of criminals," she says.

Slowly, I rub my palms together, my skin gone clammy. "And the ritual we did? With the candles and all the chanting?"

A faraway look from Gia. "Vaguely. Pretty sure it's a law in the rule book of girls. Bloody Mary in the mirror, all that woo-woo ghost story stuff."

"We pricked our fingers, said some silly chant, and afterward we all had bad dreams."

"Wait, I do remember. And Becca insisted it was all real, didn't she? Then got mad at you when you said it wasn't?"

"Mmm-hmm."

"I can't believe we never got caught sneaking in." She sets her fork down, picks it up. "I can't believe we never told."

"Why would we have, though?" I say.

"True, but I'm just surprised Rachel didn't say something, especially after all the stealing drama."

She looks at me like I should know what she's talking about, but I can't help frowning.

"The stealing?" It sounds like a bad eighties horror flick.

She's frowning now, too.

"Didn't you know?" she says. "Rachel's dad caught Becca taking cash out of his wallet. Apparently money had been going missing for a while and they figured it was one—or *all*—of us. But they weren't sure, not until he caught Becca in the act. She said Rachel told her to do it, which was a lie, but it turned into this huge thing, and afterward they wouldn't let us hang out with her anymore."

I sit back. Rake through my hair. "But . . . I thought it was because of the stories."

"The stories?" One corner of her mouth lifts. "Yeah, I think she ended up telling her parents about them, but that's not why they were so upset. I can't believe you didn't know. I'm pretty sure all our parents talked about it. Mine were up in arms, like yanking a five-dollar bill from a wallet was tantamount to murder."

The words hang in the air, clinging like a bad smell.

"I'm sorry," she says, blinking rapidly. "I wasn't thinking. I—"

"It's okay," I say.

"I mean, I may not have kids, but I can't imagine hurting your own. Did she ever tell you what was going on? Back then?" Her eyes are filled with genuine curiosity.

"No, she didn't," I say.

You can't ever tell anyone.

My fingers curl toward my palms, the edges of my nails digging into my skin.

"Would you like a refill?" the waitress says, holding a carafe, and Gia and I answer by sliding our mugs toward her.

After she leaves, Gia runs a hand across her breastbone, pinkening the skin. "I don't remember talking about it much when it all happened. Do you?"

"No," I say.

Given her quick swallow, I wonder if she's remembering how we didn't speak once I returned to school, many months later. We would sometimes say hi if we passed in the hall, but never more than that.

She shifts in her chair, plucks her napkin from her lap. If she leaves on this note, with this past darkness hovering over the table, we probably won't ever talk again.

"Okay, enough," I say. "No more morbid talk. We're supposed to be catching up and having fun."

"I second that."

The rest of the conversation is safe. Innocuous. Recommendations of restaurants, niche stores, parks. Long after our plates have been cleared away, the pause before imminent goodbyes lingers.

"We have to do this again," she says. "Please tell me you want to too?"

"Definitely."

When she hugs me, she presses her palms tight into my back for a brief moment. And then we're going our separate ways. I start my engine but leave the car in park. I want this to have been a normal brunch with an old friend. No ulterior motives. Would she sit with me, eat with me, talk to me, if she knew what I did?

I text Ryan. ON MY WAY HOME.

HOW'S NICOLE?

I feel a pinch of guilt as I reply SHE'S GOOD. Telling him I was meeting an old friend would've been fine, but it was easier to lie. Fewer questions to answer.

I call my parents, and after his greeting, Dad says, "Hey, guess what? You know the old field? The county sold the land to a developer."

I grip the phone even tighter. The field sold? No, that can't be right. "Are you sure?" I say.

"Uh-huh," Dad says. "They're going to build townhouses. Big ones with garages on the bottom floor. Probably have them built in a weekend the way they do things nowadays, but better houses than an unused field, I guess."

I try to come up with something to say, but words won't come.

"Hey, your mom's here, so I'm turning over the phone. Love you."

"Love you too," I manage.

Mom says hello twice, and I shake my head hard. One disaster at a time. "Did Becca ever steal from us?"

"What?"

"I remembered something, and I'm not sure if it's right or not. Did Becca steal money from you and Dad?"

"You're serious? You called to ask that?"

"Did she?" There's a long silence. "Mom?"

She sighs. "Yes, we had money go missing a few times."

"You never told me."

"Because it wasn't much. The two of you were already having problems when we found out, so we made the decision not to say anything. Why?"

"What do you mean?"

"Why are you asking? What does this have to do with your patient?"

She's got me there. "Stealing can be a sign of a troubled kid," I say. It isn't really an answer, but it is true.

"You need to let this go. There's no reason to be so fixated on it," she says.

"I'm not fixated, I'm—"

"You are," she says. "If that's all you needed, I have to go," she says, not waiting for me to say goodbye in return.

What the hell? That was weird. All I did was ask a simple question.

I try to focus on driving but rub my palms over and over again on the steering wheel. Construction. In the field. I never thought that a possibility. And before they start building, they'll dig. I have to go back and look for the knife again. If I can't find it, time will surely have erased anything leading back to me. Fingerprints, DNA—there should be nothing left but rust. Even if they find it, they won't know what it was used for. They'll toss it out.

But what about *her*, and why can't I remember?

My hands keep moving. Hell is murky indeed.

*   *   *

When I pull into the office parking lot, only a few spots are occupied, including one bright-red SUV taking up two. The SUV belongs to an accountant in a firm on the top floor. One of those loud, abrasive men who drops sexual innuendos into every conversation and tells women to smile. He tried the latter with me once; I gave my best professional *leave me the hell alone* face in return. He hasn't done it again.

The air holds a chill, a promise of the autumn days to come. The sky is a darker shade of blue, daylight slowly creeping in. I catch movement from the corner of my right eye and whirl around, apprehension cemented in my chest. Nothing but parking lot and a few cars. Another bit of movement, farther to the right.

Dogwoods, their leaves turned burgundy for the season, border each side of the lot. I scan the trees and surrounding bushes. Nothing out of place. No one moving. The morning shadows offer only scant concealment, but I can't shake the chill or the sensation of being watched. Cars move on Route 100; a woman calls out a cheery "Good morning!" in the parking lot on the other side of the dogwoods; leaves rustle. My name travels the same breeze. A low, indeterminate voice. I jolt backward, my heel wobbling on a loose pebble. I did not hear that. There is no one here but me.

There is no one.

My skin feels too small, my shoulders curling painfully in. I'm not sleeping well, so I'm on edge. Seeing and hearing things.

A maroon sedan pulls into the parking lot, and I will myself to walk into the building with my back straight, strides even. My mouth remains dry on the elevator ride up, but once inside the office, the fear bleeds out. I've squeezed my keys tight enough to mark my palm with jagged grooves, a strange set of semi-stigmatic wounds. Gauging from the light peeking beneath Christina's closed door, she beat me here. I stand at my window, peering through the slats until I see Ellie get out of her car. Then I twist the blinds open hard enough to make them rattle and shake. Happy fucking Monday.

After my second patient leaves, I make a quick trip to a nearby home improvement store for a shiny new shovel, and when I come back, there's dirt on the floor near my desk and the filing cabinet. A scattering of brownish-black. Dry and mostly atop the carpet, not embedded. Butter-flies gather in my belly. I know it's just dirt, but it wasn't there before. I don't have any plants in my office. Nothing's on my shoes. And I locked my door before I left.

I open my desk drawer, shuddering an exhale when I see the half-heart necklace. Then I roll my eyes. My patients are kids. Kids often have crud on their shoes. I sweep up, tipping the dustpan over my trash can. The pattering sound the dirt makes when it strikes the crumpled papers inside makes my fingers twitch. All I can think of is being trapped in a hole while the dirt falls down and down and down.

A little while later, I'm organizing my inbox when Ellie brings in the mail. After the delivery, she remains by my door, leaning against the frame.

"Do you need anything else?"

"Oh, no, sorry," she says, flushing. "I'm running across the street to the deli to grab some lunch. Want anything?"

"No," I say. "I brought leftovers, but thank you, and Ellie, was anyone in my office earlier while I was gone?"

"No," she says, shaking her head. "Your door was shut, so I assumed you locked it. Everything okay?"

"It's fine," I say. *Kids*, I remind myself.

She closes the door, and I nudge the mail with my elbow. A toppling Jenga tower, envelopes slide every which way across my desk. On one, my name and address written in neat capital letters. I don't need to pull the other envelope from the drawer to know it's a match. Time halts; the buzz of the fluorescent lights amplifies until it's all I hear.

This envelope is larger than the first, yet no less generic. Standard brown, nine by twelve inches, with a gummed flap. Same black ink, no smudge this time. No return address. Smeared postmark. Deliberately smeared, without a doubt. I can even imagine how it happens: the postal worker stamps it at the counter, the sender asks to check the address and runs a thumb across the fresh ink, the postal worker takes it back without looking and tosses it in the proper bin.

The contents aren't heavy, but bulky, crinkling slightly when I push. In my mind, I throw it out, carry the trash can to the dumpsters behind the building, toss it in with all the other rubbish. Brush my hands, banishing it from skin and thought. I don't need to see what's inside. It's nothing I need or want.

I dangle it by one corner over the bin. But I can't let go.

I don't even bother with the letter opener. Inside is a piece of sketch paper, folded many times into an irregular rectangle. Slow and careful, I unfold it, the paper crackling. It smells of time—old basements and musty attics. It smells of childhood dreams gone wrong. Of wishes made on birthday cakes that never come true.

It's a drawing of Becca and me from the back, our hands clasped together, walking toward the empty house. I rest my elbows on the desk. Prop my fingers beneath my chin. Try to keep memories from rushing in. Try to keep from screaming. The drawing was there in the house that night. She'd hung it on the wall. I'm the one who took it down.

Becca and I are in the foreground, the house farther back than it was in truth. Done in colored pencil, it's faded where it was creased, yet faded in old creases too, where it's been folded even smaller, small enough to perhaps fit into a pocket. I hold it close to my nose. In that instant, I feel her hand in mine, hear our tandem breath, see her eyes and the conviction there.

Even with the passage of years, some of the pencil marks still appear sharp, defined. Our hair was drawn loose, but where Becca's is flat against her back, mine is swirling in tendrils, as though I'm walking through my own private windstorm. And there are no marks of delineation on our hands, so they appear as one. Guilt claws at my heart, ripping holes too big to ever stitch closed.

You were a child, the clinical part of me says. *A child.*

And so were the two ten-year-olds who beat a toddler to death in England. So was the teenage girl in Missouri who strangled her nine-year-old neighbor because she wanted to know what killing someone felt like. So were the girls who lured their friend into the woods and stabbed her nineteen times in the name of Slenderman.

But I wasn't like them. Not even remotely similar. Some people are born with an innate cruelty; others have to work at it. And even if they're successful, it doesn't mean it will ever occur again.

I close my eyes and see images of us laughing, of an angry face in a dark basement, of blood and a knife, of running across the field. How quickly it all seemed to happen.

When things begin to fall apart, they do so with shocking speed.

There's no doubt as to the picture's authenticity. On the bottom right corner is Becca's signature with its distinct curlicue. *Every artist has a signature.*

She drew us wearing calf-length dresses and shaded the ground beneath our feet red, so we appear to be stepping in, or out, of blood.

"Why are you doing this to me?" I say, hunching forward with arms folded over my belly. "What do you want?"

*   *   *

Two hours later, Cassidy is sitting in the cartoon chair, staring at the floor. "And the princess ran away, but she couldn't run fast enough, and—"

Even though I have the volume down, the light on my office phone begins to blink. "Cassidy, honey, can you hold on for a second? Miss Ellie needs to talk to me."

When I call up front, Ellie says, "I'm sorry, but there's something here from Dr. Carlson that you need to sign for."

To Cassidy again, I say, "I'll be right back."

I return with an envelope of patient notes for a referral to see Cassidy standing next to my desk, holding several pieces of paper. Irritation flashes bright, but I tamp it down. It's my fault for not wanting to touch Becca's picture again, for covering it with other papers instead of putting it away. Out of sight, not of mind. Part of it must've been exposed, and Cassidy has an eight-year-old's curiosity.

"Who's the lady in the window?" she asks.

"Where?" I ask.

"See?" She points to the window at the top left of the house. "Right here, peeking through the curtain."

I grip the edge of the desk tight. Cassidy's right. There's a figure drawn in the upper window, partially obscured by the fading and a crease. The more I stare, the clearer she becomes. Beside the half-open curtain, a hint of red, a pale face, dark hair. Drawn as though she's watching me and Becca as we approach.

"She looks hungry," Cassidy says.

"What?"

"The lady. She looks hungry, like maybe she's not a lady at all but a monster wearing a lady face. That's how they trick you, monsters. They put normal faces on so you think they're real, but they're not. And when you get too close to run away, they show you their real ones," she says, eyes serious and far too knowing.

My fingers spider to the hollow of my throat. Is the woman's mouth open a bit, revealing not teeth and tongue but darkness? Or is it simply a smudge in the pencil?

"Is she going to eat those girls?"

"I don't think so. See that girl?" I point. "That's me."

"But you don't have long hair."

"I did when I was a little girl."

"How come you don't have it now?"

I shake away an image of scissors, of long strands stark against the white curve of a sink.

"It takes too much time to take care of, and I'd rather spend that time taking care of other people, like you."

She smiles, but it's fleeting. "I still think she's going to eat them. Monsters can do that without taking you away. They eat you in here." She touches her chest.

I mimic her gesture to quell the ache in my heart. She's right. Sometimes they do.

"Who drew the picture?" she says.

"A friend drew it a long time ago. The other girl in the picture."

"Did the monster eat her?"

My stomach clenches. "No," I say. "Why don't you sit back down so you can finish telling me your story?"

"Will I be okay, Dr. Cole?"

An unexpected—and odd—question, but I nod. "Of course you will."

Is there any crueler lie we tell kids? Regardless of what happens, of how deep the scars might run, we say they'll be okay and they believe it. They trust us. But what else are we supposed to say? *Hey, kid, childhood is a bitch and she leaves marks*?

I fold the picture and shove it in my desk. Cassidy starts talking again, peeking through her lashes. Innocent and trusting. I may have done a monstrous thing, but I'm not a monster. I'm *not*.

I believed that once. I wish I could believe it now.

CHAPTER TEN

THEN

The used bookstore in Timonium had a big horror section, way bigger than the mall. They had two copies of Stephen King's *The Dark Half*, which I hadn't read yet, and I grabbed the one in better shape. I picked out five more books, and since my dad wasn't finished looking, I went to Becca's favorite section, mythology, and found one she didn't have, thick and heavy with pictures and descriptions. Another looked good, too, about ghosts and folklore. Halfway in, there was a picture of a woman in a long red robe. A ghost in Alabama, not a witch. Maybe not Becca's Red Lady, but she reminded me of her. I tucked it under my arm. My dad wouldn't mind; I had some of my allowance with me.

I'd called Becca to see if she wanted to come with us, but her mom had said, all slurry and garbled like I woke her up even though it was after breakfast, that Becca wasn't home.

On the way home, we played license plates, where you had to make up words beginning with the letters on the plate of the car in front. Dad made me laugh with Stinky Cat Butt and Dog Poo Brain, and I made him groan with Fart Cheese Balls and Monkey Gut Bomb, but on my next turn the letters were TRL. All I could think of was The Red Lady, so I said I was stuck, but it was okay. We were close to home.

He dropped me off at Becca's so I could give her the books, but no one answered. I didn't just want to leave the books, but since her mom had said earlier she wasn't home, I had an idea where she might be.

Even thinking about going inside the empty house made my palms slippery and my skin hot, but I didn't need to be scared. The Red Lady wasn't in the house that night. It was only my imagination. Because of the stories Becca told, because of the candles making me sick.

The door was locked and I thought knocking would scare Becca, so I walked around the side, crouching beside an overgrown bush next to a basement window. With the branches pushed out of the way, I tried to peek in, but the curtains were shut tight. Staying low, I crept to the next window, also mostly hidden by another bush. But there was a tiny gap in these curtains, a hint of light. I knuckled the glass.

"Becca, it's me," I said.

The curtain twitched. I rocked back on my heels and fell on my butt. "Geez," I said. "It's Heather."

The light went out. I knocked on the glass twice more, but the light didn't come back on. I sat for a while, expecting her to come outside, but she didn't.

"Fine," I said. "Be that way."

I walked back, scuffing my feet on the pavement, left the books by her front door, and went home.

She called when it was starting to get dark. My parents were across the street at a neighbor's and I was slouched on the sofa, flipping through television channels.

Instead of hello, she said, "Did you leave books at my house?"

"Uh-huh," I said. "I found them at the used bookstore in Timonium. Did you like them?"

"Yeah, they're cool."

"Want to come over?"

The phone got quiet, and then she said, "Okay, but only for a little while. I'll come up the alley."

I waited in the backyard. When we were little, me, Becca, and my dad had camped out here with a tent and sleeping bags. I'd once asked if we could do it alone, but Dad said it wasn't safe. Too many roaming perverts. But no one was ever completely safe anywhere. I knew that from the books in Becca's house.

When she came in, she plopped down on the grass with a muttered "Hey." The bruise on her cheek was turning green at the edges. I told her about the books I got, but when I stopped talking, she stayed quiet, too.

"So you really liked your books?" I said.

"I told you I did."

"Just checking," I said.

A lightning bug flew past me, flashing as it did, and I caught it in my palm. Its legs tickled as it traveled the side of my hand before it flew off.

"Remember last summer when Rachel's brother smooshed one and rubbed the light all over his arms? Then he cried because it wouldn't come off?" she said.

"Yeah."

"He said it was an accident," Becca said, flopping back on her elbows and talking to the sky. "But I bet it wasn't. Lots of people say things are accidents when they aren't. Or they pretend they are when they really wanted to do them in the first place."

I plucked several blades of grass. "Didn't you hear me today at the house when I knocked on the window?"

She blinked a couple times. "I wasn't at the house."

"But the light was on in the basement, and after I knocked, it went out."

"It wasn't me."

"It's not a big deal," I said. "I just—"

"I said I wasn't there."

"So who do you think it was? Your mom, maybe?"

She made a sound in her throat. "She was in bed all day. She wasn't *feeling well.*"

"Oh," I said, sticking my hands underneath my thighs. "Maybe another real estate agent?"

"Does it matter?" she said. "I said it wasn't me."

"Sorry. I didn't think anyone else was supposed to be there."

She tipped her head back. A few stars were starting to appear, but not enough to make out any constellations yet. Not that I knew many, other than Orion's Belt and the Big Dipper. Gia knew a bunch and always got frustrated when the rest of us couldn't find them.

"I have to go," she said, rising to her feet as if pulled by a string.

"But you just got here."

"I have to get back before she gets mad."

"But you said she was in bed. How will she know you're not home?"

She glanced over her shoulder, expressionless. "You know that ghost isn't her, right? The one in the book?"

I plucked more grass. "Yeah, I guess so."

"She's so much better than a ghost," she said as she slipped out the gate.

"Well goodbye then," I said to myself.

I tried watching TV, but there was nothing on that I wanted to see, so I went to my room and read until I was tired.

In the middle of the night, I woke up, gasping for air. It felt like my mouth was full, but the only thing in it was my tongue. I had a vague impression of a person standing behind me, saying my name, and then the dream faded. Becca always remembered hers. I hardly ever did. Once when she spent the night, she had a nightmare. She woke me up, too, and we stayed up until the sun rose.

I rubbed my face. Something moved beside me. I whipped my head around, but nothing was there. I rolled onto my side, facing the wall, but I couldn't fall asleep. I hated the way things had changed between me and Becca. Hated the way she was someone else now, someone who wasn't my best friend anymore, someone who didn't even like me very much. And I didn't know what I'd done wrong. I was the same Heather. All I wanted was my friend back. I started crying and buried my face in my pillow so no one would hear.

* * *

I walked super slow to the front door of the empty house, almost wanting someone to see me, to yell at me to get away. Maybe if they did, if we weren't allowed to sneak in anymore, Becca would act like Becca again. But there was no one around to see me or yell.

The door was unlocked and everyone else already downstairs, sitting in a circle. No candles or anything else. Rachel and Gia seemed okay, and they scooted to make a space in between for me, but Becca barely said hello.

Rachel was the one who'd told me we were hanging out here tonight, and the only reason I'd even come was because she'd said it was a meeting of the Dead Girls Club.

I said, "Did you see about the lady in Florida?"

Becca rolled her eyes and made her lips thin.

"What lady?" Rachel said.

"You didn't see it on the news last night?" I said.

"I never watch the news," Rachel said.

"Me either," Gia said. "It's boring."

Becca made the face again, but I knew she watched it sometimes. She'd heard when my dad told me it was important for me to know what was happening in the world.

I swallowed, waiting to see if Becca would tell me to shut up, but she didn't, and I said, "She got attacked outside a store by her old boyfriend. They broke up, but he kept calling her and showing up at her apartment, and the police couldn't stop him. He followed her shopping, and they got into a fight in front of the store because she told him to leave her alone. Then he stabbed her a bunch of times, right there, out in front. He left and people walked by and saw all the blood and didn't even help. She was alive for a long time, too. People even saw him stab her and didn't do anything at all."

"Did they call the cops?" Rachel said.

"I guess," I said. "But by the time they got there, she was dead."

"How could you not try to help?" Rachel said.

"Maybe they didn't know she was hurt," Gia said.

"They said there was a lot of blood," I said. "No way people didn't know. They just didn't want to help. It was like that story you read, Becca, about the woman in New York, that woman Kitty."

She blinked at me, but nothing else.

"Did they catch him? The boyfriend?" Rachel said.

"Not yet," I said. "They showed a picture, and he looked totally normal. He didn't even have psycho Ted Bundy eyes, just regular eyes."

Rachel's forehead got all scrunchy. "Is he—"

"Has anyone seen anything weird?" Becca asked. "Or had any more dreams?"

I pinched my lower lip between my teeth, Rachel chewed a fingernail, and Gia played with the laces on her shoe.

"I thought somebody was in my house the other day," Gia said, talking fast. "Nobody else was home, but I heard somebody in the kitchen."

"I keep having the dream," Rachel said.

"Am I the only one who cares?" Becca said.

"About what?" I said.

"About what matters."

"The lady in Florida mattered," I said.

"But we aren't here to talk about her," Becca said.

"She's a dead girl, right? So she counts. There's more things to talk about than the Red Lady," I said, and I didn't even pretend not to be angry. I didn't care if it would make Becca mad. It felt like she was always mad at me lately anyway, no matter what I did or said.

"Maybe I don't want to talk about them," Becca said.

I hoped Rachel and Gia would back me up, but they turned away. To Becca, I said, "Why are you acting so weird? It's like you hate me all of a sudden, nothing I do or say is right."

"I don't hate you."

"You're acting like you do," I said. "All I did was tell a story. I thought this was an official meeting. I thought telling the story—"

"I'm the one who tells the stories," Becca said.

"But I asked if you heard about her first, and you didn't say anything."

Becca hit the floor with a fist. "Maybe you should've waited."

"Waited?" I said. "For what?"

"Hey," Rachel said.

"For me to tell you what we were talking about," Becca said.

"You don't make any sense," I said. "Why do we have to talk about someone specific? We never did before. You never got mad at me this way before, either."

"Hey," Rachel said. "Please don't fight."

"And no, I'm not having any dreams or seeing anything," I said.

"How come?" Becca said.

"How come what?"

"How come you're not having any dreams?"

"I don't know," I said. "Because I'm not. Why does it even matter?"

"Maybe the Red Lady hates you," Becca said.

I sighed, openmouthed. "Who even cares? What's she going to do? Come and haunt me or stick dirt in my mouth? I'm not scared of a story."

And that's all she was. The rest was just my imagination. If I believed in her—or said I did—Becca would keep talking about her. She'd never let her go. I just wanted it to be over. I wanted my best friend back.

"She might," Becca said, meeting my gaze. "You never know."

The floor above creaked. All four of us jumped. There was a second creak, then a third.

"Did you lock the door?" Becca whispered.

"No," I said. "I didn't know everybody was here. I just shut it all the way."

Becca moved toward the steps. Rachel grabbed her arm, but she shook her off. Her feet made tiny noises as she crept up.

"Come up," she said, after what felt like an hour. "You need to see this."

I went first, my ears pulsing. I wasn't sure if I was afraid to see whatever she wanted us to or to see her still mad or maybe both. Gia was snuggled up tight behind me. In the kitchen, Becca was crouched near the entryway to the hall.

"Look," she said, pointing.

There was a wide streak of dark red on the linoleum. I peeked down the hall, but there was nothing there. It was only in the kitchen.

Becca fingertipped the mark. "It's wet."

"Is it . . ." Gia said.

"Yes. It's blood."

Rachel pulled her cheeks down. "Like in the stories. She was here?"

"I guess so," Becca said.

"It's your fault," Rachel said to me. "You started it. You said she was just a story."

"Whatever," I said. "That's probably not even real."

"It is," Becca said.

The air changed, thickened. Rachel spoke, but her words were distant. She doubled over, clutching her belly; Gia sagged against the counter, fingers splayed over hers. Becca hunched her shoulders. I felt pain, too, but in my side, a sharp sensation that snarled my breath.

The air snapped back to normal, like a vacuum cleaner had sucked all the thickness out. The pain vanished. We were all quiet, like no one wanted to go first.

Then Rachel said, "I think I just got my period."

Gia wrinkled her nose. "Me too," she said. "Like right this second."

Becca said, "Me three."

"All of us at the same time?" Rachel said.

Their gazes swung toward me. I shook my head. "Not me."

"You made her mad," Rachel said. "That's why she did this."

"If she was mad, then why do it only to you, huh? Why not me?"

"I don't—"

There was a creak from the second floor.

Rachel was first to run; Gia second. I was third and didn't check to see if Becca was following, but I heard her footsteps. Outside, Rachel and Gia were already nowhere in sight, but I waited by the hedge until Becca came out. She ran right past me. Didn't even look back.

When I got home, I went into the bathroom, knowing what I'd find: my underwear sticky with a brownish-red smear. I covered my mouth. It didn't mean anything. It didn't mean anything at all.

CHAPTER ELEVEN

NOW

Ryan's working late, so I don't need to come up with an excuse for not coming home right away. Unfortunately, I leave the office at just the wrong time and fight traffic all the way to Towson. By the time I near the field, every nerve is screaming *I'm a fool, I don't need to do this, I won't find anything*. But I have to at least try.

I park on the same street as the last time. Check to make sure no one's watching before I fetch the shovel from my trunk. Once I'm on the field itself, there's no sound save the weeds my soles are destroying and the grass whisking against my legs. I nearly step in a fresh pile of dog crap so rancid I hope there's a vet visit scheduled soon. It's chilly tonight, and I'm glad I wore a jacket.

When I get close to what I think is the right spot, I see several darker areas around the base of the hill. Drawing closer, I recognize them as holes. But that can't be right. A few steps closer reveal five, neatly—newly—dug, about eight inches wide and a foot deep, surrounded with scattered reddish-brown dirt. I spin, ears ringing, guts hot and liquid. I drop the shovel with a thump. Try to swallow, but my throat clicks.

This can't be a coincidence. I kneel beside the closest hole. Slip my fingers in, find only freshly turned soil. Still crouched, I scramble to the next, ankles protesting. I find the same. And in the next. And the next.

And the next. Dirt spills between my fingers, dirt and nothing more. I sit back on my heels. Pan from left to right. I'm still alone. This is the correct spot. It's where I remember kneeling. And digging.

I shovel the first hole deeper. Drive my fingers into the new space, sifting through the loose soil. I move to the next hole. Do the same. I turn all five into ragged, open wounds, scattering earth every which way, no longer caring if anyone sees. Then I tackle the solid ground between the holes, jabbing with the point of the shovel. I dig deep, tossing rocks and pebbles, lifting scoops of dirt in my palms, flinging it away. I stab the ground again and again, biceps, wrists, and forearms aching. Nothing. There's nothing.

Nothing here, or nothing to find because someone else already found it?

The shovel slips from my grasp, and I press a dirt-covered hand to my forehead. Sweat slicks my skin. Then there's no ground beneath me; my fingers and toes are numb; a gray haze clouds my eyes. My heart is a tattoo gun. I throw my head back, take in gulps of air as my fingers clutch the earth. The purpling sky watches, indifferent.

No one knew about this. If anyone else saw me back then, they would've said something. They would've done something. I was crying. Frantic. Trying to be quiet, maybe, but no doubt failing—because I was twelve goddamn years old.

With the shovel bouncing bruise-hard against my side, legs moving in an uneven gait, I race to my car. Fling the shovel into the trunk. Fling myself into the driver's seat. The visor mirror reveals a woman with flushed skin and dilated pupils. A woman slowly being driven mad. A woman who soon won't have any fight left, who will only be able to curl in a ball and wait for it to end.

* * *

When Nicole texts to ask if I want to meet for drinks after work, I lie and tell her I have a late patient. I do end up working a little late—my last session runs over—but once it ends, I pack up and go to close the window blinds. And there, in the parking lot beside my Jeep's passenger door, is someone standing in dark clothing. Hunched over. I gasp, slamming my palm against the window frame. The person walks on, arm swinging free, car fob in hand. I choke back a humorless laugh.

Still, as I leave the building, I scan the lot. Make a quick walk around my Jeep to check the back seats. It's only when I'm inside and have the doors locked that my shoulders loosen, my fingers uncurl.

The drive home is uneventful, and although Ryan didn't text me that he was working late, his truck isn't here. The next-door neighbor pulls into their driveway the same time I do, and we offer cursory waves. A warm front moved through the area this afternoon and at least a few people are taking advantage of it—I smell hot dogs on a grill and hear the rhythmic bounce of a basketball.

Shifting the weight of my bag on my shoulder, I reach into the mailbox, and my fingers sink into something soft. Yelping, I yank back. Bend down in slow motion to spy gray fur. A bushy tail. A squirrel.

"Okay," I say, stepping back a few feet.

We've had squirrels in the attic but never in our mailbox. I wait, but it doesn't come out. Then I smell it. Rot and decay, sweet and thick. My guts churn. Did the squirrel climb in there to die? *Think, Heather. Think.* I fetch a pair of rubber gloves from the kitchen and a contractor bag from the garage, but when I reach into the mailbox, I shudder and drop the bag, my arms like electrified worms.

Returning to the garage, I scan the tools for something small but not sharp. Lightbulb moment. From the shed in the backyard, I find a small gardening shovel. There's enough room for me to slide it in the mailbox, above the squirrel. I lower it until there's resistance, burying my mouth in my shoulder to keep from inhaling the stink any more than I have to. With my other hand holding the open contractor bag below the mailbox, I pull the shovel forward. The carcass emerges. The smell intensifies and I step back, fighting not to vomit.

I bend forward. Exhale. I can do this.

When the squirrel comes free, I jump back in surprise. Both animal and shovel tumble to the ground, not inside the bag. My arms worm-wiggle again. The squirrel is on its belly, its bottom half flattened, imprinted with tire marks.

I hiss out a watery moan. Fight the urge to puke again. The squirrel couldn't have survived being run over like that, let alone climbed inside our mailbox after the fact. Someone had to have put it there. Mouth into shoulder again, I use the shovel to push the squirrel into the bag but misjudge the amount of effort needed and flip it instead.

Sticking out of the animal's chest is a small knife with a plastic handle. I back away, arms rigid, and return with hesitant steps. There's very little blood around the wound. It's not *the* knife. It's too new—the bit of blade I can see is shiny—but the implication . . . I'm not reading too much into it. It's a clear message. They know. They fucking know.

An engine rumbles nearby, and I scoop the squirrel, knife and all, into the trash bag. Gloves, too. This isn't anything like a picture sent in the mail or a ribbon left on my car. This is a threat.

Or a promise.

I need to call the police. It's what anyone with a modicum of intelligence would do. A dead squirrel with a knife in its chest is not a friendly message in any way, shape, or form. But what the hell would I say? How can I point them toward anyone specific when I don't know who's behind it? Not really. They'll probably decide it's kids playing a sick prank. If the knife weren't there, I'd think the same myself.

Fuck, fuck, fuck. I stomp to the trash cans on the side of the house and head inside for disinfectant spray.

If I don't call, am I putting myself at risk? But haven't I been at risk since the necklace arrived? Maybe I didn't want to see it, but it's more than apparent now. What are they going to do next? They obviously have the advantage. They know where to find me, and I have no idea where or even who they are. That has to change. The rules of this game obviously have.

* * *

On Wednesday I'm sitting in the parking lot outside Alexa's office when Corinne leaves for lunch, and then I'm inside the building's elevator faster than I can think about it. This is the easy—and legal—part. My guess is Alexa doesn't realize how much she's let slip over the years. Nothing important. Small things like Corinne choosing to eat lunch out of the office every day or her office partner's habit of leaving his keys in his coat pocket. I don't even recall the conversation where she brought it up. At the time it was insignificant. Now it's paramount. And it means I have a good chance of getting in, getting what I need, and getting the hell out.

The warm front blew out as quickly as it arrived, and it felt downright cold this morning. Fingers crossed it was chilly enough for Clark to wear a jacket. Fingers crossed he still takes a late lunch every day. Fingers crossed the outer door is unlocked. If it isn't, I'll have to try again a different day. But I can't waste any more time. Alexa won't be in Florida forever, and I need Lauren's address.

There's a bitter taste in my mouth when I open the outer door. I'm not breaking in, technically, not yet, anyway, but this isn't morally right. Still, no time for second-guesses or cinematic pauses in the doorway. Only time for a peek down the hall confirming that Clark's office door is closed.

My luck holds. He wore a jacket *and* left his keys. It only takes two tries to find the spare to Alexa's office, and I close the door behind me as quietly as possible. Exhale.

No keys to her cabinets on the ring. Of course not. What was I thinking? Why would she leave them while she's away? Corinne might have them, though. I kick off my shoes. Run to the front. No keys anywhere. Back in Alexa's office, I double-check the drawers in her desk. All locked.

Then I eye the cabinets. We have the same model. I wonder . . .

I take hold of the top two drawers. Give a hard yank. Nothing. Another yank, even harder. *Please don't let Clark hear. Please don't let this be a defect with my cabinet alone.*

It isn't.

I scan the files fast. *Shit.* Not in this one. I move to the next. Repeat the drawer trick and nothing happens. *Shit, shit, shit.* I yank hard as I can. The lock disengages and the drawers open with a metallic rattle. I freeze, prepared to see Clark bursting through the door, demanding to know what's up, but it doesn't happen.

I find what I need three drawers down. I flip open Lauren's file and snap a picture of her address with my phone. Alexa was telling the truth; Lauren lives almost an hour away from me. We wouldn't have run into each other. There's also a note inside regarding Lauren's employment at a hotel. Housekeeping. I recognize the name of the chain. Not a five-star, but respectable. I take a picture of that, too.

Without the key I can't relock the cabinet, but it is what it is. Holding my shoes, I lock Alexa's office, open the closet, return the keys. I have one shoe on and the other in the process when the outer door opens. Corinne. Back early.

Fuck.

Her brow furrows. "Dr. Cole?"

"Hi. I was nearby and thought I'd stop in to see Alexa." I finish putting on my shoe. "Sorry, I caught a pebble on the way in."

"She's in Florida," she says. "I'm quite sure I mentioned it when you called."

"I know. You did and I forgot. I realized it once I got here."

She doesn't believe me. It's there in her pursed lips. It's in my rapid pulse.

"Maybe I should call Dr. Martin," she says, moving too close.

What the hell is she going to do? Physically try to restrain me? I step back. "No worries at all," I say. "I'll come back when she's back in town."

And I'm out. Heart thudding, I take the stairs, my heels tattooing panic on the vinyl tile. I keep waiting for a door to slam open, for a security guard to tell me to stop. But even if they search me, they won't find anything. They won't think to look on my phone.

I drive away from the building like a bat out of hell. Triumph bubbles from my lips with a hysterical edge, but I don't care. I got Lauren's address. I really did.

"I got you," I say.

I should go right now. No time like the present. No time to worry or chicken out. And I wasn't at Alexa's as long as I thought I'd be. I even moved two sessions to come today. With an airy grunt, I pull over on the side of the road and punch Lauren's address into my GPS. If I drive fast and don't spend hours there—and why would I?—I should be okay. Or I could wait until the end of the day. Then I wouldn't have to worry.

I square my shoulders. No. No more waiting. Between the holes in the field and the dead squirrel, I have to do this. I have to know if it's Lauren. I have to look her in the eye.

The ride doesn't take as long as I thought, and by the time I get there, my palms are so sweaty the steering wheel is hard to hold. Gauging by the aged brick, the double-hung windows, the apartment complex is an older one. No balconies here. No separate entrances or loft ceilings. Probably built around the same time as my parents' house; they share the same neat, no-frills appearance. I wonder if it makes Lauren feel more at home.

There's nothing in my purse I can use to defend myself, if needed, and although the shovel's still in my trunk, I can't exactly walk to the door with it over my shoulder. I slip a key through my first two fingers, the way most women do when facing a dark parking lot. I wish I could say it makes me feel better.

What if Lauren hurts me? No one knows I'm here. She could open the door and shoot me straightaway. If the door's made of wood, she wouldn't even have to open it. But she's a felon. She can't own a gun. I wrinkle my nose. No, she can't buy a gun legally. Doesn't mean she can't get one. But the likelihood of her shooting me out in the open is slim. She wouldn't be that foolish. And if she invites me in, I don't have to go. Anyway, if she knows what I did, she's probably afraid of me. Never mind the implied threat of the knife, a squirrel in a mailbox is passive.

I'm not afraid, I tell myself. I'm not afraid of her. I try to shake away the chill and pretend it works.

In spite of carpet worn threadbare and walls in need of new paint, the inside of the building is clean and tidy. No random flyers spilled below the neat metal mailboxes on the wall. One is labeled L. Thomas. I can't tell if the handwriting is an exact match to the envelopes, but it's close. I swallow hard. Wipe my palms.

From an open door, there's the steady tumble of clothes in a dryer and the smell of fabric softener. Somewhere else in the building, a muted conversation, maybe a television.

Lauren's apartment is on the second floor and I hold tight to the railing, walking on the balls of my feet. Even so, my steps seem like elephant thuds, my knock on the door even louder. I hold my breath. No footsteps. No click of a bullet sliding into a chamber. No answer.

I knock again, same result. Rock back and forth on my heels. My mouth like sandpaper and dust, I turn the doorknob, but it's locked. The third knock results in a door creaking open behind me. I spin around and there's a young girl—about ten, I'm guessing—peeking out. Her skin is pale, save for a bit of red around her nose, her hair lank around her shoulders. She's in pajamas and striped socks.

I put on a professional, calming smile. "Hello, how are you?"

She starts and takes a half step back.

"It's okay," I say. "Is your mom home?"

Worry circles her eyes, but she doesn't move to close the door. "Not yet," she says with a sniffle.

"Your dad?"

She stands a little straighter. "He . . . doesn't live here."

"Okay. I was just looking for Miss Lauren, who lives across the hall. Do you know her?"

"Uh-huh."

"I'm Anna," I say, the lie rolling easily off my tongue. "I'm sorry if I was knocking too loud, especially since you're sick."

"'S okay," she says.

"And what's your name?"

There's a slight hesitation and another sniffle, but she says, "Mikayla."

I crane my neck, listening. The last thing I need is someone else coming out of their apartment to see what's happening, but there are no other doors opening. "Mikayla, I'm Miss Lauren's boss. From the hotel," I say, silently thanking Alexa for having that information in Lauren's file. "Have you seen her today?"

A quick shake of the head. She rubs the top of her foot against the back of her ankle.

"I really need to talk to her, but maybe I should just come back later. Do you know if she's usually home at night?" If Lauren works the late shift, my ruse is toast.

"I don't know. Sometimes, I guess? Is she in trouble?"

"No, not at all," I say. "Has she had any visitors here lately?"

Mikayla blinks a few times. "Is this about the fight?"

I don't have to feign my surprise. "The fight?"

"Uh-huh," she says. "She had a big fight with someone. My mom even went over to make sure she was okay."

"And was she?"

"Uh-huh. My mom said it was just a fight with words, not hands." She does a quick double-blink, arcing her shoulders forward.

I crouch so I can look her straight in the eye. "Mikayla, this is important. Do you know who she was fighting with?"

"Uh-uh."

I couldn't get that lucky, could I? "Do you remember when the fight happened?"

"Uh-huh. It was on Sunday, because my mom always makes meatloaf on Sundays and we were eating."

"That's very helpful, thank you," I say. "Is your mom friends with Miss Lauren?"

"I don't know," Mikayla says with a shrug. "Mostly she just gives her a ride to work sometimes because she doesn't have a car."

"Does your mom work at the hotel, too?"

"Uh-uh. She works in an office."

She sniffles and wipes her nose on her shoulder.

"Okay," I say, standing straight. "I think maybe you should go and get some rest. Will you do me one favor, please? Don't tell anyone I was here, okay? I don't want Miss Lauren to think she did anything wrong."

"Okay," she says.

I lower my voice and say, "And I promise I won't tell anyone you were home by yourself. We don't want your mom to get in trouble, do we?"

"Uh-uh," she says, wariness settling on her features.

"I hope you feel better soon," I say.

She shuts the door without saying anything else. I try Lauren's doorknob one last time, just in case, then head back to my car, my stomach a hive of angry bees.

I promise I won't tell.

I rest my forehead on the steering wheel. How could I say such a thing? It goes against everything I am. I saw the way she acted when mentioning a fight, the way she said her dad didn't live there. She's witnessed domestic violence, but she trusts women. She would've closed the door right away if she didn't. I can't pretend my words didn't hurt her. I saw the flash of alarm. The betrayal.

But I knew exactly what I was doing.

CHAPTER TWELVE

THEN

"We have to go back and clean it up," Becca said.

With the phone tucked between my ear and shoulder, I stirred through the milk in my bowl, trying to scoop Lucky Charms marshmallows without the cereal. I was in my pajamas, had cramps, and didn't want to go anywhere, especially not the house, but if I said so she'd know I'd lied about my period.

"But if someone's there?" I said.

"We can check first. But we have to clean it up or she'll know. She has someone coming to look at the house this afternoon."

"She won't know it was us," I said.

"But she'll be extra careful with the keys. We might not be able to get in ever again. And since it was blood, she'll call the police. And if they find our fingerprints, we'll all get in trouble, not just me."

They wouldn't really check for fingerprints, would they? It hadn't been that much blood. And maybe it would be good if we could never go there again. Maybe without the house . . .

But if I didn't go, she'd probably never talk to me again, no matter how many times I apologized. Rachel and Gia wouldn't either, not if Becca told them not to. And they were my best friends. Without them, I'd be alone.

I dropped the spoon in the bowl, sloshing milk on the table. "Fine, I'll come."

"Meet us on the field. Bring some paper towels, too," she said, hanging up without a goodbye.

I dumped my bowl in the sink and went to change, grabbing a roll of paper towels on my way out. At least my mom was at work so I didn't have to come up with an explanation.

The three of them really were waiting for me. When I was still too far away to hear, Rachel leaned over and spoke in Becca's ear. Becca responded with a sharp look and a quick shake of her head. Not quite a *no*, more like a *shut up*. A cramp tightened my belly.

Rachel and Gia both had bottles of cleanser; Becca, a trash bag. We walked the rest of the way in silence.

As she unlocked the front door, Becca said, "Let's check the rest of the house first."

We followed her upstairs and checked every room and every closet. All empty. Empty on the first floor, too. Walking into the kitchen, Becca stopped so fast I banged into her and Rachel and Gia banged into me. Becca grabbed the wall to keep from falling.

"What is it?" I said.

She moved aside. The blood was gone.

"What happened to it?" Rachel said. "It was there. We all saw it."

Nods all around, even from me.

"It disappeared," Becca said.

"Just like in the stories," Rachel said, all pug eyes.

"Maybe it's still there and we just can't see it," Gia said.

Becca sprayed cleanser and I gave her the paper towels. Her lower lip caught between her teeth, she wiped the linoleum. Nothing on the paper towels. Not even a speck. "See?" she said.

"We should go," Rachel said.

"Yeah, I need to get the key back," Becca said. The rustling of the plastic bag as she knotted it was loud in the hush.

On the way back, after Rachel and Gia split off, Becca pulled my arm. "Now do you believe in her?"

I tongued the corner of my lips. "You came back and cleaned it all up."

"I swear I didn't."

Her eyes held truth, but I didn't want to believe her. Someone had to have cleaned it up. Blood didn't just vanish on its own. And it probably hadn't even been real, just the fake stuff they sold at Halloween.

"Why won't you believe she's real?" she said, half sad, half angry.

"Because she's just a story, Becca."

She was. She had to be. Witches weren't real. Friends were. I wanted everything to go back to the way it was. I wanted Becca back the way *she* was.

She stepped so close the green edges of her bruise were blurry. "I think you know that's not true. I think you believe in her as much as we do, you just don't want to admit it."

I stepped back, blew air through my nose. "I can't admit to something that isn't true."

"Anyway, it doesn't matter whether you admit it or not. I know you saw her."

"Oh, and how do you know?"

"I told you, she talks to me. And she said you did."

"You're crazy if you think that."

She poked my chest with a finger. "Don't you say that. Don't you ever say that. I'm not crazy."

She walked away, her feet heavy. I called her name three times, but she didn't even turn. I stood, thumbs crooked over my waistband, until she turned the corner and I couldn't see her anymore. Then I waited even longer to see if maybe she'd come back, but she didn't.

* * *

I waited two days before I called Becca. I didn't like that I was scared to talk to her. Didn't like that I almost hung up when she answered. But, like normal, I said, "Want to hang out?"

"I can't," she said.

There was talking in the background; she covered the phone and spoke, but I couldn't hear what she said.

"Who's that?" I said.

"The television. I just had to turn it down."

I heard a familiar giggle, a *Rachel* giggle. If she was there, Gia was, too. I wiped tears away before they fell, so they didn't count.

"Maybe later, then?" I said, trying to sound fine. I bit the side of a cuticle, ignoring the sharp sting.

"Sure," she said, then added in a whisper, "It was their idea not to invite you. Don't be mad at me. Why would you want to hang out with me anyway? I'm crazy, right?"

With that, she hung up. I hugged myself tight. What were the three of them doing right now? Were they talking about the Red Lady, or were they talking about me?

*   *   *

When my mom started vacuuming and told me to scoot, I took a book to the playground. There was a mom with a little kid near the slide, but by the time I climbed to the top of the monkey bars, they were on their way out. Swinging my legs, I read a few pages, the sun warm.

A trill of laughter broke the quiet. My fingers clenched the bars; my stomach knotted. On the sidewalk passing the playground, Becca, Rachel, and Gia were walking together. I drew air to call out but clamped my lips shut. I was right there. All they had to do was look to the side. Then Becca did look. Her gaze caught mine, then she cat-blinked and looked away. I told myself it didn't matter, but it did. It mattered more than anything in the whole world. I closed my eyes, not wanting to cry, and when I opened them again, my friends were gone. I felt like I had a huge hole inside me. If I'd told the truth the night of the second ritual, everything would be different. Becca would still be my best friend, and she'd be walking with me, not Rachel and Gia.

My side ached with a sharp pain in the wrong place to be a cramp. Hands in fists, not caring if anyone heard, not caring that *she* wasn't real, I said, "You took my friends away from me; isn't that enough? You made them hate me. Just leave me alone."

I stayed at the playground for a little while longer, but every time I tried to read, the words jumbled in my head. I spent the rest of the day in my bedroom with the door closed.

For dinner, it was only me and Mom. Dad went to the Orioles game with his work friends. I pushed my peas in small circles and dragged my fork through my mashed potatoes. My mom started eating, but she kept sneaking peeks. Usually it was cool when it was the two of us, because we'd talk about stuff like periods and bras. My dad never cared if we talked about it around him, but it was easier when he wasn't there.

"Is everything okay?" she said. "You seem a little down lately."

I stared at my plate. "It's nothing."

"You know you can talk to me about anything at all."

"I know," I said.

I made myself eat, but everything tasted like nothing.

"You haven't been hanging out with Becca much lately," she said. "Did you two have a disagreement?"

I traced my initials in the condensation on my glass. "Sort of. She wants to hang out with Rachel and Gia instead of me. Like we're not even friends anymore."

My mom clasped her hands beneath her chin, elbows on the table. "Sometimes friendships change, sweetheart. Sometimes people's interests change and they get closer to one friend or another for a little while."

"But they're not supposed to change like that. Becca's *my* best friend," I said.

"She can be friends with Rachel and Gia and still be your best friend."

"Not if she doesn't even want to talk to me."

"Maybe you need to give her a little bit of time," she said. "I'm sure everything will be okay, especially once school starts."

All I could think of was sitting alone in the cafeteria. I'd rather die. My throat got thick, but I swallowed iced tea until it stopped and I had brain freeze. I didn't want to cry in front of her. She acted as if she knew, but she didn't. Maybe she could have a fight with her friends and be fine, but it wasn't the same for me. She hadn't seen how Becca'd looked at me, then looked away. Everything would not be okay. Not in a million years.

I tried to read for a while, but the story wouldn't stick in my head, so I took a walk, ending up at the empty house. I knew they'd be there, even before I sneaked to the side and saw light peeking through the basement curtains. I didn't want to go in. Didn't want to sit outside either. Mostly, I didn't want to fight anymore. I didn't want them to be mad at me. I decided to tell them what I'd felt the night of the ritual. I'd tell them I hadn't admitted it because I hadn't wanted her to be real. I'd tell them whatever they wanted to hear so we'd be friends again.

The door to the house was unlocked, like they knew I'd be coming, but I kept my footsteps light so I wouldn't scare them. Laughter pealed out from the half-open basement door, first loud, then muffled, and I leaned against the doorframe.

Rachel said, "I think it's better with Heather not here."

Gia said something I couldn't hear.

"Yeah, she's been . . ."

"A bitch?" Rachel said, her whisper sharp as a nail.

They all giggled.

"I don't understand why she's been acting so weird," Gia said.

"She's dumb," Rachel said.

Becca said, "She said I was crazy. Do you think I am?"

Rachel's and Gia's *no*s were clear as day. My fingernails bit into the wood. I didn't think that. Her thinking the Red Lady was real was crazy. There was a big difference. She knew it, too.

"Maybe the Red Lady doesn't like her," Becca said. "Maybe that's why she didn't see her, why she didn't dream about her."

"Maybe we shouldn't like her either," Rachel said.

"Maybe we shouldn't," Becca said.

My eyes went all teary. How could they say those things? I'd never talk about them that way. I wanted to stomp down the steps and start yelling, but then they'd hate me even more. I wanted to run out of the house, but that would make me a chicken, so I called out, "Hello? Are you here?"

There was a bunch of furious whispering. Then Becca said, "Yeah, we're here."

I made sure to act normal. They were all sitting close and didn't make a space for me, so I sat a little off to the side. "How come you didn't tell me you were coming here tonight?"

Rachel and Gia shot side-eye looks at each other.

Becca shrugged. "We didn't think you'd want to come, since we were talking about the Red Lady."

"But maybe I would've. You could've at least asked. I mean, if you don't want to be my friends anymore, just tell me."

Rachel opened her mouth like she was surprised, but it was faker than fake. "We never said that."

Gia said, "I don't even know why you keep hanging out with us. It's not like you want to do the stuff we want to."

I waited for Becca to say something, to tell her she was wrong, but she didn't. She looked at me, then past me like I was nothing. Like I wasn't even there. That hurt most of all.

"I heard you," I said. "I came here to say sorry, to try and make things right, and you're talking about me? It's better with me not here? I'm dumb? We're supposed to be friends."

Rachel put her head down, but I saw her smirking.

"If I didn't want to hang out with you anymore, I'd tell you," I said. "I wouldn't be a chicken, sneaking around and acting like you didn't exist. I wouldn't walk past you on the playground and pretend I didn't see you." I looked straight at Becca. She didn't turn away. Didn't look embarrassed or guilty, either.

"You don't care about the Red Lady. We do," she said. "You don't even think she's real, so when we're talking about her, you make faces and think we're idiots for believing in her."

"I do not."

"Yes you do," Gia said, bobbing her head with each word.

"It's not our fault," Becca said. "So stop acting like it is."

"Then whose fault is it? Everything was fine until you started telling those stupid stories." I flung out an arm.

"See?" Rachel said. "You think they're stupid."

"Why do you even care?" Gia said, pulling her chin down to her chest. "You should go home."

"Yeah, go home," Rachel said.

I waited, hoping Becca would tell them to shut up. She opened her mouth to speak, but coughed. Her eyes grew wide and she coughed again, pressing her forearm to her mouth. The back of my throat tickled, but I swallowed against it. Rachel's and Gia's mouths worked, too. Becca coughed a third time, thick and muffled, as though her mouth was full.

I felt dirt in my mouth and nose. I could taste it, dry and crumbling and mixing with my saliva into a thick paste, choking me, cutting off my air. I rolled onto my hands and knees, hanging my head low. Laughter filled my ears, a weight pressed on my chest, and that strange, sharp pain coiled in my side. I clawed at my face, trying to pull out something that wasn't there. Rachel and Gia were doing the same. Becca was on her side, fingers curled at her throat.

My head went swimmy. The laugh grew louder, the pain sharper. Everything hurt and the weight pushed me down and down and down. Someone touched the back of my head and spoke against my ear, but I couldn't hear through the choking. Then, in the span of a blink, the dirt was gone. I shoved two fingers past my teeth, sure I'd find dirt or a ragged stump where my tongue should be.

Gia tugged the ends of her hair. Rachel hugged her stomach. Becca was pale, with shadows under her eyes. Rachel started crying, softly at first, then harder, her shoulders shaking back and forth. "Was that her?" she said.

"I don't know," Becca said.

"Why would she do that to us?" Gia said. "Why would she hurt us?"

"It's her fault," Rachel said, pointing at me. "Everything was fine until she showed up."

My gaze locked on Becca's, and her lips curled, the same thing she did when she got away with telling her mom a lie. Something crumpled inside my chest like a paper cup beneath a sneaker sole. I wished she'd really choked to death. I wished they all had. If my skin were laced with poison, I'd touch them and leave them writhing on the floor.

I bounded to my feet, took the stairs two at a time. I didn't shut the door, didn't care if anyone saw me leaving, didn't care about anything except getting away. I ran across the field, kicking up dirt, and my chest hurt by the time I turned onto my street. My parents' car wasn't there, so I raced into the house and flipped the lock.

In my room, I stood in front of the mirror, still shaking, and opened my mouth as wide as I could. My tongue was there and there was no dirt, but I could taste it. That wasn't the worst part at all. Inside, I was scooped out and filled with lava.

I unhooked the half-heart and threw it in my trash can. "I hate you," I said. "I hate you all." After a couple minutes, I fished the necklace out and put it in my dresser drawer, underneath a bunch of old T-shirts.

"I thought you were my friend," I said. The lava kept bubbling and burning, and I wanted to pour it all over the three of them until they were nothing but a pile of charred bones. I didn't even feel bad for thinking that. Not even a little. I hated them more than they could ever hate me.

* * *

"Becca's on the phone," my mom said, peeking in my bedroom.

I lowered my book just below my eyes. Yesterday she was talking about me behind my back and now she wanted to talk *to* me? Not even funny. "Can you tell her I'm taking a nap?" I said.

"You sure?"

"Yeah, I don't feel good."

Her eyebrows went up, wrinkling her forehead, but she shut the door. A little later, she came back and perched on my bed. "Sit up," she said.

"I don't want to," I said. "I'm reading."

"But I want you to," she said.

I sighed, but did as she asked.

"Move closer, please, and turn around." When I did, she gathered my hair together and ran her fingers through it, catching on the tangles. "What a mess you've got here."

Slow and careful, she brushed the ends, working out the tangles one by one. Her hair wasn't as long as mine, but it was thick, too, so she knew how to do it so it wouldn't hurt too much. She didn't talk while she brushed, but when all the snarls were gone, she said, "Now count to one hundred."

"Mo-om," I said.

"Hea-ther," she imitated. "Count."

"One, two, three . . ."

I kept counting as she kept brushing, long, even strokes from my scalp to the bottom. She stopped when I reached one hundred and kissed the top of my head. "Feel better?"

"I guess so," I said.

"Good. Counting was the only way you'd sit still when you were little."

"Not true."

"Yes, very true," she said. "If I wanted you to sit, I had to get you to count."

"How come you've never told me that before?" I said.

"Pretty sure I have."

"I would remember."

"Hmph," she said. "Not if you didn't want to, you wouldn't."

"Hmph," I said, and she bonked my shoulder.

"What's that on your finger?" she said, pointing to blue smears on my index finger.

"I don't know. Ink, I guess. Next you'll tell me how I used to draw on myself."

She gave a little laugh. "And how you did. Luckily only once with a permanent marker. And I know I've told you *that* story."

"Yeah, I remember that one."

"See? All right, I need to throw some laundry in. Your dad's out of underwear and we don't want him running around the house naked."

"Mom! That's gross."

She took my hand again, and I tried to curl my fingers in so she wouldn't see the ragged cuticles. She didn't speak, just kissed them one by one, as if she was wishing away the hurt, and I did feel better, a little.

*　*　*

The phone rang while my parents were grocery shopping, and L. THOMAS flashed on the caller ID. Was Becca going to call me every day until I answered? Were her and Rachel and Gia giggling and calling me names, waiting for me to pick up? But I did anyway, waiting until the fifth ring. "Hello?" Everything was quiet on the other end, and I said louder, my stomach tight, "Hello?"

"Heather?" Becca said.

"Yeah?"

"Um, I . . . can I come over? I . . ."

Her words melted into a puddle of sadness. *Yes* rolled on my tongue, but I shoved it between my cheek and teeth, remembering the way she looked at me, the way she didn't defend me. The lava boiled to the surface again, so hot it scorched my throat.

She kept sniffling.

"Please," I said. "You're so faking. Is this supposed to be a prank call, because hello, it's ridiculous."

"I'm not. I swear I'm not."

"So why don't you call Rachel or Gia?" I said. "They're your new best friends now."

I could be cruel, too, but the words hurt me deep inside.

"Please be kind," she said.

And rewind, I mouthed, but hung up before I could say it aloud.

I started jumping every time the phone rang. I wasn't sure if I'd talk to her if she called again, but I wasn't sure I wouldn't either, even if it was a trick or if all she wanted to talk about was the Red Lady.

I missed my best friend so much that after brushing my teeth one night, I put the necklace back on as though I could magic our friendship back together via the heart.

Propped up with my pillows, I opened *The Dark Half*, the last book from the used bookstore I had to read. On the first page, the words HELP HER were written in the margin. It wasn't the first used book I'd found with writing in it. Most of the time it was jokes or doodles, and once a note said THIS BOOK WAS TERRIBLE. DON'T READ IT. I flipped through the rest of the pages, but there was nothing else.

I tried rubbing the words off, hoping they were pencil, but no such luck. Then I rolled closer to my nightstand lamp. The writing was sort of wobbly, but the loops on the *h*'s were squishy and fat the way I wrote mine, and the rest of the letters were messy. My teachers always said my penmanship was terrible. Yet I knew I hadn't written this. HELP HER. I traced my thumb over the words again and shivered, even though I wasn't cold at all.

CHAPTER THIRTEEN

NOW

When Ryan gets home that night, I'm in the bathtub, the water hot enough to turn my skin scarlet. Thanks to a third glass of wine, I'm feeling fuzzy around the edges. Sinking deeper in the water, I mull over a movie for Ryan, desperate for routine and normalcy. Yet my mind returns to what Mikayla said, to Lauren arguing with someone. The other woman who was looking for her? Is she involved, too? Or is she trying to make Lauren stop?

I promise I won't tell.

I drain my glass and the water and wrap myself in a robe. I can't think about this any more tonight. My head hurts. I'm tired.

Ryan's in the family room, pacing, cell phone to ear. I watch from the doorway.

"Maybe it would work, I don't know. We have to do something. Heather's—"

I jolt, my glass clinking against the doorframe.

Ryan turns and his face shifts into a grin, but it's a little too wide, with too many teeth. "Hey, can I call you back later?" He doesn't say goodbye.

"Everything okay?" I say.

"Uh-huh," he says. "What about you?"

I hold up my glass. "It would be better if I had another."

"I think we need some food, too."

"Sure. I think we have enough leftovers. Or we can order in."

"Okay," he says, but the way he's looking at me feels close to an inspection.

"Before I forget," I say, aiming for the cinematic. "In a world where the impossible becomes fact, an offhand prophecy comes true, and a hunter becomes the prey." The clue might be too vague, but I have faith he'll figure it out. He always does.

"Finally she remembers," he says, eyes lighting up. He stares off in the distance, then nods. "That's a good one. I'll have to think about it a bit." Something else flashes across his face, too fleeting to settle.

While we make dinner, we talk about our days and a video he saw on YouTube, and although he seems fine, there's something I can't put my finger on. Some sort of tension between his words. I tell myself it's the wine, the visit to Lauren's apartment, what I said to Mikayla. And who knows? Maybe I'm right.

After the day I've had, it's no surprise that my sleep is restless and I'm wide awake when the corners of the room begin to lighten. My mouth tastes sour, and there's a small ache behind my forehead, but my thoughts are clear. In my dream, I was in a hole, shoveling the dirt out while someone unseen shoveled it back in.

Ryan rolls onto his stomach. Over his shoulder, I spy his phone on his nightstand. He didn't make any other calls last night, nor did he receive any. His call, his mention of my name, was nothing, I'm sure. But why the quick hang-up?

I try to banish the questions but end up tiptoeing to his side of the bed. The name of his last caller isn't one I'm expecting at all: NICOLE. A hundred questions flood my brain, and though I'm tempted to wake him up and ask, I return the phone and get back in bed.

Why are they talking? What are they talking about? I heard my name, but there's no way either of them is involved in this. They never knew Becca. Never knew a thing about her.

Are they having an affair? That's laughable. But I get back out of bed and check his phone again. No texts between them, but there were two other phone calls. Also a few calls from local numbers I don't recognize. Ryan sighs and I freeze. I wait a few seconds, then replace the phone.

*   *   *

Pretending to be a guest, I call the hotel where Lauren works. On the verge of gushing, I say that Lauren did a wonderful job cleaning my room. The clerk on the phone says she'll pass along the message. Then I ask to speak with Lauren to tell her myself. There's a heavy pause, then she says it's hard to find the housekeeping staff. I say I understand. Smart woman. I could be anyone.

My day is a busy one, and I arrive for my four thirty meeting with Rachel with only five minutes to spare. Once the receptionist shows me to a small conference room, I tap my foot on the floor. Is this a mistake? Will I be convincing? Should I pretend to be pissed off? Should I cry? How do women on the verge of divorce act? The urge to bolt is strong. Wouldn't take much. The door isn't even closed. One quick right, then past the front desk. I wouldn't even have to run. Could say I got an urgent call, will reschedule. No one would be the wiser.

Rachel walks in, banishing any thoughts of escape. Her hair, a little more red now than blonde, is fashioned in a tight bun. Gray pants today. Pale-blue V-neck. The professional, confident walk. Moleskine notebook and Cross pen. A polite expression, then recognition. I rise from my seat, but instead of moving in for a hug, she extends a hand.

Once seated, she says, "I thought the name looked familiar, but I wasn't sure. You kept your maiden name."

It isn't a question, but I say yes anyway.

"It's been a long time," she says.

"Very long. How have you been?"

"I'm well, thank you, and you?" she says.

"Good. Well, mostly."

"How did you find me?"

The phrasing throws me off, but there's no menace in the words or on her face. "When I was looking for an attorney, I saw your name and . . ." I shrug. "I thought I might be more comfortable talking to someone I know. Or knew."

She tips her head and glances at her watch. "Let's get started, shall we?"

We go over details small and large—mortgage, bank balances, property, cars—and by the time we're finished, I'm mentally exhausted. The notebook is filled with pages of figures and notes, her handwriting heavily slanted to the right, the letters getting messier as the appointment went on. Not a match to the envelopes.

She caps her pen. "This all seems quite straightforward. As I mentioned, if you can agree on property division, it will make it much easier. Once you've collected all the documents I mentioned earlier—and we'll email you the list if you like—we can start on the paperwork. I don't see anything that will cause any difficulties." She splays her fingers. "Of course, it's hard to predict how a spouse will react, so you might want to prepare yourself for the possibility that things won't go as planned."

"Thank you. I will. So other than helping people through their divorces, what have you been up to?"

She gives a smile that isn't one at all. More like a cringe. "I'm married, one child."

There's an awkward silence where typically she'd ask the same of me.

"Do your parents still live in the old neighborhood?" I say.

"No, they split and sold the house right before I left for college."

"I'm sorry to hear that. What about your brother and sister? Are they still local?"

"Yes," she says, the word terse.

"You'll never guess who I ran into recently. Gia, of all people. She's living in Annapolis now. Small world, right?"

For the first time there's a softening to her features.

"We ran into each other at the bookstore, of all places," I say. "We got to talking about the old days. Remember the house and the club? All the stories we told?"

Her face stills. She doesn't blink. The temperature in the room changes. Then she says, peeking at her watch, "Only vaguely. It was a long time ago." She rises from her seat.

I get the point and stand as well. "It was good to see you again."

"You, too." She clasps my hand for barely a second, doesn't even look at me as she speaks, and walks me to the front with quick steps.

I tell her I'll be in touch, and she says okay, already moving away. She most definitely didn't want to talk about our past. But does that really mean anything? Maybe she wants to keep the relationship strictly professional and doesn't want to be overly friendly. The way she acted doesn't have to mean anything. It doesn't not have to, either.

*   *   *

I don't forget to pick up Starbucks on my way to Silverstone, and when Nicole sees the cups, her eyes moon and she finger-claps. Doesn't look like an act, either. I don't wait for an invite to sit. Her sage-green blouse highlights her eyes, the color a near match for the pinstripes in my button-down.

After a few sips of coffee, she says, "Did you have a good week? I texted you a couple times, but . . ."

"Sorry, it was busy."

There's a strangeness in the room between us. Not quite tension, but an awkwardness I can't remember ever feeling with her. Did I even see her texts this week? Did I truly not respond? It seems strange that I wouldn't, but I honestly can't remember.

"Doing anything fun tonight?" I say.

"I don't know yet. You?"

"No plans as of yet. If we go out to dinner or anything, I'll let you know?"

"I'd like that."

I get up to leave, but halt with one hand on the doorframe. "Hey, have you talked to Ryan lately?"

"No," she says. Her brow doesn't crease, eyes don't veer off to the side. "Why?"

"Oh, I thought you two were on the phone the other night."

"Wasn't me," she says. "Must be the other Nicole."

"My mistake, then. Time for me to get to work before the boss notices I'm slacking."

"Thank you for the coffee."

"Of course," I say on my way out. She's almost as good a liar as I am. But not quite.

In my office with the door closed, I scroll through my phone. Two texts from Nicole I don't recall reading, although they both say READ. One missed call as well. Huh. Maybe I didn't have my phone close when she rang. Maybe that's why she called Ryan? But why lie? You only lie when you have something to hide.

My phone chimes with a new text. From Gia: BEFORE I FORGET, WE'RE HAVING A PARTY NEXT SATURDAY AROUND 7-ISH. NOTHING FANCY. A FEW FRIENDS AND NEIGHBORS. PLEASE SAY YOU'LL COME!

Say no, I tell myself, but I write back, with little hesitation, SURE. CAN I BRING ANYTHING?

A BOTTLE OF WINE? AND YOUR HUSBAND, TOO! WE'D LOVE TO MEET HIM!

WILL DO, I text back. Whether or not I really do remains to be seen.

My sessions at Silverstone run smoothly—no problems with Samantha or anyone else—and the same goes for my private patients. Once Ellie's left for the day, I lock my office door, mute my phone, and bury myself in paperwork. Ryan's having dinner with his brother, and I plan on eating leftovers or grabbing something on the way home.

I'm not sure how long I'm sitting there before I hear the hum. It's low. Rhythmic. I stand in the middle of my office, head cocked to one side. The building is old, and we've had issues with odd sounds carrying from floor to floor through the ventilation system. But this sound isn't mechanical. It rises and falls. It whispers.

My arms go all-over goose bumps. Now that I hear it, I can't *unhear* it. It's a voice, soft and barely audible, but a voice nonetheless. And I can't tell where it's coming from. It's everywhere and nowhere all at once.

Blood rushes in my ears. One hand skitters to my chest. I peer into the hallway. No one's there, but still the whispers continue.

I fumble through the papers on my desk for my phone and keys, finding neither. And all I hear is the voice. It isn't right, it shouldn't be, but it's growing louder. I dig in my bag; same result. Press fingertips to my temples. No one's in the office save me. Ellie said she'd lock up when she left. I pat my pockets. Empty.

The voice gets louder still. And it's not human.

Does the air smell of smoke and candle wax? I spin in a circle. There's nowhere for anyone to hide in my office. I shake my head, a shriek clamped tight behind my clenched jaw. But it doesn't matter, because there's someone here with me and I have to get out, get away. I shove a small pile of papers, and as they cascade to the floor, my keys catch the overhead light. Another paper dislodges, revealing my phone. Both go in my pockets while I unplug my laptop, eyes on the door.

Did I relock it? I can't remember. When I pass beneath the air vent, the voice rises in pitch. I stagger to a halt, neck craning.

Heather.

I run, my fingers fumbling as I try to lock the door. And from behind me, someone says, "Heather?"

I spin with a shriek. And there, peering out from her own office, Christina.

"Are you okay?" she says.

"I heard something," I say, verging on hysterical.

"Oh, crap. Was it me? I had Netflix on while I was working," she says, flicking her fingers open beside her head. "I didn't realize you were still here."

Netflix? What I heard wasn't a movie. It wasn't.

"I heard it in my office," I say, aware I sound utterly unlike myself.

"I did have it fairly loud. I'm sorry."

She's wearing a touch of embarrassment, a pinch of amusement. I curl my fingers until my nails dig into my skin.

"It's fine," I say. "I feel incredibly foolish. I thought . . . well, I don't know what I thought, but I was afraid since I was alone . . ." It's my turn to lift a hand.

Although my pulse is no longer racing, when I exit the building I run for my car and lock the doors as soon as I'm inside. I sag back against the seat. Squeeze my lids closed. The voice wasn't from Christina's movie. It wasn't from anywhere.

Red Lady, Red Lady.

No. She isn't real. She wasn't ever real.

*   *   *

"Today, Dr. Cole," Ryan says, placing a cup of coffee on my nightstand, "You are mine. All day."

"But I . . ."

"What?"

I don't want to go anywhere, except perhaps to the hotel where Lauren works, but I can't say that aloud.

"Babe?" he says.

"No buts," I say with as much enthusiasm as I can. "It sounds wonderful."

"Good, because I wasn't taking no for an answer. So drink your coffee, get a shower, and get dressed. It's going to be nice today; not too cold, not too hot."

My smile fades from view as soon as he does. No way I'm getting out of this. How can I pretend everything's okay? How can I pretend *I'm* okay? But I empty my mug. Take a shower. Get dressed.

He drives my Jeep to Grump's Cafe for breakfast, a quirky place with silly signs on the walls and paint streaks on the floor. Not too crowded, either, which is surprising for a Saturday. Afterward, he gets on 50 West, and it takes a while before I figure out where we're going.

The Smithsonian National Air and Space Museum's someplace we've talked about visiting for ages, and we spend hours looking at the old airplanes, the space shuttle *Discovery*. We eat burgers and fries at the

McDonald's on site. Buy refrigerator magnets and freeze-dried ice cream from the gift shop. I'm even able to relax a little. I'm safe here with Ryan, with the crowds of people all around. Surely I'm allowed that, aren't I?

On the way home, we get caught in traffic. I kick off my shoes, put my seat back. "Before I forget, we were invited to a party next Saturday. You don't know her, but Gia and I grew up together. I ran into her at the bookstore, and she and her husband recently moved to Annapolis."

"Sounds good."

"So," I say. "What prompted today?"

"I do notice things, you know. You're having bad dreams, getting up in the middle of the night, you're distracted all the time, and"—he reaches across the center console for my hand—"this."

I curl my fingers, attempting to hide my ragged cuticles.

"Even without the rest, I'd know something was wrong. You only do this when you're upset or stressed."

His words are gentle, but I can't help the heat coiling in my gut. He's just being a good husband, but I pull away nonetheless.

"I have a patient who reminds me of a girl I knew when I was a kid. It's stirring up old memories, that's all."

"And?"

And nothing, I think, even shaking my head a little, but my mouth has other plans, with too many words to hold in. "I knew her when we were little. Her mom was an alcoholic, and she was abusive." The weight of what I said—that I said anything at all—sits like a stone upon my soul. I trace a circle on the armrest. Cross my legs. Uncross them and pull one foot up on the seat. "Anyway, it's not . . . ."

"So what happened?" His fingertips piano the steering wheel.

"What do you mean?" I say, the weight now a boulder.

"With her mother?"

"It's not important," I say, dropping my foot, pulling up the other.

"Well, did she get help? Your friend's mom or—"

"Can we talk about something else, please?" I say, my words clipped at the ends.

There's a pause, and then he says, "Okay, sure."

"Thank you," I say, staring straight ahead. The car feels too small. Part of me wants to open my door and disappear into the ocean of brake lights, swim into all that red. Drown in it. The other part wants to scream until my voice is gone. Until I'm gone.

I fist my hands, remembering the gritty feel of dirt beneath my nails.

Blood on my hands. Dirt beneath my nails.

"Maybe you should recommend another doctor."

"What?" I say.

"For your patient. Maybe she should see another doc." He shoves his shirt-sleeves up, revealing a scratch on his right forearm, the scab fresh.

"It's fine."

"But if it's bringing up all these old memories, which are obviously unpleasant, it isn't fine. Would it be the end of the world if you sent her to someone else? What about Christine, the other doctor in your office? She sees kids too, right?"

"It's Chris*tina*, and no, that's not necessary. I'm an adult; I can handle a few old memories."

There's a long silence, then he says, "Can you?"

"Who's the doctor here?" I say, and my words are razors. "Pretty sure I know what I can and can't handle."

His fingers flex on the steering wheel. "Right. Okay. But since you brought it up, I thought you wanted to talk about it, maybe try and get some things off your chest."

"Well, you thought wrong. I don't want to talk about it."

And I don't. Not to him. Not to anyone.

"Are you sure? Because I'm here, and if I can help you in any—"

"Stop," I say. "Just stop and leave it. I said I don't want to talk about it."

"Okay, I'm sorry."

But he steals a glance toward me, and I sense he's going to try again. Just like him to think a fucking battering ram is the best way to tackle any problem.

"What happened to your arm? The scratch?" I ask.

He looks down. "Oh, I probably banged into the corner of some drywall or something."

"Has she paid you anything yet?"

"No, not yet," he says. "Look, this won't be like the Kanes. Mrs. Harding's not hurting for money."

I run my thumbs down an imaginary line in the center of my thighs. "How do you know? The Kanes didn't seem to be either. Isn't that what you said?"

"Yes, but—"

"But what?"

"Nothing," he says. "No matter what I say, it won't matter."

Anger boils inside me, anger at myself for turning the conversation this way, for picking an argument, for the outstanding check, for being stuck in this fucking car with the fucking traffic. An apology lingers on my tongue, but it's bitter and sharp and I keep it to myself.

* * *

Ringing yanks me from sleep, and I fumble for my phone. It's not mine, though, but Ryan's. A local number, no name. When it stops, there's a long pause, then a chirp. I flop back on my pillow, wide awake now. Ryan's going to help his youngest brother install some shelving, but I was planning to sleep in.

I did end up apologizing before we got home yesterday, and he accepted, but both were contrived. The sort of things you say because you should. All I had to do was bridge the gap, one small touch on his shoulder or the center of his back in bed, but I rolled onto my side, staring at the wall until long after he was asleep.

Now, the shower in the master bath shuts off, and a minute later Ryan steps out amid a wave of eucalyptus-scented heat, a towel draping his waist.

"You're awake," he says with a mix of surprise and hesitation.

"Your phone woke me up. Somebody called you."

"I'm sorry." When he looks at the display, he blinks a little too quickly and says, "Don't recognize the number. Probably a scammer."

A legit assumption. I get regular calls from the "IRS" claiming there's a tax bill and an arrest warrant. "They left a message," I say around a yawn, rearranging the sheets to cover my shoulder.

I listen to him finish getting ready and walk down the steps, trying to be quiet. When the garage door rumbles down and his engine recedes, I throw off the sheets, pushing sleep-twisted hair from my face.

He recognized the number on his phone. I saw it. I knuckle a cheekbone. I know my heightened suspicion is due to my own perfidy. *Transference* in psych speak. Finding fault with him to avoid my own.

Not bothering with a shower, I pull on leggings and an old, stretched-out sweater. Make coffee. Flop on the sofa in the family room, ankles crossed, foot tapping, flipping through television channels but finding nothing to capture my attention. I toss the remote aside and Lady Macbeth my hands. I need to do something other than sit and brood. Or I might have another panic attack, the way I did in the field.

No. That was not a panic attack. I do not have panic attacks. It was a momentary spot of alarm. Anyone in my situation would feel the same way.

I stop moving my hands. The skin is streaked with small red smears from a rubbed-off scab. I close my eyes, but even after several rounds of deep breathing, I feel as though an electric current is thrumming beneath my skin. "To hell with this," I say.

I risk calling the hotel again. One more time can't hurt, can it? This time it's a man who answers, and he sounds bored. I use the same tactic as before, but instead of shutting me down, he puts me on hold. After a few minutes he returns with the helpful message that Lauren isn't working today or tomorrow but she'll be there on Tuesday. Did he not even consider the potential danger in giving out that kind of information?

I can't risk going to her apartment again. Not on a Sunday. Too many people around. Too many chances of being spotted. But I have to do something. I finally remember that we have daffodil bulbs inside the shed. I think it's the right time of year to plant them, but I don't really care whether they take root or not. I find them next to a bucket of gardening tools. On my knees, skin protected inside soft gloves, I start on the flower bed to the right of the flagstone patio. I weaponize the tools, stabbing and spearing the dirt, tossing it aside in messy piles, creating a series of holes resembling small graves.

I'm the dirt and Lauren—or whoever—is the metal, piercing and pricking and tearing me apart. What will be left when they're done? And who? I press the base of my palms to my brows. Banish the thought.

The bulbs go in and I smooth the dirt over top, repeating the entire process on the bed running along the left side of the patio. In the end, it looks like a toddler was playing here. Dirt's on the stone edging the beds, on the patio, in the grass. I try brushing it with the gloves, but it doesn't help much.

Back to the shed for the outside broom, but I trip over the bottom lip as I step up. "Shit!" I say, dropping the bucket and flailing for purchase. The gardening tools tumble out with heavy metal clinks, but I keep myself from falling. And in the far corner I spy a metal detector partially hidden behind the weed trimmer and a tarp. But we don't have a metal detector. We've never had one.

I strip off my gloves and rub my temple with a knuckle. Is it possible it's been here all along and I just haven't seen it? But I've been in this shed dozens of times. It was never here before. Why would we even have one?

I think of the multiple holes in the field. If you were looking for a knife, a metal detector would find it. Or at least indicate where a person should dig. No, that's utterly foolish. Even if someone used a metal detector there, it wouldn't be Ryan. I'm creating a link where none exists. *Transference*, I remind myself, then dart inside for my phone. I know it's absurd, but there's no harm in asking him, no matter how illogical it seems. It'll make me feel better. But I pause before dialing. I can wait a few hours, can't I? He'll be home soon enough.

But I want to know now.

He answers on the third ring, his tone guarded. "Everything okay?"

"Yes, but I was in the shed and found a metal detector. When did we get one?"

"Huh?" he says. "You called me to ask—"

"Just tell me," I say. "Please."

"O-kay," he says. "It's my dad's. Karen borrowed it for the kids. She gave it to me the other night to give back, but I needed the room in my truck, so I put it in the shed for the time being."

"The kids needed it." My voice is flat. Unemotional.

"Yes," he says.

"And you didn't use it?"

"Why would I use a metal detector?" There's a muffled thud, then he says, "Hold on, don't . . . hold it—Heather, I gotta go before Sean hurts himself."

"Okay, goodbye," I say, but I'm speaking to empty air.

I turn the phone over and over. Now I have my answer. Nothing nefarious or sneaky. A perfect logical explanation. So why do I still feel uneasy?

Maybe because there was a dead squirrel in my mailbox? Because someone else was digging in the field? Because I broke into my colleague and friend's office? Because someone knows what happened in that basement? Knows what I did? Plenty of options there.

"Enough," I say.

But my hands won't stop moving. My thoughts won't stop connecting dots they have no business connecting. Dots that don't connect at all. And then I put the phone down and take to the stairs.

I start with the small drawer in Ryan's nightstand. Nothing but old receipts and a few forgotten gift cards. In his dresser, drawer by drawer, I sweep beneath each folded pile of clothing, patting them down, seeking anything out of place. Underwear, socks, T-shirts. I leave nothing untouched. On his side of the walk-in closet, I do the same, examining jacket pockets and shoes. I return to his dresser and undo his socks, checking each one individually before wrapping them back into each other.

I go through the closet in the guest bedroom and each drawer of the dresser there, checking through the extra blankets and sheets. In Ryan's office, I rifle through the stack of papers on the desk. Store receipts, his business credit card statement, the balance higher than I would've thought, and the most recent bank statement for his account, the balance considerably lower.

I turn on his laptop. Go through his folders, his browser history, skim his email. Nothing, there's nothing. I catch sight of my reflection in the screen. My teeth are bared, my hair sticking up in every direction, my skin suffused with a rosy glow. Shame pushes even more warmth through me, and I sit in his chair. Let my head droop. Will myself calm. I should be happy I've found nothing. So why aren't I?

A laugh pierces the air, so sharp and startling I lurch forward. It takes a moment to register that the sound is coming from me. It sounds nothing like me, nothing like humor or human. It's guttural, bestial, and I can't make it stop. I cover my mouth, grinding my lips against my teeth. Still, it spills out. And out and out.

I jerk to my feet, sending his chair spinning, and shamble to our bedroom. Collapse on the bed and scream into my pillow. I give it all my frustration, my worry, my fear. I give it everything I don't have a name for. Tears rush out just as fast, and I don't even try to hold them back.

When they stop falling, I strip the pillowcase, sodden with snot and sorrow, and sit on the edge of the bed, head in my hands. What the hell is happening to me? Searching through Ryan's things? Sneaking into Alexa's office?

Who the hell am I becoming?

I sense that the walls are moving closer when I'm not looking. The ceiling dropping, the floor rising. Eventually I'll be trapped in the very center of a small cube, with nowhere to go and no way out.

With robotic limbs, I return to Ryan's office and put his chair back in its proper spot. I double-check, making sure it all appears as it did before. I can't do this again. I can't fall apart. I finish cleaning up out back. Take a shower. Afterward I feel a little stronger. A little more in control. I settle in with a book in the family room. Wait for Ryan. Keep calm. Everything's fine.

He doesn't mention my phone call when he gets home. Neither do I. We order Chinese takeout and watch *Godzilla: King of the Monsters*. It feels normal and right and safe. I want to bottle this moment and trap it forever.

My phone chimes with an email's arrival, and I grab it from the coffee table. And there, in my inbox: LAUREN THOMAS. The sender, not a subject line. The latter is blank.

I click it open.

IT'S TIME WE MET. I WANT TO TALK ABOUT BECCA.

That's all there is, but I hiss in a breath. Did Mikayla mention someone was there? Did Lauren put two and two together? Is that why she's sent this now?

"Everything okay? Heather?"

"Oh, yes," I say. "It's from a patient's mother."

"Bad news?"

"No, not exactly. It'll be fine. It'll all be fine."

Another question sits on Ryan's lips, but he doesn't ask, simply turns his attention back to the characters on the screen. I can't pull mine away from the characters on mine.

It's time we met. I want to talk about Becca.

Much later, in the small hours of the night with Ryan softly snoring beside me, I pick up my phone, type YES, LET'S MEET, and hit send.

CHAPTER FOURTEEN

THEN

"I had an odd phone call from Rachel's mom," my mom said.

We were sitting at the dining room table, her face serious, the way it had looked two years ago when she told me Pops, my dad's dad, had died.

"O-kay," I said, picking at a cuticle, a lump growing in my throat. Mom cleared her throat, and I tucked both hands beneath my thighs.

"She overheard Rachel, Gia, and Becca talking about something and called to find out if I knew about it. I didn't, so I thought I'd talk to you."

"Why doesn't she just ask Rachel?"

"She did. Would you like to tell me about the Red Lady?"

I couldn't read her expression. My fingers spidered free from my legs, curled around the sides of the seat, and held tight, as though the chair might levitate or drop through the floor.

"She's from a story Becca told."

"A story?"

"Yeah, nothing major," I said, but my cheeks went hot. Had Rachel's mom made her tell about our club, too? She couldn't do that, could she? It wasn't anyone's business except ours.

"It must've been some story. Rachel's been having nightmares and her mom caught her sleepwalking, which she hasn't done since she was little."

I knew about the sleepwalking. The second time everyone stayed over at my house, I'd overheard my mom telling Rachel's she'd found Rachel in the kitchen, holding a loaf of bread. After everyone went home, she'd told me about it.

"It was pretty scary," I said.

My mom's face stayed the same way. Not angry, not even worried, sort of . . . nothing.

"Okay, it was really scary and kind of gross, but she's only a story."

I tongued the back of my teeth and held the seat even tighter. My mom circled her hands on the table, like she was wiping away leftover thoughts.

"And there was some kind of ritual? You cut yourselves?"

If they knew about the ritual, then they knew about the house. I'd be grounded forever. But Rachel wouldn't give that piece up. She wouldn't. Being grounded was one thing; being arrested was worse.

"Not like that, Mom," I said, but my words were too sharp, too insistent. "We used a pin, that's all, and stuck our fingers. We were playing a game, like Bloody Mary." I had deodorant on, but I could smell onions and knew the stink was coming from me.

Now my mom looked upset, but I couldn't tell if it was angry-upset or sad-upset. It was sort of both.

"And you've been talking about serial killers, too?"

"Ugh, Mom, it's not a big deal."

"Be that as it may, it all obviously affected Rachel, and her mother is upset. Upset enough that Rachel isn't allowed to hang out with Becca anymore. And she talked to Gia's mom, who came to the same decision."

"But that's not fair."

"Maybe not," she said, raising her eyebrows and doing the weird sweeping thing across the table again. "But it was Becca who told the story, right?"

"But we all wanted to hear it. Even Rachel. Becca didn't force us to listen."

"Maybe so, but Rachel is her daughter, and she gets to make decisions she's comfortable with. That's part of being a parent."

"She's not a little kid." I crossed my arms, chin down. "So I guess you're happy we're not hanging out anymore?"

"Sweetheart," she said. "I never said that. I also know the sort of books you've been reading forever. Scary and gross things don't seem to bother you much. But Rachel isn't you, and I'm not Rachel's mom."

I was about to ask if I could go when she said, "So is this story part of the reason you and Becca aren't talking?"

"No," I said, the lie bitter on my tongue. "It's not. It's something else you wouldn't understand."

"You could try me. I was twelve once."

I shook my head.

"Okay," she said. "Do you have anything else you want to say?"

And there, the trap. I kept calm on the outside, but the onion smell grew stronger. When Becca and I were ten, we'd found a can of spray paint in her basement. On a brick wall bordering the entrance of the alley at the top of her street, we wrote MATT WILLIAMS IS A JERK and tossed the can in a neighbor's trash. Later, my mom called me in and asked what we'd been doing. I said playing. She made me tell her where and what we were doing and then said it: "Do you have anything else you want to say?" And of course I did. I broke down and told her everything, even though she already knew. If we'd written something else, we might've been okay, but the day before we'd been in Gia's backyard and her brother had turned on the hose, spraying the four of us.

But I wasn't ten anymore, and we hadn't damaged the house. There wasn't any proof we'd even been there, so I sat up straight and said, "Nope."

Her mouth twisted a little to one side, but she said, "Okay."

I went back to my room, so tired I wanted to sleep for a year but happy the house was still our secret. I was happy, too, that I wasn't the only one left alone. It served Becca right. Everything was all her fault.

*   *   *

I'd finished *The Dark Half* and was rereading *The Shining* propped up in bed with pillows behind me. I was at the part where they first got to the hotel and Danny and Mr. Hallorann were talking in their minds. I was thinking it would be fun to do when my eyelids got heavy. I should've turned off my light, but it was only a little after nine, so I kept reading.

I woke up, wincing in the bright, my hand sore. Loosened my fingers from the pen in my grip, confused. The book was open on my lap, the spine broken so it would remain flat. My mouth went dry as I thumbed the pages. Scrawled in the margins, over and over again, the words HELP HER, all messy, but definitely my handwriting. And the side of my hand was smeared with blue ink.

With the book at arm's length, I slipped from bed, thinking of Rachel's sleepwalking. This was so much worse. I would never write in any book, let alone my favorite. Never. I took *The Dark Half* from my bookcase and opened it to the writing inside. Compared it to the writing in *The Shining*. Identical. But I hadn't done it. I swore I hadn't.

I stuffed the books under the sweaters in my dresser. It seemed safer to keep them hidden.

My handwriting. Mine.

But it wasn't me. It was her. She'd made me do it.

No. Uh-uh. She was a story. She couldn't make me do anything.

She. Wasn't. Real.

I licked the ink on my skin. Wiped it on my pajamas, but only a little came off. Heat flared in my chest, spreading out until my entire body felt afire and the hairs on the nape of my neck rose, as though a thousand eyes were watching me. I squeezed mine shut. Counted to ten. The sensation slowly lessened.

There was a soft knock on my door, and I bumped into the edge of my desk.

"Are you okay?"

"Fine, Mom. I just hit my desk."

"It's after eleven, so get some sleep, okay? I love you."

"Love you too."

The shadows of her feet remained in the gap between door and floor. I just wanted her to go away and leave me alone. A few minutes later, she did.

I pushed a T-shirt under my door to block out the light, careful not to shove it out the other side. I opened my closet and pawed through my clothes, all the way to the wall. On my knees, I looked under my bed; the only things there were shoes, a plastic container with old stuffed animals, and dust. Sitting with my back against my dresser, I watched the shadowy space beneath my bed. I checked the corners. I even craned my neck at the ceiling. I knew no one would crawl out from under my bed or drop from the ceiling. It was just the creeps.

When my parents had to be asleep, I took out *The Shining* and tore the pages, first one by one, then two at a time, then more, gaining speed as I went. My mouth was thick with unshed tears, my nose running. I wiped the snot on the shoulder of my pajama top and kept ripping pages until every single one was out and in a pile.

I packed them in the plastic container, all around the stuffies. Crammed it back where it was and climbed in bed, the light on. But I was afraid if I closed my eyes, someone else would be there. I was afraid *she'd* be there, with her handless arms and her horrible black eyes and her long hair trailing through the blood.

This was all Becca's fault. For telling the story, for making us do the ritual, for pretending she was real and making me think she was. I wasn't going to help her. No matter what.

* * *

Because of the humidity, sitting outside felt like breathing underwater, even early in the morning, but I didn't want to stay inside. I walked the neighborhood, kicking pebbles out of my way, ending up at the edge of the field. When I got to the top of the little hill, Becca was on the other side. Once she was gone, I ran after, crouching next to the open spot in the hedges.

She darted across the lawn, bent over like an old lady. She was carrying her backpack by one strap, practically dragging it on the ground, and when she reached the front door, she shot a glance over her shoulders. I tensed, but she didn't see me. Once she slipped inside, I crept from my hiding place and knelt near the basement window with the curtain gap. I couldn't see Becca, but I heard her moving. A heavy thump sounded, close to the window.

I felt light-headed and everything went gray, like I was caught inside a raincloud with no way out. I didn't panic. I didn't do anything. I couldn't. When the fuzziness vanished, there was a circle of mist on the glass with HELP HER scrawled across it, already beginning to fade. The fog was on the outside, and I recognized the handwriting.

I scrambled to my feet, but my ankles tangled and I landed on my butt, a branch scratching my upper arm. With a yelp I couldn't bite back in time, I scrabbled away from the window as the mist disappeared. On rubbery legs I took off.

Once I turned onto my street, I slowed down, trying to act normal, but my chest hurt. Sweat poured down my back, ran down my forehead and into my eyes. My fingers were shaking and I held them out as though they were strange, disconnected things with minds of their own. On my index finger, a smear of grime. I scrubbed it on my shorts. Scrubbed it again and again, long after the dirt was wiped away.

I hadn't written on the window. I knew I hadn't. I kicked a stone from the sidewalk. And what was I supposed to do anyway? Becca didn't want to be my friend. She didn't want my help.

But what if she did? What if she hadn't been faking at all when she called? I bit the side of my thumbnail. It wasn't my fault. What was I supposed to think? She shouldn't have shut me out. She shouldn't have acted the way she did. Most of all, she should never have told us about the Red Lady in the first place. And if the Red Lady was real, if she was so powerful, then she could help Becca. They didn't need me.

When I got home, Mom was going to the grocery store for milk, so I went with her. In the magazine aisle they had a shelf of paperbacks, and I thumbed free a copy of *The Shining*.

Mom glanced at the cover when I asked if I could get it. "I thought you had that one?"

"I did. I dropped it at the playground and a bunch of pages ripped."

"Toss it in the cart. And sweetheart, your finger's bleeding again."

A narrow strip of my cuticle from the side of my nail was peeled all the way back, past the top of the nail. When I licked away the pearls of blood, she made a small sound and rummaged in her purse.

"Here," she said, offering an adhesive bandage. "You know, staying mad isn't always the best thing to do."

I pushed the cart down the aisle. "I thought you just needed milk."

"Yes, but while I'm here I thought I'd pick up a few more things."

One of the wheels squeaked as I turned the corner into the next aisle. My mom grabbed a few cans of soup, then fixed me with a pensive look. "You know, you could call her first."

"Mom, stop," I said, glancing around to make sure no one else was listening. "I don't want to talk about it."

She glanced at my finger long and hard enough that I tucked my arms behind my back. Home, with the groceries put away and Mom upstairs, I picked up the phone. But after I dialed the fifth number, I hung up. I wasn't the one who'd decided we weren't friends. She was. She could call me if she wanted to talk.

*   *   *

I stood in semidarkness, my mouth a desert, my fingers ice. Shaking, I turned around in every direction. I was alone in the kitchen. But I didn't remember waking up. Didn't remember getting out of bed and coming downstairs. Was I sleepwalking? But I didn't do that. I never did that. A sound, half sob, half giggle, slipped out, and I covered my mouth. My lips went grainy and rough, and I scrubbed them on the sleeve of my pajamas as I turned on the overhead light, blinking to clear the bright. My skin was dusted with white, and on the table the sugar bowl was overturned, the words HELP HER traced within the sweetness. A sharp pain in my side drove the air from my lungs and my knees buckled. I sank, a deflated balloon, to the floor.

"Please," I said. "Stop."

The pain flared anew as if in answer. I was afraid to stand, afraid my legs wouldn't support my weight, but I was more afraid my parents would come down and find me, so I gripped the edge of the table to pull myself up. I scraped my index finger through the words, cutting them in half.

"Why don't you help her?"

I touched my side in anticipation, but there was no pain. Crying, I held the bowl next to the table, swept the sugar back, and wiped the table with a dishrag. Too afraid my parents would hear if I turned on the water, I used the rag to clean myself, too.

Finally I turned off the light and said to the darkness, "Fine, I'll talk to her."

CHAPTER FIFTEEN

NOW

When Nicole calls midmorning, I push my chair away from my desk, give my computer my back. We chat about nothing in particular, then she says, "So, is everything okay at work?"

"Why wouldn't it be?"

There's a funny little pause. "You've been . . . different the past few weeks."

"Oh?" There's a challenge in the word that I don't mean. Or maybe I do.

"It's like there was some strange seismic shift. One day you were fine, the next not. All I can think is something must have happened, and we're—I'm—worried about you."

"We're?" Definitely more than a challenge now.

"Ryan called me because he was worried and thought I might know what was going on."

"So you have been talking to Ryan," I say. "You lied to me." Each word is blunt.

"Yes, but only because we were trying to figure out what's wrong. We love you, Heather. What happened? You haven't been answering my calls or responding to my texts. Does it have to do with the old friend? The one with the abusive mother?"

It takes effort to swallow. Ryan told her? I barely even mentioned it and he fucking told Nicole?

"Stop prying. Please." I do my best to make the last word sound at least a pinch sincere.

"I'm not prying. I care. "

"I'm fine."

"You're not fine. It's obvious you're not. Come on, this is me, your best friend. You can talk to me about anything."

I'm half tempted to say, *My last best friend? I killed her.* Would Nicole still care about me then? Would anyone?

"I said I'm fine. I need to get ready for my patient." I spin to my monitor and hit refresh. Nicole's in the process of saying goodbye as I disconnect the call.

What a wonderful conversation to have on a Monday morning. I jump from my chair, sending it skidding across the plastic floor mat, and grab my mug. Past the reception area is a small kitchenette, and I jam a pod in the Keurig, striking the tile with my heel while the coffee brews.

As I skirt Ellie's desk on my way back, my sleeve catches on one of the leaves of the plant in the corner. I try to grab it, fingers splayed, while keeping my full mug balanced. No luck. Coffee splashes and the plant tips over the edge, dirt spraying as the pot thumps on the carpet.

"Ah, shit," I say.

Ellie jumps from her seat. "It's okay."

I set my mug on the corner of her desk, and kneeling side by side, we scoop up the soil.

"I'm sorry," I say.

"No big deal. If you want to kill it, you'll have to try harder next time. I did it myself last week. The knocking over, not the killing."

She's smiling, but her words send the hairs on the back of my neck prickling. I think of the dirt I found in my office. And the day I found Ellie at my cabinet. The way she behaved, as if caught in the act. But of what?

She wipes off the pot and returns it to her desk, moving things around to place it a little farther in, away from errant sleeves.

"See? Good as new," she says.

Is it my imagination or is her expression slightly off-kilter? How much do I really know about her? She was vetted by the temp agency, but they were concerned with professional references, experience, and the like. She's too young to have known Becca, but is it possible she knows Lauren? But from where?

"Dr. Cole?"

"Oh, sorry," I say.

My nails are crusted with dirt, gritty and dark; there's more stuck to my skin, courtesy of the spilled coffee. Under the fluorescent lights in the bathroom, I turn on the hot water, soap up, and begin to rinse, working my hands against each other. Soap bubbles glisten on the tiny pool of water near the drain; dirt speckles the stainless steel.

Blood on my hands. Dirt beneath my nails.

Dirt in her mouth. I put dirt in her mouth.

I remember running home, washing away the dirt and blood, all of it swirling down the drain. I remember thinking my skin would never be clean and everyone would see, everyone would know, so I used the pot scrubber on my nails, tearing already ragged cuticles, washing away my own blood, knowing there would be no absolution, no matter how much I bled. I remember the slick of the dish soap as I upended the bottle over my palm again and again. Scrubbing until my skin hurt.

As it does now.

With a half-uttered curse, I yank my arms back. The soap is long gone, my skin bright red. Blood pearls from a torn cuticle. But at least the dirt is gone.

My eyes are haunted still; I can only imagine how they appeared then. You can't hide guilt with makeup. How did no one suspect, especially my parents? How did I hold it in? I rotate my shoulders and arch my neck until my muscles release some of the tension. In the mirror, dark shadows notwithstanding, I appear fine. I *am* fine.

Back in my office with the door closed, I see a new message in my inbox. From Lauren. TOMORROW NIGHT. 9 O'CLOCK. Along with an address, not hers. All the warning bells are ringing, but Google reveals a building in a small business park not far from her apartment. A business park means good lighting. Open spaces. Security guards.

I'LL BE THERE.

I spend the rest of the day in a mental fog, rehearsing what I might say, deciding yes, that's it, then having it all flutter away. The fog clears the minute I get home and see Ryan's forgotten to check the mail. Again. My thoughts narrow in on the conversation I had with Nicole. I should take a long bath, maybe have a glass of wine before bringing it up, but my husband and best friend have been chatting about me behind my back. Why should I wait?

He's in the family room, drinking a beer and channel surfing. I drop the mail on the coffee table, enjoying the wince it brings. I remain on the other side, arms crossed.

"I talked to Nicole this morning."

"Uh-huh. Hi to you, too."

I ignore the barb. "What did you think you were doing, talking to her about me? About my old friend? It wasn't something for you to run around telling everyone."

His face contorts briefly, then arranges itself back again. "First of all, I didn't run around telling everyone, and I didn't know it was some great secret. I just assumed Nicole knew. And second, I talked to her because I thought she might know what was going on with you. You won't talk to me, so what else was I supposed to do?"

"If I'm not talking to you about it, then there's nothing to talk about."

"Or nothing you *want* to talk about."

"The proper response would be to let it go then, not sneak behind my back with my best friend."

"I was not sneaking," he says, rising to his feet and circling the table to cup my upper arms. "I love you and I'm worried. She is, too. It feels like there's more going on, more than just a patient who reminds you of someone you once knew. Could you talk to me? Please?"

Although there's a haze of anger in the air, there's nothing on his features. I could tell him everything. I could tell him what's happening to me. I could tell him the truth.

Fuck. That.

I pull free from his grasp. "There's nothing to talk about."

He says nothing, but it doesn't matter. I'm already walking away.

* * *

The hotel where Lauren works in downtown Baltimore is easy to find, and there's plenty of available parking in the garage below. My heart's already pounding, and despite the fact that it's cold enough for a light coat, sweat glues my shirt to my back. I tie a navy-blue scarf around my head a la Audrey Hepburn before I get out of the car. Not much of a disguise, but it's the best I can do. I'm not planning on getting too close. I just want to see her before we meet tonight.

Once I reach the hotel's lobby, a modern open space, all gray, black, and glass, I press the button for the elevator, peeking around while I wait. A businessman waiting at the front counter. A clerk with an ornate updo. Another with winged eyeliner. A man in cook's whites crosses the lobby, entering the restaurant off to the side. A middle-aged security guard in a crisp uniform, military haircut, arms crossed over a broad chest. I smell coffee and furniture polish, a not-unpleasant combination.

The car arrives with a cheery *bing* that makes me jump, and I ride to the top floor—the twelfth—alone. The hotel is shaped like a large rectangle with a center hallway running the length. Easy to see from one end to the other. There are no housekeeping carts on this floor. Only closed doors and quiet. Old nicotine ghosts cling to the air.

Down to the eleventh—one cart. A too-young-to-be-Lauren housekeeper. Gray uniform shirt with the hotel's logo on the left side, black pants. No old-cigarette smell, only lavender air freshener.

No carts on the tenth floor, but there are two on the ninth, with two housekeepers about my age chatting beside one.

One cart on the eighth floor, the housekeeper out of sight. I pass by and peer into the open door. A woman emerges holding a bottle of cleaning fluid. She's older, thin, short, with salt-and-pepper hair, but she has dark eyes. Wide hips. Not Lauren.

"Do you need something?" she says.

"Oh, no, thank you," I say. I scurry down the hall toward the elevator, feeling her watching the entire time. When I get on the car, I catch sight of myself in the mirrored front panel—my skin is blotchy, my eyeliner has smudged. I force myself to calm down, but I'm running out of time. If I don't find Lauren soon, this was a wasted effort.

I step out of the elevator on the seventh floor, but there are no carts here. I'm back in the car and the doors are halfway shut when an arm halts their movement, an arm belonging to the security guard I passed on the way in. There's a half smile on his lips, but it stops there. His stance is solid, feet wide. His gaze sizes me up from head to toe, not in a sexual manner. I fight the urge to smooth my hair, stand straighter.

"Are you okay?" he says.

I swallow hard and say, "I'm fine. Just late for a meeting and I got turned around somewhere. I've never been here before."

He nods and joins me in the elevator, tipping his head toward the number panel, where the six is illuminated. "The meeting rooms are on the second floor." He even pushes the button for me.

I can smell the mint mouthwash he recently used. Can he smell the bitter adrenaline spiking in my veins? Hear the pounding of my heart? Is his showing up simply a bad coincidence on my part? Or did someone call him to investigate a panicky woman running from floor to floor? But I can handle this. I've done nothing wrong.

"My boss is going to kill me," I say, glancing down at my feet as I Marilyn Monroe my voice. "And it isn't even my fault. He didn't tell me where the meeting was. His assistant did and she told me the wrong floor, and I can't lose this job. I just can't." My act has the intended effect. He shifts his weight, leaning away from me. His jaw relaxes. And when the doors slide open on the sixth floor, there's not much I can do. I stay put, making a show of looking at the time on my phone. When we reach the second floor, he remains inside the elevator.

"Hey," he says, hand on a door to keep it from closing. "Are you with the health care guys or the lawyers?" His voice dips just a touch on the last word.

"The lawyers," I say, adding a wince.

"Good luck," he says.

"Thank you." I dash away as the doors shut.

I race for the stairs at the far end of the hallway, passing a group of thirty-somethings in business casual who watch my progress with amusement. Two at a time, I take the steps. By the time I reach the sixth floor, my lungs are shrieking in protest.

The hallway here is empty. Back to the stairs I go. There's one cart on the fifth floor, at the opposite end of the hallway. No housekeeper in sight. I'm about ten feet away when a uniformed woman emerges from a room. Pale skin and hair, small stature. She grabs a roll of toilet paper from her cart and disappears again. I step closer.

She returns to her cart. This time, she sees me. "Did you need anything?" she asks. No smile, but a helpful mien.

And it's her. It's Becca's mother. Here, only six feet away. Her hair is white now, not blonde. Her skin holds a prison-pale luster, the wrinkles faint. In spite of her hair, she looks much younger than I expected. There's something in her face, something sad and tired and . . . broken. She's a far cry from the woman who staggered into the kitchen while Becca and I made ice cream. The woman who scared me with her slurred speech and the way she touched my hair. But she's here, doing her job like nothing's wrong, like she hasn't turned my world upside down and inside out, like she doesn't even know who I am.

"Why?" I say, the word tumbling like a brick from my mouth.

Her brow creases. "I'm sorry?"

Breath coming too fast, I tug the scarf from my head. "Why did you send me the necklace? The picture she drew? Why did you leave the squirrel in my mailbox?" My voice isn't as strong as it should be, but it's as strong as I can manage.

Lauren's lips part. Her eyes widen. She's a rabbit in disaster's head-lights, but I know she recognizes me.

"Why are you doing this to me?" I say. "What do you want?"

"You need to go now," she says. "Please. Not here, not now." She glances around, takes a half step back.

This isn't going the way I thought it would. She isn't acting how I imagined she would. Why isn't she sneering? Why isn't she threatening me with worse? Why isn't she demanding to know what I did to Becca? Or revealing that she already knows?

A couple emerges from the elevator, dragging their wheeled suitcases and loud conversation toward us. Lauren moves her cart aside, still not looking at me.

"Please go," she says.

"Fine, but I'll see you tonight," I say, not waiting for her reply.

*   *   *

Google didn't reveal that the business park is abandoned. The five build-ings, all four stories with narrow windows, some broken, others pocked with bullet holes, appear as though they've not had tenants in ages. Graf-fiti streaks across the brick and concrete. Weeds jut from cracks in the parking lot asphalt like deformed Chia Pets. There should be security fencing, but there isn't. Half the lights are burned or maybe shot out. The whole place feels like a set from an apocalyptic movie. Maybe one with zombies.

I navigate an obvious pile of shattered glass and pull into a parking space in front but leave the engine running. I drain half my water bottle, but my mouth is still parched. No way am I getting out of the car until Lauren's here.

I'm five minutes early, but I check my email, just in case. Nothing new. I pull my coat tighter around me. As far as Ryan knows, I'm down-town meeting Gia for drinks. I trace the edge of the steering wheel from top to bottom. When I saw Lauren at the hotel, I was all panic and surprise. Tonight, though, I'm prepared. I'm going to stay calm and not ask questions. I'm going to let her speak first. And if she tries the timid-old-woman act again, I'm going to call her out on it. Because it had to be an act. And it was good, I'll give her that. It almost had me convinced. But I had her cornered at her job, a job she can't afford to lose with her prison record, so what else could she do? Alexa Martin can only pull so many strings.

Her email said she wanted to talk about Becca, so we'll talk about Becca. But I don't care if she reveals she made herself invisible and was in the basement with us that night. I'm not going to admit a damn thing. Besides, if she thinks she knows, why hasn't she gone to the police? Why this game?

The minutes tick slowly by. At nine, the parking lot's still empty. Five more minutes pass. No Lauren. I worry the steering wheel over and over again. At quarter after, I open my car door, swinging one leg out.

"Hello?"

The word echoes on and on. And there's not a sound in return. I don't understand. Why set up a meeting and not show? I told her at the hotel I'd see her tonight. Did she change her mind? Is she watching me from somewhere? Maybe she's in one of the buildings. But I'm here, so why isn't she coming out?

I step all the way out but leave the door open. Stand with arms akimbo, fingers wide. Spin in a slow circle, aiming for nonthreatening. *Here I am. Come and get me.*

I sense movement behind me and spin around. There's someone standing at the window. Someone on the side of the building. I look closer. Only shadows and nothing more. More movement, behind me again. The suggestion of a shoulder, of an arm, hiding behind the front door of that building? My skin prickles with goose bumps.

No.

This is my imagination running wild in the darkness. There are too many gaping windows. Too much broken glass. This was pointless. No one's here. It's twenty after nine. She said nine o'clock. I'm not going to sit here all night. Fuck that. Fuck her.

Back in my car, I slam the door. My heart is racing; my mouth is filled with bitter panic. I tap the side of the phone on my lower lip. Should I email and ask where she is? Why she isn't here? Is this a new game or part of the same? Does she really think I'll wait forever?

More movement to my left, but it's nothing. A whole business park of nothing. My tires kick arcs of pebbles as I drive away. Before I turn out of the lot, I give it one last scan. No Lauren. No one at all.

*   *   *

I call the hotel first thing but hang up before anyone answers. I've already called twice. Sure, I got lucky because I called on different days and spoke with two different clerks, but I doubt people call about the house-keepers on a regular basis unless it's to bitch about something missing from their room or not enough towels during their stay. And I sincerely doubt they call about specific housekeepers.

Instead, I send Lauren an email: I WAITED FOR YOU, BUT YOU DIDN'T SHOW UP. By the end of the day, there's still no reply.

It's Ryan's turn to meet with someone tonight—his brother—for drinks after dinner. Or maybe this is our new code for lying about our evening plans. *Pot, this is kettle.* I pick up dinner from Panera on my way home.

In the kitchen, I set the bag on the counter in front of the toaster oven, our usual spot for takeout. The bag slips off the edge. I grab. And miss. There's a liquid thud, and the side of the bag goes dark. Goodbye, French onion soup and Greek salad. Hello, whatever I can scrounge from the cabinets and fridge. A wad of paper towels later, I figure out the reason behind the mishap: the toaster's about six inches away from the wall.

Thanks a lot, Ryan.

He also pulled out the fruit basket and the coffeemaker. I don't see anything different with the backsplash or the counter, and I think he would've mentioned a problem he had to repair, even with the way things are between us right now. Unless he just forgot.

But upstairs in our room, one side of my dresser is tugged forward an inch or two. The same with my nightstand. The comforter on my side of the bed is folded back. Yet I made the bed neatly this morning.

The clothes in my top dresser drawer seem fine, but in the second drawer my T-shirts are leaning toward the center, as though someone placed a hand there and whisked it around. The clothes in my other drawers show signs of being touched as well. Everything is in its place in my jewelry box, even my half of the heart necklace. But the chain looks different, in a messy pile whereas I had it coiled. I step back, fingers quivering.

Holding the railing tight, I run back downstairs. In the family room I stand with hands on hips and look. Really look. The coffee table is angled, revealing a divot in the rug below. Same with the sofa, the throw we keep draped over an arm unfolded over the cushion. In the breakfast nook, the table's been pushed back nearly a foot. The napkin holder in the center is no longer parallel to the window but perpendicular. In the dining room, the chairs are pulled out from the table, and the glass bowl in the center sits off to the left now. In the formal living room, the front corners of the end tables are angled toward the sofa. Several books in the bookcase are turned spines in. Every change is slight, easy to miss. If it had been only one thing, I probably would've. But this is calculated. Not noticing is impossible.

I push my hair off my forehead. Toe the floor.

Someone's been here. In the house. And they wanted me to know. No, not they. *She.* She wanted me to know. I scrunch my toes, curl my fingers. She was in my house. Sweat pools between my breasts. I pat my pockets, but my phone isn't there and I can't remember where I left my bag. I scrub my face, smearing the last traces of the day's makeup. I need to call the police. I need to file a report and—

I can't. A report will lead to an investigation. And then? Maybe eventually to Becca. To the truth. I'm trapped and she knows it. My knees lock. So what the hell am I going to do? A voice of reason slips in. *Straighten up before Ryan gets home. Put everything back. Do that first, then take it from there.*

Like a spider on fire, I scurry through the living room. End tables. Coffee table. Books. It doesn't take long. In the dining room I stub my big toe on a chair leg and stork-stand until the throbbing ceases, attempting to blink away tears. They're still falling even after I check the kitchen—in the cabinet, the canned goods were turned so the labels faced the back—and the nook. By the time I head for the stairs, they've progressed into hitching sobs I can't stop.

Halfway up, I stumble, yelping as I bang a shin against the tread. I crouch with my back against the wall and pour my fear and rage into my palms. I can't do this. I can't do any of it anymore. It's all too much.

How the hell did she get in? We have solid dead bolts. We keep the doors locked. There was no broken glass. Sometimes we forget to lock the door leading into the house from the garage, but we've never had a problem before. It would take a Herculean effort for someone to physically raise the exterior garage doors. And Lauren is small. So how did she get in?

I don't know how long I sit there, but when the sobs reduce to quiet sniffles and my skin is sodden and snot-sticky, I trek the rest of the way upstairs to wash my face. A stranger peers back from the mirror. Eyes purpled with fatigue. Hollows beneath the cheekbones. Skin ruddy with anxiety. She isn't me. She isn't anyone I know. I rest my hand atop the reflection, one eye visible through the gaps in my fingers.

Red Lady, Red Lady.

Don't look in her eyes!

Arms at my sides, I stomp into Ryan's office. My childhood wraith isn't the issue here. His pens have been removed from the mug in the corner, strewn like pickup sticks atop design sketches. My office has fared worse: my papers have been rearranged higgledy-piggledy, so I gather them into a neatish pile for later. Even the bathrooms—shower curtains opened, towels puddled on the floors, toothbrushes left in the sinks—were touched. Instead of replacing the brushes, I toss them out.

Once again I stand in the middle of the family room, searching. If I miss something small, Ryan won't notice. Hell, he might not miss something large, but I will. I go from room to room again, fingertipping every piece of furniture. Once I'm sure I've fixed it all, I run upstairs and strip the bed. Throw the sheets in the washer with extra detergent. Then I scour all the flat surfaces with disinfectant wipes. When I'm done, the house smells of lemon cleanser and dryer sheets. I stink of sour sweat.

My stomach growls, but the thought of food makes me queasy, so I drink a glass of wine. A brilliant move. Once it hits my empty stomach, it makes a reappearance in no time flat. I don't try anything else, just brush my teeth with a spare I found in the closet—safe in its packaging—and climb in bed.

I checked the French doors, didn't I?

But when I planted the flower bulbs on Sunday, surely I locked the doors when I came back in. That was five days ago. I don't think I've been out back since. Has Ryan?

I slip out of bed and tug on my robe, tying it tight. Down the stairs one at a time, mouth dry. What if the doors are unlocked? What if she's out back, waiting for me to realize that? What if she's hiding somewhere in the house?

"Stop," I hiss through clenched teeth.

My steps grow slower as I approach the French doors, not wanting to see what's painfully obvious: the thumb-turn lock is in the disengaged position. I jam it to the right, tugging on the handles to make sure it's secure. Now I know how she got inside, but I wish it made me feel better.

I rub my upper arms and do a quick check downstairs. I do the same on the second floor, but I'm alone. I'm safe. But something tugs at the back of my mind. It doesn't make sense. Lauren played her fearful act at the hotel yesterday, didn't show up for our meeting last night, then broke into our house today to move things around? It doesn't feel right. Am I missing something painfully obvious? Have I somehow fallen into a trap I can't see?

Back in bed, I pull the covers to my chin, but sleep refuses to claim me for its own. When Ryan comes in, I know he knows I'm still awake, but he pretends I'm not. We both do.

* * *

It's easy enough to act like everything's normal while we're getting ready for the day. Or maybe it's because we're moving in different direction and rarely cross paths. At least not until we bump into each other in the kitchen, both with designs on the coffeemaker.

As I'm pouring milk into my travel mug, I say, "Did you leave the French doors unlocked yesterday?"

"No, I wasn't out back. Why?"

"They were unlocked when I got home. I probably did it, but I wasn't sure."

"Do you want me to go check?"

"No, I locked them." But he's already out of the kitchen. A few seconds later, there's the distinctive rattle.

"Locked tight," he says when he comes back in.

"Okay," I say.

I feel his gaze on my back, sense the weight of an incipient conversation, but as soon as I'm done making my coffee, I toss a quick "Have a good day" over my shoulder. There's a pause before he says the same in return. But everything will be okay eventually. I know it will. I just have to get through all this first.

When I get into the office, I've an email from Rachel waiting. I steel myself—for what I don't know—as I open it, but it's from her assistant, asking if I've had a chance to compile the requested information yet. It takes me a second to realize what she's talking about. Financial documents pertaining to my supposed divorce. I should write that I've changed my mind, but I close the email without responding.

Nothing from Lauren.

Still nothing after my first patient leaves. The same after my second. Every time I close my eyes, I envision her sneaking through my house, moving my things. I have a little over an hour before my next patient session. It's time enough. Clutching my car keys, I tell Ellie I'll be back shortly and get on the highway, driving toward Lauren's. It's probably not the wisest move and she probably isn't even home, but I need to know why she didn't show for the meeting. Why she came to my house. And if all this is a trap of sorts, she won't expect this. At least I hope not.

The drive's an easy one, but when I draw near her street, a group of people are huddled on the corner. A red news van is parked at the far end. A few feet away, a reporter is speaking into the microphone, gesturing toward the building. What the hell's going on?

I find a parking spot one street over and casually walk toward the group. The air is mild today, but I wish I'd remembered my jacket. In front of Lauren's building, bright-orange cones are blocking off a section of the road, and inside the rectangle are a sedan, police cruiser, and white van. A woman in a button-down, shiny badge clipped to her waist, disappears into the building.

Most of the people around me are gray-haired and sun-spotted, wearing elastic-waist pants and floral prints under windbreakers, but there are two younger women with babies in strollers. There's a current of dark energy here, that hope of catching sight of something illicit, along with the smell of menthol and artificial roses. I maneuver around until I'm next to a sharp-eyed woman in a yellow cardigan.

"What happened?" I say.

"A woman got killed."

"Killed?"

Not looking at me, the woman says, "Yes."

Another woman, her hair a frizzy halo, says, "They found her last night." She glances at me, frowning slightly at my creased slacks, my fitted jacket. "They had the whole street blocked off. You couldn't even stand here."

The two younger women are whispering to each other, their heads close. I carefully step toward them.

"You know who it was, right?" one says. "What the news said? If they're right, then she deserved it."

"Yup."

Is it possible?

When I step a little closer, they both gift me with withering gazes. Flushed with warmth, I move back near the woman in the cardigan and say, "Do you know who—"

My phone rings, and everyone in the groups shoots a glare. I say, "I'm sorry," and mute the call. Ellie can wait. The officer with the badge at her waist emerges from the building, glances around, then heads toward us. Shit. I can't be seen here.

Phone to my ear, pretending to be engrossed in a conversation, it takes all I have not to run. With every step away, the fear of hearing a command to stop increases, and I don't allow myself to breathe normally until I'm back in my car. I want to check my browser, but what if even now the women are telling the cop that I was asking questions?

I'm careful to obey the speed limit as I navigate out of the neighborhood, but once I've left it well in my rearview mirror, I pull into a gas station. Open a browser on my phone. "Come on, come on, come on," I say as it slowly loads.

On the main page of the Baltimore newspaper: CONVICTED KILLER NOW A VICTIM, with the beginning of the first paragraph below: LAUREN THOMAS, WHO WAS RELEASED EARLIER THIS YEAR AFTER SERVING NEARLY THIRTY YEARS FOR THE MURDER OF HER DAUGHTER . . .

I click the link and skim the rest, each detail a sharp little shock. Found by a neighbor in her apartment on Wednesday morning. Killed Tuesday night. Blunt-force trauma. No suspects. Police still gathering evidence. Asking anyone with information to call the tip line.

I sit back, hands clasped together on my steering wheel. Dead. That's why she never showed up for our meeting. Someone was bludgeoning her to death.

I bite back a sound. Will Mikayla tell the police I was there? I tap my fingers. Remember the flash of fear. No, I don't think she will. Even if she does, I didn't give her my real name. And I didn't see anyone else. No one in the group of rubberneckers today will think of me as a threat. An outsider, yes, but a threat?

A tiny thread of hope winds its way through me. With Lauren dead, am I safe? Is it over? I scroll to the photos of her address and the hotel information in my phone. Hit delete. Check the gallery to make sure they're gone.

But what about fingerprints? If I left any in the hallway and they find them, what will I say? I went to see Lauren and she wasn't home? It's the truth, but then they'll want to know why.

Wait, wait, wait.

I don't move. Don't blink. Don't make a sound.

If Lauren was killed Tuesday night, it means she wasn't in my house yesterday. No. That can't be right. Maybe it was a misprint. Or the police are wrong about the time of death. Lauren could've come to my house in the morning, and then someone killed her after she got home.

I'm still sitting there when an email arrives. From Lauren Thomas.

Fingers like ice, I click it open. The message reads WHAT DID YOU DO TO MY DAUGHTER?

CHAPTER SIXTEEN

THEN

I stood on Becca's porch, arms at my sides after knocking. She might not even answer. Might not even be home. But the door creaked opened a few inches and she peeked out. Her hair was grease-slicked to her scalp and her clothes hung loose on her frame, like her bones were a cheap hanger twisted out of shape. Her gaze flitted from right to left behind me, then settled on mine. Her pale eyes appeared almost colorless.

"Becca?"

"Duh," she said, moving aside so I could come in. "Who else would I be?"

As I passed by, I smelled her, sour and biting, but I kept from wrinkling my nose. "Are you okay?"

"Come on up," she said, not waiting for me to respond before she took to the stairs. "She's not home."

She was barefoot, the soles of her feet grubby. The curtains and blinds in her room were closed, and the overhead light was off.

"Sorry," she said, flipping the switch.

In the bright, she looked even worse. Her skin was pasty-white, her lips cracked, and sleep grit was collected in the corners of her eyes.

"She said you'd come," she said.

Even her voice sounded wrong. Raspy, yet barely there. Unused.

Before she'd had a few drawings on her walls. Now they covered almost every space from floor to ceiling in a chaotic, overlapping wallpaper. All the Red Lady. And more were on top of her bed and her desk, piled haphazardly.

"What's all this?" I said.

"Just drawings."

"Becca, this isn't just drawings. It's, it's—"

"I know you're still mad at me. I know you're only here because she told you to be. I didn't think you'd come, I really didn't, but she was right. She's always right."

Sweeping one foot back and forth, I fought the urge to run back downstairs and out the door. I tried to ignore the drawings, but from every direction, black eyes bored through me, arms outstretched and ready to grab.

"That's not true," I said, but my words didn't sound convincing, even to my own ears. I picked at a cuticle. "I heard about Rachel and Gia."

"Doesn't matter. They were never important."

I rubbed the back of my ankle with the toe of a sneaker. "What do you mean?"

"They were only my friends because of you." She paced from one side of the room to the other, her movements strange and jerky, a puppet on invisible strings. "I never took mine off," she said, lifting the half-heart. "See? I don't blame you, though."

Cheeks burning, my fingers inched along my bare neck. She kept moving, patting things along the way with her fingers. Desk, headboard, nightstand, dresser, and the same in reverse.

"What's wrong?" I said.

"You have to swear not to tell. Do you?"

"I don't—"

"No! You have to swear. Swear on your mom and dad's lives. Your life, too." She didn't stop moving, and her words mushed together. "You can't ever, ever tell. You promise. You swear you'll never tell. I'll know if you do."

"But I don't—"

She stopped. "Not ever," she said.

"I swear I won't tell."

But in the back of my mind, I was trying to figure out how I'd tell my mom what was wrong when I didn't even know. Becca seemed like an alien or a pod person, not like Becca at all.

"Good," she said, raking her hair back. She turned and lifted her shirt. Bruises ran left and right and up and down, underscored with several thin scratches in varying states of healing. She pushed up her sleeve, revealing bruises on her upper arm, too, in the shape of fingers.

I gasped. I didn't want to look at the marks, the bruises, but I couldn't look away either.

"Lauren did it," she said. "She's worse than ever now. As soon as she comes home, she starts drinking. Then she gets mad and tells me everything's my fault. It's not so bad on the weekends because she drinks until she passes out, but during the week she's angry all the time and I don't even know if she knows she's hurting me. But she is, Heather. She hurts me a lot here"—she held out her arm—"and here." She pointed to her chest. "And there are other things, too, but I can't tell you—"

I blinked a bunch of times. Her mom did that to her? But moms weren't supposed to hurt you like that. It was wrong. "We have to do something," I said. "We have to tell my mom."

"No! You swore you wouldn't." She came right up to me and pressed two fingers gently against my lips, her breath like spoiled milk and rancid meat. "If you do, I'll hate you forever and never talk to you again." She paced back across the room, elbows cupped in her palms. "But she's going to help me. The Red Lady's going to make things right. And I need your help, too.

"Rachel and Gia were lying. They didn't see her or hear her. I know they didn't. They just pretended to, but I know you really did. She said so. Once we do what we have to, everything will be okay. She promised."

Her eyes were wild, darting like lightning bugs. Her mom hadn't just hurt her body, but her head, too. She must have, to make Becca say things like that. To make her think a made-up story would help her. We *had* to tell my mom. *I* had to tell her, no matter what Becca said. But part of me wanted to run away right now, because I was scared. Her bruises scared me. She was scaring me, too.

"Please, stop," I said. "Please just stop."

"No, this is way too important. She's too important."

"She's just a story." Even if Becca couldn't see that, I could. But my mom was real and she could fix it.

Becca spun on her heel and stalked toward me. She got so close I could feel heat coming off her body. "Don't you say that! You know she isn't. You know she's real. Know how I know?"

I held out my hands, not wanting her to get any closer. "I don't want to talk about her anymore. Please, please, let's talk about something else, anything else."

"No!" she yelled, her heat burning me up. "We have to talk about her. There's a lot we have to talk about."

I backed toward the door, away from her eyes, her fire. I felt shaky and sick.

"She knows you felt her. She told me you did."

"I didn't. You have to stop all of this. We can talk to my mom. We can figure out a way—"

"And if you don't help me, if you don't do what she wants, she won't leave you alone. She won't ever leave you alone." She grabbed my wrist, and I cried out. "Do you understand?" she said. "You have to help me.

"There's something I didn't tell you about her. I didn't tell any of you. Before they put her in the hole, a woman who was her friend, who was afraid to speak up because she knew they'd kill her too, gave her a hug. But she didn't just give her a hug. She stabbed her in the side, so she would die fast instead of being buried alive, instead of suffocating under all the dirt. But you already know that, don't you? She said she showed you that, too. She had to, to make you understand."

I shook my head, hard, and yanked my arm free. I touched my side, remembering the sharp pain I'd felt when I woke up in the kitchen. When I crouched by the basement window.

"You're lying. I can tell. I've known she was real since the first time she came to me. Everything else was to prove it to you, Heather. To prove to you she's real."

"She's a story," I said, the words small and powerless. "And stories aren't real. They're not."

"But she is real, whether you want her to be or not," she said, her cheeks red and spotty. "She's more real than almost anything." She caressed one of the pictures, stroking the Red Lady's face, her own soft, the way a mom looks when she's holding a newborn baby.

"Stop it, stop it, stop it," I shouted.

I stomped over, pushed past her, and ripped down the picture. "She isn't real!" I tore another free, and another, and another. Becca stood to the side, watching. When I had one wall half bare and a pile of torn paper on the floor, my legs went rubbery. I sank down on top of the shreds.

She knelt beside me. "The pictures aren't that important. I can draw more."

I burst into tears. I didn't want her to be this way, and I didn't know what to say or do. She put her arms around me, like she was a mom and me a kid, and I kept crying. After I stopped, she brought me a wad of toilet paper for my face and nose. Maybe if I did what she wanted, every-thing would be okay. She'd understand that the Red Lady couldn't help her. Then we could talk to my mom.

"What do you want me to do?" I said, my voice still thick.

"Nothing yet. It isn't the right time, but soon."

"I don't understand," I said. I wanted to go home. Hide underneath the covers and pretend I hadn't come here, hadn't seen Becca this way.

"I know. I'll tell you everything, but not now. And you can't help me here. It has to be at the house."

I shook my head. "No, uh-uh. I'm not going back there."

"We have to," she said. "That's where we have to finish it."

"Finish what? You're not making any sense."

"The ritual."

I groaned. "But we did it already. I don't want—"

"This is a different one. One that'll fix everything. You have to trust me, okay?"

Next to me, the Red Lady stared up from a torn scrap of paper.

"Fine," I said. "But after this, we're done with her, okay? You have to promise me. When this is over, no more drawings or telling stories about her. We go back to the way things were."

"We can't ever go back."

But when I opened my mouth, she held up one finger. "No more drawings or stories, okay. You should go home now. I have some stuff to do, and if Lauren comes home early, I don't want her to see you. She'll get mad. Meet me at the house Friday night after your parents go to bed."

She practically pushed me down the stairs. I stood on her porch with my arms crossed, thinking maybe she'd open the door, telling me it was all a joke and I fell for it. I waited, but the door stayed shut. I should tell my mom, but Becca was my best friend. I wanted everything to be okay. I wanted her to be okay. I'd do anything to make that happen. I'd do almost anything at all.

That night I changed into my pajamas early. My mom was in the bathroom, taking off her makeup, and I stood in the doorway, wiggling a little.

"I have to pee," I said.

"Come on in. You won't bother me."

When I finished, she moved aside so I could wash my hands.

"You okay?" she asked. "You've been awfully quiet tonight."

"I'm fine," I said, looking down at the water in the sink, not at her.

"All right. Hey, next weekend we'll go school supply shopping."

"Ugh."

"And after, we can stop at Friendly's and get ice cream sundaes, like we did last year."

But it wouldn't be like last year. Becca had been with us then, and we'd eaten so much ice cream our stomachs hurt for hours. My mom probably wanted to wait until after payday, but I wondered, too, if she wanted to give me more time, in case I wanted to ask Becca to go. I thought about her bruises. Wondered if her mom would take her shopping or not.

"Hey, Mom?"

"Uh-huh?"

"I . . ." Pain darted my side, one fast jab gone almost as quick as it began. I swallowed hard. Turned off the faucet. "Never mind."

She passed me a towel. "If you want or need to talk to me, I'm here. Oh, and before I forget, your dad will be working late for the next couple of weeks because they're running behind at the job site. They still haven't even filled in the hole where the other man fell. So you and I will have plenty of girl time, just in case you decide you do want to talk."

"Okay," I said, hanging up the towel and going back into my room before I could break my promise to Becca, no matter how much it hurt.

CHAPTER SEVENTEEN

NOW

I drive back to the office in a daze. My patient is waiting, and although I'm not even that late—it's not my fault they arrived early—her mother gives a look so full of disapproval I feel as though I'm a student with incomplete homework. Having had no time to fully prepare for the session, I do my best to ask the right questions and listen, but when the hour's over, patient delivered back to her mother, I sink down in my office chair.

It's not Lauren.

It's not her.

Was it ever? I thought her timidity at the hotel was an act, but what if it wasn't? What if she had no idea why I was there or what I wanted? What if she never did anything to me? Never did anything but try to salvage what was left of her life?

So who's behind it all? I'm back to square one, which is even worse now, because it made sense for it to be Lauren. Now, anyone else seems unlikely. But maybe that was my problem all along. Lauren made such perfect sense that I didn't expend enough energy looking anywhere else. Sure, I followed Gia to the grocery store and met with Rachel, but I didn't really do anything.

I don't know what to do or where to look. I feel as though I'm falling through the dark into a great gaping maw. I want—

I scramble for my phone and dial, barely letting my mom say hello. "What are you up to tonight?" I say, summoning every bit of calm I can.

"Not much. I was planning to go to the Avenue to do a little shopping," she says. "Why?"

"Want some company?"

There's a pause, then she says, "Sure."

But she doesn't sound sure at all. I tear at a cuticle. It's me, I know. There's nothing wrong with her tone or her words. So I tell her I'll meet her there, and she says that'll be nice.

For the rest of the afternoon, I focus on my patients. It's a pleasant fiction, but it makes me feel better to think so. At the end of the day, I pack up and text Mom to let her know I'm on my way. I turn the music loud in the car, attempting to drown out my thoughts, but I can't stop thinking about Lauren's wary eyes, about someone bludgeoning her to death, about the bystander who said she deserved it. About my house with everything moved out of place.

Mom's waiting outside Starbucks, so I wipe away the worry, and we get coffees before puttering around Old Navy. We're next to a display of skinny jeans in autumn colors when she touches my forearm.

"So what's wrong?" she says.

"What?" I say, inspecting tags to find my size.

"Sweetheart, I know you better than I know myself sometimes. For you to want to come shopping, something must be wrong." She's watching me closely, and I shrug.

"Work stress got a little unbearable today," I say. "But this is helping. Plus, I just wanted to spend some time with you."

Her gaze bores through me, and I feel caught with the cookie jar. I tug a pair of pants free, hoping they're the right size. But I'm not lying. Not completely. Here, with her, I do feel a little better.

After Old Navy, we grab new mascara and lipstick at Ulta, a few books from Barnes & Noble, and slices of pizza for a quick dinner. I don't want to leave, so I order a cannoli. After I finish it, I suppress a groan and the urge to unbutton my pants.

"So how did Ryan's meeting go?" Mom says.

"His what?" I say, head cocked to one side.

"His meeting last Wednesday."

Did he have a meeting? I don't remember that at all. "I . . . have no idea," I say, pinching crumbs between my fingertips.

"Oh, when I ran into him at Grinds—I was meeting Cathy there—he was wearing a suit and said he had a meeting. Didn't he tell you he saw me?"

"No," I say, but hasten to add, "Work's been busy, and he's been getting home late."

I don't recall him wearing anything to work recently other than his usual jeans, T-shirt, and boots. I catch the sidelong look Mom is giving me, but the waitress interrupts with the check.

As we approach her car, I say, my voice as bland as I can make it, "Did you happen to see the news?"

She stiffens. "Sure, why?"

"Did you see that Becca's mom died? That she was killed?"

She says nothing, puts her bags in her trunk, and turns, face tight. "Is that the real reason you wanted to come with me? To talk about this? Still?"

"No," I say. "Not at all. But I saw the news, and someone killed her, Mom." *And someone's coming after me.*

"So it's over and done with, then."

"But—"

She stalls my words with a chop to the air and slams her trunk shut. "Stop this, I mean it. I don't understand why you're doing this to yourself. It isn't good for you, you know that."

My thumbnail finds the skin of my index finger. Begins to scrape. "I'm not doing anything, Mom."

"You're a terrible liar, sweetheart. Always have been."

How wrong she is.

She presses a quick kiss to my cheek and says, "Let it go."

I give her a half-hearted wave as raindrops start to spatter. So much for the nice weather. By the time I get on 97, it's raining in earnest and visibility is nearly nonexistent. People drive like assholes: going too fast, tailgating, or zipping around people who've slowed down. It's like no one ever took a driving lesson. But having to concentrate on driving and the rhythmic *thump-thump* of the Jeep's wipers help keep the thoughts out of my head.

Not far after the Veterans Highway exit, visibility goes from bad to worse, forcing everyone, even the assholes, to slow down. An old grayish-blue car pulls into the middle lane behind me, drawing too close to my bumper for comfort. I try to keep distance between us, but it keeps edging close. As soon as space opens in the left lane, I scoot over. Being rear-ended is not on my agenda. A quarter mile later, the old car, a Chevy, pulls behind me again. Again, it moves too close.

I have the chance to pull ahead, so I do. A silver Beetle sneaks between me and the Chevy. I cringe, waiting for the squeal of brakes and the crunch, but it manages to avoid us both. A minute later, the Beetle changes lanes again. The Chevy draws way too close, our bumpers almost close enough to tango.

It's too dark to make out the driver, too dark to make out the license plate number either, but it's a Maryland tag. At least I think so. The car seems familiar. I rack my memory and it hits me. I think it's the same one I saw outside the townhouse where one of the wrong Laurens lived.

Speeding up again, I angle into the next lane, even though the spacing makes it closer than I'd like. When I do the same to get to the far right, the Chevy moves into the middle. A minute later, directly behind me.

"Go away, go away, go away," I say.

Palms clammy, I hold the steering wheel tight. Flick my gaze from road to rearview mirror and back. The rain lightens a bit, and traffic begins to open. I slowly increase my speed. The Chevy sticks with me, only one car length between us. I reach into my purse, rooting for my phone, cursing myself for not putting it in the cup holder the way I usually do. To my left, a car lays on its horn, and I swerve back into my lane.

The Chevy edges even closer. Half a car length away now. *What the fuck?* I refuse to get any closer to the car in front of me, and there's a car next to me in the lane on my left. To my right is the shoulder where cars sit periodically, waiting out the storm. The Chevy draws even closer. The grille looms in my mirrors; lights strobe the interior. The deluge begins again, killing all visibility in front of me and wrecking my chance of gunning it. The Chevy is so close now, I'm sure our bumpers are only inches away. I speed up a little. The Chevy does the same. Brake lights flash, dim, flash again. Horns blare, bleat, cheep. My wipers slam back and forth, offering scant glances of the road between slashes. In front of me, brake lights turn the world red. I slam on mine. Behind me, the Chevy's does the same, but they're so close I can't even see the grille. A fluttery feeling creeps beneath my skin.

And the dark shape behind the wheel seems to grow even larger. A presence so large I'm too scared to look close, too terrified to look away. It's her. The Red Lady. She's here and she's real and she's come for me. After all this time, she's come back. I choke back panic. Shake my head hard. No. She isn't real. It isn't her. No matter what, no matter who.

It. Isn't. Her.

The car in front of me starts moving faster. I do, too, getting too close to their bumper but opening space between the Chevy and me. Not for long, though. It gets closer and closer, then scoots into the middle lane and slows down. A horn chirps, but the Chevy keeps slowing, keeps falling back.

Lights brighten my side mirror as it surges forward. Then it starts pushing into my lane. Shouting, I pound the horn, and they edge back. They scoot up again and we drive side by side. No matter how many glances I snatch, I can't see anything other than an amorphous shape in the driver's seat.

Then the car pushes into my lane, so fast I can't hit the horn, can't do anything but yank the wheel to get away. My tires slide and I cry out as the wheel skids from my grip. The car judders to the right on the shoulder and I jam on the brakes, slamming my body forward in the process. There's a dull metallic crunch as the Jeep meets the guardrail, a second jerk of my body, the seat belt yanking me back tight and tearing the air from my lungs. Pain flares in my shoulder, my hip, my wrist.

The Chevy is still moving ahead, but in moment or two, its lights are swallowed by the rain.

"You fucking bitch!" Sweat beads my forehead, my back, between my breasts. My vision turns hazy. My heart is racing so fast it feels as though it's not beating at all. And the air is thick and viscous. They ran me off the road. They wanted to hurt me. Or worse.

Car in park, I cup my face. Slowly—too slowly—my world stops shaking. And I shriek at the windshield as loud as I can, rage and fear turning my voice hoarse, collapsing against the seat when I'm done. I feel like a coward. I feel weak. Incapable. And it feels like hell.

I don't know how long I sit there. Long enough for the shock to turn to numbness, long enough for the rain to cease and traffic to begin moving at a normal pace. My right wrist throbs, but I can still move it. My left shoulder aches, and I can already see the mark of the seat belt stippling my skin. My hip is sore.

I get out to inspect the damage, and the right side of my car is scraped and dented from the driver's side door back. With a shaking hand, I call Ryan, and flashing lights appear behind me the same time he arrives. I give the officer and Ryan the same story—I slid in the rain.

"So no one else was involved in the crash?" the officer says. "The person who called it in said there were two cars."

Here's my chance. All I have to do is say yes. It's provable now. There's a witness. But I've told so many lies, I'm not sure how to untangle myself. And Becca's death sits at the very heart. One misguided yes could become the end of everything. I can't. I want to, but I can't.

"No," I say. "They were wrong. It was just me. My tires . . . The rain . . ."

She finishes writing up her report and gives me a copy before leaving.

"Are you sure you don't want to go to the ER?" Ryan says. "Get some X-rays of your wrist?"

I shake my head. "I'm sure. The ER will be a waste of everyone's time. I can tell it's not broken. I'll wrap it once we get home."

"All right. Stay in the right lane and I'll follow you."

We make it back home without incident. On the kitchen counter is a vase with sunflowers, orange lilies, red roses, and the many-petaled flowers that resemble daisies but aren't. The sight of them hurts. He comes behind me, circling my waist with his arms. I make myself relax as I lean against him.

"I bought them before you called me," he says. "I'm sorry I talked to Nicole. I shouldn't have, but I thought she'd know what was wrong. I wanted to help, that's all."

Once again, the story pushes at my lips, wanting out, wanting to be told, but I can't do it. Not to him, not to anyone. I wiggle free from his grasp and give him a quick hug.

"They're beautiful, thank you. I'm going upstairs to take a couple Advil and go to bed."

"Want me to bring you anything?"

"No," I say. "I'm good."

I hold tight to the railing as I ascend, feeling his attention on my back the entire time.

*　*　*

After Ryan leaves for work, I stand beneath a hot shower, soaking some of the stiffness away. The marks on my shoulder and upper chest are a livid shade of purple-red. The one on my hip, too. My wrist is a touch swollen and sore, but I'm still positive it's not broken.

In our walk-in closet, I stand in front of Ryan's clothes. He has only one suit—a charcoal-gray all-weather we picked out together a few years ago for a wedding. I reach for the jacket sleeve and pause. I know my mom wouldn't lie, but . . .

With one fluid movement, I tug the jacket free and press my face to the fabric. I smell, or at least think I smell, coffee. A fresh smell. No perfume, no lipstick on the collar. Nothing in the pockets.

There's probably a simple explanation. Maybe he met with a potential client he wanted to impress. Didn't say anything to me because the client hasn't decided yet, or worse, decided to go with someone else.

My fists clench, balling up the fabric, my right wrist giving a twinge of pain. All I have to do is ask him who the meeting was with, but I'm afraid he might not answer the way I want him to and it'll turn into another argument. I'll unleash all my frustration and anger about the Chevy, the person in our house, the person who wants to hurt me, on him, and I won't be able to take it back. I feel it all, a huge weight atop me, a mound of dirt, pressing me down. I'll say things I'll regret. Or I'll say something I should keep to myself. I shake out the jacket and return it to its hanger, making sure it's in the same spot it was before, then move to my side of the closet.

My Jeep looks even worse in the daylight. I follow the speed limit, checking my mirrors frequently, eyeing every grayish-blue car, hands like vice grips on the wheel. No cars follow me or get too close, but I drive a wide circle through the neighborhood around Silverstone before pulling into the lot and I practically run to the door. They sky is still overcast, but there's a brightness at the edges hinting at a clearing in the near future.

Nicole's office door is shut, thankfully, and I'm unlocking mine when my phone rings. *Alexa.* My mouth goes dry. I think about letting it go to voice mail, but not answering will look more suspicious.

In lieu of a polite greeting, she says, "Did you see the news about Lauren?"

No point in pretending. "Yes, I saw it. Regardless of what she did, it's awful."

She makes a sound I can't decipher. I lock the door behind me and set my bag on the floor beside my desk.

Another sound, this one her throat clearing. "What were you doing at my office?"

I steady myself with a palm on the wall. A three-second blink. "I stopped in to see you, that's all."

"While I'm in Florida."

"I know, I completely forgot," I say. I try to make my words convincing, but I've a suspicion I fail. This is Alexa, after all.

"It's a little strange, don't you think? Your visit and then Lauren dies?"

My knees feel like marshmallow and I stumble to my chair. She can't possibly think I had something to do with it. She knows me. "What are you saying?"

"I'm not saying anything, hopefully, only that the timing seems strange. Strange, too, Corinne finding one of my filing cabinets unlocked."

"Alexa," I say. "How would I unlock your cabinet?"

Silence on the other end. If she knows about the lock defect, my comment is a moot point, but either she doesn't know or doesn't want to say it aloud.

The anxiety I'm feeling gives way to a rush of hot anger heavily laced with guilt. "If you want to know if I hurt Lauren, why not just ask?" I say, unable to keep out my emotions. "Here, let me state it for the record. I. Did. Not. Hurt. Her."

"Heather—"

"No," I snap. "That's what you wanted to know, so now you do. And if that's all you wanted, I have to get ready for my patients."

As soon as she says a weary goodbye, I disconnect the call. Is she going to contact the police? Is Corinne? If either one mentions the unlocked cabinet, the cops might decide I'm a serious suspect. And if they contact me, what will I say? My fingers dig into the chair's arms. I'll tell the fucking truth. I did not kill her.

No, only her daughter.

I cover my mouth to hold in a broken laugh that turns into a wheezing sort of cough. When I get myself under control, my wrist is aching again and it's nearly time for my morning session. I swallow two Advil, grab a notebook and pen, and hightail it to the session room. It's way too warm, and while everyone gets settled in their chairs, I adjust the temperature. Samantha's sitting next to Abby again, with Hannah, the oldest in the group, on her other side.

"Today we're going to talk about changes," I say, balancing my notebook on my knees. "Specifically the changes you'll need to make when you leave here." Groans all around.

"What kind of changes?" Samantha says, leaning far forward, the points of her elbows on her thighs, fingers beneath her chin.

"That's what we're going to figure out. I'm not talking about a full game plan. Think small things, things that might not seem important but can have a big impact."

She flounces back in her seat.

Willfully obtuse, I'd call her comment. Pushing buttons.

Hannah clears her throat. "What Dr. Cole means is *we* need to come up with the answers."

Hannah starts talking again, and I tap my pen on my notebook, letting her voice fade into the background of my mind. I need to come up with a new game plan. No matter who's doing this to me, if they're willing to come into my house, to run me off the road, I should be ready for anything. It's clear they want more than to make me remember. Maybe they want a life for a life. What can I do to stop it? I can watch my back, look over my shoulders, but I can't do either twenty-four/seven. And what if—

A girl jumps to her feet. A chair thuds on its side. Hands grab. An open palm meets a cheek. A girl curses. Shouts. Another girl shrieks. Like a stop-motion film, each thing happens a little too slow, the whole thing a little too unreal. I blink once, twice. Someone's calling my name, begging me to help, to stop it.

I stand, notebook sliding to the floor, and the chaos rushes in full-speed. Samantha has Hannah on the floor, knees pinning her in place, slapping and punching and pulling her hair, yelling names every girl and woman knows too well. Hannah's crying and trying to get away. Abby's grabbing Samantha's arms, attempting to pull her free. The other girls are shouting. I push someone out of the way. Grab for Samantha. But she's an eel coated in olive oil; no matter where I touch, my grip slides right off.

"Get security!" I say to the nearest girl.

It doesn't take long. It also takes forever. By the time the guard arrives and she successfully peels Samantha off Hannah, the latter's cheeks are dark red, one eye is swollen shut, and her lower lip is split, the blood running bright down her chin. She seems dazed. All the girls do, except Samantha. She looks triumphant. Smiling with one side of her mouth, blinking like a milk-fed cat. The guard is holding her tight, but she isn't trying to squirm away. She's standing as if waiting for a bus and doesn't look back when the guard leads her out.

The room smells of sweat, musk, and adrenaline. Abby's by Hannah's side, and when the nurse comes for her, Abby stays behind, standing like a lost child. The other girls are huddled together on the opposite side of the room, and once I have myself under control, I say, "Everything's going to be fine."

One steps forward, looking down at the floor. When she does glance up, it's in tiny increments, and she says, whisper soft, "Why didn't you stop her, Dr. Cole? The things she was saying. Why didn't you make her stop?"

Knives in the gut, those words. I should've been paying attention. Yes, it could've been so much worse, but it shouldn't have happened at all. If I'd been doing my job, it wouldn't have.

From behind me, Nicole says, "Everyone okay?"

My first thought: *I hope she didn't hear what Claire said.* My second: *I hope Claire doesn't repeat it.* My third: *I can't believe I'm even thinking this way.*

"What happened?" Nicole asks.

"Samantha was saying shi—stuff to me," Abby tells Nicole, "and I guess Dr. Cole didn't hear her. Then she tried to hit me, and Hannah grabbed her arm and stopped her. Then Samantha just attacked her."

When Nicole looks at me, I nod my agreement, even though I'm collapsing on the inside. It's all I can do. I should've noticed as soon as things went south. I should've stopped them before things got too far. I should've sent for security faster. It's my fault. One thousand percent. And I can see Nicole thinks so, too.

"Girls, we're going to end the session early, so go ahead to the common areas or to your rooms. I'll talk to each of you a little later." To me, she tips her head, and I follow her to her office.

I sit first. Fingers wrapping the armrests, Nicole lowers herself down. Exhales once she gets there and fixes me with a gaze, all heat and coiled energy. "What the hell happened?"

"One minute we were there, talking, and the next . . ." I rake my fingers through my hair. It sounds like a pitiful excuse. It sounds like a lie.

"And what Abby said? Did you not hear what Samantha was saying?"

"I didn't, I'm sorry. It happened so fast, I didn't realize what was going on. I guess I . . ."

"Wasn't paying attention?"

"I didn't say that."

"Your face said it all." Her mouth twists as though she's bitten a lemon. "I told you to keep an eye on her. I told you she was antagonizing Abby."

"They seemed fine, Nicole. They've even been sitting together. I didn't think it was a problem."

She leans forward. "Then you weren't paying attention."

I open my mouth to deny it, to lie, but I can't do it. I know I'm wearing the truth on my face. This isn't private dysfunction. It's public destruction. Maybe not a nuclear war, but a promise of the chaos to come.

"I did my best to grab her, but . . ." I hold up my wrapped wrist, feeling the flimsiness of the excuse settling like a gauze veil.

When she speaks again, her words are faded at the edges and falling in the middle. "I think it would be a good idea if you took a few weeks off. The worst part of all this is that I knew something was wrong. I thought about pulling you from the sessions but didn't think it was necessary, so this is on me, too."

The knives in my belly twist. "I'm sorry," I say. "I—"

"Please leave all your session notes on your desk before you leave."

"Okay, but—"

"Heather," she says, and the word's a guillotine. "Just go."

There are no notes from today in my notebook. Nothing a few pages back either. I must've used a different one, but when I find another in my bag, there's only a page of circular doodles, another with slashes. I know Nicole. She won't forget her request. But I pack my things as quickly as possible, grateful that her office door is shut when I pass.

I manage to get out of the driveway before the tears hit, but it's a near thing. I manage to drive safely to my office. That, too, is a near thing.

There, I open Cassidy's file, looking for recent notes and finding none. Not from this week or last week or the one previous. There's a sheet with pen marks, that's all. I check another patient's file. Nothing. And they're not the only ones. I can't find any recent notes in any files. I nibble at a cuticle. Tear it free. Do the same with another. This time, there's blood. I forcibly pull my hand from my mouth. I need to get a handle on myself. This isn't okay at all.

I'm not okay.

CHAPTER EIGHTEEN

THEN

I sneaked a can of Coke upstairs—my mom didn't let me have it late—and drank it when I got tired. Reading made me way too sleepy, so I sat on the floor, back against my bed, and listened to my Walkman while waiting for my parents to finish their movie and come upstairs.

I snapped awake with a jolt, headphones and the house silent. Panic made a Greyhound of my heart, but it was only a little after midnight. I slipped on the necklace, and it was strangely heavy, but comfortable, too.

My parents' door was shut, the gap beneath dark. Holding my shoes, I took a step and the floorboard creaked. I froze, but my parents' light stayed off. Baby steps took me downstairs. I was afraid the front door would make too much noise, so I crept down to the basement. Even though I had to wiggle the key in the dead bolt, the back door opened without a sound and closed the same way. Key in pocket, I darted across the backyard. The latch on the gate slipped, clanking shut, and I crouched beside it, my whole body shaking. No lights turned on anywhere, so I lifted the latch again, pinching it tight between my fingers. With only crickets to notice my passage, I ran through the neighborhood to the field. Halfway across, a possum trundled by, hissing at me.

My steps slowed when I got near the house. By the time I sneaked through the hedges, I was practically dragging my feet. The front door was unlocked and the hallway was dark, but there was a pale light in the kitchen from the open basement door. I went down the stairs quietly, but not so quiet she wouldn't know I was there.

She was on the floor with her back to me, her hair in a ponytail. Her pillow and blanket rested near the wall, with a collection of juice boxes and crumpled granola bar and Pop Tart wrappers, a box of vanilla wafers next to them. A few books sat in a pile. A drawing hung on the wall of the two of us from the back, holding hands and walking toward the house.

Along with the basement stink, I smelled dirty feet, sweaty armpits, and unbrushed teeth. I stood perfectly still, afraid it wasn't Becca at all. I tried to say her name, but it stuck in my mouth like peanut butter.

She turned. The grease was gone from her hair. Her clothes were clean, and while circles still marred the skin below her eyes, they weren't as dark. Her eyes were bright, not dull and vacant.

"Have you been sleeping here?" I didn't need to ask; the answer was in front of me.

"Sometimes, when Lauren gets really bad. It's safer here. I was afraid you weren't coming."

"I'm sorry," I said, toeing the carpet. "I fell asleep waiting for my parents."

Her gaze found my necklace. "Best friends?"

I gripped the heart between my finger and thumb. "Forever." I sat, legs crossed. "So what do we have to—"

"Not yet," she said. "Can we just be friends for a while, and talk the way we used to?"

I smiled so wide it made my cheeks sore and I felt like crying, but in a good way. "Sure."

She smiled, too. "Do you remember when Kyle peed his pants in first grade? And said he spilled water from the water fountain?"

"And how mad he got when Mrs. Jackson sent him to the nurse?"

It was silly to remember that after so long, but it was okay, too. We kept talking about kids in school, about books, about music, about everything. Leaning back, arms straight, I thought things would be okay. I didn't think this was the ritual, but it was sort of one all by itself. Maybe it would be enough. I felt like I had my best friend back. Finally.

Then she tucked her knees beneath her chin. "Sometimes I hate everything, but I hate myself most of all, and the feeling never, ever goes away. I want to scream and kick and punch everyone, but I almost don't even care anymore. Anyway, what difference would it make? At the end of the day, I'd still be me. And no one wants me."

I hunched forward, not sure what to say, not sure if I was part of the "no one." But she had to know I wanted her, because I was here with her.

She cocked her head to the side, as if listening. "Okay," she said.

I was afraid she'd start jumping around like she had in her room, but she stayed put. She was almost the old Becca, but different, too. More grown-up, which seemed silly to think. But her eyes were different. Not scared or stormy. Peaceful.

"Okay what?"

She linked her fingers together. "Everything will be okay tomorrow night."

"What do you mean, tomorrow night?"

"Tonight I had to be sure."

"Sure of what?"

"Sure you were really my friend. If not, the ritual won't work." She yawned. "You should go now. It's really late. Want me to walk you home?"

"No, I'll be okay," I said, my voice small.

She walked me upstairs and leaned close at the door. "Promise you'll come back tomorrow night?"

"I promise."

"And you'd do anything I asked, right? If I told you it would help me? Even if it didn't make sense?"

I looked her right in the eye and said, "Yes." I meant it, too.

*　*　*

Sneaking out was easier the second time. I wasn't even scared.

All the trash was gone from the basement. Becca's blanket and pillow, too. Everything save the picture on the wall. She was sitting on a towel inside a circle of unlit candles, her head down, hair loose, a red ribbon as a headband.

"Don't get upset," she said.

"What do you mean?"

She lifted her chin, and I gasped. The skin around her eye was purple and red, and blood was crusted beneath her nose. Her lower lip was split, beginning to scab. I stepped over the candles and dropped to my knees, my hands making frantic designs in the air.

"I went home to change," she said, "and Lauren was there. I didn't do anything. She just started yelling at me and she pushed me down and I fell and she didn't even care."

"Becca—" This was awful in a way I couldn't describe. Her face. How could her mom do that to her? How?

"It doesn't even hurt anymore."

She was lying. She had to be. And I wasn't sad. I was angry, angrier even than when I'd thought Becca hated me. "We can't do nothing. We have to tell some—"

"You promised you wouldn't. You can't take back a promise like that." Her words were calm, but unyielding.

I hung my head. I had promised, but I didn't think I could keep it. Not after seeing her like that. But I'd come up with something so Becca wouldn't know it was me. I'd tell my mom not to say I told her. Even if Becca hated me forever. What her mom was doing wasn't okay at all, and she couldn't just get away with it.

"She tried to save me once when I was little," Becca said.

"Who?" I said.

"The Red Lady, but I didn't know it was her. She used magic to hide her real face. I know now, though. Lauren was too strong then, but she isn't anymore."

"What are you talking about? I don't understand." And I didn't. The Red Lady had tried to save her? When? How? But she wasn't even real.

"It's okay," she said. "We don't have time for me to explain it anyway. There's one last story I have to tell."

I scowled. "But after this, no more, okay? No stories or pictures, like *you* promised?"

"After this, I won't need to."

She lit the candles and turned off the overhead light. Shadows danced on the wall, and soon enough, I could smell only the candles, all fruit–vanilla–pine trees. I sat with my arms and legs crossed, not wanting to hear the story, just wanting it to be over.

"The Red Lady's friend, the one who helped her die fast instead of slow? She left the village in secret. When she came back, everyone was gone. She went to the Red Lady's house and saw her there, waiting. She apologized and cried, saying she should have stopped everyone, she knew it was wrong, but the Red Lady said it was okay, she did what she could, and it was better now because she was stronger. They both were.

"Her friend said she'd tell everyone the whole story so it could never happen again, but the Red Lady said no, she had to promise not to. She didn't want anyone to know. She said no one would believe her, and it was the truth. Then the Red Lady told her to go. When she got to the door, she looked back, but the Red Lady was gone."

I rubbed away goose bumps. "Did she keep her promise not to tell?"

"She did. Because when you make a promise, you keep it forever. She thought about telling the story once and even started to, but stopped before she got to anything important. The next morning there were foot-prints by her bed. She knew it was the Red Lady, reminding her not to ever tell."

"But wasn't the Red Lady her friend?" I said. "She wouldn't have really hurt her, would she?"

"Maybe, maybe not, but she didn't want to take a chance." Becca unfolded a corner of the towel, revealing a plastic baggie filled with red-dish dirt and a small knife. "Don't worry," she said.

"I'm not," I said, but I swallowed hard, my throat sandpaper. The knife had a dark wood handle and a small blade glimmering orange-yellow in the candlelight. My mom used one like it to peel vegetables. "What's the dirt for?"

"It's for later. Remember how the Red Lady will help you, but you have to give something up?"

"Uh-huh," I said.

"She can grant your most secret wish—the one you never tell anybody, not even your best friend—but there's a catch." She bit her lip. "You have to die first."

"That's not funny, Becca." My voice was shaking.

"It's not supposed to be. I wanted to tell you before, but I was afraid you wouldn't come back if you knew." She stretched out on the towel and held out the knife. "You have to be my friend. Best friends forever, you said."

"What are you talking about?"

She pulled up her shirt. Pointed to a spot on her side. "You have to do it right here. Right here exactly."

"What?" I said, the word wavery. "You're kidding, right?"

"I'm not. This is how it has to be done. Trust me, I won't die. I mean, I might, but I'll come back. She'll bring me back and everything will be okay."

"You want me to stab you?" I said. "That . . . no . . . I can't do that." I was angry all over again, my skin hot. It had to be a test, but I wasn't sure what for. Wasn't it obvious I was still her friend? I was here, wasn't I?

She didn't get up. "You said you'd do anything. This is what you have to do. I can't do it by myself. It won't work. It has to be you."

I shook my head so hard my ears rang. She was serious. It wasn't a joke. It wasn't a game. "I can't."

"You have to. You promised you'd help me. She said you would."

"No! I didn't promise to do this." I bent over her, punching the floor next to us. "Please, you don't need her. You have me. I can help you. We can go talk to my mom."

Indecision flickered across her face. Her mouth worked and tears glittered.

"I can help you," I said, pounding the floor again.

She swiped at her eyes with angry hands. "You can't. It's too late. No one can help me. No one but her." She grabbed my wrist. "Don't worry. She promised everything would be okay."

I shook my head, unable to speak, and jumped up. Running, I made it upstairs, down the hallway, to the front door, but as my fingers met the doorknob, a pain in my side drove me to my knees. It was fire and ice, and I couldn't think, couldn't move. It went on and on and on, and when it faded, I was curled into a tiny ball, shaking all over. She wouldn't let me leave. Not until I did what she wanted. Not until I helped Becca.

With quicksand feet, I returned to the basement. Becca hadn't moved.

"I knew you wouldn't leave," she said. "Best friends forever, right?"

I thumbed the pendant. "Best friends forever."

"Don't worry." She held out the knife, and this time, I took it. "This is the way it has to be," she said. "It's the only way it'll work. And you can never tell anyone about tonight. Not ever. Not even when you're an old lady. Promise?"

"I promise." My voice didn't even sound like mine.

"She's here with us," she said. "Can't you feel her? She'll help you do it the right way."

But I felt nothing and no one but Becca lying on the floor and me sitting beside her. Just the two of us. The way it should be.

Then I felt a hand, warm and light, on my shoulder. I moaned but didn't pull away. No one was there, only the air in the basement, but it felt real. It felt more than real. I sniffed back a sudden gush of salty snot.

"See?" Becca said. She sounded birthday-party happy, and it cut me into ribbons. I didn't want to be here anymore. Didn't want to feel the hand on me. She wasn't supposed to be real. I leaned back, away from Becca. The hand on my shoulder pushed me back into place. Snot ran over my upper lip and I shouldered it away.

"Becca, I can't," I said.

"Yes, you can," she said, as the unseen hand moved down my arm, guiding it where it needed to go. "That's it. Now."

"I can't," I said. But I did. I did because the Red Lady made me do it. Because Becca was sure everything would be okay. Because if I didn't, Becca would never be my friend again. There was a pinch of resistance, then the knife slid all the way in. Becca's eyes got wide and she groaned. I did, too. When I pulled the blade free, she blew out all her air. A thin line of blood trickled down her side, the wound an almost-closed mouth smeared with red lipstick. Nothing serious. It only needed a few stitches. I dropped the knife on the towel and started crying because that was a lie. I'd cut her. I'd cut her skin and her insides.

She coughed a little. "It doesn't even hurt. Stay with me, okay? Don't leave me alone. Promise me." She pulled her shirt down to cover the wound, and blood seeped through.

"I won't," I said, clutching her hand. "I promise. I'll stay the whole time. I'll be here when you come back."

"No," she said. "The dirt. Get the dirt."

I pulled the baggie close. "Okay. I have it."

"You have to put it in my mouth. Not yet, but when it's done. And then you have to go."

"I—but . . ." I glanced at her side, at the blood, and felt like I was going to throw up.

"Don't worry. It's how it's supposed to be. I'll be okay," she said, linking her fingers with mine. "Tell me about when we met in kindergarten."

So I told her the story of how I saw her playing by herself. How nobody else wanted to play with her, but I did. How she asked if I would be her friend and I said yes. I was at the part where I introduced her to Rachel and Gia when she said, "Don't forget to put the dirt in my mouth."

"I won't."

"I knew you'd help me," she said. "Please be kind."

"And rewind," I said.

Her eyes fluttered shut and her grip loosened.

"Becca?"

The room was so quiet, it hurt my heart. So heavy it pushed my head forward. Still holding Becca's hand, I tucked my knees to my chest. My pulse was thready, breath coming in little gasps. I wanted to disappear. Wanted to shatter into a million pieces and blow away.

But she'd told me I had to put dirt in her mouth, so I pinched a little bit from the bag, sprinkled it in her half-open mouth. Because I was shaking so bad, some got on her cheeks, too, the red dark against her skin. I wiped it away and tossed the bag near the knife, but I didn't want to go, didn't want to leave her alone. I wanted to be here when she got back.

I held her hand again; her fingers flopped against mine. "Becca, come back. You said she'd bring you back."

The warmth left her body in slow degrees. I sat with her and waited. And waited.

I bent close to her ear. "You have to come back now. Please. Please come back."

Then you have to go, she'd said. After the dirt, I was supposed to go. Maybe that's why she wasn't awake yet. I didn't want to leave her, but I said, "Okay, I'll go. But I'll come back. I promise."

CHAPTER NINETEEN

NOW

I'm holding two bottles of wine—one red, one white—unable to decide which to take to Gia's party. I don't even really want to go. Last night I slept poorly, and my head's still full of fading images of falling into a hole with Becca standing at the edge. There was another dream, too, of the two of us in a shadowy basement, but the less I think about that, the better.

With the bottles left on the kitchen counter, I pad upstairs, intent on removing my makeup and donning pajamas. Ryan will understand. I'll tell him my wrist hurts. Or that I'm still upset about the altercation at Silverstone. Guilt twists in my gut. He knows there was a fight, but not my part in it. He doesn't even know yet that I won't be working there for the time being. At least not from me.

He isn't in our room, but his office door is open a crack. I stand close.

"No," he says. A pause, and, "It's taking longer than expected." Another pause. "By the end of the week."

The door opens.

He looks down as he slips his phone into his pocket, and when he looks back, his lips are set into an easy smile. But worry nestles in his eyes.

"What's up?" I say.

"Just work stuff," he says, kissing my cheek. "You look beautiful."

I'm wearing my new forest-green skinny jeans. A black V-neck. Suede peep-toe ankle boots. Crimson toenails. A ton of concealer to hide the dark circles.

The worry remains, though, and I feel an accusation building. Not that I have a reason or any idea of what to accuse him of, but tension gathers inside me like a storm. I might not want to go to the party, but I don't want to stay home either. Not feeling like this. I'm tired of fighting with him. And with Lauren dead, Gia's back on the suspect list, as ridiculous as that seems, so I can't squander tonight's opportunity.

"Should we take red or white?" I say.

"Red."

We're halfway to Gia's house, Ryan driving us in his truck, when he says, "Can I get a hint?"

"A hint for what?"

"How quickly she forgets," he says, pressing our linked fingers to his chest. "A movie hint, for the one you gave me?"

My mind goes blank. I know I came up with something, but . . . I run my tongue along my bottom teeth. It seems like something I said a lifetime ago. The movie comes back to me, but I've no idea what else to say. I think of various scenes, discarding the obvious choices of electric fences and green Jell-O, and say, "Vomit."

"Vomit?"

"Mmm-hmm."

"You might stump me this time."

"That'd be a first," I say.

When we get close to Gia's, I flip down the visor. My makeup looks as it did when we left. Of course. I slide my hands under my upper thighs. Nip the inside of my lower lip between my teeth.

"You okay?" Ryan says.

"Mmm-hmm."

"You seem nervous."

"Maybe a little anxious. We won't know anyone. What if they're all boring or heavily opinionated or drunk and belligerent?" I add good humor to my voice.

"If they're terrible, we'll leave. Sound like a plan?"

It does. But my fingers dig into the backs of my legs.

Gia's curtains are open, lights bright and welcoming, matched by the cheery message on the mat. I square my shoulders as I knock. A stranger opens the door, and Gia comes running, giving me a hug first, then Ryan. She's in dark jeans and a paisley shirt. Flats with lacing at the ankles. She turns to the room, to the dozen people milling there. "Everyone, this is Heather, who I've known since we were kids, and her husband, Ryan. Ryan, Heather, this is everyone."

People say hello or wave and Gia leans close. "I'm sorry I'm not introducing them all individually, but I can't remember some of their names." She points toward a table in the corner topped with a collection of liquor bottles. "Trying not to create too many bottlenecks, so mixers are there, and there's beer in a cooler on the back deck."

I try to picture this woman behind the wheel of a battered Chevy and fail. I try again. Fail a second time.

Ryan holds up the wine.

"Wine's in the kitchen. Follow me," she says over her shoulder. "And you can meet my husband, Spencer."

The downstairs layout is fairly simple—living, dining, kitchen, small family room in the back, half bath. A staircase to the left of the front door. No basement, common in houses in Annapolis. It's decorated in shades of gray with bright splashes of color—teal throw pillows; sea-glass-green tablecloth in the dining room, almost completely covered with bowls and trays of food; a glossy red Keurig on the kitchen counter.

I recognize her husband from the Facebook photos as he extends a hand. Gia gives us two wine glasses and leaves us in the kitchen while she greets another arrival. Spencer tells us to please eat, so we wander into the dining room, where other folks are piling food onto heavy-duty paper plates. Deli meats, baked ziti, Caesar salad, fruit salad, Caprese skewers. Tortilla chips, salsa, guacamole. A massive charcuterie tray. And a sideboard filled with a whole slew of desserts.

Ryan and I eat and exchange pleasantries with the other guests. Most are coworkers. One couple lives next door. The conversation rises and falls, a roller coaster of thoughts, opinions, and random observations. Expressions hold polite interest. I visit the half bath, which is clean enough to dine in, and peek in the cabinet under the sink. Extra rolls of toilet paper, bowl cleaner, a packet of what Ryan calls butt wipes. Advil, Band-Aids, tweezers, and Neosporin in the medicine cabinet. I soap off the guilt. Even if Gia's the least likely suspect, there's no harm in looking.

When I return, Ryan's nowhere in sight, and I wander around until I catch sight of him through a sliding-glass door. He and Spencer are chatting up a storm, so I refill my wine glass and step out a side door to a small empty porch with three steps leading down. The closed door dulls the hum of voices. It's verging on cold tonight, but I don't mind. Out here I don't have to feign good nature. Only a few minutes pass before Gia comes out with a glass of her own.

"An escapee!" she says.

"Catching some air," I say.

She plants herself on the middle step. "Yeah, more people came than expected, even a bunch who said they weren't coming, and it's getting crowded."

When I sit, she scoots even closer so we're crowded together like kids. I want it all to be real. Our reconnecting. Our growing friendship. It has to be. She couldn't fake the sort of kindness she's shown. Something would give it away. Leaning against each other, we sit for a time talking about Annapolis and such, and then, her glass empty, she says, "I'd better get back in before Spencer comes to find me."

After a few minutes, I return myself. Don't want to be too conspicuous with my absence. The conversations seem louder, the cheer more boisterous. I leave my glass on the counter. Weave through the rooms to the staircase. The bathroom on the second floor is done in black and white, and all the bedroom doors are open, which makes finding the master easy. Shoving my guilt into a small, dark place inside me, I close the door almost all the way, blocking the view from the hallway. The tops of the dressers are uncluttered. The nightstands as well. There are two closets. Men's clothes, men's shoes in the first. In the second, Gia's. I don't even know what I'm looking for.

I hear voices, flick off the closet light, and position myself behind the bedroom door. I keep still, but it's only a few people waiting for the restroom. Doesn't take long for them to finish. The doorbell rings as I'm halfway down the stairs, and in steps a gray-haired man. The same man who knocked on my car window when I came to Gia's neighborhood. I swear he's even wearing the same blue polo.

I will him to look in any direction but mine. Will him to walk toward the kitchen. But he remains by the front door, surveying the crowd. A few people glance at him with mild curiosity. A couple in the far corner wave. He does the same in response. Just when I think I've bypassed the inspection, his gaze locks on mine.

Shit.

Shit, shit, shit.

I can't tell if that's recognition or not. Tongue sticking to the roof of my mouth, I continue down and aim for the small porch again. A few people are already there, so I wander to the larger back porch and find Ryan with Gia's husband and several others, talking movies. There's another smaller group on the opposite side of the deck talking politics.

The door opens again and the man in the polo emerges. I move closer to Ryan, and he slips an arm around my waist. The newcomer joins the other group. From time to time he glances over; I do my best to look involved in the conversation. I'm about two minutes from asking Ryan if he's okay with leaving when the man in the polo walks over. The group opens to let him join.

Go back inside, I silently will. *Leave us alone. Leave me alone.*

"I'm Gus," he says. "I'm in charge of the Neighborhood Watch here."

Peachy. Just my luck. I pocket my fingers to keep them from wandering to my mouth. Everyone else does a quick introduction. Ryan takes care of us both. The conversation returns to movies; this time, horror. I do my best to tune them out.

Cupping my elbow, Ryan leans close to my ear. "You okay?"

"I'm a little tired," I say. "Maybe we can go soon?"

He looks surprised but says, "Sure."

Gia comes out, arms outstretched for a hug. "I'm so glad you came tonight," she says.

"How do you two know each other?" another woman—Eileen, Ellen?—asks.

"We grew up in the same neighborhood," Gia says. "And after Spencer and I moved here, we ran into each other at the bookstore. Talk about wild, right?" She beams at me.

"Definitely wild. Hey, I'm going to get more wine," I say, brandishing my almost-empty glass. "Anyone else need a refill?"

I duck into the house and take my time, rinsing my glass and drying it with a paper towel before examining the bottles. I've finished pouring a red blend when there's movement beside me. Gus, standing a touch too close for comfort.

"Still thinking of moving here?" he says.

"Excuse me?" I say, painting my features with confusion as I step back.

"You said you were thinking of moving here."

"Sorry, I don't know what you're talking about."

His eyes narrow. "I don't forget faces, especially one like yours. You were sitting outside in your car a couple weeks ago and I knocked on the window."

I shake my head. "You have me mistaken for someone else."

"You drive a black Jeep, right?"

"Whoever you're talking about, it wasn't me." There's a touch of amusement in my words to make it convincing. My palms are damp, though. Armpits as well.

"I'm not in the business of lying."

"Didn't say you were, but you're mistaken." I'm trying to stay calm, but there's a quaver in my voice, and heat splotches my cheeks and sternum.

"No, I don't think so," he says, moving even closer and blocking the way.

"Excuse me, do you mind?" I lift my glass. "I'd like to pass by."

"I remember you, remember what you said."

I say nothing.

"What kind of game are you playing?" he says. His gaze bores into mine. His foul breath pushes into my face. "I know it was you."

I'm so tired of it all. Tired of this man, his suspicious eyes, his reeking mouth. Tired of the bullshit and my aching wrist. Tired of everything. I step forward, forcing him to take one back. "So what the fuck if I did? It's no crime to park on the street. Did I hurt anyone? No. So why don't you back the fuck off, asshole."

He recoils, mouth working silently. He definitely wasn't expecting that. Over his shoulder, I spy Gia standing at the entrance of the kitchen. One hand touches her lips, the other palms the doorframe. A little behind her, Ryan, his brows arced into sideways commas.

"Heather?" Gia says. "What's going on?"

Fuck. How much did she hear? How much did they fucking hear?

Gus crosses his arms. "She was sitting in her car outside on the street a couple weeks ago, right before the big yard sale. Just sitting. Said she wanted to move here. She didn't like me talking to her, that's for sure. Wasn't happy to be seen, and she hightailed it out. I should've gotten her license plate number—that would prove it—but she drove too fast." He points, then turns to Gia. "And now she's here in your house? Doesn't that bother you at least a little bit? 'Cause it bothers me."

Gia says, brow creased, "I don't understand."

She's glancing from Gus to me and back again. I open my mouth to speak, to tell her it's a misunderstanding, and Gus speaks over me, burying my reply.

"You two just *happened to run into each other* at the bookstore, you said. You sure about that?" Gus says, spittle in the corner of his lips. "Maybe you did, maybe you didn't, but when I told her I remembered her sitting outside, she said it wasn't her, then she admitted it and told me to fuck off. You heard that part."

Gia's eyes meet mine again.

"So why not tell us why, huh?" He rounds on his heels, jabbing a finger toward me, almost touching me between my breasts. "Why were you here?"

"Okay, I think that's enough," Ryan says, stepping around Gia to grasp Gus by the upper arm. "This is between them, okay?" Gus snorts and tugs his arm, but Ryan doesn't let go.

When Gia and I are alone, she blinks away the sheen of tears. She can't blink away her expression, though. It's the look of a dog expecting a treat and getting a kick; a child anticipating ice cream but being sent to their room. In that moment, I know she had nothing to do with the necklace, with any of it.

"Gia, I—"

"The big yard sale was before we ran into each other. Was that meeting an accident, or did you already know I was here in Annapolis?"

"I can explain," I say. "Really, this is just . . . Gus is blowing it all out of proportion."

She runs her thumb along the counter. "I think maybe you should go."

I step closer. "But if you let me—"

"I said go, Heather," she says, her words painted with anger. "I don't understand this, but I don't want you here right now."

"Okay," I say. "I'm sorry, I'll go."

Ryan's waiting by the front door. I pretend not to hear the whispers, not to see the looks, as I make my way, but my face is hot. Gus is near the steps, wearing a smug frat-boy smirk. I'd love to walk over and slap him. How dare he. How fucking dare he.

We drive out of Gia's neighborhood in silence, and at the first light, Ryan says, "What the hell was that about?"

"I wasn't doing anything wrong," I say, tapping my knuckles on the window.

"But you were sitting outside her house?"

"It's not how it sounds."

"I hope not, because it sounds irrational. It sounds like something—"

I slam both palms on the dashboard. "I don't want to fucking talk about it!"

"Jesus Christ, Heather. It's like I don't even know you anymore."

"Oh, please," I spit. "I'm not the one sneaking around in my suit going to secret meetings."

"What are you talking about?"

"My mother saw you on Wednesday at Grinds," I say, because obviously I haven't done enough damage today. "You were dressed up. In your suit."

He scratches his chin. "Not sure what you want me to say."

"How about the truth?" I say.

"Are you kidding me? You want to talk about the truth right now?"

"Since when do you wear a suit to work?" I say. "And why didn't you say anything about seeing Mom? Why did I have to hear it from her? Why are you being secretive about the phone calls you're getting and so evasive about the missing check? Not to mention going behind my back with Nicole. Seems like every time I turn, there's something else." There's too much anger painting my words, shading the syllables wrong.

A muscle twitches in his jaw. "Am I hearing this right? What exactly are you accusing me of?"

"Why were you wearing a suit, Ryan? What are you hiding from me?"

Irritation shifts the planes of his face. "Fine. Yes, I talked to Nicole. I already told you I shouldn't have. I already apologized. I haven't talked to you any more about the Kanes' check because it hasn't shown up. And yeah, I saw your mom at the coffee place. Yeah, I was wearing my suit because I went on a goddamn job interview."

"A what?" The word holds the ghost of humor.

"A job interview," he says.

"But you own your company."

"Yeah, I do," he says. "But I've been thinking of closing up shop, letting someone else handle the business end of things."

"But," I say, "you've worked so hard for so long, I don't understand. Why would you want to work for someone else? You've never said anything. Isn't this something we should talk about or—"

"Heather, there are a lot of things we haven't talked about lately. I didn't say anything about this because you've been so stressed and distracted and I didn't want to add any more," he says. "But right now, I don't want to talk about it. I don't want to talk about anything. I just want to get home."

"But I—"

"Please." The word slices the air.

He turns on the radio. I stare out into the night. And the space between us grows larger and larger.

*   *   *

Sunday is a study in polite replies and pauses heavy with all the things we're not saying. I try to bring up the job interview once, and he says, "Not now, please." I let it go. Maybe it's better this way. It gives us both time to think. I still can't believe he didn't say anything about his job. He always talks to me about things like that. Always.

Dropping my car off at the dealer and picking up a loaner takes less time than I expect. Since I sent Ellie an email letting her know I'd be late, I stop at Starbucks, but even after a cup of coffee and a scone, I'm earlier to the office than planned. The main office door is unlocked, but Ellie's not at her desk and Christina isn't here yet.

I stand in the hallway, staring down at my office door, my half-open office door. There's a shuffle of papers, a sliding drawer. Someone's in there, going through my files. I stand still, clutching the strap of my bag. Did Alexa call the police? Thank god I deleted the picture of Lauren's address. But if the police are here . . .

Hello hangs on my tongue, but I don't let it go. No way this is the police. There'd be an officer stationed by the door. If they were investigating me, this isn't how it would happen. So who the hell is in my office and what do they want? I don't keep anything personal there.

Are they looking for the half-heart necklace? It's safe, locked in the top drawer of my desk. Safe, unless they know how to pick locks or have a key.

I take baby steps. By the time I draw near, my heart is a painful knot in my chest, my fingers clenched so tight they hurt. Beneath the elastic bandage, my wrist is thumping. From inside my office, there's another rattle of paper, a sniff, a soft murmur. I can't take it anymore. I rush forward and peek round the doorframe to see—

My receptionist sitting on the floor next to my cabinet, crying with a file open on her lap. What the hell? Yes, she has spare keys in case of an emergency, but she typically waits for me to unlock everything.

"Ellie?"

She jumps to her feet, swiping away the moisture on her face, holding the file tight at her side, the triangled corners of several pages jutting from the manila folder.

"Dr. Cole," she says. "Hi, I didn't think you'd be here so soon."

"It didn't take as long as I thought. What are you doing in my office?" I say. "Whose file is that?"

"I'm . . ." She looks down.

I close the space between us with wide steps and snatch the file, enjoying her slight recoil. It belongs to a former patient, Kerry Wallace, who committed suicide several years ago.

"Why were you looking at this?" I say. Ellie's perfume is cloyingly sweet, and I want her out of my office. But I also want an explanation.

"I wasn't. I was putting away another file and dropped that one, so I had to pick it all up and reorganize it. It was easier to just sit down." Inching her way toward the door, she wipes at her reddened eyes. "Sorry, my allergies are acting up."

Is that what I saw? Something doesn't feel right. "Wait, please," I say, stopping her in the doorway.

She turns slowly.

"What file were you putting away?" I say. She toes the carpet. She knows I know she's lying. "Just tell me the truth."

Her shoulders slump as she exhales. "There wasn't a file. I came in to look at Kerry's, to read the notes. I was hoping I'd be done before you got here. I'm sorry. I know I shouldn't have, but I just wanted a quick look."

I frown, my top lip curling. "I don't understand. Why would you want to read my notes?"

"Because Kerry is—was—my cousin," she says.

Confusion gives way to a bit of clarity. "Your cousin was my patient?"

"Yes," she says. "I wanted to ask you about her, but I was afraid. And I knew you couldn't legally tell me anything."

"Is that why you took the job here?"

She shakes her head hard enough to pendulum her ponytail. "No, uh-uh. I promise. I swear I didn't know at first you were her doctor. My aunt never said your name. A few weeks ago I was at her house and I saw an old calendar. Your name was there, and so I . . ."

I gesture to the chair and she takes it, gaze down at her folded hands. When I unlock my desk, the half-heart is in the top drawer, chain coiled around it, as I left it. "So you decided to sneak in here this morning and read her file," I say.

Her chin jerks up. She swallows. "I . . . yes." The tip of her shoes makes another small circle on the floor. "I tried to look a couple other times, too," she says, emotion thickening her words. "I thought you knew—I left dirt on the rug because I knocked my plant over like you did that one time and stepped in the mess—but then you didn't say anything, so I . . . I know it was wrong, but Kerry's parents, my aunt and uncle, it tore them apart. I thought if I could find something, anything, maybe it would help. I don't know. I wasn't thinking, not really. I just—"

"Take a deep breath," I say. "Now take another. Good."

"I'm sorry, I'm so sorry. I just wanted to do something." She holds out her arms, lets them fall back down.

"Sometimes there isn't anything anyone can do," I say, as kindly as I can.

"The kids at her school were cruel, and nothing ever happened to them. Nothing." Ellie's words dissolve into tears.

The kids *were* cruel. I remember the hurt in Kerry's eyes when we spoke of them. A hurt she couldn't escape. I remember hating the kids who'd wounded her so. I also remember reminding myself they were children, too. I offer Ellie a tissue and close my office door. Twenty minutes later, I have her smiling through her pain. Stories about her cousin in happier days. Stories that can't erase what happened but remind her Kerry's life hadn't always been terrible. By this point, Ellie's gone through half a box of tissue, and she surprises me with a hug. I stand with stick-figure arms, then embrace her back.

"Thank you so much, Dr. Cole, and I'm so sorry I didn't tell you the truth."

"It's okay," I say.

When she leaves, I sit cradling my wrist. Maybe I should still be mad at her for sneaking in, but I'm more relieved that I helped her. A sudden wash of sorrow fogs my vision. How long has it been since I felt this way?

*   *   *

When I come back from lunch, sitting in the middle of my desk is a small package the size of a trade paperback, wrapped in brown paper. Generic brown paper. Black ink. Now-familiar handwriting. Inside the box, beneath a mound of crumpled tissue paper, is a book. A simple thing of construction paper folded in half and stapled unevenly along the edge. On the front cover in red magic marker: THE WITCH BY REBECCA LILIAN THOMAS AND HEATHER MARIA COLE.

The edges are ragged; a corner of the back cover is missing. The interior pages are in better shape but wear the passage of time with rips, creases, water stains. I don't remember this particular book or story, but it's unmistakably ours. We must've been only seven or eight when we made it. Her drawings, my writing, but she was the storyteller; I was the scribe.

The writing is legible, barely.

Once upon a time there was a witch. Her real name was Sarah. Everyone was mean to her. They ignored her. One day she got sick and died. No one came to her funeral. Then everyone got sick and started to die, too. When there was only one person left, someone

came into the room. It was the witch! She was alive the whole time!
She killed everyone because she was so mad!

I half laugh, half sigh. The drawing on the last page shows a witch in a typical pointed hat, standing in a graveyard, her long hair coiled on the ground beside her. The precursor to Becca's later stories, the drawing in my desk, and all the others I recall. The genesis of the Red Lady, here in old ink. A story. Just that and nothing more.

I gather up the torn brown paper, and there's a blank space where a postmark should be. I turn the rest of the paper over and over. No post-mark at all.

I practically run down the hallway and skid to a stop in reception. "Ellie, the package on my desk, was it delivered?"

"A woman dropped it off for you a little while ago. She said she was a friend."

"Did she leave her name?" I say, my entire body rigid.

Ellie bites her lip. "No, sorry, I should've asked, but then the phone rang and I—"

"What did she look like?"

"Is—"

I thump a fist on the edge of her desk. "What did she look like!"

She blinks fast. "She was sort of short and thin and had blonde hair to about here." She taps the middle of her upper arm. "She was wearing—"

"When did she drop it off?"

"Um, about ten minutes or so, I think." She glances at the wall clock. "Yes, ten minutes, because I looked at the clock right before she came in."

The air feels as thick as an August day.

"Dr. Cole, is something wrong? Should I—"

But I'm halfway out the door. I jab the elevator button, hiss air through my teeth, and decide on the stairs, my heels clattering all the way. Short with blonde hair? It sounds like—

This isn't possible. It isn't.

Under a sky the color of an old wool blanket, I scan the sea of cars in the lot. A man in a gray suit; a red-haired woman in a floral dress; an older couple walking together, a dark-blue folder under the man's arm. My feet kick pebbles as I hit the nearest row, peeking in cars. I see pale hair in a driver's seat and stumble to a halt by a green Honda. The door opens. A woman emerges, all highlighted waves and red lipstick.

Ignoring her frown, I start moving again, blood rushing in my ears. A car pulls out of the lot, spewing a wide fan of gravel, and I squint, trying to discern the driver's shape, but the sedan moves too quickly into the flow of traffic. I walk the bumper lines, glancing from left to right.

Then I feel someone watching. Not a passing glance but a stare, a magnet drawing my gaze across the four lanes of traffic on Route 100. And there, standing near a café, a petite woman with pale hair. In spite of the weather, she's wearing a pair of dark sunglasses.

I break into a run, adrenaline thrumming in my veins. The blonde doesn't move. I reach the end of the lot. Now only a bit of grass, a sidewalk, and four lanes of moving traffic separate us. I step off the curb, but pull back as a car nears. This time of day, traffic chokes the air with exhaust and the rhythmic hum of tires on asphalt. The woman remains where she is. *Becca* remains where she is. Because it's her.

But I killed her.

A childish giggle escapes my throat. My stomach churns with disbelief, shock, elation, and I breathe her name. How is this even possible? I blink, but she's flesh and blood, not a mirage. I wave, the small gesture laden with hope and trepidation. She doesn't wave in return, but she wouldn't stand there if she didn't see me. Didn't know me.

Finally, she nods. Tears pricking my eyes, I do the same. The world falls silent. No rushing cars, no distant rumble of airplanes, nothing at all save two women who were the best of friends when they were girls. It feels like a million years ago. It feels like yesterday.

I point toward the light less than fifty yards away, hoping she'll understand, hoping she'll wait until I can cross. A hundred questions crowd my mind, each pushing to the front of the line.

She touches the side of her glasses, and I go all-over cold. I see an eyebrow, the top of an eyelid. My lips part, the word *stop* on my tongue, but I swallow instead, scared and confused at my reaction. At the hot sweat dampening my body. At every last hair now standing on end. I barely understand it, but I don't want to look in her eyes.

They'll find you in the morning with a mouth full of dirt.

An old pickup truck the color of hammered steel pulls out of the lot on her left and trundles by, obscuring Becca from view, and when it passes, she's gone.

The spell shatters like an elbow to the gut. No. She can't be gone. Not now. Not yet. I run toward the light, the distance stretching in cinematic slow motion, every click of my heel on the sidewalk echoing in my head. All the while, I steal glances at the café and its parking lot, even when I'm too far to see anything but the side of the building. There's still no sign of Becca, but I know I saw her. I know she was there.

Inside, I'm a tangle of fear, worry, excitement, and a dozen other emotions swirling too fast to name, all fighting for dominance and threatening to pull me under. I push them away and focus on moving.

"Come on, come on," I say as I wait for the light to change, shaking out my fingers. As soon as the walk symbol illuminates, I'm moving again, the fabric of my pants whisking between my thighs, my gaze darting back and forth from road to café, café to road. My shoe pinches the baby toe of my left foot and I'm gasping for air, but I slow only when I draw close enough to touch the brick. Through the plate-glass windows, I see the employees in their matching green polos and a few customers. Catch a flash of pale hair in the far corner, but as I crane my neck, the patron turns her head to reveal wrinkles and sagging jowls.

She isn't in the parking lot either. I start scanning the windows of the cars. How could she disappear? It didn't take me that long to cross the street, but even as the thought resolves, I know it was time enough to get in a car and drive away. And if she left via the exit in the back, I wouldn't have been able to see her go. I wring my hands. Why wouldn't she stay?

I run into the café and go up and down the aisles between the tables, checking every seat. No blonde hair. No Becca. At the counter, I clear my throat. "Did anyone see a woman, short with blonde hair, a few minutes ago?"

Heads shake, shoulders shrug.

"Please, it's important!" My words are sharp with panic.

"No, I didn't see anyone," the woman behind the counter says. She looks at her coworker, then back to me. "Is everything okay? Should we call 911?"

I smooth my palms together. "No, no, it's nothing like that, sorry," I say. "I had someone leave my office upset. I thought they came here. Thank you." I say, exiting before she can say anything else.

I run back to my office, ignoring Ellie's "Is everything all right?" With the door locked, I pace back and forth. Becca. Alive. Why didn't she stay? Why didn't she want to talk? Was she even here? I choke down nervous laughter. I know who I saw and my eyes aren't liars. Becca's alive. She's been alive the entire time. How? How did she get out of the basement? Where did she go? Did someone help her? I need to talk to someone. I need to tell them what I saw. Instinctively, I think of Ryan, but I can't. He won't understand.

My mom picks up on the second ring. "I saw her, Mom. I saw Becca. She was here, right across the street." I'm sobbing as I speak, choking out the words.

There's silence on the other end, then she says, "Heather, this isn't funny."

"I'm not trying to be funny. It's not a joke. I saw her."

"Stop it, Heather. Stop it right now, I mean it."

"I swear, Mom. I swear on my life. It was her. It was Becca. She's alive. She's okay."

"Heather, you need to get hold of yourself. I have no idea why you're harping on this, on her, but you need to stop."

"Would you fucking listen to me! I saw Becca and she. Is. Alive!"

More silence, but of a different kind. The call's been disconnected. I call back, but it goes straight to voice mail. I toss my phone aside. I shouldn't be surprised. How could she understand? She didn't see Becca.

Before my next patient's arrival, I check out the window, scanning the lot and the street, just in case. I flip through the book again, inhaling the memories. I do the same after the patient leaves, too. And before and after the next one as well until, somehow, it's the end of the day. I stand by my car for a long time, waiting and hoping. No Becca, though.

When I walk in the house, Ryan's sitting in the breakfast nook, a letter open before him, elbows on the table, upper body curled over, his face serious. But I'm sure he's fine. He's always fine.

"You'll never guess what happened today," I say, gripping the top rail of one of the chairs, barely pausing between words. "It's the strangest, most amazing thing, and—"

"When were you going to tell me?" he says, his voice thick.

"Tell you what?" I say.

"That you want a divorce?"

My hands tighten, the force momentarily lifting the front legs. "What are you talking about?"

He picks up the sheet of paper, heavy stock with an embossed logo. "This. From your fucking attorney. Asking if you've gathered the rest of the requested information yet. The *rest* of the information? That sounds pretty clear-cut to me."

A letter from Rachel's firm. Today of all days. "I can explain," I say, reaching forward.

He yanks the paper away. "I'm sure you can," he says. "It all makes perfect sense now, the way you've been acting, how you've been treating me. Never in a million years did I think things would end like this, that you wouldn't even say a goddamn word. I didn't even know you were that unhappy. Why didn't you just talk to me? Why?"

"Please, listen to me. Yes, I went to see her, but only because I knew her when I was a kid. I needed to see what she was like now and I wasn't sure how else to do it." I touch his hand, but he pulls away. "It sounds ludicrous, but someone's been following me, and the other night when I crashed the Jeep, someone tried to run me off the road. Then today, an old book was delivered to my office and it was from my friend I told you about. The one with the alcoholic mom. I didn't tell you that she went to jail for killing her, for killing my friend, but she isn't dead, like I thought. She isn't." My words rush and crash, and even I can tell the story's tangled and doesn't make sense, but if I can just get him to listen to me, it'll be okay. We'll be okay.

He shakes his head. "Are you even listening to yourself? What you're saying makes no sense. You're being followed? Your dead friend isn't dead?" He waves the letter again. "And this isn't real? Jesus Christ, I don't even know what to say."

"Please, none of this is what you think. It's not. I don't want a divorce. I've never wanted a divorce. I went there for her, not for us."

Palms out, he backs toward the front door. "Stop it. Just stop. I've been as patient as I can be, but I'm done. I have nothing left."

Then I see the duffel bag on the floor. Its implication falls like a ton of bricks.

"You're leaving? But the letter— Please, I told you, I don't want a divorce." I can barely get the words between my tears. "I went there for . . . for research. Rachel, she's the lawyer, I needed to see her and there was no other way. That's why I was outside Gia's, too. Please don't leave. I need your help. Please."

There's a hush between us, and his face shifts from anger to confusion and back again. "I can't stay. I'm sorry. I love you, but I can't. I'll call you in a few days and we can maybe talk when we're calm." But there's a look I've never seen. Disbelief. In me.

After he leaves, the silence in the house is deafening.

CHAPTER TWENTY

THEN

I didn't feel good, so I stayed in my room all day. Mom took my temperature, said I had a slight fever, and brought me chicken soup I couldn't eat. I wanted to stay in bed, but after my parents were asleep, I sneaked out through the basement once more.

Becca had to be awake by now. I hoped she wouldn't be mad because I'd waited until now to come back. I was halfway across the field when I heard footsteps. I crouched super low and listened hard, but heard nothing else. When I stood up, I didn't see anyone either. But I felt like someone was there, watching me.

What if Becca had just been playing a game the whole time? The knife could've been fake. The blood, too. What if they were all trying to trick me? With each step, I got angrier and angrier, stomping through the grass, swinging my arms. If it was a trick, it would be one of the meanest ones ever and I wouldn't talk to her again for a long time. Wouldn't talk to any of them.

The basement was dark, so I turned on the overhead light. Walked like a little kid down the stairs, one foot down and then another on the same stair. The candles had burned down to nothing. Becca was in the same place, the same position. She looked like she was sleeping.

"Becca?" I said, steeling myself for the jump up, the *Gotcha!*

She didn't move.

"This isn't funny anymore," I said.

I counted to twenty, then crossed the room and knelt beside her. Her shirt was stuck to her skin, the blood dried to a hard brown crust. When I touched her arm, it was like ice. I yanked my hand away. Scrubbed my eyes. Touched her again. Poked her with a finger. Poked a second time, even harder. She didn't flinch, didn't do anything because—

No, no, no, no. She'd said she would come back. She'd said the Red Lady would bring her back. I shook her arm. "Becca, please. You have to open your eyes now. I'm here, so you can wake up now."

Even if she jumped up and scared me, I'd forgive her. I'd forgive her anything if she would just open her eyes. But she didn't move. Didn't blink. Didn't breathe.

Because she was dead.

I pulled away with a hiss and covered my mouth. She was dead. I'd killed her and now she was dead. Hands still over my mouth, I rocked back and forth on my heels. She couldn't be dead. Not Becca. Not my best friend.

With a loud shriek, I jumped to my feet. "She said you'd help her! Please, you have to help her. You have to bring her back." I turned in a circle, peering past the flickers of light into the shadows beyond. "She believed in you," I shouted, not caring if anyone heard. "She said you'd help her. She said you'd save her. You lied to her. You lied!"

I crouched by Becca's side and shook her again. And again and again and again. She had to come back. She had to.

But she didn't.

She was never coming back.

I let her go and cried until my chest ached. Until my shirt was slicked with snot. Until I had no more tears to cry.

The Red Lady had tricked her. She'd tricked us both.

My shoulders sagged. And nobody was going to believe me. I'd go to jail, and I'd never see my parents again. I'd never see anyone.

Becca weighed a lot less than me, so I could pick her up, but I wasn't sure where to take her. Back to her house? But I couldn't do that. Her mom would see me.

Could I hide her in the field? I scraped wax off the side of a candle and flicked it off my fingers. I gathered the rest, shoving them in her backpack, on top of a bunch of folded clothes and a wad of money. I took down the picture, folded it, and put it in the backpack, too. People would think she ran away from home. I picked up the knife, staring at the blood crusted on the blade.

Becca's fingers twitched. With mine splayed on the carpet, I crouched beside her, weight on the balls of my feet.

"You came back," I said. "It worked. It really worked."

But she didn't move again. My stomach tightened. "Becca?"

The room grew heavy with the smell of a hundred wet pennies, and I was suddenly sure someone else was there. *She* was there.

Don't look in her eyes!

I squeezed mine shut. My chest was a tornado, my heart a tiny building in its spiral. I couldn't move, couldn't think.

Don't look in her eyes, don't look, don't look!

I staggered toward the stairs, arms waving in protective arcs. My foot banged against a riser; my elbow struck the railing. I caught a sliver of light and clamped my lids even tighter. I crawled up, palms and soles slapping against the wood, my shins striking every edge. When I was halfway up, I heard something like a laugh or a cry, but it wasn't Becca.

I didn't stop. And I didn't look back.

I paused in the field, trying to catch my breath, still gripping the knife. I threw it down with a cry and turned back toward the house. But I couldn't go back. And I couldn't leave the knife. Kneeling, I dug a hole just deep enough, tossed it in, and covered it back up.

Then I ran the rest of the way home. Stood at the kitchen sink, my flesh speckled with dirt and dried blood. I used the pot scrubber and dish soap, and red swirled into the water. Even after it ran clean, I kept washing, expecting my parents to wake and come see what I was doing. Inside I was cold. Empty.

Skin burning, I crept to my room, climbed into bed, and pulled the covers over my head. The Red Lady had lied, and I didn't understand why. I'd done what Becca said she wanted. And she *had* been there. I'd felt her. I hadn't pushed the knife in by myself. I couldn't have done that to Becca. I couldn't.

She was my best friend.

* * *

I didn't remember hardly anything for the next few days because I had a fever so bad my mom kept putting cold cloths on my forehead, chest, and neck. I had lots of bad dreams, the kind that disappear as soon as you wake up. I guess my mom talked to my dad about taking me to the hospital, but then my temperature dropped. When she told me Becca was missing and a police officer wanted to ask me questions, I was in bed, holding a book but not reading.

"What do you mean, she's missing?" I said, my voice as dry and cracked as the corners of my lips.

"I'm sure everything's fine," Mom said, but her face didn't match her words.

Blanket clutched round my shoulders, we went downstairs. Mom held my arm the entire way. Did the police already know what had happened? Were they going to arrest me right now, even though I was sick?

By the time we reached the bottom step, my mouth was so parched I didn't think I'd be able to speak at all. But the police officer smiled when I sat next to her on the sofa. She was sort of young and pretty and was wearing regular clothes, not a uniform. She had on a jacket, too, probably to hide her gun and handcuffs so they wouldn't scare me. Or so I wouldn't think that's why she was here.

"Heather, I'm Detective Harris. Thank you for coming downstairs. I know you're not feeling well. We're trying very hard to find your friend, and I want to ask you a few questions, okay?"

"Okay," I said.

"Can you tell me the last time you saw Rebecca?"

I peeled my tongue from the roof of my mouth. "She doesn't like her whole name. She goes by Becca," I said.

"Okay, thank you," Detective Harris said. "When was the last time you saw Becca?"

"I don't know," I said, staring at my lap. "It was a while ago."

"July," Mom said. "It was in July."

The police officer gave her a side-eye, and Mom cleared her throat, cheeks pink.

"My mom's right. We kind of stopped hanging out." It wasn't completely a lie. I pulled the blanket up to my neck, turtled down into the fabric, and told Detective Harris how Becca had started hanging out with just Rachel and Gia. I kept thinking she was going to call me a liar, but she didn't. She just listened, and her believing me was almost worse. She asked about places Becca might go, and I told her about the playground and how sometimes we'd had picnics in the field. I told her she'd spent the night at our house a lot, my voice trapped halfway in tears and snot.

"I only have a few more questions," she said. "Did you ever see her mom hurt her?"

I shook my head; I was crying too hard to talk. I wasn't lying either. I'd never seen her do that. I'd only seen what it looked like after.

"Did you ever see bruises or other marks on her?"

I pulled my voice free from the tears and said, "Sometimes."

"Did she tell you how she got them?"

I went still. *You can't ever tell anyone about her.* And I'd promised I wouldn't.

"She said she fell down or bumped into a cabinet," I said.

"Can you think of anything else that might help us find Rebe—Becca?"

I hunched down even more. "Uh-uh."

"Okay, I think that's all I need right now. Thank you very much for talking to me, and I hope you feel better soon. I promise, we're doing everything we can to find Becca, okay?"

I wiped my cheek on the blanket. The truth fizzed inside me, salt on a slug. Why couldn't they see it? Why didn't they know I was lying? All they had to do was shake my shoulders and it would all spill out.

"Go on upstairs, sweetheart," Mom said. "I'll come check on you in a few minutes."

Detective Harris waited until I was almost upstairs before she spoke to my mom, but it was so low I couldn't hear the words.

I went into the bathroom, let the blanket drop, and picked up my hairbrush. When it caught on a tangle, I yanked hard until it came free, trailing several long strands of hair. One grabbed the chain. I tugged it back and ran my fingers over the heart.

Was she still in the basement? Was she waiting to see if I'd come back? I started crying again, without making a sound. I kept brushing, ripping out the snarls, not even caring it hurt. I counted to one hundred, my cheeks wet and my nose running. I wanted everything back the way it had been when summer break first started. I wanted my friend back. We were best friends forever. We'd said it, both of us. She had to come back. She had to.

I opened the medicine cabinet and removed a sharp pair of scissors from the bottom shelf. No matter how much you wanted to, you didn't get to go back. Not ever. Tongue between my front teeth, I pulled out a hank of hair and chopped it off a few inches away from my scalp. *Wildebeest*, I thought. I grabbed more hair. Cut again, lips pressed together so I'd stay quiet. I kept cutting until the sink was filled with long strands and I couldn't see through the tears.

Fingers aching, I dropped the scissors and stumbled out of the room like a mummy in too-tight wrappings. My mom was coming up the stairs, and when she saw me, she rushed to my side.

I offered my hands, hair draped over my palms. "I didn't, I didn't, I . . ."

"Oh, sweetheart." She put her arms around me, rocked me back and forth, and whispered against my head the way she had when I was baby. "Everything will be okay," she said over and over again. "I promise. Everything will be okay."

I couldn't speak. Couldn't tell her she was wrong. She didn't understand. She didn't know what I'd done. Nothing would ever be okay again.
I wanted to tell her the truth, but I couldn't. When you made a promise,
you had to keep it. No matter what. You had to keep it forever.

CHAPTER TWENTY-ONE

NOW

With Ryan gone, every room's a cavern, every hallway a tunnel. I pace the first floor, sure I'll find him somewhere, never mind that I watched him walk out the door an hour ago. He said he'll call me in a few days. I can be patient. Can give him his space. Once he's calmed down, he'll understand.

I must still be on my mom's shit-list, too, because she's not answering my calls. *Ryan is gone and Becca's not dead.* The words play in my head until they become a chant I can't banish.

Why did she leave? She went through so much trouble, so much theater, when she could've simply called. *Oh, Heather, guess what? You're not a murderer. Sorry to leave you hanging for so long.* Sure, I might not have believed her at first, but it would've been easy enough for her to prove she was who she said. Remember our club? The serial killers? Please be fucking kind?

I cross my arms again, drum an arpeggio on my sleeve. After all the dramatics, she shows up, and then . . . nothing? It makes no sense. I was right there. I waved, for god's sake. Did she chicken out? That doesn't seem like the Becca I knew. Then again, it's been a long time. But something doesn't feel right. The dead squirrel? The Chevy? Were they random events, pranks, not connected to her at all? And what of her mom's death? Would she have . . . ?

It's too much to unpack.

But now I know why her body was never found. I wasn't a "super-clever-best-hiding-spot-for-a-grave-ever" kind of kid. I definitely remember burying the knife and running home, but after, there's a gray area. I assumed it was one piece my mind hid too deep to find. When you don't know the whole story, you piece it together, fill in the gaps.

That last night, we were in the basement on a cold floor. I thought I killed her, so my mind made her dead. I remember staying beside her for a long time, but what's a long time to a kid? A few minutes at best? I tap my fingers even harder.

And when I went back, she must've been pretending. That's all. She was smart and clever. She could've fooled me if she wanted to. And after I left her there alone, what the hell happened? Did she get up? Was she cold and hurt and scared? If so, even if she didn't want to go home, why didn't she come to my house? How did she survive the knife wound? Where did she go? What did she do? Did someone else save her? And if so, who? Why didn't she ever let me know? Too many goddamn questions. It bugs me.

Red Lady, Red Lady.

I got caught up in her, too, believed she was real. Now I know better. Mass hysteria crops up now and again in all parts of the world. The dancing plague, the Tanganyika laughter epidemic, the West Bank fainting epidemic. All documented. It explains the coughing, the blood in the kitchen, the cramps. The writing in my books, in the sugar, all messages to myself, borne of guilt and helplessness. I didn't remember writing them because I didn't want to. That's why I still can't remember some things.

But I do remember that Becca really thought she'd save her.

I shake out of my stare, releasing an airy grunt. There's a pang in my chest, not for what I don't know, but for what I don't have, for what I haven't had since that summer. Not even Ryan knows me the way Becca did. All the good, the bad, the ugly, all the parts that made me *me*. She's still inside, that twelve-year-old girl, still reaching out a hand in the darkness, still whispering *best friends forever*.

Please be kind . . .

Becca's not dead.

And Ryan is gone.

I pace the first floor again. I can't stay here right now. Can't sit in the house by myself. Not tonight. It's all too much. I grab my keys and my jacket and slip on my shoes. I have no destination in mind, but after driving aimlessly around downtown Annapolis, I pull into an available spot on Main Street near Kilwins Ice Cream Shop. With a scoop of sea salt caramel, I sit in a rickety chair out front, then make my way to City Dock. A wooden boardwalk surrounds the water on three sides, a parking lot and the Harbormaster's Office flanking one side and restaurants the other, a wide promenade at the end.

The night's a cool one, but a few bars have their doors open, letting out music and chatter. People are milling around, occupying the boardwalk benches, looking at the expensive boats moored along the waterway known as Ego Alley or sitting near the Kunta Kinte-Alex Haley Memorial at the harbor's head.

I keep my pace slow. At the end of the promenade I stand, overlooking the creek, watching the water slosh around the pilings. Now and again glances fix on me, linger, then dart away. I see worry, pity, alarm. Then I feel the moisture on my cheeks, the lurch in my shoulders. Hear the hitching sobs. Swallowing embarrassment, I scrub my skin dry with my forearms. Pin my emotions in place.

And I feel someone watching me. The hair on my arms stands at attention, a legion of soldiers at the ready. Behind me, a small child cries over a spilled bag of Swedish Fish. A young couple kisses. Two men in khakis exchange a rowdy high-five. A woman waves to someone aboard a boat. No familiar faces, no one staring, but the sensation is too strong to shake.

On my way to the car, while waiting at a crosswalk, I see Nicole leaving Middleton Tavern. Our gazes meet and hold. And she turns away. The light changes and people push their way around me. I finally shake myself out of my stupor—if she wants to be that way, so be it—and pretend her rejection doesn't hurt.

When I return home, the first floor smells of candle smoke, faint enough to have trailed in from the outside, but I call Ryan's name anyway. Of course he doesn't answer. We have three candles clustered on one end of the fireplace mantel; I press my thumb into each, and it sinks a bit in one. The wax isn't liquid, but I swear it's warm. Did Ryan have a candle lit earlier? Even if he did, wouldn't it be cool by now?

Wielding a fireplace poker, I stalk from room to room with a sense of déjà vu, but this time everything's in its place. There's no one on the first floor, no one on the second. I even check under the beds and the closets. No one's here but me.

I double-check all the windows and the doors and carry the poker with me, along with a glass of wine, to the bedroom. The lock is only a flimsy push button, but I press it anyway. I check under the bed again, then sit on the edge of the mattress, drink my wine, and listen to the quiet.

When the glass is empty, I open my email and find the last one from Lauren. BECCA, IS THIS YOU? I type. I wait for a long time, but there's no response.

*　*　*

I do something I've not done in years: I call in sick. I don't even talk to Ellie, simply call early enough to leave a message for her to cancel my appointments. Once that's done, I set the phone to silent and roll over. When I wake again, I'm tangled in sweaty sheets, my mouth bitter. I shove the dreams from my thoughts and unwind my legs.

It's sunny outside, but I keep the blinds shut. No need for cheer in this house. I return the fireplace poker and, while coffee is brewing, check my phone. No calls or texts from Ryan or Mom or Nicole. Only a response from Ellie that my appointments were canceled and she hopes I feel better. I fill a mug. Put together some yogurt with blueberries and granola but toss most of it out uneaten. Send Ryan a quick text apologizing again. In a few moments, it shows as read, but there's no response. I wrap my arms around myself and rock.

I send my mom a message, too. In her case, it shows as delivered, not read. Then I send one to Gia, apologizing, telling her I can explain. Delivered. Read. No response.

I scratch my scalp. Refill my mug. Dump it into the sink and return upstairs. The sheets smell sour, but I don't care. Nearly an hour of flopping back and forth from belly to back like a beached whale later, I climb out of bed again. This time I shower.

I'm in the hallway, hair in a towel, when I hear the patter of soft footsteps. I stand, fists clenched tight. Someone's in the kitchen. Robe belted tight, I toddler-step to the first floor, pausing at the landing. And there, a single footstep. Careful, cautious.

No fireplace poker in sight, but I raise a fist and run in, voice a hero's war cry. But the kitchen's empty. The breakfast nook, too. The entire first floor. I let my fist drop. Walk the rooms again, twisting my hands together, but you can't out a damned spot when you're the one who's damned.

I change into leggings and an old hoodie. Fuzzy socks. I don't know where the day went, but the sun's already dropping below the horizon.

On the back patio, I drag the fire pit a little closer to the house and light it up. Inside, I open my bag and remove the ribbon, the drawing, our construction paper book, and Becca's half of the necklace. I fetch mine, too. In the family room I catch movement from outside, a flash of pale darting near the glass, disappearing again. Skin? A dress? A plastic bag tumbled by the breeze? Armpits damp, I tiptoe across the room. There's enough light left outside to make out the edge of the yard, the river beyond, its surface like a sheet of glass today. Nothing and no one else.

The fire has built up nicely, blue and orange flames dancing in the shadows. It's time to say goodbye to my childhood ghosts. To my guilt. Time to put myself and my life back in order. I feed the ribbon to the fire pit first, closing my eyes as it burns. The book goes second, and although tears are coursing silent tracks, I manage a small smile.

She was alive the whole time!

I hold the drawing for a time, then feed it to the fire as well. The necklaces are cheap metal, but I doubt this blaze is hot enough to melt them. The water behind our house beckons, and feeling much like old Rose in *Titanic*, I carry them down. Unlike Rose, I can't bring myself to let go. These I'll keep, to honor our friendship. I turn back to the house, and there's someone standing near the fire pit. Not just someone. *Becca.*

The necklaces fall to the grass. My steps are slow, faltering. I'm not sure what to think or feel. She's here. At my house. But she's not smiling. Fear tightens my belly, but I keep moving forward. She's not frowning, either, just watching me, her face impassive. I stop a few feet away.

"Hi," I say.

"Hey," she says. She's wearing jeans and an old olive drab jacket. Boots with scuffed toes. A battered tan messenger bag slung over one shoulder. I step closer and give her a hug, my vision blurry. I can't help it. She's alive. She really is. She smells of old smoke, a hint of mildew, and musky earth, not patchouli, but a scent in a similar vein. At first, she's stiff and awkward in my arms, then she relaxes and gives a squeeze before we let go.

Wiping my eyes, I say, "I can't believe it's you. It's you and you're here and . . . oh my god." I say, touching the hollow of my throat. "Do you want to go inside? Do you want some wine or water? Or anything?"

"I'd rather stay out here, and no, I don't want anything."

"That's fine. We can— Here, let me pull the lawn chairs closer."

"Sure, yeah."

I sit first. She so strongly resembles Lauren, it's startling. She's about the same height, but thinner. The angles of her cheekbones are sharper, her chin more pointed. And she looks older than she should. Much older. She drops her bag on the patio and shrugs off her jacket, revealing a faded red long-sleeved Henley. She's even skinnier than I first thought. And not the healthy-eating-and-consistent-exercise kind. Her collarbones, the tendons on the backs of her hands, speak of ill health, of days without enough food. The firelight reveals weathered skin, a chipped front tooth. I feel a surge of guilt for my own physicality. Limbs made stronger in the gym, skin clearer in the bathroom, belly full of healthy options. Doctors and dentists within easy reach.

"I have so many things I want to ask you," I say, crossing my ankles under the chair. "I'm not even sure where to start. I guess . . . how have you been?"

"I've had some rough years, you know, but things are starting to work out." She glances at the house. "Looks like you're doing okay."

Guilt rises again. "I'm a psychologist," I say. "I work with kids, but I guess you know that?" She makes a small sound, but I can't decipher its meaning. "What about you?" I say, flicking the cuticle of my pinkie with my thumbnail.

"Nothing important. Just a job that pays the rent," she says, gaze darting from side to side, foot bouncing.

I tuck my hair behind my ears. Lean forward with elbows resting on my thighs. "Why didn't you call me? Tell me you were okay?"

She shrugs. "Never seemed like the right time."

She pushes up her sleeves, yanks them back in place, but not before I see the thin tracery of scars patterning her skin. Now I understand. She's an addict. Recovered, though. There's a clarity she wouldn't have if she were still using. Hello, more guilt. It hurts to see her this way. To know her road has been potholed and cracked.

"I got the things you sent," I say.

Something akin to a grimace darts in and flickers away so quickly it might not have been there at all. There's a tension in the air, rubbing like sandpaper on skin.

"The book . . . remember how many we made?" I say. "Do you still draw?"

"Uh-uh," she says, looking down, rubbing her palms together as though she's cold. Her foot ceases its movement.

"You were so good. Everyone said so, remember? The drawing you made of Roxie? I kept it on my wall for a long time," I say. "It's still packed away somewhere in my parents' attic. I think I might've loved it as much as I did Roxie."

Her brows pinch together. The tension grows larger.

"Please be kind," I say, watching her closely. Something isn't right here. She isn't right somehow.

She blinks. Scratches her arm. The frown deepens. She has no idea what I'm talking about. I can understand her forgetting about my old dog, but our catchphrase? It hits me like a punch in the solar plexus. This isn't Becca. I don't know who she is or what the hell she's doing here, but she's not Becca.

She sits back with her arms folded over her chest. "I wondered how long it would take you to figure it out."

"Who are you? Why did you let me think you were Becca?" My chest aches at the cruelty. The callousness.

"I'm Sarah, her mom."

I go rigid. "That's not possible. Her mom is—was—Lauren Thomas."

"No, Lauren was her aunt. I'm Lauren's sister, Becca's real mom."

I shake my head. "I don't understand." And I don't. Becca had an aunt, I remember that, but she was dead when we were kids. Or so I thought.

"It's not that hard, doc. I got pregnant when I was fourteen. Lauren was just supposed to take care of Becca until either I got my shit together or my mom finished chemo. Lauren was thirteen years older than me, see. But it didn't happen like that. And my mom . . . well, her chemo didn't work so well."

My mind is reeling. I can't make these puzzle pieces fit because I don't know where the corners are.

"Look," I say. "You should go. My husband will be back and—"

"The same husband I saw all packed up and leaving?" She stares until I wither beneath the weight. "Yeah, that's what I thought."

"So, my sister told Becca I was dead," she continues. "Guess she thought it was the best thing to do, I don't know. I did get clean for a little while and I tried to see Becca, but Lauren wouldn't let me. One Halloween I even tried to take her, but I was a mess then, not even eighteen yet. Lauren and I ended up getting into a pretty ugly fight."

A piece falls into place, and I say, "The angel."

"Huh?"

"Becca told me a story about almost being kidnapped by an angel. I thought she made it up."

Guilt ages her at least five years. In the firelight, she turns skeletal. "She remembered that?"

"At least some of it."

"Yeah, I thought with the costume Lauren wouldn't know it was me. Like I said, I was a mess. I was a mess for a really long time. When Becca called me . . ." She looks off toward the water.

"She called you? When?"

"Yeah, the summer she . . . disappeared. She found out the truth and she wanted me to come get her. Said things were bad with my sister. The drinking and the hitting. But I couldn't take care of myself, let alone her and me. She called me a couple times. I kept telling her I couldn't help. The last time she said I needed to come and get her that night or she might die. But I couldn't get to her for a couple of nights. I went to her house, figuring I'd talk to Lauren. Maybe she'd let me see Becca."

Her words are stones in my heart. "Lauren said no, didn't she?"

"Wrong. No one answered the door. So I left. Then I saw the news, and that was that, right?" Sarah tips her chin down, peeks up through her lashes. Not coquettish, but sneaky.

I meet her gaze as evenly as possible. Keep my composure.

"I would've helped if I could," she says. "I would've taken Becca away." But she looks to one side when she speaks.

I can't imagine how Becca must've felt finding out her mom wasn't her mom, and then finding out her birth mother wouldn't help her. No wonder she was such a mess that summer. And after she realized she couldn't rely on either one, she turned to the Red Lady. She didn't understand the how and why. How could she? Her birth mother's name—Sarah—the name of her childhood invisible friend, the name of the witch in the book we made, the name of the Red Lady. All those dangling threads twisting into one. All because of this woman.

"I never saw Lauren when she was in prison," she says. "But once she got out . . . She really did think she killed Becca. She was having black-outs and remembered that they had a fight and she hit her, but nothing after that. So when the cops said she killed her, she just went along with it. No fucking way would I plead guilty to something I didn't remember doing, but Lauren . . . she was weak.

"I got to thinking, what if Lauren didn't kill her? I guess if you knew her the way I did, you'd understand. I made her go over everything she did remember, and one thing kept bugging me: Becca said someone was going to help her. Lauren didn't want to tell me who, so I had to convince her it was the right thing to do. She said it was you. You were supposed to help Becca."

My hand fumbles toward the pocket in my hoodie, but my phone's inside. I glance from Sarah to the house. She's in the chair closest to the French doors, but if I run, I should be able to make it inside fast enough to shut and lock the door. Should being the operative word.

"From there, I just had to track you down. Wasn't too hard. I even found your picture in the paper. I called you a couple times but figured you wouldn't talk to me. So I had the idea to send you the necklace. Lauren wasn't real happy about it, said she wouldn't be involved, said you never would've hurt Becca, but it wasn't her decision to make."

Wait. This piece doesn't fit, no matter which way I turn it. How did she even have Becca's necklace? It was around Becca's neck, and she was in the basement. Sarah wasn't there. "Where did you get it?" I say.

"Get what?"

"Becca's necklace," I say. "And her drawing and the ribbon. Where did you get them? How did you get them?"

She purses her lips. "When I went to her house, there was a backpack on the porch and her stuff was inside."

Becca's things . . . and the stolen money. That part makes sense. If Sarah was using, the cash would've been impossible to resist. But how did the necklace get in the backpack? How did the backpack get on her porch? Something's missing. Something's wrong.

Sarah snaps her fingers. "Earth to doc, come in, doc. We're not talking rocket science here."

And something else pops to the forefront of my mind. "But why send them to me? If Becca meant so much to you, wouldn't you want to keep them?" I say. I know I shouldn't make her angry, but I can't help it. Hands on the chair's arms, I set my feet firmly on the patio, once more gauging the distance between me and the door.

"Never been arrested, have you?" she says. "Ever seen a cop show?" At my confusion, she rolls her eyes. "Jesus. See, if the cops have evidence and want to find out if you know anything about it, sometimes they'll have you in a room and bring it in, see what you do. It's a good trick, yeah? And it works most of the time.

"Besides, I didn't really have a whole lot of other options. If I'd just asked, would you have told me the truth? I kinda hoped Lauren was right. But it was pretty obvious you knew something. And when I put the ribbon on your car, I saw how afraid you were. So, what are you hiding?"

I am not telling her a damn thing. She has no proof that I did anything wrong.

"Was it you that night in the rain? In the old Chevy? And outside the apartment?" I touch the bandage on my wrist.

She smirks. "That's not really important right now." She opens her messenger bag, withdraws an envelope, and every muscle in my body tenses. "But this might be."

Out slides a knife I wish like hell I didn't recognize. I press the back of my hand to my mouth. The handle, once a uniform shade, is bleached gray in some spots, oily dark in others. Time has pocked the blade with speckles of rust, and dirt crusts where metal meets wood. It's a paring knife, the blade only about three and a half inches long, so much smaller than in my memory. Impossible as it seems, it still appears sharp. Becca didn't stand a chance.

I feel Sarah watching me and my hand drops. I try to appear calm, but it's too late.

"I wondered what you were doing in the field," she says. "What you were looking for. When I found it, I knew. So it's real easy. What did you do to her?"

No, no, no. I am not doing this. I'm not admitting anything. I do that and I'm as good as dead.

"I don't know what the hell you're talking about," I say. "You show up at my house, pretend to be my friend from thirty years ago, and pull a knife? You think my acting strange after you left something on my car means I'm somehow guilty? Who wouldn't be freaked out by that? You need to go. Right now." I stand up fast and she does the same, grabbing my arm.

"What did you do to Becca?" she says.

She's stronger than she looks, and I can't tug free. "I didn't do anything. Your sister killed her."

She pulls me kissing-close, then pushes me away. The backs of my legs hit the chair, and I pinwheel my arms to stay upright.

"My sister was nothing like me. She couldn't kill a spider, let alone a person," she says. "She used to cry when we passed dead animals in the road."

"After I went to see her at the hotel, did she tell you to leave me alone?" My words are soft. "Is that why . . ."

Her eyes are flint. "What happened to my sister was an accident. She fell. But she died thinking *she* killed Becca. Even after I showed her the knife, she said you wouldn't have hurt her. She died defending you. How fucked up is that? But she was weak and stupid. Now tell me the truth. What the fuck did you do to my little girl?"

Anger pumps through my veins, and I realize that not only is she unstable, she doesn't really care if I'm guilty or not.

"Your little girl?" I say, my voice ice. "How dare you. Where were you when she needed you? She called you for help, and you said no!"

She puts a booted foot on the edge of the fire pit and shoves it in my direction. The logs, still aflame, roll every which way, one landing near the partly open French doors. Sparks dance across the stones.

I run for the house.

Just inside the family room, Sarah grabs my shoulder, yanking me back. Curled fingers dig into my upper arms, and she flings me against the perpendicular wall. My teeth snap together with a painful, audible click. My wrist shrieks.

Tiny flames are creeping near the doorway, licking toward the floor mat only a few inches away. I freeze at the sight. We have a fire extinguisher hanging on the wall in the garage. I need to—

Sarah grabs me again and drives me farther into the room. I clamber over the sofa as she comes around, wielding the knife. My phone is on the coffee table between us, but before I can get it, she hurls it away with a swipe of her arm. The knife goes flying, too. With the table protecting me for the moment, I move as fast as I can. If I can get to the front hallway, I might be okay, but I have to get away from her or she's going to—

She kicks me in the back of my knee and I shout, falling forward, still in the family room. I roll onto my back and prop myself up on my elbows, ears ringing. She looms over me, and this close, I see the lines grooving her mouth into a puppet's. Her eyes are slits, her jaw tight. I smell the rage on her skin, sour and bright.

There's another smell in the room now: smoke. And a low popping. *Oh no. Please, no.*

"Can't you smell that?" I say. "We have to—"

I rear back just fast enough to keep her fist from slamming into my nose, and the blow glances off my cheekbone. I scramble to my feet. There's no getting away from this, from her. Bracing myself with bent knees, I punch her in the face. I've never hit someone like this, and the impact of my fist on her cheek is like nothing I've imagined. For one thing, it hurts. I cry out as my injured wrist goes hot and cradle it to my chest. She reels back. And she smiles.

We're about three feet from the hallway now. Behind us, an orange glow. A soft push of heat. A low purr. A gray haze hovering near the ceiling.

She charges. Her head strikes me in the sternum, driving me back against the wall. One foot against the plaster for leverage, I shove her away. Her head hits a framed photo, sending it to the floor in a shatter of glass and splintered wood. She growls like a caged animal. Charges again. This time I bring a knee up, catching her in the belly. She staggers back with a shout. Yet another charge, this one so fast I can't do anything. Her fists pummel my belly, my sternum, my ribs. I grab one of her wrists; she breaks free with ease. She's too strong. Too determined.

The low purr grows louder. The air is heavy with heat and I smell the burning. Flames are licking the French doors, turning the exit into a devil's mouth. Fire is consuming the sofa, devouring the rug.

"Can't you tell the house is on fire, you fucking bitch!" I elbow her sideways, catching her off guard, and bolt for the hallway. She hooks the edge of my hood, catching my windpipe. Her fingers twist in my hair, nails scraping channels in my scalp as she drives me to the floor.

"I don't fucking care!" she hisses in my ear. "Tell me what you did!"

I land on my chest with a grunt, hands coming up in time to keep from kissing the wood, palms stinging from the impact. I flip over, kicking out once, twice. The second lands above her knee; her leg slides out from underneath her and she tumbles.

I run into the hallway. Her footfalls go the other way. The door is six feet away when she hurtles into me, launching me forward. I slam into the floor, wheezing a scream. Turn, fists up. And she has the knife again.

She grabs a fistful of hoodie and flings me into the wall, but I hook her ankle, dragging her down with me. She drops the knife. Using *her* hair, I lift and drop her head, hoping it works like in the movies, hoping it'll knock her out.

It doesn't.

I jerk to my feet. She follows suit. We're both openmouthed and panting. I don't want to do this anymore. It has to end. The knife is beside us on the floor. Closer to me. I snatch it up and hold it high. But her back is to the front door, mine to the family room. And the fire.

"So now what are you going to do?" she says.

Before I can think, she tackles me, and it's like being struck by a school bus. I shout as we collide with the floor, the knife flying. She pins my arms to the sides with her knees. Lowers her face to mine.

"Tell me what you fucking did to her!"

Then her hands are on my neck, squeezing. I wrench my right arm free, try to pry her fingers back, try smacking her wrist, pounding her forearm, but nothing works. I can't pull her off. Can't get up. Can't breathe.

My head gets swimmy and everything starts to fade. I spider my fingers along the tile for something, for anything. My fingertips meet something hard—the knife handle. My wrist screams in pain when I grab it, but I hold tight.

She might be stronger, but I'm taller and heavier. I thrust with my hips and twist my chest, and her grip on my throat breaks. Sucking in air, I roll, and the momentum carries us both over. Fury has twisted her into a nightmare. Clutching the knife two-handed, I raise it high overhead and slam it down as hard as I can.

Her eyes widen, holding my gaze. I go cold all over, down to the marrow, and scrabble off, skidding away. Her hands twitch toward the knife, nestled between her breasts in a Rorschach blot of red. She opens her mouth, but nothing emerges. Then she stills.

What have I done to her? What have I done?

More smoke, darker now, wisps down the hallway, turning the air caustic. The heat from fighting, from the growing blaze, slicks my skin with sweat. The family room is impassable and flames dance along the walls of the hallway.

I stumble to the front door and yank it open. Run to the front lawn and fall to my knees, wheezing, my chest and throat aching from the effort it takes.

From ground to roof, the house is destruction. Shingles tumble like dying birds. Broken glass glitters. The fire roars. I curl into a ball and rock back and forth. I'm numb. Terrified. Nothing and everything and all that's in between. I ache from neck to belly to wrist. I ache even more inside, where no one can see. Voices rise and fall, say my name, tell me help is on the way. The wail of sirens pierces the night.

"I killed her," I say, but the words are lost to grief. When the first responders arrive, I'm still crying.

And the house continues to burn.

EPILOGUE

TWO WEEKS LATER

I dream about Sarah, about sliding the knife into her chest, how dreadfully easy it was. I wake, fall back to sleep, into a different dream: Becca and I in the house holding hands and chanting *Red Lady, Red Lady.* When I wake again, I sit on the edge of the bed, waiting for the sun to rise.

After it does, I send a text, receive a brief one in response. Traffic is heavy, but not horrible, not until I get to 695 anyway.

Her eyes wary, my mom opens the door before I can knock. Two mugs wait on the kitchen table, curling steam into the air. "I wasn't sure if you'd want me to make breakfast," she says, "but I have blueberry muffins if you're hungry?"

"No, I'm fine," I say, sitting in the closest chair, the one that was my spot when I was a kid. "Where's Dad?"

She sits, cupping her mug. "He's with a friend. I told him you wanted to come over and talk."

"Does he know why I'm here?"

She winces and looks away. "No, he doesn't."

I sip my coffee. Beneath the smell, there's another lingering in the air: the sour bite of anxiety. Of fear. When Mom asks about the house, about Ryan, we both know what—who—waits in the pauses between. I don't want to have this conversation either, but I want it all to be over. Inasmuch as it can be.

I rub the cast on my wrist. I spent the night of the fire in the hospital, but there was no permanent damage to my lungs or throat. In addition to the hairline fracture, I've a map of fading bruises and a stiffness in my lower back when I turn the wrong way. It could've been much worse.

I tried calling Ryan that night, but he didn't answer. He showed up at the hospital the next morning, though, but it wasn't a tear-filled reunion with hugs and promises of forgiveness. That only happens in the movies. It was strange and awkward and it hurt, but we spoke, mostly about what happened that night and the events that led up to it, not including what really happened to Becca. We've talked several times since then and even met for dinner two nights ago, but what's between us is a fragile sort of peace. He's still angry, understandably so, that I didn't tell him what was going on, but there's still love there, too. And concern. But right now he's staying with his brother while I'm in an extended-stay hotel near my office.

After dinner we kissed and I came very close to asking him to come back to the hotel with me, but I was afraid he might say no. I will next time, though. I'd like to think we'll be okay, eventually, even if the road there is rocky. We've been together a long time. You don't just throw something like that away.

In spite of the firefighters' best efforts, our house is gone. I've driven past it twice, and the haphazard pile of charred timber doesn't look like it could ever have been anything else. I know it's replaceable, but it hurts more somehow than the bruises on my skin.

The official story: Sarah was stalking me and I didn't tell anyone because I thought it would make it worse. She showed up at the house and attacked me, the house catching fire sometime during the struggle. I had bruises all over my body and finger marks on my throat. She had a history of drug abuse and assault. They also matched her DNA to the crime scene at Lauren's apartment. There was a blip in the paper, the sort of blink-and-you'll-miss-it write-up.

Nicole saw it, though, and called me. Alexa did, too. I haven't called either one back yet; I'm not quite ready for that. Maybe it's because of everything that happened, everything I did. Maybe it's because of the genuine concern in their messages. Alexa even apologized for accusing me of doing anything wrong. I don't know if I'll ever be able to look her in the eye again. And even if, out of pity, Nicole asks me to come back to Silverstone, I've decided to resign there and focus solely on my private practice and my patients. If she and I don't work together, maybe we can salvage our friendship. I hope so, anyway.

This week I returned to work, and I took more notes than I can remember taking in a long time. I listened to my patients, too. Really listened. I'm grateful that I have them, even if everything else falls apart.

I still don't remember anything after running out of the basement that last night with Becca. I still don't know where her body is. But now I think I might know why, no matter how improbable.

"Were you there that night?" I say finally. "Did you see what happened to Becca?"

"No." The word is barely audible, and she clears her throat, her attention still on the table. "No," she says, louder this time. "I heard you sneak out the first time, and the second, when you came home, you were crying. The third time, I followed you—you were sick that night and I was worried—to the house. I waited outside. And after you ran out, I went in."

When she looks up, I see truth. I can't believe she's known all these years. Can't believe I never knew she knew.

"Mom, I—"

"It wasn't a secret the two of you were fighting. When I found her, when I saw, I assumed it got out of hand or there was an accident of some kind. She had bruises on her face, and I didn't know what to think. There was nothing I could do, do you understand? She was already gone. She'd been gone for a little while."

Because I killed her. Not the Red Lady. Me.

"I knew it was wrong, but I panicked. I just wanted to protect you. That's what mothers are supposed to do. If I'd called the police—I didn't know her mother would be blamed. I thought people would think she just ran away. Kids do that. If I'd known what would happen, I would've come up with something else. I swear I would've. But I saw her there and I couldn't do anything to help her and I was afraid you—I wasn't thinking, I just knew I had to . . ."

"I need to tell you what happened, okay?" I wait for her to nod. "It was a game, sort of. And it started with a story."

Slowly, the truth tumbles from my lips. All of it. The house. The Dead Girls Club. The bruises. Lauren's drinking. The Red Lady. And those final nights in the house.

When I'm finished, my chest hurts, but I feel twenty pounds lighter. Just to tell it, to let it all out. "It sounds outlandish now, but it made perfect sense then. We thought she'd be okay. I swear we did. I never would've hurt her, not like that. Not to really hurt her."

"I know." Her voice is gentle.

It's a struggle to find words. "Does Dad—"

"No, and he never will. Do you understand?"

"Yes." I also know we'll never speak of this again. "This might sound odd, but did you leave her bag on her porch? Her backpack?"

She cocks her head. "I did. I accidentally left it in my car and didn't know what else to do with it. I knew I couldn't keep it there, couldn't throw it out. Why? How did you know?"

"Just a guess," I say. "And her necklace? The half-heart? Did you put that in her backpack, too?"

She starts and visibly swallows. "Yes. It-it caught on something in the-in the trunk, and when I went back to the car, I saw it there." She shakes her head. "I wasn't thinking. I wasn't thinking at all. But how . . . ?"

"Mom?" I don't want to ask, but I need to know. The words are so small, but so heavy: "Where is she?"

* * *

The Coleman building is twelve stories of glass and brickwork. Pretty, but still functional, it sits next to an old cemetery dating back to the

1890s. I find an open spot on a nearby street, pay the meter, and walk. There's a small park across the street from the building, and I plop down on a wrought-iron bench. It's cold today, too cold to sit outside for any length of time, but I pull my coat tighter. Ignore the chill leaching from the metal into the backs of my thighs. The sky is an angry shade of blue-gray that can't tell in which direction it wants to tip. I smell frying chicken from a fast-food restaurant, burgers from another.

I think of all the people in the building, in their offices. I think of Becca beneath all that weight, all that dirt. Tucked away. Hidden. I think of her being so sure I'd help her. I think of her in the basement, her eyes shut, her skin cooling, me by her side.

I think of my mother putting her here, knowing they were finally about to pour the concrete. Hiding Becca beneath rubble with no way of knowing if she'd be found or not. Hoping she'd be safe. Hoping I'd be safe, too. I think of my dad, never knowing, not when he was working on site and not now.

I wish I could rewind the days and change it all. I wish I could bring her back, but what's done is done. A thousand apologies can't change that. She's gone, and she's been gone for a long time. Part of me is gone, too. Has been since that night. You can't do what I did and come out on the other side unchanged. Undamaged. But I would've done anything for her, anything at all.

I remove the half-heart necklaces from my purse. When I went back to see what remained of the house, I found them on the ground near the water.

Best friends forever.

I think about that last night in the house, how sure Becca was that the Red Lady was going to fix it all, that everything would be okay. But nothing was okay. Nothing was ever okay. She was only a story, but once we fell in there was no way out.

The sky darkens and the chill settles deeper into my bones. A breeze touches the back of my neck, and in that caress, I hear the whisper of my name. Sense someone standing behind me. Smell freshly turned earth and the coppery tang of wet pennies. My muscles lock, and I can't move. Can't think.

And then it's gone.

But I won't look. I won't ever look.

ACKNOWLEDGMENTS

Some novels are problem children and require a little more work to get right than others. This was one of those novels. Thank you, Chelsey Emmelhainz, for your wonderful editorial advice, your dedication to Heather and Becca's story, and your patience while I got it right. And to Heather Flaherty, my agent extraordinaire, thank you for your guidance as well as *your* dedication and patience, too. (I'm also incredibly grateful that you didn't freak out when I sent you the query letter featuring a character with your first name.) I don't know what I'd do without the two of you on my side. I do know that this novel would be a very different animal, and I quite like the beast it turned out to be.

Thank you to the entire Crooked Lane Books team. It's been a genuine pleasure working with all of you.

Thank you, Kristi DeMeester and Paul Michael Anderson, for reading a much earlier draft, when I was still struggling with how to tell the story. Every comment you made helped me find my way through the fog. And Kristi, extra thank-yous for helping keep me sane during the revisions and for inspiring me with your work.

Thank you to my yoga crew for sharing my excitement and for supporting me along the way.

Thank you to my family for their love and encouragement, especially to my daughter, for letting me go on and on about Heather and Becca as if they were people we knew; to my husband, for listening to me endlessly brainstorm and babble about edits and deadlines while on our daily walk with the dogs; and to my son, for minding said dogs while we took a much-needed break.

Hugs and love to the littles—Jeremiah, Chloe, Tristan, and Madison—for making me smile and laugh all the while.

And last but never least, thank you to my readers. Without you, none of this would be possible. There are many books published every day. Thank you for picking up mine, for choosing to spend your time with my characters. I hope you enjoyed their story.